A
Million
Bullets
and a Rose

Praise for *A Million Bullets and a Rose*

This is a compelling and riveting narrative, executed in a haunting style. Akachi Adimora-Ezeigbo writes with the ferocity of a barbed arrow: straight from the quiver of the heart to the target of another heart. The result is a lyrical tale that is experientially rich and enriching, a veritable mosaic of the human condition.

James tar Tsaaior, Ph.D.

A Million Bullets and a Rose Roses takes us right into the experience of war: its divisiveness, the pain caused by untimely and violent death, and the humanity that prevails in spite of pain and violence. It comes from a voice of experience, providing depth and insight into a traumatic period in Nigeria's life in a most moving, graphic way. In reading, we live a little along with the characters, sharing both the trauma and the hope of new life.

Pat Bryden, Edinburgh, Scotland

A Million Bullets and a Rose is the most realistic fictional description of the Nigerian-Biafran War I have encountered. Ginika's life is a symphony of love, war, death, pain, bliss and betrayal. Adimora-Ezeigbo is dispassionate, profoundly candid and devoid of the pretentious bias common among authors of similar stories.

Nwachukwu Egbunike,
Editor, Fast Edition and Feathers Project

Akachi Adimora-Ezeigbo's *A Million Bullets and a Rose* distinguishes itself among the best of Nigerian Civil War novels. It is a beautiful human story about an ugly (inhuman) war. Tearful and heartrending.

Odili Ujubuonu, author of *Pregnancy of the Gods*

. . . Poignant, insightful and deeply moving. Akachi Adimora-Ezeigbo's new novel captures an era and its people so well. A story of despair yet filled with so much hope.

Jude Dibia, author of *Walking with Shadows*

A Million Bullets and a Rose

Akachi Adimora-Ezeigbo

Abibiman
Publishing

New York & London

First published in Great Britain in 2022 by Abibiman Publishing
www.abibimanpublishing.com

All rights reserved. Published in the United Kingdom by Abibiman
Publishing, an imprint of Abibiman Music & Publishing, London.

Abibiman Publishing is registered under Hudics LLC in the United
States and in the United Kingdom.

ISBN: 978-1-9989958-1-3

Cover design by Gabriel Ògúngbadé

Printed in the United Kingdom by Clays Ltd.

Also by Akachi Adimora-Ezeigbo

Novels
The Last of the Strong Ones
House of Symbols
Children of the Eagle
Trafficked

Short Story Collections
Rhythms of Life, Stories of Modern Nigeria
Rituals and Departures
Echoes in the Mind
Fractures and Fragments

Poems
Heart Songs
Waiting for Dawn
Cloud and Other Poems for Children
Come to the Hills with Me & Other Poems for Secondary
Schools
Singing in the Rain and Other Poems for Children

Plays
Hands that Crush Stone
Barmaid and the Witches of Izunga

Children's Fiction
The Buried Treasure
The Prize
Alani the Troublemaker and Other Stories
Asa and the Little Stream

Whisker the Brave Cat
Red One and the Wizard of Mula
Sunshine the Miracle Child
Snake Child and Star Baby
Ezezemale and the Tree Spirits
Adventures of Anum the Tortoise
My Cousin Sammy
Fire from the Holy Mountain
Ako the Storyteller
Zoba and his Gang
The Slave Girl
The Dwarf's Story
The Return of the Thief
The Boy and his Dog
Mina the Shy Girl
Toki Learns the Hard Way
Seyi's Strong Voice
Kidnapped at Noon
Ona and the Dwarf

Non-Fiction

Fact and Fiction in the Literature of the Nigerian Civil War
Gender Issues in Nigeria: A Feminine Perspective
A Companion to the Novel
Artistic Responsibility: Literature in the Service of Society
Snail Sense Feminism: Building on an Indigenous Model
The Literatures of War (edited with Liz Gunner)
Wings of Dawn (edited with Ronnie Uzoigwe)
Literature, Language and National Consciousness: A
Festschrift in Honour of Theo Vincent
(edited with Karen King-Aribisala)
Things Fall Apart @ 50 (edited with Adetokunbo Pearse)

In memory of Joseph Adimora,
Samuel Ogbuefi and Nathan Ezeigbo
who died fighting in the Nigeria-Biafra War

Theirs is not to make reply,
Theirs is not to reason why,
Theirs is but to do and die
– Alfred, Lord Tennyson

Older men declare war.
But it is the youth that must fight and die.
– Herbert Hoover

Part One

THE BEGINNING

1

Ginika watched the man drive off in the pickup truck and disappear round the corner of the dirt road. She surveyed the brown envelope he had just delivered to her and felt a slight tremor in her heart. A folded scrap of brown paper, no doubt, but intuitively she felt it possessed the power to pulverize her peace. The threat was not the letter but the one who produced it, she thought. In the distance, some children played in the grass. They looked charmingly happy; free as birds released from a cage and allowed to take wing.

Children would be happy anywhere, she thought, as long as their parents were around, as long as they had other children romping around them. Ginika lifted her eyes as if she was searching the sky. The sun was shining; the weather was fine. The July sun, she mused, was always sweet to the skin, its heat moderated by the ever-present rain clouds. Certainly, a time to be happy, but many things had gone far wrong in the land and war had just broken out . . .

Ginika turned and entered the house. It was the biggest of the many bungalows tucked away down a street of mango and cashew trees on the outskirts of town. These were the staff quarters of St Augustine's College. She was the sole occupant of one of the five rooms in the house. She slipped unobtrusively into it to read her letter. Gingerly, she opened the envelope as if it was a letter bomb waiting to go off.

> *"Ginikanwa, I want you to come home immediately. I want my family to stay close together. Your brother has returned from university. I wonder what you are doing in Enugu and why you did not come straight to Mbano when schools closed. I wish you were here without waiting for my letter. Sometimes I think you act wilfully just to annoy me or get me in a temper. Don't I deserve to be treated with filial affection and respect? You are my only daughter and I care for you more than you realize. I doubt if what I say sits comfortably with you. Anyway, get your things ready; I will come over to pick you up as soon as I can get away for a few days. Kindly show this letter to your aunt and her husband. I am sending it through Doctor Ufo Ndefo, a friend who is returning to Enugu . . ."*

Ginika stopped short; there was little else to read, anyway. Just his name written in full, rather than signing himself 'Papa' or 'Dad' as she thought other fathers would probably have done.

Soon she heard a barely audible tap on the door and waited. The door, yielding to a gentle prod, yawned open. Ginika sensed, rather than saw, a figure stalk in to disrupt her moment of introspection. In the past fortnight she had been under the illusion that for once she could and would do what she really wanted to do and be allowed to do it. Now she knew it had all been sheer delusion.

"What are you reading?" Ginika's aunt asked, her ample

frame teasing the door. "You look awful. What is the matter?" She left the doorway and gravitated closer to the bed where Ginika was sitting. The light from the open window revealed an oval face and a finely chiselled nose as that of a bespoke *agbogho mmuo* mask. The woman was well-rounded and shapely even after four pregnancies.

Ginika looked up in relaxed recognition and thrust the sheet of paper forward. "Auntie Chito, here, have a look at this. It's from Papa." She sighed deeply at the thought and shut her eyes.

A moment of awkward silence ensued as Chito read the letter. Ginika flicked a nervous glance at her aunt, searching for her reaction. In her anxiety, her deeply furrowed eyebrows contracted. She kept her hands folded in her lap. But the next moment, they had begun to circle the surface of the bedspread in some absent-minded childish prank. Again her eyes burrowed their way into her aunt's face.

Her aunt's face was expressionless when she finally spoke.

"*Hmm*, this certainly is an order . . . Well, he's your father and has a right to ask you to come home."

She returned the letter to Ginika, patting her right shoulder.

"You're barely eighteen." She chuckled. "When you're twenty-one, I believe you'll be freer to do as you wish. He did not say when he'd be coming?"

"No. But it should be any day from tomorrow, I think."

Ginika sighed deeply as she folded the sheet of paper.

"Auntie, I don't want to return to Mbano. Perhaps I will later, but not now." Her eyes clouded over with misgiving as she gazed at the older woman. "I like what I'm doing here. It's all I want to be doing now. Auntie, I want to stay and help . . ."

"Yes, I know," her aunt said sympathetically, "and I agree. It's a shame you have to leave. You've been so helpful with the dry pack. Where did you learn to make cookies so well? The women are all praising you. I am sure our boys are enjoying our snacks."

Encouraged, Ginika persisted, "I love it out here. I want to remain in Enugu. Helping to prepare delectable snacks for our soldiers at the Nsukka front is my own win-the-war effort. Auntie, can't you and Uncle Ray persuade Papa to allow me to stay here?"

Chito hesitated, sighed. "I will try." She did not sound quite enthusiastic and Ginika's hope plummeted. "You know your father. Getting him to change his mind on any issue is harder than climbing _Ugwu Nwosa_ – that dreaded hill in Ama-Oyi." Chito burst into laughter, tickled by her own witty analogy. But when she glanced at Ginika's thoroughly miserable face, she stopped.

Ginika was determined to fight for what she wanted. She was not going to give up so easily. She would make her aunt see how important it was to her to be allowed to remain in the town. How her happiness depended upon it.

"I know but I want you to try," she begged. "If Papa forces me to go with him, I'll run away from home. Auntie, you must help me, please?"

"Okay, I'll do my best. Come with me, lunch is ready. The kids have eaten and are in their rooms. We won't wait for Ray; he'll eat when he returns from work."

"I'm ready for lunch," she announced and followed her aunt out of the room. She was sure her support and Uncle Ray's would perform the miracle. She would definitely put up a fight when her father arrived. She was not just going to pack her things and follow him just like that.

THE KITCHEN was small; a table, pots and plates took much of the space. Two mortars – one big, the other small – two pestles resting on a wall, brooms and a plastic container filled with forks and spoons, adorned the room. Everything was scrupulously clean. Ginika admired the way her aunt ran her house. Even without a housemaid or domestic help, she coped pretty well.

Chito dished the food out while Ginika laid the table in the dining area: an extension of the medium-sized living room. Ginika returned to the kitchen and watched her aunt scoop *agbono* soup into a bowl. She watched the older woman's deft moves, believing that one day she would perhaps also be a wife and a mother. But that would be much later, after she would have completed her education and secured a good degree like her aunt. But, of course, she wouldn't want to be a teacher. She didn't think she was cut out for that. She just didn't have the patience: she had told herself this, again and again.

Her task completed, Chito washed her hands and wiped them up with her top *wrappa*, just as Ginika thrust a dish-cloth in front of her.

"Oh, thank you, but my *wrappa* has done the job. Now, let's take the food to the table. I am so hungry I think I will gobble enough food for five men!"

"Auntie, I know you won't," Ginika guffawed. "You hardly eat at all."

"See who is talking. You think I am you who run away from food, as if you are anorexic. See how slender you are, like *ome ji*. I am going to teach this *nni oka* a lesson today." She waved her hand over the mound of corn meal which was still piping hot.

Ginika laughed until her sides ached. Sometimes she wished her father would let himself go and roar with laughter as Uncle Ray would, or make others laugh even if he himself did not want to. No one made her laugh as much as Auntie Chito. Her aunt's home was the happiest and liveliest she ever knew. Perhaps this was why she came to stay with the family at the earliest opportunity.

"We'll see who will eat more, then," Ginika challenged, setting a bowl of water for them to wash their hands.

They had burst out laughing when the blast of a car horn caught their attention. Could that be Uncle Ray? Ginika wondered. It didn't sound like him. He hardly honked his car horn. If he did, it was always a sharp or gentle toot. In fact, he would sneak up on everyone, going about the house quietly, even if he had to tug his things along. Then Auntie Chito and their four children would help him bring in the rest of the things he had brought back. And if she was around, she too would dash out and help him.

"*Hmm*, who is the lucky visitor? Perhaps the person might wish to have lunch with us? Ginika, find out who it is." She sat down and waited for her to return with the visitor.

But Ginika walked back alone. She looked at her aunt and shook her head in growing apprehension. "Oh, it's Papa!"

Her aunt pushed her chair back and got up. "Is he not coming in? Won't he want to at least eat with us? What's the hurry?" She frowned. "Ginika, come and sit down. Now, calm down. I will go and see him." She patted her shoulder consolingly.

"He's with my stepmother," Ginika said as she sat beside her. She wished her father hadn't visited that day; she had hoped he wouldn't come so soon, so that she would spend

8

a few more days in Enugu helping her aunt and the other women.

"He asked me to get my things. He said he doesn't have much time and must return to the hospital without delay."

She had prepared to put up a fight, but the way her father spoke, magisterially, with a deep menacing frown on his face had made her decision a hopeless case. It seemed she would not even be given room to put up a fight, let alone a feeble one. "Papa is completely unapproachable, utterly impossible," she whispered.

"All right, just sit here and have some food. I will be back with them soon. Remember, it is better to be calm than lose your cool; you'd think better and act more sensibly." She hurried out of the room.

At the door, she met her visitors – her brother-in-law, Ubaka Ezeuko, and his wife, Lizzy, a fat woman of about forty.

"Ah, Doc and Lizzy, how are you?" greeted her aunt. She shook his hand while she and the woman hugged. Ginika watched, detached. As her stepmother's rather large body pressed against her aunt's, Ginika thought she had gained more weight since she last set eyes on her during her holiday at home. She closely observed the three of them and thought how different they were. Auntie Chito was cheerful and homely while her stepmother was sour and bad-tempered, distant and aloof. But her father was neither cheerful nor aloof; he was somewhere in between and she could never understand why he made no effort to make people around him happy. She tried to remember when last he made her laugh, but couldn't.

She had once asked Auntie Chito why she called her father Doc, rather than his first name or something more endearing. She had replied that she started calling him Doc after he became her brother-in-law. Ginika wished that her mother had survived the birth of her third child. She had died. The baby was stillborn. Ginika would have had two brothers if the baby had lived. Would her father have been different if her mother had lived? Auntie Chito talked a lot about her, especially when she was visiting. Ginika liked that very much; she was happy to hear about her dead mother though it made her sad sometimes. Auntie Chito told her she was six years old and her brother, Nwakire, nine, when her mother died.

"Please, come and sit down, my in-law. *Ibiana*, welcome. We were not expecting you so soon. It was just this afternoon your letter got to Ginika." She made way for them to enter the sitting room.

"Chito, how are you all? Is your husband not at home?" He smiled, revealing two rows of gleaming white teeth. Ginika wished he could smile more often. She was always impressed with her father's porcelain teeth and liked to look at them when he smiled, which unfortunately was not quite often. She observed that all the men she knew – her friends' fathers – had discoloured teeth; none had clean teeth like her father's.

"Please, sit down. Do not stand at the entrance or you will bring us more visitors, as Ama-Oyi people would say." She laughed. "Ginika and I were about to eat when you arrived. There is enough food here for all of us. Please, join us." She indicated two seats, one for each of them.

"I asked after Raymond, your husband," he reminded her, ignoring the chair she had offered. "I am in a hurry. I must return to the hospital at once. We have an emergency on our hands."

Chito did not seem to know where to start. She decided

to answer his question first. "Ray is not at home; he went to work. The children are having a siesta." She glanced at the wall clock. "He should be back soon."

"Work?" he asked, surprised. "I thought all schools had closed." He accepted the chair his sister-in-law offered, and his wife sat next to him. It was a settee, flanked by single chairs in the modestly furnished sitting room. Ginika's father was not tall; he was of average height, stocky and dark-skinned. Her stepmother was a head taller than her father, though the fat she had accumulated over the years seemed to have distorted her body. That made her look much shorter than she really was. Ginika thought a man should be taller than his wife, not the other way round. She was irritated by the prevailing situation. She deeply resented their presence in the house because the tribe had come to take her away willy-nilly, as if her opinion in the matter counted for nothing.

"Yes, schools are closed, but teachers have to work," her aunt explained. "In fact, Ray goes to work every day."

Her stepmother's mascara-coated eyes raked around the room like searchlights until a family photograph hanging on the wall arrested her attention. Absent-mindedly, she responded to Auntie Chito's explanation, "He goes to work every day?"

"Yes, as principal, he does that," her aunt replied.

"We came for Ginikanwa," her father said. "Thank you for the invitation to enjoy your food, but we can't stay." Turning to Ginika, he chided, "What are you still doing sitting there? Have you packed your things? Did you not hear me say I am in a hurry?"

"Papa, I don't want to return to Mbano. Please, let me stay with Auntie Chito and Uncle Ray. I am helping with making packed lunches for our soldiers. Please, Papa, let me stay."

"No, you cannot stay. A war is going on and you want to be separated from your family? Just listen to yourself." His face instantly grew into a deep frown, highlighting his furrowed brow. His hair was greying in a most striking manner. It looked like a cock's crest, stretching from his temple to his nape.

Ginika was transfixed with shock. She was the spitting image of a shrine goddess. She was in the throes of battling knife-edge emotions. She felt as if her innards were being gutted.

Her aunt mercifully intervened. "Doc, please, let her stay a little longer. She is doing a good job with many of the young women in town. You need to see what marvels they are achieving to appreciate them. We are all involved. I promise we'll bring her back to Mbano in the next couple of weeks, if you wish."

"She is just one of the several people working with you, is she not? Will the making of packed lunches just stop if she comes home? The girls who live in Enugu can go on with the task, can't they?" He was now even more resolute in his objection.

Her aunt tried yet again. She was not going to give up so easily. "I know, but Ginika wants to be part of the action. She is as safe here as she is in her own home. I assure you we will take good care of her. You don't need to fear at all."

"I do understand. I know she's safe here, but we want her home," he insisted. "In fact, we want her to train with other young women as a special constable, in Mbano."

"Oh, you have made other plans for her?" Her aunt asked, staring at her in-law for a moment before turning to look at Ginika's stepmother, surprised they had made plans for her without consulting her.

"Yes. She can serve the new nation as a special constable." Ginika noted that his voice mellowed as he turned towards her. "Ginikanwa, you will like it, I'm sure. There are many ways to contribute to the war effort when you return to Mbano. You will be surprised when you discover what is happening there. If you prefer to go to Ama-Oyi, you would be welcome. Besides, the students' association will want you to get involved in a special project of theirs. They will be back next week. Perhaps you know their president: a young man called Eloka Odunze? He sent the students to Mbano last week. They want you to take part in a play they are producing to entertain our soldiers and to raise money for prosecuting the war. So you see, you won't be bored or remain idle."

Her father had a self-satisfied smirk on his face. He was now in his element. No one could ever hope to win an argument against him. Ginika wondered how he expected her to go along with his plans for her without seeking her opinion. If he asked her, she would tell him she preferred to remain in Enugu and continue with the project Auntie Chito and other Enugu women were undertaking. But he wouldn't ask, she knew.

Her stepmother did not speak persuasive or threatening words but compensated for her reticence by just grunting and sighing deeply. It was obvious she was on his side in this matter. "*Umm, Umm-umm, Huu-huu, Ah, Ahaa . . .*"

There was no indication that her reaction would be taken into consideration. Her hope now rested squarely on her aunt's ability to convince her father of the need for her to stay. Ginika fixed her with a blank, irresistible stare.

Chito made one more daring effort. "Doc, please let Ray return before you take her away. He will be deeply hurt if he comes home and finds her gone. Let him see her before she leaves. Let me send for him. You know his office is not far from here; just a few metres away."

Her father rewarded her aunt with a puzzling frown. Ginika's heart sank. The scowl she detected in his face could mean only one thing: he couldn't possibly understand why he should obtain Ray's permission to take his own daughter away.

"Oh, we have lingered on this matter for too long," he observed, glancing at his watch. "Chito, we have to leave now if I am to return in good time to the hospital."

Chito clung to her argument – her demand that common courtesy and good manners should be accommodated by her visitors; that all due respect must be accorded to the absent head of the family still sheltering Ginika; that the umbilical cord of the basic family decency and its sense of decorum must not be snipped off at will. She tried to make them understand her stand on the matter. That was Ama-Oyi tradition, and he needed to be reminded of it in case he had forgotten. But when his pained look deepened and he felt a jerky spasm of irritation, Chito knew it was time to give up on him. One should not cling to what did not belong to one by right. She capitulated. Her anguish for her niece was not assuaged by the course of events.

"Ginikanwa, bring your things and get into the car. We have spent far too much time here." Her father's voice bristled with punctilious airs of authority. "And don't keep us waiting." Ginika watched him as he stomped out of the room. He was followed by her stepmother who gave Auntie Chito a slight nod and a wink.

Her aunt got up reluctantly to see the visitors off. Her face fell. Her usual cheerful self lacked sparkle. Ginika fought back the tears that haunted her eyes. Her aunt had lost the argument but won her dignity. Ginika knew her aunt had done her best, but she could not help feeling shrugged off by everyone. She felt so dejected and lonely, wishing her brother, Nwakire, were around to give her a few words of encouragement. She could not bring herself to look at her aunt's face . . .

"Did you not hear what I said? Go and get your things," Ginika heard her father letting out a bellow of rage. She looked up instantly and saw him standing smack at the door. He had doubled back to find out if she was picking up her things. "Meet us in the car. I'll send Udo to help," he added.

At the mention of Udo's name, her deeply troubled heart warmed up. So, her fourteen-year-old cousin was in the car all along? She hadn't known it. Her father had met her halfway to the house when she went out, and she hadn't noticed there was someone else with him apart from her stepmother. But, why hadn't Udo come out to greet her? It was very unlike him to be so lukewarm about her. She was still transfixed with shock on her chair when her aunt came in.

"Ginika, my dear," she began in a gentle tone. "I'm sorry, but I tried. Can anyone ever succeed in making your father change his mind? It is like making a man with an unsightly protuberance dance in the market square . . . Please, get all your things together and go with him. He is *your* father and you have to obey him."

Ginika nodded rather ruefully. She had hoped against hope that her aunt would easily persuade her father to let her stay. Now she was asking to let her go. She got up gingerly as if suffering from dizziness.

"But Doc has not treated us fairly by taking you away like

this. I was appalled at his conduct today. Indeed, Ray will be more scandalised when he gets to know. Nevertheless, go and get ready." Her aunt's voice quivered with resentment.

Ginika was absolutely devastated. Full of feeling, she smarted from the tears that misted her eyes.

As she shuffled to her room to obey her father – or was it her aunt? – she almost fell over. She clutched on to the back of the chair for support. Her breath came in short gasps as she burst into tears. Her shoulders shook and shuddered involuntarily as she sobbed.

Her aunt pressed her to her bosom, held her for a while without uttering a word. "*Ozuone*, it is enough. Hold your head up and go with the ebb and flow of the tides, or they will drown you. God knows you might find life better in Mbano when you get there. Remember what I told you yesterday, always be set on being whoever you want to be. It sounds a great idea to serve your country in any other way. Go for it, dearie!"

Her head nodded in agreement. Ginika was finally forced to capitulate. It was another matter whether this was a temporary or permanent gesture of submission.

Udo burst into the room without knocking. He greeted Chito and, grinning with delight, turned to Ginika. He halted, staring at her face which looked morose. But when she glanced up quickly with a smile, he lunged forward to greet her warmly, exclaiming: "Sister Ginika, good afternoon!"

She burst out laughing, to cover her sombre mood. He called her 'Sister', to which she had no objection. It was unthinkable that, particularly within the larger family, any other term such as 'cousin' was adequate to describe their blood relationship. His father was her father's younger brother. Being much younger than she, he would not want to address her by her name. Ginika grew up to discover that in Ama-Oyi, people generally avoided calling people by name if there were more respectable terms of endearment that they could use to identify them. So, for Udo, 'Sister' it had been and would always be.

"Udo, how are you? Look how big you've grown!" Ginika cooed, pleased to see him. For a moment she forgot her misery. "You're nearly as tall as I."

Udo smiled. His eyes glowed with pleasure, his teeth gleaming white. He wore a white T-shirt over a pair of blue jeans.

"Why didn't you come into the house? I didn't know you'd come with them." She gave him a puzzled stare.

"Uncle told me to wait in the car and look after it. He didn't lock the doors and the windows were not wound up."

"Well then, come and help me take my things to the car. They are not too many, anyway."

A few minutes later, her aunt was at the door, waving them goodbye. Ginika responded, her eyes trained on her aunt until the car had turned a corner and melted away. Then she turned, facing the situation squarely, before curling up and as far removed from her father as possible. She hoped they would let her be without trying to draw her into a conversation. Her father always did that when he exerted his authority in an overbearing manner and knew he had put the other person on the spot. She was often his innocent victim. So too were her brother, Nwakire, and her stepmother – Auntie Lizzy.

Ginika blinked in the bright sunlight of instant but distasteful recall. *Auntie Lizzy*: that was the name she had told them – Nwakire and herself – to call her after she had married their father and taken their dead mother's place.

Ginika wished war had not broken out between Biafra and Nigeria. Almost everyone had thought Nigeria would let Biafra alone when Colonel Chukwuemeka Ojukwu declared the Republic of Biafra in May. How far away it seemed now, but it was not quite two months yet. How everyone had rejoiced! How they had all danced and sung victory songs, with everyone learning to sing the new national anthem!

Then Nigeria declared war on Biafra and schools were closed and students sent home. Her dream of taking her Higher School Certificate examinations in December was aborted. Only five months away. Ginika sighed deeply at the thought. It was the frustration of all her ambitions. Her shoulders heaved with gushing, unspoken emotions. But her unspoken mood swings did not go unnoticed.

Udo, who sat pensively, was fully and intensely alert to his beloved Ginika's soul-searing and agonising recollections. He sensed she was being smuggled away from her dream world of what she wanted to do and where she wanted to be. He would give anything to be able to rescue her. He also sensed she would rather be left alone to chew on her lip, so he made no effort to talk or chat as they loved to do when they were together.

Her father drove very fast, but carefully, concentrating on the road. But Auntie Lizzy did not want him to drive at that speed. "Uba, could you go a little slower? You are so fast," she cautioned. Ginika heard them. She did not care about what he did at the wheel.

"It's all right," he replied, with a nonchalant shrug. "I know what I'm doing. We must get back in no time."

"In one piece, of course," she warned. A weird sign posted at strategic points on the country's highways about how much wiser it was *to be late* for one's appointment than *to be the late* ran through her mind. "Remember, better be late than the late," she stressed, suppressing a scurrilous scowl.

He reduced speed as they approached Milliken Hill. The road was an undulating, unending and bizarre convolution of massive rock formations and cavernous gullies that snaked treacherously away into the deepening distance, in long twisting dangerous curves that boggled the mind.

"Ginikanwa, you see the trouble you have caused me. It's because of you that I have to drive on this dangerous road at this time," her father's voice ranted and raved. "I don't have to remind you that you ought to clear with me before you travel anywhere again."

Ginika had been making an effort to compose herself in her predicament. She had been telling herself that she shouldn't allow her father's behaviour to upset her so easily. She ought to be used to such shenanigans by now. After all, they were not as insidious and condemnable as the invasion of her privacy! What great lengths hadn't he gone to in order to have and dictate where she should go and should not go? But now, his carping stung her like a wasp.

"Papa, you didn't have to come, so you shouldn't blame me. If you have to blame anybody, it is yourself! You should have left me where I was."

Ginika took a deep breath. She was astonished at her sudden effrontery. What had got into her, she wondered? She had never ever spoken to her father in such strong terms.

"*Ewo*, Ginika!" Auntie Lizzy swivelled around to give Ginika a blank cold stare. She hissed at her to be quiet and turned round again.

Udo was shocked too. He cowered in his corner. He was worried, wondering what was the matter with his cousin.

"You see the way you talk back to me?" her father raged. "I will not tolerate it. As long as you are under my care, you will obey me. Remember this." He turned round quickly, stabbed Ginika with a painful stare and returned to the road. The incident took only a fraction of a second, but all his passengers were shaking with fright.

Ginika tensed herself. She had had enough. When her fearsome scream came, it unnerved all of them. It pierced the air and circled the car. Her father's hands wavered at the wheel and then steadied.

"I'm tired, tired, tired of it all!" she screamed. "Why are you doing this to me?"

"Ginikanwa, *kpuchie onu*. Shut up!" he yelled. "Are you drunk?"

This stream of abuse seemed to stoke up the embers of Ginika's anger and frustration.

She even raised her voice. "Take me back to Enugu!" she cried. "I don't want to go to Mbano! Did you hear me? Take me back to Enugu!"

"Ginika, be quiet," Auntie Lizzy hissed. "It's enough. See how people are staring at us. Can't you see the damning look in their eyes? They think we want to harm you, that we kidnapped you."

"Did you not kidnap me? Wasn't that what you did?" She started to weep uncontrollably.

The car sped up. Every now and then, people by the roadside would stop, listen and watch a girl crying her eyes out in a Peugeot 403, driven by a grim-faced middle-aged man with two other helpless, hapless passengers staring vacantly ahead. But no one made any move to stop the car or find out what was happening inside it, and why the girl was screaming blue murder.

A battle was raging on at the Nsukka front. And soldiers were dying in their hundreds, though the Nigerian government told the world that what was happening was "Police Action" to return the rebels to the fold.

At Oji River junction, Auntie Lizzy saw women selling fresh maize and wanted to buy. "Uba, please, stop. I want to buy maize."

The volume of Ginika's scream increased. She cried out, demanding to be taken back to Enugu. "I will run away from home if you refuse to let me return to Enugu. If I do, you will never see me again," she protested.

Udo turned once again and gave Ginika a morbidly curious and troubled look. She ignored him.

Her father drove on, impervious to all her thunderous tantrums, and oblivious of Auntie Lizzy's pleas. Ginika was infuriated that he showed no remorse for taking her away and trifling with her feelings and desires.

They arrived in Udi in twenty minutes. Auntie Lizzy sighted several women sitting behind tables on which *abacha*, edible shredded and dried tapioca, was displayed. Again, she asked him to stop just for a while.

Ginika, this time, was determined to annoy everyone else as much as they had angered her. To give as much as she thought she had received. She thrust her head out through the window nearest to her, and roared deafeningly. She let out prolonged and unrelenting yells . . .

Motion seemed to freeze everywhere as people turned to gaze and gawk at the spectacle. Utter astonishment mixed with growing concern was discernible on every face. Nonetheless, the occupants of the car maintained a dignified inscrutability, gazing straight ahead, turning neither left nor right. Her relentless, single-minded father drove steadily on.

He spoke only once. "Sorry, Lizzy, I cannot stop. How can I, with Ginikanwa bellowing like a raging bull?"

After Ginika had expended all her energy and let out her pent-up feelings, she shut her mouth like a burst dam suddenly brought under control. She lay back in her corner, on the back seat, and did not utter a word to anyone until they arrived in Mbano. It was about five in the evening. No one spoke to her. In fact, no one spoke to anyone until they reached their house.

2

The next day, Ginika rose early as she always did when she was in Mbano. It had been the same when she was at school. The bell rang at five in the morning and you woke up whether you liked it or not. It had become a habit she did not think she would break. Five o'clock it was, every morning whether at school or anywhere else. Even in Auntie Chito's house in Enugu. Her aunt would often ask, "Why do you wake so early?" Ginika would laugh and say she liked it that way. "Suit yourself," Auntie Chito would reply with a shrug.

In Mbano, you did not need a bell to ring to wake up in the morning. Birds would do it for you. They sang out so insistently outside the house in the surrounding trees that you could not but wake up. You couldn't help listening to their singing. You couldn't help having your fancy tickled. Above all, you couldn't help enjoying it. She did not even know the names of most of the birds. One of them looked so beautiful and adorable that each time she looked at it, tears filled her eyes. At Ama-Oyi, they called it *nkelu*, but she did not know what Mbano people called it. Did it have the same name here as in Ama-Oyi? Ginika wondered why she never really tried to find this out though she had friends here who would be glad to satisfy her curiosity.

This morning, her favourite entertainer was a lively playful fellow who thought the entire house belonged to her. She sang loudly enough to rouse the curiosity of the whole house and even the neighbourhood. She sang lustily as if warbling to a distraught lover. But, how did Ginika know it was a 'she' not a 'he'? Well, only a female could sing so sweetly and with such a clear lilting voice, she rationalised. So the bird had to be a female. Flinging open her window, Ginika whispered, "Be my guest, little bird," as if it could hear. She searched for it. The bird was up in the avocado pear tree close to her window. It must be tucked away in the thick green foliage, Ginika thought. Sing on, birdie dearie, I need your happy song to heal the wounds in my heart. Her father had hurt her so deeply, she told herself. But a good night's sleep had partially calmed her stormy nerves. She was a trifle worried about how far she had gone in her carefully orchestrated war of revenge. All that screaming and shrieking and screeching, was it necessary? Well, she hoped it signalled to them that she was no longer ready to be treated as a child. Papa had it coming, she mused.

She felt much better, almost herself again, after cogitating about the recent past. Yesterday was a nightmare and she wanted to bury it in her subconscious. She detested tension revolving around her relationship with people, least of all members of her family. She would give anything to live in peace with people. If only her father would not bully her so. She thought that malice was a stranger she detested entertaining, so she was willing to forgive her father.

After all, he was the only parent she had, having lost her mother at a tender age. Besides, he had been good to her too in his own way, and in some other special ways. He had made sure she was given sound education in the best secondary school for girls in eastern Nigeria, now renamed Republic of Biafra. And she knew he had plans to send her to the university where Nwakire was already being educated as a future medical doctor. This would not be the first time she was angry with her father nor would it be the last, she was certain.

Tightening her dressing gown around her slim figure, she adjusted the sash that held it in place. Ginika suddenly tore herself away from the bird and its music and headed for the kitchen. Monday, the houseboy, had beaten her to it. He was perched on a stool, rubbing his eyes. This one did not seem to have had enough sleep, Ginika thought, looking at him with a sneaking suspicion.

"*Daa* Ginika, good morning," Monday greeted. He added '*daa*' when he greeted a female older than himself, and '*dee*' or '*dede*' if it was a man. She remembered she had once asked him why he did so. He had replied that it was the custom of his people.

"Where are you from?" she had wanted to know.

"From Mbawsi," had been the prompt reply.

Two years had passed since Monday joined the family and by now everyone in the house was used to being addressed as either *Daa, Dee or Dede*.

"Good morning, Monday. Why don't you go back to bed, I'll prepare breakfast myself?" Ginika's eyes focused on the big tear in the right knee area of Monday's black trousers. "Let me have *that* later to mend for you!"

"Thank you, *Daa*."

"That's all right. You may go now. Leave breakfast to me. Do we have bread and eggs in the house?"

Monday scratched his completely bare head. He must

have had a recent haircut and the barber made a good job of it.

"No, I wan cook for *oga* doctor now. I don sleep finish."
He scurried off and returned shortly with a big tuber of yam.

"Is this what we are going to have for breakfast?"

"Yes, Madam say make I prepare yam porridge for everybody this morning."

"Okay, you win, get on with the porridge. Let me know when you finish so that I may share the food." She looked forward to serving her father. It was time to call a truce, and she was willing to initiate it.

An hour later, Monday tapped on her door. "*Daa*, food don ready," he called.

She followed him to the kitchen. He had tidied up and washed up the utensils. He was always neat, thought Ginika. The kerosene stove still smoked, its smell, hot and stuffy. But it had dissipated enough for Ginika's nose to sniff out the strong but pleasant smell of the porridge. Monday was a good cook; this was not the first time she was relishing his culinary skills. "Good job, Monday. This sure smells nice. It had better taste nice."

"*Daa*, thank you. Am happy you like the food."

Ginika felt his pidgin was as half-baked as his English, yet Monday had insisted on speaking this bastardised English since he caught Ginika and Nwakire one day making fun of his Igbo dialect which was totally different from the Ama-Oyi dialect which the family spoke. With time, everyone had learnt to accept Monday's English, especially as it helped him to communicate well enough with the Ibibio man who was teaching him carpentry. This was the trade he had preferred to learn rather than the one the family had suggested. He had bluntly refused to learn bricklaying.

Udo sauntered in as Ginika was sharing the food. He had just finished washing the 403 and brought in the metal bucket, the brush and cloth he had used.

"Just on time, Udo," Ginika announced. "Here's your breakfast."

"Thanks, Sister Ginika, I'll put these things away and then rejoin you."

"Take the plates to the table," she instructed Monday. "I'll call Papa and Auntie Lizzy."

Ginika knocked gently on the door of her father's bedroom and waited. She was not surprised that her heart palpitated a little, but there was nothing to be afraid of anymore. Once upon a time, even thinking of that room spawned nightmares. The edge of her memory had become so blunt it couldn't possibly cut her now.

"Come in," was the curt reply.

She pushed the door open and entered. "Papa, your food is ready. Do you wish to eat now?" She gave him a big smile.

The first thing Ginika noticed about the room was that the bed was unmade and his pyjamas were lying across it where he had dropped them before having a bath. A table at the right-hand corner was cluttered with books, medical journals and sheets of paper. The house had no study; her father's bedroom served this purpose. Some of his books were carefully arranged on the big bookcase in the sitting room.

"Thank you." He glanced up from the papers he was scanning through. She could see he was utterly pleased that she was jolly and affectionate, after what transpired yesterday.

"What did you prepare this morning?" he asked.

"Yam porridge, but you'll like it."

"I'm sure I will. I need to eat well this morning; we have

a marathon session of surgery today. My first comes up at nine o'clock. Five cases of hernia and one of appendicitis . . ."

He stopped himself short, wondering why all these disclosures. Perhaps a way of expressing relief after her outrageous behaviour yesterday. Was he steadily weakening with age? He should be angry with her if only to impress upon her that such an appalling tantrum should not be displayed again.

"Papa, what is hernia?" Ginika had never heard of the ailment. She was pleased her father was in a communicative mood and was talking about his work in the hospital. He never ever mentioned his cases nor discussed his patients with the family.

"Oh, that is a long story. Let's keep it for another day. I must not be late to work. Now think of my suggestion that you enlist and train as a special constable."

Ginika nodded, withdrew and shut the door. She walked to her stepmother's door to tell her it was time for breakfast.

IT WAS quite hot in the afternoon. Ginika decided to retire to the back of the house and have a nap under one of the avocado trees. She loved to look at the trees and flowers in the compound. They soothed and calmed her nerves whenever she was in low spirits. The war had brought its own uncertainties and anxieties. She asked Monday to assist her to carry a mattress outside and place it on a mat she had spread out under the tree. She lay on the mattress, her eyes roving around the premises. They were not focusing on any object of particular interest for more than a second or two. The boys' quarters – BQ, as everyone referred to them – were some distance away, at the far side of the compound.

Often Ginika had to walk that short distance to call out to Monday when he was needed in the main house. It always struck her how the former occupiers who designed and built the houses in the living quarters had thought of virtually everything: the trees, the hedges and the rest of the landscaping which made the houses around here look so beautiful, so serene, so magnificent. She had heard it said that the original occupiers were white people who had managed the hospital in colonial times. Now all the doctors and nurses in the General Hospital were locals. Her father had worked as the Medical Director in the hospital for four years. The other two doctors and their families lived nearby, in similar quarters.

Ginika's eyes caught a lone avocado nestling among dark green leaves. She could hardly believe her luck, for it was tucked away from view. Where was Monday? He must come and pluck it for her. It was big. A seemingly meaty and luscious variety which this particular species produced. What a real find!

As she lifted herself to a sitting position, she saw Udo striding towards her, his handsome face sporting a smile, his crewcut accentuating his charm. How the war had disrupted everyone's education, she mused. Udo was in Form Three but now no one knew when the war would end. No one could say when schools would reopen. The war had only just started. The news last night was that Biafran soldiers were holding their own in the Nsukka sector and the Ogoja front.

"Sister, you have a visitor," Udo announced, giving her a knowing wink. "A friend, I think."

"A friend? What's the name of this friend?" She stared

blankly at him. "I don't have many friends here, really, and who among them knows I'm back anyway?"

Since her best friend, Anna Nwoke, moved to Umuahia last year, Ginika had no intimate friend in Mbano. Mrs Nwoke had moved to join her husband and had taken her children with her. How she missed Anna. "Male or female?" she asked Udo.

"Male. He said he came from Port Harcourt and that it is urgent."

"What's his name?" When he shook his head, she cried, "You mean you didn't ask him his name?"

"Should I go back and ask?"

"No, I'll see him. But next time, always ask for the visitor's name. It helps to prepare one. Sometimes one may not even want to see the visitor. In that case, it's more practical if you know who has come."

"Okay, Sister," Udo said.

He was tall and well-built, and was already seated when she entered the sitting room. She had come into the house through the back door and gone to her room to freshen up and change into more presentable clothes. She wore an open-necked white blouse and a maxi skirt made from flowered cotton material.

He sprang to his feet as soon as she entered the sitting room. He accepted the hand she thrust forward and shook it firmly. "Miss Ezeuko, *kedu*? How are you?" His eyes blinked his astonishment; she had changed a lot, with a fuller figure. He wondered if she still remembered him; their meeting had been so brief.

"I'm all right," Ginika replied, gingerly withdrawing her hand. "*Ibiana*, welcome. Please, sit down." She promptly recognised him, though he was taller and his figure more muscular than when she met him years ago.

"Thank you."

He took the chair nearest to the door as if he wanted to leave as soon as possible. Ginika sat at the other end of the room, near the large radiogram which occupied the space between the book-case and a table. She waited for him to speak, to explain his visit.

Her mind turned to the past and she recalled a skinny boy striding to where she sat, waiting for her father after the annual Thanksgiving Service in Ama-Oyi. She was thirteen then and had felt quite uncomfortable, with him standing there and talking to her. Apart from meeting him on that single occasion, she knew next to nothing about him.

"Miss Ezeuko, I'm not sure you remember me . . ." He paused, his eyes glued to hers.

She gave him a friendly smile, wondering if that was supposed to be a statement or a question. She decided to wait for him to say more.

He shook his head. "No, I don't think you do, but we've met before. It was a long time ago and only briefly, in Ama-Oyi. My name is Eloka Odunze, the President of Ama-Oyi Students' Association. Your father might have told you I sent two of our members to meet you but they weren't able to see you. Your father did tell them you were expected the following day. I decided to come myself, considering the delicate nature of our proposition." He paused as if to gauge the effect his words had on her.

Ginika felt she should say something at this point.

"Yes, my father told me about the visitors, but not the detail of their mission. Perhaps you should tell me now."

"Certainly," he said. He sat back in his chair and crossed his legs. "Our association is producing three plays and we want you to join us. Someone recommended you and said you were the best person to act one of the parts. Now that I have seen you, I agree with her." He laughed softly.

Ginika stared at him. "Who recommended me and what part am I supposed to play? And what makes you think I'm the best person to play the part?"

"Too many questions," he teased. His eyes seemed to disappear in their sockets when he laughed, and he laughed easily.

"Well, you must answer all of them if you want me to listen to you further." She was thinking: *You have a wonderful laugh and your teeth are the whitest I've ever seen.*

"Lucy, your school-mate recommended you. She said you are a good actress and acted in many plays in your school. As for the part we want you to play, you have a choice. You can either play the heroine in Shaw's *Arms and the Man*, or the mermaid in a play written by one of us entitled *Mammy Wota*. The other play is *No Place Like Home* and the cast has already started rehearsing. So which will it be?"

"You have not answered the third question," she reminded him.

"Why I agree you are the one to play either of the parts?"

"Yes," she confirmed, watching him.

"Do I need to say it? You know what I mean: you are beautiful." His eyes bore into her, challenging her to deny that she was beautiful, that this was the first time she heard someone say so. She laughed and looked away from him quickly to hide her embarrassment. But she was pleased that he considered her beautiful.

His eyes were still fixed on her when she rose, exclaiming, "How terrible of me; I haven't offered you anything. Will you like to drink a beer, Fanta or Coke? Or would you prefer oranges?"

"No, thanks," he said. "Please, sit down. You haven't answered my question. And, please, do not say no. I brought copies of the two plays with me so you can see we mean business."

"I cannot give you an answer now; I have to think about it. I have to discuss it with my father. Besides, I am already enlisted for training as a special constable. There are many girls in Ama-Oyi who can act these parts, I believe."

He could not hide his disappointment. "Miss Ezeuko . . ." he began.

"Please, call me Ginika," she said. "And may I call you Eloka?"

"Sure. Ginika, please, you must not say no. We are counting on you. There are many girls out there, as you put it, but not all of them can act. It might interest you to know that we had an audition and were disappointed with the result."

She thought about it for a moment and shrugged. "You may leave the scripts if you can spare them. But, please, don't give up your search for suitable hands. I'm not sure when I'll be free to leave Mbano, or if I'll be able to leave at all. I will definitely train as a special constable. If you will have me after that, I'll try to come down to Ama-Oyi."

He sensed she would not shift her ground. "All right, keep the copies; they are yours. If you allow me to choose for you, I would like you to play Mermaid, the sea princess. I believe you will make a perfect fit or match."

"Okay, I'll play the Mermaid," she finally agreed.

When this matter was settled, they talked about other issues. He wanted to know what she had been doing in Enugu, and she wanted to learn more about him, too, what life was like in Port Harcourt, how they were preparing for possible evacuation from the town.

"Can I have that bottle of beer you offered me?" he said. His mouth must have felt as dry as a bone.

"Yes, you can." She glided across the room while he followed her with his eyes. She too felt he was a bit dry. The beer was cold.

As he poured it carefully, he answered her question. "No one is thinking of evacuation from Port Harcourt, so there is no preparation for that eventuality. Certainly none in my family. My father thinks Port Harcourt is impregnable. He goes on and on about the power of Biafran *shore batteries* – the deadly mines planted on our seashores – that would repel every attempt of the enemy to enter either Port Harcourt or Calabar. If I try to disillusion him by saying that this is war and so nobody can be sure of anything, he may get angry and call me a pessimist. My father has strong views; sometimes I think he is rather difficult to deal with. He wants the war to end soon so that he can get on with his business and expand his empire; yet any time I raise the issue of joining the army, he flies into a rage, ordering me not to mention the subject again. He wants the war to end, but does not want his son to fight."

"I guess none of us wants to hear negative news about the war; your father is no exception. As for joining the army, many people don't want their children to fight for fear they would get killed. My father gets angry when my brother mentions joining the armed forces. He says he will not permit his only son to fight in the war."

"That's true, but isn't that self-delusion? If the war is to be won, people will have to fight. I'm in the same predicament: I'm an only son. My mother gets hysterical when she hears me talk about the army."

Ginika smiled at him sympathetically, as if to impress on him the fact that she perfectly understood his situation.

"Is your electricity here working?" he asked, changing the subject. "The beer is cold."

"Not really. We use a kerosene refrigerator. The hospital has a generator and we also get a supply of electricity in the quarters but only at night. In the morning it disappears."

"This is my first visit to Mbano," he admitted. "Is it a big place? A town?"

"I wouldn't call it a town. It's not like Enugu, Aba, Port Harcourt or Calabar. It's a county council made up of a number of communities. We live in the county headquarters where the General Hospital is located. There are also county council offices headed by a District Officer – DO. Each community has one or two colleges."

"What's life like out here? Do you like it?"

"What kind of question is that? This is where my family lives so I have no choice. War has now broken out, but I was in school most of the time apart from the holidays."

"Okay, maybe I put it wrongly. I meant to ask if you had a social life here before the war."

"Yes, quite a lot of it – church activities, students' gatherings and parties, local festivals of all sorts. Life was never static here. There were lots of activities to keep one busy. But the war has changed things. People are not as cheerful as before. Everyone is thinking of the war; many of the boys are talking of joining the army. Things like that."

"Can we listen to the news?" he asked, changing the subject. "This morning there was a rumour that our people were having a really bad time in the Nsukka sector and that Enugu is threatened. Radio Biafra denied it, of course."

"Yes, let's do that." Ginika ran out and came back with a transistor radio. "This one gets not only Radio Biafra but the BBC and Radio Kaduna."

She fiddled with it until she got the station she wanted. A voice was giving the news in Igbo and was saying that Biafran forces were repelling enemy attack at Opi Junction. It also announced that the fight was still raging in Gakem, in the Ogoja axis.

She tuned in to Radio Kaduna and it was screaming that Enugu had fallen into the hands of Federal forces. When the mind-bending shouts of 'O Shebe' assailed the air followed by the jingle 'To Keep Nigeria One is a Task that Must be Done', Ginika quickly turned off the radio.

"What about the BBC?" asked Eloka. "Can we also listen to it?"

More fiddling from Ginika - and the station came alive. It had nothing new to report except to tell them what they had already heard: Enugu was threatened and Gakem was about to fall to Federal forces hell-bent on invading Port Harcourt.

They sat in silence for a while. Ginika was upset. She rarely listened to news, for she always felt sad afterwards. The feeling was worse if she tuned in to Radio Kaduna. Yet she couldn't help listening, for she wanted to know what was happening, to find out which towns and villages were threatened and which had been evacuated. She felt sure Biafra's territory was largely intact, that the claims of victory made by Radio Kaduna were mostly false. She was a little uneasy though about the pronouncements of Radio Biafra. Were they all true?

"Where do you live in Port Harcourt?" she asked, trying to restore the cheerful mood that had enveloped them before.

"My family lives on the outskirts of town, on a large farm managed by my parents. We live between the city and Umukoroshe."

"A farm?"

"Yes, my father is a farmer; he bought huge tracts of land from the locals and has been farming the land for years. We grow cassava, maize, yams, cocoyams and all sorts of food and cash crops. A section of the land is used as a palm plantation; we grow pineapples too, and there is an orchard."

"It must be a wonderful place," she marvelled. "How do you feel surrounded by nature? The air around you must be fresh all the time?"

He laughed. "Like here, you mean?"

"Better than here, I'm sure. Do you do a lot of farming yourself?"

"Yes, I love the land. I used to assist my father a lot, but since I got into university, I have little time for farming. But I love gardening and still do much of that. I love growing flowers, especially roses. You need to see my rose garden."

Ginika gazed at him as if he was a creature from another planet. She had never met anyone who said he grew roses. She tried to imagine what a garden full of roses would look like. She was sure it would be beautiful, fascinating. She marvelled at him. He was a man of many parts, it seemed: a farmer, gardener, playwright, producer, director and actor, rolled into one.

"What course are you studying at university? And, by the way, which of the universities are you in?"

"Oh, I didn't tell you? I'm at Nsukka studying electrical

engineering. You don't have to tell me the name of your school. I know already."

"How did you know?" she asked, smiling.

"I told you: your schoolmate said a lot about you. I even know that you are majoring in the arts, studying literature, history and geography. I also heard you are the president of the Dramatic Society in your school and that a play you wrote was produced by one of your teachers last year and that you acted in it. You can now see why I was desperate to get to you, to persuade you to join us. I know an expert when I see one!"

Ginika doubled up on her chair, laughing so much he feared she would hurt herself. "You are a very cunning man," she cried.

He laughed. "Have you been to Port Harcourt?"

"Yes, we used to live there years back when I was in primary school. My father worked at the General Hospital."

"So you know the town well?"

"Not really. I was too young at the time." They both sat in silence for a while. "Do you know my brother, Nwakire?" she asked. "He's also a student at Nsukka but is based in the Enugu campus. He's studying medicine. Like father like son." She laughed.

"Yes, our paths have crossed once or twice again in Ama-Oyi. We hardly know each other, though. Like you, he is not a member of our association. Is he around?"

"No, he's visiting our uncle at Aba."

"I should run along," he announced. "Thanks for the beer and for agreeing to be part of our project. I look forward to seeing you again here or in Ama-Oyi. It will be a pleasure to show you my rose garden in Port Harcourt or Ama-Oyi. And my rabbit-hutch. Did I tell you I keep rabbits?" He wanted her to answer. "So, where will I see you, in Port Harcourt or Ama-Oyi?"

"In Ama-Oyi more likely," she said. "You speak our dialect so well. I'm ashamed to say I don't have your competence."

"I'm sure you would if you made the effort. What dialect do you speak at home when you are with your family? Or you speak English all the time?" He got up, his eyes still focused on her.

She answered him while still seated, "We speak a mixture of dialects – Ama-Oyi, Ikwerre, Mbano, Onitsha and a smattering of Owerri dialect introduced in the family by Auntie Lizzy." She laughed. "These are mostly places I have lived in. I take a bit of every dialect and get them together. Silly of me, you think?" She was laughing, challenging him to confirm her statement.

He smiled. "Your words, not mine." He stretched out his hand and pulled her up. "Come and see me off. Unless you want me to change my mind and spend the day and night with you and your family?"

She freed her hand from his grasp and walked towards the door; he was right behind her. "We have enough rooms for you to stay in if you choose," she teased. "But what happens to you afterwards is your own concern."

"Like what?"

"I leave you to figure that out."

He had come in a 404 Estate car. He got in and waved to her. "See you soon," he said. "It's a pleasure getting to know you." He gazed at her for some time before he started the engine. His words were an understatement compared to what his eyes were saying.

Ginika squirmed at his naked gaze, but she was glad he did not drop it.

"Bye." She waved as he drove off.

Throughout the day and evening, Ginika's thoughts were full of Eloka Odunze. She could not get him out of her mind even if she tried her hardest. His image cast a shadow she could not ignore – a lively and vivid mental picture of a figure after her heart. She tried to imagine a possible scenario where she would act in a play written, directed and produced by him. He had told her he wrote *Mammy Wota*, a political allegory of the war between Nigeria and Biafra. He was talented, a fully rounded individual, perfectly capable of doing so many things that made life worth living. She was pleased they both shared a common interest in writing plays and acting, as well as in horticulture.

She smiled a knowing smile. So, he had found out about *Adanma Chooses a Husband*, a play she wrote a year earlier to commemorate her school's Silver Jubilee. It was the first of such an attempt in the school, and the principal was over the moon. Ginika had felt a tinge of regret that the play was amateurish. But her literature teacher, Miss Miriam Taylor, had produced it, improvising on its features where necessary, to make it a successful production. Small wonder that everybody in the school started to call Ginika 'Dramatist'! She was not surprised when she was voted president of the school's Dramatic Society. Their next play had been Synge's *Riders to the Sea* in which she had participated as Bartley.

When her father returned from work, Ginika did not mention that Eloka had visited her. And she had no objection later when he sent for her and told her she could start training as special constable the next day. He was in the sitting room with Lizzy and two visitors – the District Officer in charge of Mbano County Council and his wife. It was the DO's office that organised the training programme which was run in batches. Ginika was to join the second batch.

"You will find it interesting," her father concluded. Ginika was leaning against the door, listening attentively.

"Precisely, it is a way to keep the youths busy and involved in the war effort," the DO concurred. His name was Ifeje Bosah, a thirty-five-year-old native of Onitsha and a graduate of sociology trained in the University of Edinburgh, in Scotland. He had only been recently posted to Mbano, the first graduate ever to head the County Council. He was determined to introduce changes in the way the County Council was run and to infuse new life into the system. Not even the war would discourage him from going ahead with his plans.

"Keeping them busy and focused is so crucial," Ebele, the DO's light-skinned, attractive wife put in. "Their energy is stupendous. Did you see what they did last week in front of the County Council office?" She shuddered at the thought. "They almost killed Mr Amadi because, according to them, they had heard he was arguing insistently that fighting a war was not in the best interest of Biafra, that Ojukwu and the other leaders should stop the war. They dragged him out from the office and were beating him up badly when Ifeje intervened, pleading with them to exercise restraint. I had gone to the office to collect something from Ifeje. I was so frightened. They were singing such war-songs as: 'Biafra *nwe nmeri*' and 'Ojukwu *nye anyi egbe*' . . . *Hmm*, if you saw their faces burning with anger, you would run. They were demanding guns to fight the invading army. If they had guns, they would have shot the terrified man." She wiggled her shapely body to the right, as she demanded confirmation of the incident from her husband. "Ifeje, is it not true?"

"You're right. They would have killed Mr Amadi or inflicted serious injury on him if they had had their way. It was a difficult task restraining the attackers. We need to keep this gang of youths busy, no doubt."

Ifeje Bosah had started going prematurely bald. The signs were there for anyone to see, though he still had a shock of hair on his head. Ginika considered it such a waste that much of this splendid crop of hair would disappear before long.

Lizzy shook her head in disbelief. "The dead will soon grow weary of sleep. The youths will have more than enough time to fight the war."

Ginika slipped out of the house unnoticed. They had virtually forgotten she was there. She told herself she would be there among the youths tomorrow, and looked forward to enjoying their company. On her way out, she almost collided with Monday who was hurrying to the sitting room with a plateful of guava. She knew they were for Ebele Bosah who was crazy about fruit, especially guavas and mangoes. Lizzy sated her regularly with loads of fruit gifts. And Ebele reciprocated by sending Lizzy a generous pack of chickens, eggs and goat meat which her husband had received as gifts from people in the various communities in Mbano. Ginika recalled hearing Ebele mention that she virtually lived off fruits and vegetables, and was sad no fruit trees grew in their quarters.

Back in her room, Ginika embarked on a desperate search for appropriate clothes for the training session. She would almost certainly need a pair of trousers or shorts. She did not usually wear these in Mbano, as most people considered them strictly men's clothes and frowned upon a girl wearing or appearing in them. So, she had to search thoroughly before stumbling across a pair of trousers Nwakire had given her as a birthday present two years ago. She had never ever worn them, for such an outfit was not allowed in school. She could not resist a hearty laugh at the thought that the war had made most people less conservative and more accommodating. The sight of a girl in trousers or shorts had now ceased to provoke a resentful stare or malicious criticism as in the past.

Times had changed, she thought, as she pulled out an old trunk from under her bed.

3

Ginika thought it was not wise to go too early to the field at the back of the County Council Office, where the training would take place. She knew nothing ever started when it should among her people. If someone told you to be somewhere at twelve noon, you should be there at two o'clock, two hours behind schedule. People have a name for this odd manner of telling the time – African time! She often wondered why this appellation was given to the habit. Did it mean that this was the common practice in other parts of Africa, say in Ghana, Ivory Coast, Kenya, Ethiopia or Zambia? She had never travelled abroad, so she could not find the answer to this puzzle. Suddenly, she belonged to a new country, Biafra.

This habit persisted in the new country, just as it did in Nigeria. She was struck by this sudden thought and she began to reflect on it. She was now a Biafran, not a Nigerian any more. So, Nigeria was now a foreign country to her. *Hei*, how life could be strange, unpredictable. As a little girl in primary school, she was taught to recite and sing Nigeria's national anthem. Now she was obliged to recite and sing the new Biafran anthem. Yes, life was full of surprises!

She got dressed slowly. She had found the trousers,

after a long search, in a raffia basket with a firm lid. She had shoved them in there when they came. She pulled the trousers in place and took a look at herself in the mirror hanging on the wall. They were black with two horizontal stripes of red material running from the waist down to the ankles. She liked the way they clung on tight to her body and perfectly fitted her natural contours. The tail tapered to a rounded tip, reaching the ankles without extending to her feet. It was certainly a ravishing dress.

She knew this was the style in vogue. In the past, loose trousers had been quite fashionable. She had seen them in magazines, but now they were made to fit closely. She had chosen to wear a red T-shirt Auntie Chito had bought for her. She drew back a little to see how perfect was the fit. She eyed the firm swell of her well-formed breasts, accentuated by the cotton fabric of the T-shirt. Was it too sassy, too eye-catching? Well, there was nothing she could do about it. She chuckled at the memory of how Miss Miriam Taylor had screamed about her voluptuous breasts that made it difficult for her to pass for a man when she played the part of Bartley in *Riders to the Sea*. When the play was eventually staged at the Shell BP Headquarters in Umumasi, Port Harcourt, a strip of cloth was used to damp down and flatten her breasts.

Well, this was the challenge a producer faced when plays were produced in girls' schools, where all the actors were female. Ginika did not think this problem would arise in a school for boys, as she supposed it was easier to fake a girl than a boy. Suitable pads of foam could be layered in someone's chest to look like breasts. She chuckled again; giggled this time on remembering how, in primary school, she used to put two small oranges, inside her dress, on either side of her chest, pretending they were her breasts. She would then stand in front of a mirror and cavort up and down like a fashion model she had seen in magazines Auntie Lizzy bought and left in the sitting room. One day, Nwakire had caught her at it and had laughed so uproariously that she scampered away in shame. She never ever played the game again. Pulling her canvas shoes from under the bed, she put them on.

When Ginika arrived at the training ground, there were already many people there. But as she rightly guessed, the exercise had not started. In fact, the instructors were nowhere to be seen. She saw many young women dressed in trousers as she, but they were by far fewer than the men. She scoured the large area for a familiar face. There were at least two hundred young men and women asked to assemble there. She decided to slog around from one side of the field to the other, hoping to find someone she knew. The youths had gathered in groups, discussing the war, making claims and counterclaims about Biafra's successes and Nigeria's losses. Some of them said the war would end soon and were sad they might not have the opportunity to fight, to show the enemy what they could do, and teach Gowon and his men a lesson. One skinny young man of about twenty beat his breast and boasted he would be an army officer before the war ended.

Ginika heard another youth shout him down. "*Mechie onu gi*, shut your mouth! You will for sure catch a leopard with bare hands, you coward! When the time comes, you will run 'four-forty', the race of a lifetime!" The aggressor was short and stocky, twenty or twenty-one years old.

Everyone present roared with uncontrollable laughter.

"Who are you talking to like that?" the aggrieved youth demanded, soured and disillusioned. "What did I say wrong to attract your scorn and venom?" Turning to the others, he complained, "You all heard him. I was not talking to him. Why should he put his *akputu* mouth into something that did not concern him, eh?"

"Who has *akputu* mouth?" the stocky young man cried, coming forward with vengeance. "Tell me, which of us has *akputu* mouth? You or me? Look at the thickness of his lips, like the lobes of a fat woman's buttocks."

Laughter exploded all around. People were sent reeling backwards and bursting into peals of mirth. Soon, the two combatants engaged each other in a slanging match, enduring each other's taunts about their mutually identifiable physical deformities. The stocky one called the other *ogwu azu*, fish bone. They let fly at each other with a stream of abuse, like two cocks fighting to the death. However, bystanders separated the two men before they could hurt each other.

"Stop this nonsense!" one other youth shouted them down. "Reserve your energy for the enemy; it will not be long before you are called to confront him."

Ginika moved away gingerly, for she had just seen someone she recognised. It was Bobby Unogu, the second son of one of the doctors in the Mbano General Hospital. They were friends and he often visited her at home during the holidays. Bobby was tall and slender, with a physique that was more feminine than masculine. He wanted Ginika to be his special girl, as he had put it, in a special relationship that would be more romantic than platonic.

"Be my girl," he had urged and pleaded. "For me alone." She had asked him what he meant and he replied by pulling and holding her close to him and pressing his cheek to hers. Ginika had shoved him off and screamed, "Are you out of your mind? What would my father say?"

She was then in Form Four. And she had not liked any lad being chummy with her. However, Bobby's misadventure had not ended their friendship, but it had left it just where it was when it started. They had met, talked generally about school, laughed and parted without so much as holding hands. Like her, he was preparing for the higher school certificate examination when the war broke out.

When their eyes met without flinching, he strode along to meet her.

"Hello, Bobby," she greeted.

"Ginika, so you're back? I was wondering where you had been and why you didn't come home after schools had closed. When did you get back?" He shook gently but warmly the hand she had offered him.

"Fine face," she teased. "Are you still growing?" she looked him up and down. His handsome face was beginning to sprout a mustache; a fine line above his upper lip that enhanced his good looks.

"Yes, I guess, I'm still growing." He was laughing. "I'm nineteen this year and my father said I would continue to grow until I am twenty-one."

"Well, make sure you don't become Goliath or you'll find no one to marry."

"I thought I had found someone already?" He was still laughing, looking into her eyes with romantic longings. She turned back to look at him, but there was no fire in her eyes.

A loud call diverted their attention. A man was trying to draw everyone's attention and telling them to gather in the centre of the field. Ginika and Bobby gravitated towards his gesticulations and he turned out to be a militiaman. But it was rumoured that they hated each other – the regular army and the militia. Reports were rife that they revelled in petty jealousies and antagonisms. Ginika did not know if these reports were true. There was always a rumour circulating: if it was not about the war front, it was about what happened in the government, or about the activities of the immensely powerful individuals who controlled Biafra and dictated her pace of action and direction. Some of these people were said to have committed their enormous resources, both inside and outside Biafra, to ensure her survival.

Ginika noticed that Ifeje Bosah was among the three men approaching from the direction of the office. He addressed the youth.

"We are pleased to see so many of you responding to the national call. Biafra counts on you, on every citizen, and wants you to do your best to ensure that the war is won, that the war ends quickly in our favour. You are the second group destined to receive training as special constables. No doubt, many of you will go beyond this assignment and join the armed forces later. But this is a good beginning for all of you. You will be called to higher service if you perform well in this one."

He paused and surveyed the crowd. "We encourage you to maintain discipline and self-control. If you behave badly, you will definitely be disciplined by the teacher trainers. So, forewarned is forearmed, as the saying goes. I wish you well in your training."

A shout of joy rent the air as the crowd hailed the DO.

He waved as he took his leave, followed by one of his aides. The other two conferred with the militiaman. Three men detached themselves from the crowd and joined them. Ginika felt that those men must be the trainers. She watched them.

The crowd was still in jubilant mood. The speech had stirred them into action and fired their zeal. Some of them were yelling, "Biafra, win the war! Victory to the Rising Sun!" Ginika knew they were referring to the Biafran logo – a bright yellow image of the sun rising from the east. She was ecstatic and joined in the jubilation, sandwiched, as she was, between Bobby and another tall man. Though averagely tall, she was virtually dwarfed by the two young men beside her.

She heard a man behind her say, "My prayer is that everyone will be allowed to undergo the training, including some of us who cannot speak *oyibo*, English. I am absolutely illiterate." Another voice replied, "Why should they not allow us? Do people use *oyibo* to shoot the enemy? Does the gun speak *oyibo*?" A third voice added, "I wonder! Have you not heard that many of the enemy soldiers do not speak *oyibo* at all, especially those they call *gwodogwodo*? I heard they speak only Hausa; they say they come from Niger Republic and are helping Nigeria to fight us." Ginika turned round, nodded and smiled at the men. "My sister, am I lying?" the last speaker asked, returning the smile. "No, you are not lying," she confirmed.

Soon the training session began. Six groups were formed and designated squads: altogether six in number. Ginika was in Squad One, while Bobby belonged to Squad Five. Each of the six trainers took charge of a squad. The militia officer was responsible for Ginika's squad. Thirty people were in Squad One and eight of them women. The militia officer seemed to find Ginika attractive and did not hide his feeling for her. From the beginning, he paid her extra attention and encouraged her more than he did the rest.

"Yes, Miss Ezeuko," he once remarked, "you are doing

very well. Good." To the rest he would say, "You must emulate her; she learns fast."

Ginika was delighted to be considered the best, but she would not want the officer to create a situation where the other trainees, especially the girls, envied or resented her. She had overheard one of them grumble about this growing resentment among them. After all, weren't they there to learn and not seek to be elevated above others? Ginika wanted to maintain a cordial relationship with everyone, including the officer, but nothing more than that. Most of them looked rustic and she was sure they did not have her kind of educational background. So she kept it a closely-guarded secret. She got to know that one of the girls called Alice was a barmaid and another named Aku traded in second-hand clothes. Ginika was excited about the possibilities of the militia experience. She was surprised how little she remembered or thought about Eloka Odunze. She wondered if he was in Port Harcourt or Ama-Oyi now.

The training programme that first day was taken up by an introduction to military terminology, followed by marching drills on the grassy field. The officer explained terms like platoon, company, battalion, division and such abbreviated ones as 'recce', meaning reconnaissance and 'sit rep', meaning situation report. Ginika grasped the importance of these terms easily and responded eagerly to questions, while most of the others struggled along.

"Left, right; left, right . . . About turn . . . One time, mark time, *Hudee* . . . One two . . . Stand at ease!" intoned the officer who had introduced himself as Lieutenant Kanu Ofodile. When he said *hudee*, he dragged his right foot and allowed it to meet the left where it stood still, a little in front. He took two or three steps forward and the squad followed him in a four-line formation. His lithe figure was a spectacle to behold as it stepped forward, swivelled around and moved forward again.

Some of the girls giggled nervously at the ace performance. They were clearly revelling in the music of his military jargon. It sounded as if he was saying, "Lef, rai. Lef, rai. Abou tua . . . Tanda taiz!" They enjoyed the nonsensical sound of the drills better than the intellectual appeal of the training course or menu that required them to memorise technical terms and explain them when asked to do so. All the girls and some of the men had good, if not rumbustious, fun marching up and down their section of the field. Two particular girls wiggled their bottoms and shook their waistlines loose, as if they were doing a riotous dance routine.

"Stop it!" roared Lieutenant Ofodile. "Are you dancing or marching? Do you think we are here to make a joke of this business?"

Alice, the barmaid, giggled at his intervention.

"You, come here!" bellowed Ofodile. "Idle civilian! Common, hold your ears and do frog-jump until I tell you to stop." He showed her what to do and she obeyed, all smiles wiped off her sweaty forehead.

The rest of the squad were shocked at the officer's instant reaction and became more serious and resolute. Alice failed to turn up the next day. In fact she never showed up after that first day. Ginika made friends with one of the girls who came from Umuduru, one of the neighbouring communities. Her name was Philomena. She told Ginika she had lived in Lagos before the war and had worked as a sales girl in a petrol station. She had an interesting story to tell about how she escaped being killed when Igbo people were hunted down and murdered in Lagos and other cities, especially in northern Nigeria.

After one week of training, the squad was introduced to the use of a gun and live ammunition. Lieutenant Ofodile brought a rifle for the exercise. They had been practising with sticks which they handled and wielded as if they were guns. Nonetheless, Ginika was afraid, and reluctant to handle the gun.

"Common, try it," Kanu Ofodile coaxed at first, and then bellowed, "There is nothing to be squeamish about. You want to be a soldier? You must carry a gun; so, you have to learn to use it!"

At this point, she was lying face down in the bush behind the county council office, while the other members of the squad stood and watched. They all wore garlands of leaves on their heads, and had twigs stuck into the waist-bands of their trousers and into their shoes as camouflage.

Ginika took the gun gingerly. She was relieved when he told her that there was no bullet in it yet. But before the end of the training period, each of them had to learn to fire a gun with a live bullet. Kanu Ofodile lay beside her, his body pressing her side. She could feel one of his legs on top of hers. Frowning, she shifted uncomfortably where she found herself, but did not lose concentration. She held the gun with her left hand and he guided her right to practise squeezing the trigger. Soon the others took it in turns.

The training was to last four weeks, but after two weeks, another officer took over Squad One while Kanu Ofodile was asked to proceed to Orie-agu to train the youths of that community as special constables. In his report, he wrote that Miss Ginika Ezeuko was the best candidate in all the squads and requested that she should be promoted to join him in training the youths at Orie-agu. The DO was pleased with the report and immediately sent the good news to Ginika's father. His messenger was none other than Ebele, his amiable wife. She paid a visit to the Ezeukos in the evening. When she left an hour later, Monday trudged after her, weighed down with a basket of oranges Lizzy had given Ebele.

After dinner, Ubaka sent for Ginika. He was happy she had distinguished herself and felt justified that he did the right thing by bringing her back from Enugu to Mbano.

"Ginikanwa, you've done really well," he declared. "You have my permission to join the officers who will train Orie-agu youths." His smile was big and broad enough to reveal his perfect white teeth.

Ginika smiled in return. She wished her father could smile some more. He looked less intimidating when he smiled.

"I'll go if you want me to, Papa." She, Lizzy and Udo were sitting together with him in the living room.

"Yes, I want you to. You can see it was not a bad idea after all, taking you away from Enugu." His smile broadened as though he was telling himself that, by and large, parents should make decisions for their children, and that it would amount to sheer irresponsibility to allow them too much independence before they reached maturity.

"But how will she get to Orie-agu?" Lizzy asked. She was picking her teeth with an improvised toothpick. "Orie-agu is more than ten miles from here."

"That has been taken care of. The DO has given instructions that she and the officer, Lieutenant Ofodile, be taken to Orie-agu each day by the county council's Land Rover."

"Sister, may I come along with you?" begged Udo. He had longed to go with Ginika for the training ever since it started, but she said he was too young for that.

"You are too young to train," she told him again. "Boys of your age are not allowed to participate. How many times will I tell you that, Udo?"

"Okay, I've heard you." He picked up a book on his lap and began to read.

"Oh, I forgot to tell you," said Ubaka, "Enugu fell to enemy troops today. It was broadcast on the BBC earlier today and Radio Biafra also admitted it in its news bulletin this evening. It's a big setback for Biafra."

"My God, what about Uncle Ray, Auntie Chito and their children?" wailed Ginika. "Papa, do you think they are safe?" She began to cry.

"I don't know," her father replied. "We will not know until after some time. Somebody I met this afternoon said people have been streaming out of the town since yesterday. The roads, I understand, were heavily congested as vehicles and people struggled to escape from the beleaguered town which was under heavy shelling by Nigerian forces. He told me he had not seen such heavy traffic in all his life. I thank God this did not happen the day we went to Enugu to pick you up, Ginikanwa."

"God saved us," Lizzy said. "Our eyes would have seen our ears if it had happened that day. God is good."

Ginika was not listening to them now: her concern for her aunt was choking her. "What are we going to do to reach them, if they are safe?" she moaned. "Papa, may I go in search of them as far as Udi or Awka?"

"No, I am afraid not," Ubaka said firmly. "Nwakire will be back tomorrow. I will send him to Ama-Oyi to find out if Ray Akah and his family are there. I believe this is the most sensible thing for them to do, head for Ama-Oyi, after evacuating from Enugu."

Ginika was worried and frightened for her aunt and her family and prayed for their safety. She clung to the hope that they would head for Ama-Oyi. She agreed that it was an option they could take if they managed to escape at all from the town. She knew there was nothing she could do but wait, as her father had said. She was somewhat relieved that her father would do something, that he would send Nwakire to Ama-Oyi to see if they were there. She knew she would not be able to feel completely at ease until there was news, credible news, about them and their safety. But now she had to be patient and wait for that. She was frightened though that the war was adding a new dimension, an unforeseen angle, to their overburdened lives.

4

Eloka sat behind the wheel but there was no sign of Osondu, the farmhand. He waited a few more minutes and honked impatiently. He had many things to attend to today before moving to Ama-Oyi. He did not have time to waste and here was Osondu forcing him to do just that.

Osondu ran out of the house in a moment, his unbuttoned shirt revealing his hairy chest. "Sorry, Brother Eloka," he apologised as he got into the seat next to Eloka. "*Oga* called me back to do something for him as I was about to come out. That is why I am late."

Eloka nodded, "All right. We can go now; there is so much I have to do today. Did you put the machete in the boot?"

"Yes, I did that this morning when I washed the car."

In a moment they were driving out of the compound, leaving a cloud of dust billowing out behind them. Eloka glanced at the rear-view mirror, saw the moving cloud of dust and reduced speed. He thought that if anyone was standing by the road, he or she would be covered by the rising dust. Perhaps it would be best to have the road tarred. But would his father want to do this even if he could afford it? He did not believe that money should be spent on projects that were not crucial. Tarring the driveway to his farm was not his priority, especially now that a war was raging. He was more concerned about the fate of his farm. But what would happen to the farm if Port Harcourt fell into the hands of the enemy?

The old man, as Eloka often referred to his father – though he was not really old, just a little over sixty – was also worried about how to begin and where to move his property, especially the livestock if ever a time came for an emergency evacuation. His thoughts were interrupted by Osondu who informed him a vehicle had just passed and a man inside it was frantically waving to him.

Eloka looked at the side mirror and saw that a car had actually stopped and a man was getting out from the driver's side. He too stopped and allowed the car to roll to the side of the road, ensuring he was not causing any obstruction. It was his friend and classmate, Etim Usoro, and he was sauntering towards Eloka as if he had all the time in the world and expected everyone else to be in his shoes. Eloka checked his watch and thought he really had to get going.

"Hi, ole boy," Etim hailed him from a short distance. "Where are you heading? I was actually going to your house. Good I came this way or I would have missed you."

Eloka had left the outskirts of town where the farm was and had just entered the metropolis. He had almost reached his destination, Kingsway Stores, before Etim stopped him.

"Hey, man," he greeted. "I'm in a hurry, running errands for my mother." He was still sitting inside the car. He noticed that Etim, who used to be clean-shaven, had grown a beard. It was short, but it was there. "Hey, are you imitating His Excellency! Look at that beard."

Etim laughed. "No, I'm not imitating anyone, just sheer laziness." He bent from the waist and they shook hands.

"How are you doing?" Eloka asked. "Did you hear Enugu had fallen? Very bad news, very bad." He shook his head.

"This is the problem," Etim said. "Things are not going well. I'm bored with life at home, hardly anything to do all day except listen to news or visit friends. I'm even tired of hearing people discuss the war. They either make you sad or raise false hopes in you."

"Well, we are at war and these things are to be expected. The news about Enugu was shattering, to say the least." Eloka looked away, his right hand caressing the steering wheel.

"Look, I'm tired of all this uncertainty," Etim blurted it out. "I'm thinking seriously of joining the war; perhaps joining the Biafran Army Engineers Corps that gives logistics support to the infantry battalions. What do you think, my friend?"

When Eloka said nothing, Etim continued, "Man, you are luckier than I. You have your father's farm to keep you busy; I have nothing tangible to do all day. I might as well be useful in the war front."

"Have you discussed this with your father, with your family?" Eloka asked, softly. "Do so before you make a move; that's my advice." He paused and then added, "I've got to go. I have to leave Port Harcourt later today for Ama-Oyi, and there is little time left. I don't know what else to say to you, but I'm becoming very realistic about this war. Most of us might eventually join the army; it's a matter of time. We may lose contact with friends for a while or even forever. Who knows how many of us will survive the war?"

"Now, you are being damn pessimistic," Etim said with a short laugh. "I believe the war will not last too long." He straightened himself up, patting his low-cut hair which was parted in the middle.

"What makes you think so?" Eloka stared at him. "I haven't seen any sign that this is going to be a short war. I'm just being realistic. Anyway, I'm leaving Port Harcourt today. Take care of yourself whatever you decide to do. Hopefully, we'll meet some time in the future." Suddenly, Eloka felt terribly sad. He was not sure when or where he would see his friend again. On impulse, he extended his hand to Etim and he grasped it. They shook hands again, more warmly and for a longer time.

"Bye, Eloka, my friend, and take care as well." Etim was dispirited as he contemplated himself returning to his home in the government reserved area, GRA, where he hung out all day doing nothing.

Eloka watched him enter the car and drive off. He himself pulled out and continued on his way to Kingsway. "What are you thinking about?" he asked Osondu, who had listened to the conversation between the two friends.

Osondu smiled faintly, scratched his head and replied in the Ama-Oyi dialect, "Nothing important really, but I was just thinking about the war that is gobbling up many heads. I was also thinking about what you said – that most people will end up fighting in the war."

"*Ehe*, it has come to the time of doing, not just talking! Can you fire a gun yourself?" Eloka asked, still speaking in typical Ama-Oyi parlance.

"Brother Eloka, your question bugs me. That is really my problem." The smile had completely deserted Osondu's face, leaving it rather grim. "I am not a fighter; I have never fought anybody since I was born. How then can I fight a war? Fear alone will kill me before I even fire the first shot. Moreover, someone told me our army does not enlist short people. As I am as short as *ikpi nku*, a stump so to speak, do you think they will even look at me let alone test me for suitability?"

Eloka burst into laughter. He had almost passed Kingsway before he realised it and had to brake to a halt, before negotiating the road that led to it. "Osondu, so you are a coward?" he asked after he had parked the car at the Kingsway parking lot. "You must not say what you have just told me to anyone else or they will laugh scornfully at you. Some will even report you to the military authorities. If a young man like you refuses to fight, who then will? Women? And what is the meaning of your name, Osondu? Does it not mean 'race for survival'?"

"I hear you, Brother Eloka, but I have told you the truth. And I'm not ashamed of it. I do not want to hurt a fly, let alone kill somebody."

"Suppose a bee buzzes about you, will you not kill it? Suppose a man attacks you in order to kill you, will you not fight back and kill him instead?"

Osondu thought about it, and was still puzzling it out when Eloka locked the car and asked him to follow him. Before they entered Kingsway, Eloka turned to him and said, "This is what the war is all about. Some people have attacked us and want to kill us, so we must fight back and kill them too before they kill us."

As usual, there were many people in the store, buying all imaginable things: clothes, hardware, food, cosmetics, baby things and kitchen equipment. Eloka could understand why the human traffic was so much – Kingsway was the largest department store in Port Harcourt and attracted people from different walks of life. Eloka hated coming here to shop, but his mother often sent him on and his father asked him to help deliver vegetables, fruit and other farm products their farm supplied to Kingsway. The previous day, he had been there to supply pineapples and bananas.

Quickly, he picked up from the shelves the items he had been asked to buy. Osondu helped to move them to the counter behind which perched a buxom cashier.

"Hello," she greeted them cheerfully.

Eloka smiled and said, "Hello." He knew she was obeying one of the maxims: 'the customer is supreme and always right; be polite and attend to him or her'. He paid her and said, "Keep the change." She smiled her thanks and nodded, as they left.

He drove out of the parking lot, and headed for Diobu. There was an air of gloom everywhere and he attributed it to the fall of Enugu, the nation's capital. Naturally, people were jittery. Nobody knew what would happen next. He knew most people believed that if the enemy captured Enugu, they would next turn to Port Harcourt. This was to be expected, as Port Harcourt was not only a seaport and a major city, but also the headquarters for oil exploration. Eloka noticed there were more checkpoints on this road since last week when he used it. He was stopped three times, and he regretted not going home the way he had come, though this route was shorter. There was nothing he could do now but to endure the delay. One of the checkpoints was manned by militia-men in green uniform and black berets.

"What do you have in your boot?" one enquired politely.

"Nothing," Eloka declared.

"Let me see."

"Sure." He got out and opened the boot. The man nodded, Eloka banged the boot and returning to the car zoomed off. At the next stop, he saw two women and a man dressed differently. As they looked into the boot and searched the vehicle thoroughly, he told himself these must be the special constables he had heard about. The image of Ginika Ezeuko flashed in his mind. He remembered she had said she would train as a special constable. She had been on his mind since their meeting; he hoped she was giving attention to the script he left with her. Somehow, he thought he could not find a better actor to take the part of Mammy Wota, the water goddess. "You may go; we are through," he heard one of the girls say. He looked at her and nodded, and she freed the barrier for him. He was impressed by her professionalism, her devotion to duty and her courtesies.

He drove past Trans-Amadi Layout, past Umumasi, and finally reached Umukoroshe. He heaved a sigh of relief as he drove into the farm. In the next thirty minutes or so, he and Osondu cut leaves and *ata* grass for the goats and the rabbits from the forested and grassy areas of the farmland. These were regular chores which had to be done nearly every day. He helped out whenever he was home on holiday. Since the war started, he had become fully involved in running the farm. His father wanted it so and had actually wanted him to study agriculture, but Eloka had declined, preferring engineering. He knew his father wanted him to take over and run the farm fully on graduation. But this was not to be, and now the war had changed everything.

Back in the house, he began to pack his things hurriedly. He did not want to get to Ama-Oyi after dark, so he had to leave as soon as he could. His room was in a mess, had been so for some days since he started sorting his things out in preparation for his journey. Instinctively, he knew Port Harcourt would become a war theatre soon, so he wanted to take the things he valued most, to take as many of his things as he could carry. His father had even conceded to his request to take one of the cars along with him. He was sure it would be handy when the association started rehearsing the plays, on hitting the road for performance.

Now satisfied he had all he would need, he called Osondu and told him to put the things in the car. He was taking the estate car which was quite roomy and rugged and would accommodate everything he meant to take with him. He led the way to the rabbit-hutch and Osondu followed with the leaves and grass they had cut on their way back. As he approached, the rabbits scuttled about, excited that food had come their way at last. He surveyed the cages, wondering what would happen to the poor creatures if Port Harcourt was evacuated especially while he was away. His heart was also burdened about the entire farm, his father's business and everything else that would be ruined by the war if the city was lost. He counted the rabbits to make sure they were twenty, both the adults and the young ones. He rubbed their bodies tenderly and they slipped in and out of his arms. "Be good," he whispered, as if he was speaking to children. A big rabbit sat on its haunches, staring at him, virtually saying goodbye in its own way, apparently sensing his master was undertaking a journey. "Take care of your harem and your little ones," Eloka said to the rabbit, rubbing its ears. He picked up one of the small ones by the ears and said, "Osondu, this is how you do it; take note of it."

"Let me try it while you are still here," Osondu suggested.

"That's a good idea. Anyway, Anyanwu knows, for he took care of them when I was not around, so you can ask him if you have any problem." He watched him lift one rabbit and then put it back in the cage. "Bring me this cage," he told Osondu, indicating the smallest of the three cages. "I'm taking it to Ama-Oyi. And, Osondu, please, take good care of the rabbits and my rose garden. Take the cage to the car and join me in the garden."

He was in the garden, tending the roses, when Osondu joined him. He moved from the section where pink roses grew to where red roses grew in thick clusters. He tried to untangle some of the stems that were resting on others, telling himself the rose bushes needed pruning, but he did not have time to do it before leaving. He hoped Osondu would do it; he had taught him how to do it. The garden was a square enclosure, fenced with barbed wire, and located directly behind the main house, a storey building in which the family lived. There were three other smaller houses, bungalows, in which the farmhands, the servants, the drivers and their families lived. Some distance away was an outhouse which was used as a store. One side of it sheltered the goats and sheep. Eloka could hear the goats bleating, apparently fighting over the leaves Osondu had left for them.

He went in search of his mother and found her lying down in her room. "Mama, I am ready to leave." He went in and sat on the edge of the bed. His eyes shifted from one part of the room to the other. In one corner stood three metal trunks, one on top of the other. Eloka was sure they were full of Dutch wax, his mother's favourite brand of *wrappa*. There would also be Madras cloth popularly called *intorica*. On these, his mother and women of her circle spent a fortune, accumulating materials that would soon go out of fashion, to be replaced by others with high-sounding names that would make them sell well. The more sophisticated the name, the costlier the material, he knew.

"Nna, *ikwadone*, you are ready to go?" she asked, struggling to get up.

She called him Nna, Father, for he was said to be a reincarnation of her father, his grandfather. She touched his face lovingly, allowing her hand to slide down his chest. She looked worn out and tired as if she had not slept for days. She was on the fat side, but still retained some of the good looks she must have had in abundance in her younger days, some of which her four children – Eloka and his three sisters – inherited.

He smiled at her, noticing her furrowed brows, the wrinkles on her upper lip and the dark lines underneath her lower eyelids. "Mama, don't worry about anything," he pleaded. "I think you worry too much. The war is here and you cannot wish it away. However, we must do our best to ensure that Biafra wins it. I have asked Papa to send you to Ama-Oyi, which is quieter and safer for you. At least, there are no air raids there. I have also suggested that some of our things should be moved to Ama-Oyi."

"You are right," she agreed. "Now you are moving to Ama-Oyi, I think I should follow so that I can take care of you. I know you will starve yourself there."

He laughed. "Starve myself? Why should I do that? But I agree that you should move to Ama-Oyi. I do not like the way you worry yourself sick here in Port Harcourt. Is there anything you want me to take to Ama-Oyi for you?"

"Yes, you can take my trinkets. They are in a small box, but are you sure those militia and soldiers at the checkpoints will allow you to drive out of town?"

"Why not?" he asked. "There is no panic, and nothing is happening here to make them stop anyone driving out of town."

"You are probably right; do not mind me."

He hugged her, picked up the box and walked out of the room.

"*Ije oma, nwa m.* Safe journey," she called out to him.

As Eloka drove out of the compound, the delivery van trundled in. Behind the wheel was David, the driver. Eloka waved to him and he waved back. He gave one last glance before the farm disappeared from his view. This was where he grew up, where his father invested his money and toiled for so many years. He loved the place with its well-tended cultivated patches, its orchards and vegetable gardens, its livestock; and he cherished his rose gardens and his rabbits. How much longer would all these belong to him, to his family? He felt sad that just as the farm was beginning really to rake in money, to pay back for all the resources and sweat expended on it, the war came and threatened to destroy everything. Eloka grieved that his father might lose everything he had worked for all his life. He had paid good money to the locals to secure this property, the farmland.

WITH A SIGH, ELOKA HEADED FOR AMA-OYI, ALMOST SURE HE WOULD NOT BE ABLE TO RETURN TO PORT HARCOURT.

5

Ginika was the first to hear that Auntie Chito and her family were safe in Ama-Oyi after their dramatic evacuation from Enugu. Her scream followed by whoops of joy brought Udo flying into the sitting room, to be followed shortly by an alarmed Lizzy and Ubaka, who thought something had gone amiss. They were relieved to find her holding Nwakire, in a warm embrace, crying, "Thank God; oh, God, I thank you-o!" She was both laughing and crying, thanking Nwakire for bringing back such good news. She was the one that whooped up the good news to the rest of them, though the sight of Nwakire, his cheerful look and Ginika's profuse gratitude to God had given them a foretaste of what the scream, the wild laughter and the hysteria were all about. "Nwakire saw them," she announced. "Auntie Chito, Uncle Ray and their children are all safe in Ama-Oyi. Thank God."

Nwakire was a tall and sturdy young man, but the unexpected momentum of Ginika's embrace had almost floored him. He had had to spread his legs and plant them solidly on the carpeted floor to cushion his body from the impact of her bear hug. She had not been herself since the loss of Enugu, agonising over her aunt and her family, driving herself mad with the thought that they were trapped in the town or had been killed by the rampaging enemy soldiers. She had refused to go to Orie-agu with Lieutenant Ofodile to train the new recruits. It was a complete mood swing for her now, her face suffused with joy, her voice clear and tingling like a bell. She freed Nwakire, led him to a chair, addressing him fondly, "Kire, please, sit down and tell us what happened. How did they escape from Enugu?"

They all sat down, wanting to hear what actually took place in Enugu: how the enemy managed to infiltrate into it and capture that well-guarded city. There were rumours flying around about how Enugu was lost, about the error made by some army commanders in charge of defending the capital, and about suspected sabotage involving some indigenes. Nobody in Mbano was absolutely sure of what actually happened, so this was a good opportunity to find out. Ginika was more interested in knowing how her aunt and her family escaped. Her father was eager to learn about the fate of the capital, if all of it had been lost or if a section was still in Biafran hands. He was willing to listen to Nwakire though he was expected in hospital after the lunch break. Perhaps Ray and Chito had the facts and passed them to Nwakire.

With all eyes on him, pleading that he should tell his story, Nwakire had no choice but to narrate what he had heard from his uncle and aunt. He had not even had time to drop his travelling bag before Ginika saw him, grabbed him and almost pushed him down in sheer excitement. He was tired after travelling by public transport on some of the worst roads imaginable, after the delays on the congested roads owing to the number of checkpoints that had sprung up in all nooks and crannies of Biafra.

He sat back in his chair, crossed his long legs and began. "Uncle Ray said no one was actually sure when the enemy entered the town. There was hardly any warning before *katakata*, confusion and commotion engulfed the whole town. The result was that most inhabitants of the city fled without taking much of their property; some lost everything, taking nothing out except their lives and the clothes they were wearing at the time. He said that the first thing he knew about the threat to the city was the sound of *gbim, gbim, gbim* – heavy bombardment and shelling by the enemy.

"Did they say how the enemy entered the town?" asked Ubaka. "Was it sabotage as some people claim?"

"Uncle Ray did not think it was sabotage. He said the enemy shelled the town before they entered it. He was sure they were not inside the town when people started moving out in panic. It was the shelling, the mortar fire that drove people away and cleared the way for the invading forces to enter the town. He also said it was possible the Biafran defence between Opi and Enugu was outnumbered and completely outgunned, and this enabled the enemy to move nearer the town before unleashing the heavy shelling."

Ubaka had heard enough and had to return to hospital. "How are the people at home?" he asked Nwakire. "Did you see my brother and his family? What about Akueju and her children? Are they all right?"

Before Nwakire replied, Ginika's eyes settled on Udo and held his gaze for a moment. It was as if telling him that she loved him and empathised with him. That she was there for him and would be always. She was thinking of Udo's father who lost his life in Jos in the pogrom that took place there before the war started. His mother, Akueju, was living in Ama-Oyi with her other two children. Udo read Ginika's thoughts, smiled and then turned his attention to Nwakire in time to catch his words.

"They are all well," Nwakire was saying. "Uncle Chima asked when you'll send some of our things to Ama-Oyi: whether you do not think it is the proper thing to do in view of the war and the way people are losing property in the places they lived before they were displaced. I think he was referring to what happened to Uncle Ray and Auntie Chito."

Ubaka gave a short laugh and left the room.

"Nwakire, *nno*, welcome back," Lizzy said, as she got up to follow Ubaka.

Nwakire nodded. "Thank you, Lizzy." He called her Lizzy and had done so since he went to university and felt grown up enough to consider it ridiculous to address his stepmother as Auntie Lizzy. He then concluded that it was best to call her by her name and do away with the pretension. He recalled the first time he did this, how surprised she had looked and how offended afterwards. But he had stuck to his guns and there was nothing she could do about it. Was it not ridiculous on her part, in the first place, to have asked her stepchildren to call her aunt? Nwakire had reflected. Turning to Udo, he said, "Your mother asked after you. She asked what you were busying yourself with in Mbano. She said you must read your books whenever you have the time."

Udo nodded. He was surprised his mother should be thinking about books with the war raging and towns falling into the hands of the enemy, but he did not express his thoughts in words. Instead he asked, "My brother and sister, are they well?"

"They are well and asked me to greet you." Nwakire

yawned and realised he was hungry – he had left Ama-Oyi without breakfast.

"Kire, can I get you something to eat?" asked Ginika. We've had lunch, but some of it is still left."

"Yes, I'm famished. What did you cook?"

"Beans and plantain, your favourite food."

"Good, my darling sister. I'll take a bath, freshen up a bit and then enjoy the food. I trust your cooking. Later, I would like you to tell me more about the special constable programme you have been involved in. You merely mentioned it before I left for Ama-Oyi." He was gazing at her, laughing, feeling that it was good to be back. There was no one in the house in Ama-Oyi to keep him company or cook for him, so he had had to eat one meal in Auntie Chito's house, one in Uncle Chima's and another in Akueju's. He had never learned to cook well. Even when he was away from home, in university, he did not have to cook, as students were served delicious meals in the cafeteria. Apart from the problem of food, he found the house covered in dust and only dusted the places used during his brief stay: the sitting room, his room, the bathroom and toilet. He was glad to be back; he looked forward to Ginika spoiling him as usual.

As Nwakire slouched to his room, Udo followed him with his small suitcase and Ginika went to get his food ready.

6

It did not surprise anyone when Ginika dressed up the next morning, and announced that she was going to Orie-agu for the training of special constables which had started there in the past few days.

"Hey, look at those trousers!" exclaimed Nwakire, on his way to have a bath. He had slept late and felt better this morning. "May I come along with you?" he teased. He allowed his eyes to travel all over her body. "Make sure the male trainers do not come after you, the way you look."

Ginika laughed. "Big brother, if they do, the blame will be on you: you gave me the trousers. Remember, your gift on my birthday two years ago?" Her eyes rested on his chest which had no hair on it. Then shifted to his shoulders which were broad and muscular. He had nothing on except a *wrappa* which he tied around his waist. She wondered if he had a girlfriend, perhaps a fellow student in university; he had never mentioned one. If he had one, no one would quarrel with that. It was only when a girl had a boyfriend that eyebrows were raised, that tongues wagged. Parents frowned when they saw their daughters with boys. She would not be surprised if her brother had a girlfriend. She told herself that one day a lucky woman would claim the right to rest her head on that chest, clasp those shoulders in a hug or cry her eyes out on them. She heard him say something and her wandering thoughts turned to other issues, making her listen to him.

"Really, they still look new, as if you had only just acquired them."

"I didn't wear them in the past. The war has made them indispensable. Let me go or I will be late and miss the Land Rover."

"Off you go then," Nwakire said and thrust his toothbrush, which had a generous amount of tooth paste on it, into his mouth. He headed for the bathroom.

Ginika was about to leave the sitting room when Udo hailed her. "Sister Ginika, can I see you off?"

"Yes, come along. But we must hurry."

They walked abreast along the drive, past the doctors' quarters. She turned her eyes to Bobby's house, wondering if he was at home. She had not seen him since the day they met in the field, near the county office, though Monday told her he had visited the following day when she went to the market with Aunty Lizzy. They continued in silence until they joined the main road. In the distance, they could see the county council offices.

"Sister Ginika, *imaka*, you look beautiful in your trousers and white blouse." Udo enthused, admiring her. She wore her long dense hair braided, as most girls did. This form of hair-dressing, called Calabar style, was native to Calabar, among Efik women. Ginika used to plait her hair with black thread, but had since resorted to braiding it when she found it impossible to buy thread. This was because the Nigerian government had blockaded Biafra and hair thread could not be brought in anymore, as in the past.

"You like it?" she asked, looking down at herself. She noticed that people she passed by gazed at her; some even turned to stare.

"See the way they are turning and looking at you," Udo remarked with a laugh. "They know you're absolutely stunning."

"Oh, I think it's my trousers they're looking at," she replied. "Perhaps they are too tight. Do you think so?" she asked him.

"They are tight but not too tight," he intoned after inspecting her.

"Tight or not, they are the only pair I've got, so I have to wear them."

Ginika was lucky, for the Land Rover was revving, ready to drive off when they arrived. She waved to Udo and ran to the vehicle. Lieutenant Ofodile was surprised to see her, as he had already concluded she was not interested in the programme any more. He shifted and asked her to sit beside him in the back seat. She obeyed, and found herself sandwiched between him and another officer. A third militiaman was sitting in front with the driver.

"What happened?" Ofodile asked as the vehicle took off. "I expected you on Monday. In fact, we waited for a while before deciding to go without you." He introduced her to the men, informing her that they were helping him with the training. "You have not answered my question," he reminded her.

"I was indisposed." Ginika folded her hands in between her thighs, trying hard not to lean on either of the two men even when the driver turned a corner and the Land Rover swerved sharply. But the more she tried, the more Ofodile pressed the left side of his hard thigh against hers. His shoulder rubbed against hers. At one point when the Land Rover jolted and rattled into a pothole, his arm touched her right breast. She flinched, as if a blow was aimed at her. She wished the distance to Orie-agu would be reduced so that they could get there in the shortest time possible.

At last they were there and she heaved a sigh of relief, already thinking of a scheme that would make her claim the front seat on their way back. "This way, Miss Ezeuko," she heard Ofodile say, as he offered his hand. She allowed him to help her out of the vehicle whose elevated steps made it slightly difficult for one, especially a woman, to get in and out. "May I call you Ginika?" he asked.

"Yes." She shrugged.

"Call me Kanu," he added.

Ginika found herself in a school compound which seemed deserted. This place once teemed with pupils, she mused. The war had driven them to their various homes. The compound was overgrown with grass in many places. Kanu Ofodile led the way and took them round the nearest building to the entrance. It was after they had negotiated it and got to the other side of the compound that Ginika's breath was taken away for a moment by the large crowd that met her gaze. She was sure there were at least six hundred people standing in the crowd, men and women, though there were more men, as was to be expected. In awed silence, she followed closely behind Ofodile. The grass on this side of the compound was newly cut and she could see the heap at the end of the field. When the people saw them coming, they broke into a song.

Take my bullet when I die, O Biafra
Take my bullet when I die, O Biafra

If I happen to surrender and die in the battlefield
Biafra, take my bullet when I die, O Biafra.

Ginika's eyes misted over when she heard the song which reminded her that death was a consequence of war, the price of conflict. How many of these people in the field would survive the war? Would she survive it? Would her family live till the war ended? She did not know, but she was convinced about one thing – Biafra would win the war. Was she being too optimistic? She felt she would survive the war. It was not decreed that everyone would die; many would live to celebrate the victory. She would be one of them. The most important thing now was for Biafra to go on fighting, to beat the enemy back until they left Biafra alone.

The song sounded and resounded, attracting people who were passing by. Children especially ran to witness the scene. When she saw that Ofodile and the other militia officers had joined the singers, she did the same. It went on for a while until Ofodile raised his hand to stop the singing.

The training exercise began soon and went on for more than an hour. Three militiamen were with the group already before Ofodile and his team arrived. Altogether there were six groups; each officer had a group to himself. Ginika was pleased when Ofodile told her to join his group, for she liked and admired his style of training. She derived pleasure in watching his antics in the field. Ginika's presence, her agility and her role as instructor encouraged the young women, compelling them to put more effort into their work.

Later in the day, Ginika shared her experience with Nwakire and Udo who slipped into the room to listen to her too. "I love it," she told them.

"After this, what next?" Nwakire asked. They were in

Ginika's room; he was sitting on a chair opposite Ginika who lay on the bed. Udo sat on the edge of the bed, close to Ginika's outstretched legs.

"I don't know," she admitted. "I think most of the men will join the army or militia. The girls will probably end up at the checkpoints, in the Red Cross or in any of the other services that engage women."

"What about you, Gini?" he asked softly, calling her in that special way he alone did. Ginika's heart always melted each time he abbreviated her name in that way. She was sure if her mother was alive, she would also call her name that way. They had always had each other, comforted each other and cared for each other.

"To tell you the truth, I'm not sure, but I could go to Ama-Oyi for the play I told you about. I'm sure Eloka Odunze is waiting for me to join the rest of the cast."

"Oh, I forgot that," Nwakire said, thinking that he too should make up his mind about what he should do to contribute to the war effort. He couldn't delay taking a decision much longer. He would hate to remain in the house if Ginika left, so he had better come up with a plan soon. Being stuck at home with Lizzy and her petulance, without his sister's laughter, was not a situation he relished. None of his friends lived in Mbano, he reflected, so he was in for loneliness.

Monday knocked, entered and announced, "*Daa* Ginika, someone come look for you; she said her name be Philomena. I tell am to wait for sitting room."

Ginika's face lit up with pleasure. "Monday, please, go and bring her to my room. Has she been waiting for long?"

"No, not long at all; she come just now." He hurried out to do her bidding.

Philomena breezed in, calling out in her exuberant way, demanding why Ginika was hiding in her room, then she saw Nwakire and checked herself. "Sorry, I thought Ginika was alone," she blurted.

"Philo, come in," Ginika invited, sitting up. "Come and meet my brother." She introduced them and they said hello, shook hands and looked each other up and down. Ginika was amazed to see how guarded Philo had become, as if she was not comfortable with Nwakire being around. She was sure her brother thought the same judging from his statement.

"I'll leave you girls to your gossip," he joked. "Udo, let's get out of here." Without a backward glance, he left the room: something in Philomena seemed to repel him though he did not know exactly what. Perhaps it was her wide mouth and her flaring nostrils each of which he thought could swallow a pebble if it was pushed into it.

As soon as Nwakire and Udo left, Philomena became her exuberant self. She threw herself into the chair vacated by Nwakire. "Do you have food in the house?" she asked, "I'm very hungry. I left home early this morning not to be late for the training session; nothing has entered my stomach since then." When Ginika hesitated, she said quickly, "Don't worry if there is no food; but let me have some water to drink."

Ginika had hesitated because she was mentally considering what to give her, for she knew there was no food left in the house, and it was not yet time to start preparing supper, but she did not realise her face had been so expressive for Philo to read or misread her thought. She feared that Philo had interpreted the expression on her face as disapproval or refusal to satisfy her request, so she spoke immediately to dispel her friend's doubts.

"There's no food left in the house at the moment, but I'm sure we have some snacks if you will accept that – *chinchin*, groundnuts, biscuits – and we have some fruits. Which of these should I offer you, my dear Philo?" She was looking at Philo steadily, her face suffused with that smile of hers which never failed to lift the spirit of anyone she favoured with it.

Philo fell for it, relaxed and laughed. "Bring whichever is handy. I love *chinchin* and biscuits."

When Ginika returned with *chinchin* and biscuits and a bottle of water, she found Philomena looking at a framed photograph hanging on the wall, directly opposite the door.

"My mother," she said, as she placed the plate of *chinchin* and biscuits and the bottle of water on the table standing in one corner of the room.

"She was beautiful," Philomena remarked, her head tilted backwards, studying the picture.

"She was very beautiful," Ginika agreed, for a moment remembering her but hazily, of course, for she was only six when she died. What she remembered most about her mother was how she used to come into her room before she slept to wish her good night, sing to her or tell her a story. This was what she missed most after she lost her.

"You know, you look like her," Philomena said, turning from the photograph to Ginika. She had been to see Ginika three or four times, but this was the first time she invited her over. "In fact, you are just her carbon copy," she added.

Ginika smiled, knowing that this was not the first time she was hearing such a compliment. Someone said to her one day – someone who grew up with her mother, "You look like your mother very much. Ogochi simply vomited you." She knew this was the expression Ama-Oyi people used when they wanted to say that a child looked like his or her parent. She had felt very happy then and still did each time someone told her she looked like her mother.

"Many people have told me so," she said. "I don't remember her well enough to be certain about the resemblance, but when I look at that photo, I have the impression I do look like her somehow. Come, the snacks are here."

She sat on the bed while Philo munched her snacks. "Would you like to take a Coke or Tango?" she asked.

"No, thank you; I'm okay with water."

They sat in silence for a while, each swimming in thought. Philomena was admiring Ginika's room and all in it, while Ginika was thinking about their friendship, how they had met during their training as special constables. She had tried to puzzle out the reason for their attraction to each other. She could only attribute it to one fact: to her, Philo was everything she was not; and she was almost sure that Philo felt the same way about her. They came from different backgrounds, and moved in different circles. Ginika knew she was heading for a university education that would elevate her position further from what it was at the moment – provided, of course, the war ended and she would be able to return to school. On the other hand, Philo had not gone beyond primary school and had worked in a petrol station before the war. Ginika had more education, but Philo was more experienced in life, especially life in the street, in the world out there. Ginika found this fascinating. The freedom she was denied at home and in college was Philo's for the taking. This again Ginika found exhilarating.

Ginika knew Philo was not beautiful, but she had a figure some men found attractive – big busts and buttocks, shooting out in front and behind. In addition, she had a sense of humour that would tickle anyone suffering from depression and her laughter was infectious. Ginika enjoyed this latter aspect of her nature very much. So, she was going to cultivate and nurture their friendship. She had already rebuffed Auntie Lizzy on account of Philo. The second time Philo came to visit, Auntie Lizzy had asked Ginika afterwards, "Where did you pick up this one that looks so crude? Ginika, this girl does not measure up to your class, you know?" Ginika had left the room without responding to her stepmother's comment which she considered snobbish and spiteful.

"Thank you, the *chinchin* is delicious. Did you make it?"

Ginika nodded. "Monday and I made it last week. I'm glad you enjoyed it. You can have some more when you leave; I'll wrap it in a piece of paper for you."

Philomena rubbed her hands together to remove the tiny bits of chinchin that stuck to her palm. She poured more water in the glass and drained it. "I feel all right," she said, shaking her body. She stood up and in the manner of James Brown, the Afro-American musician, she began to dance and twist, singing, "Hey, hey, I feel all right . . . One, Two . . . Hey, hey, I feel all right!" Her breasts vibrated, her buttocks quivered. Ginika watched her, howling with laughter. Philo pulled her up and asked her to join in the dance. Ginika laughed, but did not dance. Philo held her close and started coaxing her body to make her dance. Ginika freed herself, protesting she did not want to dance.

"I have visited you four times, Ginika," Philo said sitting down on the chair. "When will you come to know our house and meet my mother? She has heard me talk about you so much that she wants to meet you. 'When will I see this beautiful friend of yours?' she asked me. 'Bring her to visit us, before you deafen me with your prattles about her.'" Philo spoke with a strange voice and Ginika laughed; she understood that Philo was mimicking her mother.

"So, when will you come?"

"Will next week be all right?" Ginika asked, mentally going over her engagements in the coming week to ensure she had time for the visit.

"Yes, next week is all right. Saturday?" Philo's smile was sunny as she waited for her reply.

"Saturday is fine."

THE FIRST day she stayed away from Orie-agu, Ginika was lying on a mattress under her favourite avocado pear tree when her father came home for lunch. She heard his voice and wanted to dash to her room, but he appeared before she could get away.

"What are you doing here?" he asked, his eyes dilating with surprise. "Did you not go to Orie-agu today?" He stood near the tree but not near enough to hear her hiss. Ginika did not want to give any explanation for her decision not to go to Orie-agu and resented his barging in to disrupt her solitude. But she was relieved he had not heard her hiss. He would have been angry if he had heard; he would have lectured her on the evil of disrespect for one's parent. She did not respond to his question; she stared at him instead.

"Ginikanwa, I asked you a question." He sighed when her silence persisted, and was turning away when she spoke.

"I don't feel well," she said deliberately, knowing she was

lying, but feeling she had a right to lie since he had persisted in questioning her. Since she did not want to tell anyone why she did not go to Orie-agu, she had no choice but to lie to her father. She would be grateful if he left her alone now, but she knew he would not: the doctor in him and his habit of probing her mind and her actions would compel him to insist on knowing more.

He checked himself, and turned back. "What's wrong with you?"

"It's my period; I have cramps in my stomach and pain around my waist," she said, looking away from him. She hated to lie like this because she was not menstruating, but he had asked for it; he caused her to lie to him. She had stopped feeling remorseful each time she lied to her father now, as she did when she was younger. She lied so easily to him now. As her feelings for him cooled over the years, she began to keep things from him, to tell what she considered harmless lies. She had, at first, learnt to suppress the emotion of guilt, but with time she completely ignored it.

"Have you taken any medication?" he asked, this time with a softer voice that made her look at him and nod, relaxing the muscles of her face.

"I took the usual pills; I feel better already."

He nodded and went into the house to take his lunch which Monday had served. In the following days, Ginika chose to leave the house before his lunch break so that he would not find her at home when he returned, so that he would not find out that she did not go to Orie-agu.

It was a sordid experience, but she had felt better after she tried to explain it away as one of the many such experiences she had had in the past. She had established a friendly relationship with Lt. Ofodile, and looked forward each morning to her trips to Orie-agu. Sometimes they chatted on the way, sometimes they sat in silence, each of them engrossed in thought. The other officers were also friendly and devoted to duty and she liked them as much as she liked Ofodile. She felt privileged to work with such disciplined and competent officers. She had started calling Lieutenant Ofodile by his first name but addressed the other two by their ranks as 2nd Lieutenant Otuka and Sergeant Ndioka.

On the day it happened, they had a wonderful session though it did not last as long as the previous ones. The training session had gone well. Everyone had been enthusiastic as usual. When it ended, two of the militia officers who rode with them asked the driver to drop them off near a market which was some distance from the county council office. Ginika thought nothing of it but later she was to conclude that it was premeditated, that Kanu Ofodile knew they were going to stop there; that, in fact, he had told them to alight there.

"Today has been most successful," he told Ginika as the Land Rover regained the road. "Why don't we celebrate it?"

"How do you mean?" She had turned to look at him. He was smiling, his eyes shining and Ginika thought she had never seen such sparkling eyes in her life.

"Oh, let's just go somewhere and have a drink," he suggested. "We won't be long. There's a bar not far from here. They have good palm wine there."

Ginika hesitated, wondering if she should accept the invitation. She liked palm wine but only when it was fresh and sweet, not when it had fermented and she knew bars sold only strong and fermented palm wine. Still it would be nice to take a sip; surely, she would not get drunk if she took a glass or two of it and the Land Rover was there to take her home anyway. With a laugh, she agreed, "Okay, just a glass or two."

The bar was a room in the front of a storey building. The door was wide open, but covered with a curtain made with beads. When Kanu led her into the bar, the beads clinked and swung in and out. There was no one in the room. She walked behind him and they sat in the extreme right corner. A short woman with a round face came in to serve them. Ginika looked round the room and saw the rows of benches pushed together and the rickety forms behind them. The room could take up to twenty people, she thought. Flies were everywhere, attracted by the heady smell of palm wine. Ginika hit out at them with her white handkerchief.

"If you drive them away, they will return in no time," the short woman said, laughing. She placed two bottles of palm wine on the bench where they sat. "They want their share of palm wine."

"Certainly not mine," replied Ginika, grimacing.

Kanu poured the drinks and raised his glass. "To Biafra!" he intoned. Ginika quickly picked up her glass and enthused, "To Biafra and to victory!" She sipped the wine and was surprised it was fresh. She wondered if the bar tender had added sugar or saccharine to it, as she heard many did to sweeten palm wine. Then she noticed Kanu's glass was still aloft. He was gazing at her. "Aren't you going to drink it?" she asked, feeling self- conscious at his relentless stare.

"To Ginika, the most beautiful special constable in Biafra!" he exclaimed. His smile widened to engulf his eyes.

Ginika's laughter was extra loud to disguise her self-consciousness. She observed that his eyes were not only swimming in mirth, but also speaking a coded language every woman would understand even if she were not experienced in coquetry, even if she had not been seduced before.

"Ginika, you are beautiful; do you know that?" he asked, his eyes smoking with desire. "Do you realize how much I desire you? I just cannot get you out of my mind since the day I met you. Do you feel the same way about me?" His gaze had not left hers even for a moment.

She was flattered; who would not be. But she was not interested in him in that way, and had not even considered the possibility of any such relationship. "Lieutenant Ofodile," she began quickly, unconsciously slipping into the formal address she was used to before he insisted she should call him Kanu. "Thank you, but, please, don't say such things. You make me feel bad because I have not thought about you in that way . . ." Her voice trailed off, for she did not know what else to say.

"You don't mean what you're saying," he countered and she feared he thought she was playing hard to get, that she wanted him as much as he wanted her – as his next statement confirmed. "Shall we go to my house? It's not far from here, you know? There is privacy there . . ."

Ginika could bear it no longer and stood up. "Please, let's go. My family will be wondering where I am." She was already leaving when he spoke again, pleading, "Ginika, come back, please," and when she returned to where he sat, he continued. "Perhaps I should give you time to think about it? I can be patient, I assure you."

"Please, believe me," she replied in a tight voice. "There's nothing to think about. I don't want any such relationship with anyone at this time. Can we go now?" She refused to look at his face, not wanting to see the emotion there, whatever it was.

Kanu Ofodile got up with force; one of the palm wine

bottles tottered, but he caught it before it hit the cement floor. The wine left in it spilled on the table, some on the ground. The flies danced and sang for joy at such luck.

Ofodile's eyes smoked. "Look, what makes you so puffed up?" he spat. "You should be glad I'm interested in you."

"I'm sorry," was all Ginika could whisper. She wished this scene was not taking place; she had had so much respect for Lieutenant Kanu Ofodile.

"Sorry for yourself," Ofodile raged. "Do you realize you are a bloody flirt? You encouraged me all along and now you pretend you did not."

"Oh, no, I never encouraged you…" began Ginika, appalled at the unjust accusation. She was sure her behaviour towards him had not conveyed any such intention. She was disappointed that he was saying all this.

"Shut up, you did." His eyes were blazing and she thought he would strike her, but he did not. He stormed out of the place. She followed a few paces behind, mulling over his accusation and wondering in what way she had encouraged him. The bar tender ran out, asking for her money.

The driver had dozed off by the time they rejoined him. He woke up rubbing his eyes and apologising, but Kanu Ofodile said nothing. They rode in silence until they got to the county council office. Before the Land Rover stopped, Ginika was already opening the door. "Goodbye, Lieutenant Ofodile," she blurted, fleeing his sight and vowing never to go near him again. As she hurried home, she thought that her parentage and the fact that she was personally known to the DO saved her from Lieutenant Ofodile's assault. The training programme had been going on at Orie-agu for almost three weeks and she decided she had had enough of it.

So when her father demanded why she had not gone to Orie-agu, she was reminded of the incident with Lieutenant Ofodile which she wanted to put behind her, and had vowed not to divulge to anyone, not even her beloved brother and confidant, Nwakire. Ginika heard the sound of a vehicle driving off and knew her father was returning to the hospital. She got up, calling Monday to help her take the mattress inside the house. Her left hand clutched the *Mammy Wota* script Eloka Odunze had left with her. She had read it and liked it and had decided to commit to memory the speeches of the water princess.

7

Ginika looked forward to her visit to Philomena's home in Anara which was some distance from the county headquarters where she lived. She thought it would be a refreshing break from lolling at home all day, now that she no longer went to Orie-agu. They had agreed Philomena would come for her and both of them would travel back to Anara, and Ginika would return alone at the end of the visit. She was sure the visit would cheer her up and that she would like Philo's family when she eventually met them. She had the impression that Philo and her mother were quite close. Philo had told her she was twenty and the youngest in her family. There were two other daughters and two sons; their father had died several years before from a bad fall while tapping palm wine. So Philo was fatherless and she, Ginika, was motherless. Which was worse, she wondered ruefully: to grow up without a father or without a mother?

Philomena was early, arriving at about eight-thirty, just after Ubaka left for the hospital and Lizzy had gone to Umuahia, the nearest city, to do her shopping. She had said she needed to buy new clothes and shoes before they disappeared completely from Biafra, with the blockade getting tighter and tighter.

"Ginika, are you ready?" Philomena called even before she entered the sitting room.

"Welcome, Philo; please, have a seat," Ginika called from her room. She was almost ready, but needed to tidy her hair. She had loosened the braids and was combing the hair when Philomena hailed her. She gathered it back, away from her forehead and held it with a band. Snatching her handbag from the bed, she hurried out of the room. As soon as she entered the sitting room, Philomena got up and hugged her.

"You look gorgeous," Philomena complimented, admiring Ginika's green skirt and yellow top. "*Igbujekwe*, you will kill the men with your looks. Remember we are at war."

"You are not looking bad yourself," Ginika reciprocated. She liked her friend's black maxi skirt though she thought the blouse was too outlandish with its plunging neck that revealed the top of Philomena's massive breasts. She thought her father would not approve of such a blouse; her teachers would have a fit if any of the students dressed as Philomena did. For a moment her mind went back to her school and she wondered if the teachers, especially the white missionaries, were still living in the compound. Perhaps they left, as most other people did, when the state of Biafra was born and after the war started.

"Sister Ginika, where are you going?" asked Udo who walked in as they were leaving the front door. He looked from her to Philomena. "Good morning, Aunty Philo," he greeted, eyeing her blouse, his face expressionless.

"Udo, what type of question is that?" demanded Ginika. "Have you forgotten I told you I would be going to visit Philo this Saturday?" She gave him a grave look, as if telling him that he was too young to forget things.

"When are you coming back?" Udo asked, not too pleased that he would be left alone in the house, as Monday had gone to the carpentry workshop where he was training to be a carpenter and Nwakire had taken off again to Aba to see his friend.

"In the evening." Ginika patted his shoulder affectionately and added. "Take care of the house. If Papa asks of me when he comes home, tell him I've gone to see my friend and will be back before sunset. Okay?"

Udo nodded and stood at the door to watch them go.

Philomena's house was a thatched building with mud walls, surrounded by trees – breadfruit, orange, *ube* and *udara* trees, all growing luxuriantly, as if the soil around them was constantly fortified with fertilizer. Ginika feasted her eyes on the numerous bunches of *udara* fruit up in one of the trees.

"Hey, Philo, how come you have never brought me some of these? You have been enjoying them alone, you selfish girl?" she teased, her head tilted backwards, revealing her graceful *ugbana* neck.

Philomena laughed. "I was reserving them for when you would visit me. Here you are today; you can have as many as you want and take some home. Some are waiting for you in the house."

"Really?" Ginika was overjoyed; she loved *udara* and she was sure Udo would welcome her with a hug, for he too enjoyed the succulent fruit with hard seeds the colour of red wine.

"Come, let's go in," Philomena said, pulling her away from the spot where she stood rooted, unwilling to take her eyes away from the fruit. "Let's go," her friend urged. "Look at that breadfruit tree laden with fruit. It's very dangerous; it often releases its ripe fruit when least expected. If it falls on you, that's the end. It can break your neck or back."

Ginika glanced at the breadfruit tree burdened with fruit that looked like balloons. She allowed herself to be led away, musing about the paradoxical gifts of nature. Breadfruit is delicious, but it comes in a deadly package.

Ginika sat on one of the wooden chairs in a central room which served as a sitting room. Four other rooms branched off from the four corners of it. Philomena mumbled that she would soon be back and disappeared into one of the rooms. When she returned, she was carrying two bowls: one had water for Ginika to wash her hands in, and the other a bowl filled with *udara*. As soon as she had washed her hands, Ginika fell to; she ate and ate until she was tired. The gummy juice of the fruit smeared her lips and she had to use her fingers to rub it off. But Philomena had disappeared again and this time came back with a small plate containing palm oil.

"Dip your finger in the oil," she instructed. "The gum will disappear and your lips will be free." Ginika hesitated, reluctant to soil her finger with palm oil. Philomena put the plate on the floor and before Ginika knew what was happening, she had dipped her index finger in the oil and had rubbed Ginika's lips once or twice. Philomena told her to lick her lips to remove all traces of the red oil from them.

Ginika laughed, did as she was told and gazed at Philomena. "You are very wise and practical, Philo. I didn't know this way of getting rid of *udara* gum. I always used my fingers and ended up most of the time hurting my lips and sometimes drawing blood. Thank you."

"One gets to know certain things if one lives in the village," Philomena explained, shrugging. "I would not have lived with this *udara* tree all these years without getting to know this fact, anyway."

"Is there no one in the house?" Ginika relaxed, kicking off her black leather shoes. She had noticed that the door to the central room had not been locked; Philo had simply given it a shove and it yielded and let them in. She knew, in her house, they would not dare leave their door unlocked when no one was in the house. She remembered that last year, someone, who was never caught, had entered Auntie Lizzy's chicken coop and taken away three of the hens. Her mind turned to the present when she heard Philomena say, "Mama will soon be back; I am sure she did not go far."

As if on cue, a female voice hailed them from the front of the house and Ginika knew it could be no one but the mother. "Philo, are you home? Did you bring your friend with you?" the voice shouted, sounding so much like Philo's, Ginika thought.

Both of them went out to welcome the owner of the voice. Ginika was taken aback; before her stood a woman who looked like Philo in every respect – the same generously endowed body, though slightly fatter; the same facial features, height, complexion, though age had darkened her skin more; and the same raucous laughter and exuberant voice. She had just thrown down the bundle of leaves she had cut for feeding her goats before they came out. The goats sensed that food was near and were bleating loudly in their pen, which was out of sight; Ginika could hear clearly the sound of their violent movements as they strove against their leash.

"Mama, welcome," Philomena greeted, bending forward to lift the bundle to take it to the pen.

"*Adanma*, beautiful daughter, welcome to my house," she

greeted Ginika, smiling to reveal teeth that were discoloured by years of chewing tobacco. Ginika had observed this habit among many men and women from Mbano communities. It was a puzzle to her that in Ama-Oyi and many other parts of Igboland, the habit rarely occurred. She had meant to find out from her grandmother why this was so, but always forgot to ask when she visited her.

"Good morning, ma," Ginika greeted, shaking hands with her, feeling the roughness of her work-worn palms.

"How are your people," she asked, her eyes looking Ginika up and down, without hiding their admiration of her. "Philo said you are beautiful; she is quite right." She dropped the hand and adjusted the scarf which covered her hair completely.

Ginika smiled, pleased with the compliment, thinking how different she felt hearing these words uttered by Philo's mother than when she heard them from Lieutenant Ofodile: from the former the words had rung true; from the latter, they had sounded throaty, rasping with lust and the desire to seduce.

"They are well," she replied to her enquiry about her people, thinking that she liked Philo's mother. Ginika was glad she had brought her a present. She opened her handbag and brought it out: three tablets of bathing soap which she had wrapped in a sheet of paper.

"*Ewuu*, all this for me? You brought me a present? God bless you, my child." She looked at the soap for a while and then called out in a loud voice. "Philo, come and see what your friend gave me. She has filled my hands with a gift." She gave her loud laugh and Ginika also laughed. How infectious her laughter was, just like Philo's, she thought! Philo hurried forward to see the present and, turning, she hugged Ginika.

Inside the room, they sat down on the wooden chairs and chatted. The room was almost bare, but warm with laughter and affection. Philo and her mother are quite close, Ginika thought, a wistful look entering her eyes, as she thought of the mother she lost too early, a mother she did not have long enough to feel or remember her warmth and affection. She had turned to her brother, Nwakire, to squander her affection on, but even this was denied her. Auntie Lizzy had done all in her power to discourage bonding between brother and sister. She had cast her shadow over them like an iroko towering over lesser trees, starving them of sunlight and freedom. She never quite succeeded, but she did enough harm not only to them but to their father and indirectly to herself.

"Philo said you are from Ama-Oyi?" the elderly woman asked, but Ginika did not hear; her mind was far away, swimming in a past that often evoked pain.

"Ginika, Mama asked you a question," Philomena said, gently, nudging her.

"Oh, sorry, a thought just entered my mind," she apologised. "Mama, what was your question?" She repeated it and Ginika confirmed her family was from Ama-Oyi, but also added that they hardly spent time there, having to live in the towns where her father worked. She also explained that since after primary school, she had lived mostly in boarding school and visited home only during the holidays.

They changed position to have lunch; there was no table around which to sit or on which to put the plates of food. Philomena spread a mat on the floor and they sat down to enjoy their pounded cocoyam and delicious *oha* soup. Ginika had not eaten so much in recent times; she thoroughly enjoyed the meal. Philo's mother had used smoked fish and some stockfish to prepare the soup.

"Mama, the food is very good. Thanks, ma," she said, washing her right hand, which had bits of cocoyam on it, in a bowl of water Philomena presented to her.

"I am happy you like it," she answered. "This is what I eat these days since the doctor that looked after me when I was ill last year told me to stop eating cassava *fufu* and change to lighter food like cocoyam or *ede-oji*. Cocoyam is cheaper, so I eat it more than *ede-oji*."

"It is soft and smooth and slides down the throat gently, unlike cassava *fufu*," Ginika remarked. "So this is what you enjoy all the time?" she laughed, as she pinched Philomena's arm.

Philomena and her mother laughed. "Is this what you call enjoyment?" the older woman asked. "Philo and I eat whatever we have, what we are able to lay our hands on. It is only when there is a man at home that complex meals are cooked. It is then that a woman scouts about looking for a special meal. When women are alone, they eat anything; sometimes they eat nothing at all. My first two daughters are in their own homes – one married a man from Amaigbo, the second married an Ihioma man. I see them when I can. My sons joined the army: two of them. I asked them if they wanted to kill me. Did I cause the war that the two sons I have should both fight in it?" Her face became gloomy, as her voice droned on and on.

"Mama, why are you talking like this?" Philomena chided. "It is enough."

"Philo, leave me alone; I talk when I see someone to talk to, someone patient enough to listen. If a child is beaten, is it right to stop her from crying? *Eh*, answer me!" she glared at her and continued. "I have not seen Cletus and Vincent for a long time; they only visited home once. If they are dead or alive, I do not know. Is this a way to live? And you say I should not complain?"

"Whom are you complaining to? Is it to Ginika? What do you want her to do?" Philomena hissed.

Ginika wished she had supernatural powers to command the two men, Cletus and Vincent, to return immediately. But she did not have such power and no human being did. The men could even be dead, who could tell. She was sorry for the poor woman. It was mostly the children of the poor that had joined the army, the ordinary people who had little at stake, people without money or property. She looked around the almost bare room and could imagine how the other four rooms were. She wondered how Philomena and her mother passed their time – no radio to listen to news about the war, no books to read, no radiogram to play occasional music. Perhaps the only music they listened to was that of the birds that chirped in the trees all day.

"Mama, do not worry," she consoled, "just pray for them. One day they will come to see you."

"Thank you, my child." The smile she gave her was a ghost of the previous ones. "I believe the God I worship will not allow the war to eat my sons."

"I believe that too," Philomena affirmed. "My brothers will not die in this war. They did not cause this war; they will survive the war."

Ginika wanted to talk about something else that would steer them away from the war and the talk of death. She decided to return to the subject of cooking which they had been discussing before the war crept into their consciousness.

"I wish I could cook *oha* soup like you, Mama," Ginika said, and she meant it. Perhaps if her mother had lived, she might have taught her to cook soup like this. Auntie Lizzy never bothered; it was from Auntie Chito that she learnt the much she knew.

"Maybe you should come for a lesson the next time we cook *oha* soup," Philomena teased. They all burst into laughter. Ginika was pleased to see Philo's mother laugh again. Like Philo, she slipped into different moods easily, especially pleasant moods.

"Maybe I will," Ginika replied, giving Philomena a challenging look. "Only I may move to Ama-Oyi before long."

"Move to Ama-Oyi?" Philomena queried; it was more of a wail than an ordinary question. "What will you go to Ama-Oyi for? There is no sign that war will touch Mbano soil; this is the centre of Biafra. If war gets here, then it is all over. So why will you leave this secure area?" Her brow was furrowed, as if the information that Ginika might go away disturbed her.

"Who told you Mbano is the centre of Biafra? Let me tell you, Ama-Oyi is the heartland of Biafra," Ginika chuckled.

"But your family is here, why would you want to leave?" Philomena persisted, as if her insistence would make Ginika give up leaving Mbano.

"I told you about my aunt who moved to Ama-Oyi with her family after the enemy captured Enugu; I have not seen them since they were displaced. I would like to go to Ama-Oyi to see them."

"So you will return after seeing them?"

"Very likely," she replied. This answer seemed to satisfy Philomena, for Ginika was happy to see her smile, to see the cloud disperse from her face.

"Would you like to take some palm nuts home when you leave?" Philomena's mother asked, changing the subject. "We harvested some few days ago."

"Yes, we cook bitterleaf soup with them. I would like to have some."

"You know, it also goes well with *oha* soup. Fresh palm nut oil is the secret of delicious *oha* soup." She was laughing as she said this to Ginika in a conspiratorial voice, as if she was divulging a secret.

When the time came for her to leave, Ginika had a big parcel of *udara* and palm nuts. She hugged Philomena's mother and thanked her profusely. Ginika nodded several times when she told her to visit whenever she felt like it. "I will," she declared.

Philomena carried the parcel and escorted her to the main road. They stood there waving to passing cars for a ride. Most of them were full, but eventually one stopped. As they raced towards it, Philomena reminded Ginika that they had agreed she would spend the next weekend with Ginika and her family. Ginika nodded, took the parcel from her and entered the vehicle, a 404 estate car heading for Umuahia. She would drop when they got to Mbano. "See you next Saturday," she called out, as the car moved. "Yes, till Saturday," she shouted back, her curvaceous body quivering, as she waved with both hands. Ginika looked back and watched Philomena waving vigorously until she could not see her anymore.

By the time she arrived home, it was nearly dark. She entered the sitting room and found everyone in there, but no one said anything to her, even when she greeted them. At first, she thought her father was angry with her for coming back so late, but on second thoughts, she knew it could not possibly be. The presence of Monday in the sitting room was rather strange. He perched on a sofa, close to a wall, his face so miserable. Ginika looked at Udo and saw he was crying.

"What's the matter? Will someone not tell me what has happened?" She was sure something terrible had happened to her brother, Nwakire, or to Auntie Chito and her family. She looked from one person to another.

"Port Harcourt has fallen. The enemy has entered it and there is heavy fighting going on there now," her father intoned.

Ginika gave a loud scream and threw herself into the chair nearest to her, shaking her head from side to side. Monday got up and picked up the parcel that had fallen from her hand.

IT WAS a sad-faced Ginika that waited for Philomena, who was expected in her home that weekend. Everyone had gone out, leaving her alone and in deep thought. She wished Nwakire was there to cheer her up with his jokes, but he had not yet returned from his trip to Aba. She wondered why he was staying away for so long, without sending them any message. The loss of Port Harcourt devastated her more than she thought possible, almost as much as the loss of Enugu. In the case of Enugu, the news of the safety of Auntie Chito and her family had doused the pain of that first tangible loss in the war. But the evacuation of Port Harcourt had brought a different kind of pain. It was Biafra's only viable seaport and the biggest city remaining, as well as the source of crude oil which Biafran scientists had already started refining.

A radio addict, Ginika glued her ears to Radio Biafra for news about the invasion of Port Harcourt. She did not get much information there and she knew it was deliberate. The information unit did not want to alarm the populace further by providing news about the situation, so the best thing to do was to withhold information. Instead, a familiar voice bleated in Igbo, "*Ogu na-agariri n'iru n'iru na Gakem* – the battle is still raging in Gakem." Ginika hissed; she did not want to hear about Gakem, in Ogoja area. She wanted to know what was happening in Port Harcourt, the gateway to the sea, the garden city. Radio Biafra was not forthcoming, so Ginika sought other options. Listening to the BBC and Radio Kaduna analyse what the loss of Port Harcourt meant to Biafra, Ginika wept bitterly; it was like rubbing salt into an injury. A jubilant announcer in Radio Kaduna cried in delight, "To keep Nigeria one is a task that must be done ...." Ginika gave a bloated hiss, hit the radio with her right palm and switched it off immediately. "Shut up!" she screamed, upset the more because she realised how impotent her anger was. She struggled to stifle the urge to dash the radio against the wall.

A loud knock on the door got her hurrying to let Philomena in; she was sure it was her friend. Ginika was not disappointed, for Philomena stood there, beaming at Ginika, a handbag in one hand and in the other, a basket containing her things. Ginika was amazed that Philo could look so cheerful after what had happened to Port Harcourt, or did she not know that Biafra had lost the town?

"Ginika, *kedu*?" Philomena greeted as she entered the sitting room after Ginika, and sensing her friend's mood, asked, "What happened? You look unhappy? Are you not happy to see me?"

Ginika gave a wry smile, and hugged her. "No, it's not you, Philo. I'm happy to see you." She disengaged from her and picked up the basket from the floor. "Come let's put your things in the room and then we'll have lunch. Are you hungry?" She told herself she must not spoil Philo's visit with her bleak mood. She had looked forward to the visit and was sure Philo had. She knew no one else in the family was enthusiastic about it, least of all her father and stepmother. However, after she told them of her invitation to Philo, they had swallowed the news without upsetting her or themselves. Her father had not warmed to Philo the day she introduced her, and had kept his thoughts to himself, though she noticed a deep frown on his face. As for Auntie Lizzy, she had not hidden her disapproval of the friendship. Ginika was not bothered about their attitude to Philo so long as they did not stop her from visiting the house.

She watched Philo rummaging in her basket, her buttocks jutting out in her bent position. "What are you looking for, Philo?"

"Looking for the thing I brought for you," Philo replied, straightening up and handing her a well-wrapped parcel. "I brought some *udara* for you."

"Ah, the famous *udara*; thank you very much." She turned the parcel over, feeling the wrappings. "Hmm, you wrapped it very well."

"I used cocoyam leaves and paper to wrap them to protect my clothes from being stained."

"Good idea; the juice is too sticky and will ruin a dress if it touches it," she agreed, remembering how Philo had used palm oil to remove the sticky stuff from her lips when she went to Anara.

After Philo had changed into a flowered dress that clung to her fleshy body, as if it was plastered to it from the neck to the knees, they went to the kitchen to get the food Ginika had prepared earlier. She had once heard Philo say that *jollof* rice with beef was her favourite meal, so she had prepared it specially to welcome her. She warmed the food before dishing it out. They carried the steaming bowl of *jollof* rice and meat and placed the food on the table in the dining room, which was a small room adjoining the sitting room.

"This room is just for eating food alone," Philo observed. "It's enough to serve as a bedroom." She sat next to Ginika who was already scooping food into a flat plate.

"Philo, this is for you. Tell me when to stop." Ginika continued to shovel jollof rice into the plate, expecting to hear Philo say "stop", but she did not hear the word and decided to stop anyway. The food in the plate was a hillock. She wondered if Philo would be able to eat all of it. She took the second flat plate and put some of the remaining food in it. She looked up and saw that Philo was already eating.

"Don't you pray before you start eating?" she asked laughing.

"I prayed; did you not see me?" Philo laughed. "I made the sign of the cross as Mama taught my brothers and me."

"We always say grace together before anyone starts to eat both here at home and in the school." Ginika also laughed. "If you eat before grace is recited in my school, you will be punished." She shut her eyes and after a moment she opened them and began to eat.

"Is that so?" asked Philo, registering her astonishment. "Why should they punish anyone for that?"

"Well, they believe one should thank God first for providing the food and it has to be done collectively, not individually. It is called table manners." She watched Philo eat; she thought she swallowed the rice without chewing it. She had already consumed half the food in her plate. The urge to laugh was strong, but Ginika smothered it. "Sometimes, we shut our eyes for over five minutes waiting for the food prefect to conclude her prayer before we can start eating. No matter how hungry you are, you have to wait patiently for her to finish praying. The most popular grace goes like this, 'Some have food but no appetite; some have appetite but no food; we have both, we thank you, O Lord.' That's the one I like best."

Philomena burst into laughter, almost choked by the food in her throat. She grabbed the cup of water near her and took a long sip. Ginika stretched her hand and rubbed Philo's back. "Don't kill yourself here all because of laughter," Ginika teased.

"If I die, remember to tell my mother you killed me by making me laugh so much." Philo went back to her food. Soon she was helping herself to more food.

"God forbid; you will not die from laughter," rejoined Ginika, amazed at Philo's huge appetite.

PHILOMENA'S VISIT partly restored Ginika's spirits. Ginika saw to it that they were always together, doing everything together – they walked to the nearby Ngene River in Umuduru to swim, and went to church on Sunday morning. Though Philomena was a Roman Catholic, she worshipped with Ginika and her family in St. Andrew's, an Anglican church. Philomena told Ginika it was the first time she had worshipped in a different church, and when Ginika asked her if she liked it, she said it was all right. The terrors of the war receded to the background though not altogether, for Ginika agonised over the bad news that filtered to them through the radio or through rumour-mongers. She knew far too many people claimed to have first-hand accounts of the war and, though she suspected many of the stories were not true, she still listened and felt elated or demoralised depending on whether it was good or bad news.

After lunch, Ginika, Philomena and Udo played Whot in the sitting room. It was a game Ginika enjoyed playing on Sunday afternoon, especially when Nwakire was around. Sometimes they abandoned Whot and played music using the radiogram. She would bring her *Record Song Book* – a compilation of the famous Pop songs by famous stars like Cliff Richard, Elvis Presley, Helen Shapiro and other singers like Mighty Sparrow and Millicent Small. She liked the love songs best and knew them well and sang along when they played the records. Millicent Small's *My Boy Lollipop* was a great hit that set her quivering with excitement each time its rhythm filled the air. The radiogram would go *boom, boom,* and she would get up and dance. She also enjoyed the music of Celestine Ukwu, Rex Jim Lawson, Victor Uwaifo and I.K. Dairo. She smiled when she recalled the battle she and Nwakire had fought before they could convince their father that they needed to have music in the house when they were on holiday. It was difficult indeed to persuade him to buy the radiogram.

Sunday was a day everyone was at home and did whatever pleased them after service and after lunch. Her father and Auntie Lizzy sometimes went out to visit friends or retired to their rooms for a nap. This was the only day her father did not go to the hospital, except, of course, if there was an emergency; he would relax in the sitting room for a while or move to the garden to potter around and watch Monday as he trimmed the hedge. Sometimes, he went into the garage and tinkered with the car. Ginika would watch him; some of the affection she had had for him in the past would flow back and swamp her heart.

Ginika watched Udo dealing out cards to everyone, and making sure he did not play any pranks or cheat in any way. She gathered her pack of cards and inspected them. "Oh, poor me, not a single Joker for me. Who has the Jokers?"

"I have one." Udo displayed his Joker and turned to Philomena. "What of you?"

"Philo, you have three Jokers!" Ginika lunged forward to snatch Philo's cards but could not as Philomena jolted backwards, out of her reach.

"Here are the Jokers. I have the three." Philomena was triumphant. "I will beat two of you."

But once they started playing, Ginika knew Philo was not as skilled as Udo and she. Before long she had lost all her three Jokers and was edged out of the game. Ginika captured one and Udo the rest, bringing his to three.

"Philo, sorry, relax and watch Udo and me." To Udo, she said, "Play, it's your turn," and then she heard Auntie Lizzy calling her and saying that it was time to prepare dinner. They dropped the cards, and then Udo began to put them back in the package. Ginika and Philomena went to the kitchen to help Auntie Lizzy and Monday, while Udo went to iron some of the clothes washed the previous day.

MUCH LATER, Ginika and Philomena retired for the night. They had sweated a lot when they were cooking, so Ginika decided to have a bath; Philomena did the same. When the generator was switched off, the whole house was plunged into darkness.

"*Hei*, I cannot see a thing," cried Philomena. "Just like last night."

Ginika laughed. "I know. It's always like this when the generator is switched off. The darkness seems thicker than it ought to be. But don't worry; there is a lantern in every room in case it is needed. Mine is under the bed."

Philomena said, "My mother lights a fire in her room all night. I sleep with her when I am in Anara; I did before I went to Lagos and now war has driven me back home. I am used to sleeping with a light on. I do not remember when I slept in a dark room last until I came here."

"Well, you have to endure it again tonight, as you did yesterday." Ginika laughed again, wondering why she did not complain the previous night, as if she was not aware of the darkness then. Or could it be that she did not feel free yesterday as she did today? Ginika knew that sometimes people's tongues loosen more after they have got used to a place, than when they first arrived there. She smiled in the dark, remembering the proverbial saying about the chick that stood on one leg the first time it was taken to a new home.

She was lying on her side, facing the wall. Philomena lay beside her, fidgeting from time to time. "Are you comfortable?" Ginika asked, realising she had dozed off, but was wakened by Philo's movements.

For answer, Philomena sighed and threw her right arm across Ginika's waist. The night had become almost chilly, a sign that the harmattan was on the way. As Philo shifted closer to her, Ginika was grateful for the warmth generated by their two bodies; she pressed backwards for more body contact. But she was dozing off again when she felt Philo's hand sliding upwards, gently, until it rested on her right breast. She held her breath, not sure what Philo was up to. She slid her hand into Ginika's night-dress and gave her breasts a gentle squeeze. Ginika froze, not knowing how to react. She felt Philo pause, as if feeling the ground, gauging Ginika's reaction. Then a more determined squeeze which set Ginika's pulse racing, her heart fluttering. "What is this? What is happening to me?" she screamed in silence, but was yet unable to repulse this strange assault or welcome it. What baffled her most was that she was not angry with Philo though she felt this was very wrong. Her lack of movement seemed to have either encouraged Philo or maddened her; she yanked Ginika's body with some force so that they faced each other in the darkness. Her mouth, hot and wet clamped on Ginika's. Like an animated object, Ginika found herself responding to the impassioned embrace; the bed squeaked as their bodies pressed on it. "Philo," she whispered, but it sounded louder than a whisper in her ears. "Shssss," Philo hushed her. "Keep quiet. Don't talk!"

Ginika heard some banging and gasped. She froze, then recoiled from Philo's arms. Philo heard it too, waited, listening in the dark. "What was that?" asked Ginika, trembling. "I have no idea," Philomena whispered, turned and lay on her back. Both of them were breathing rapidly, as if they had done a race. Ginika could not make out what the noise was or who made it, but she had heard it clearly and thought it might have been somebody standing outside her door that had banged on it. She got up and, moving stealthily to the door, placed her ear against the keyhole and listened. She heard nothing; everywhere was quiet. There was no sound from outside.

Had the person gone, she wondered? Was it her father? Was it Udo who slept in Nwakire's room? She considered Auntie Lizzy and felt it could not be her; she was a heavy sleeper. She listened again, but there was no sound from outside. Could it be a rat? Sometimes one or two of them would scurry into the house and bump against the doors or chairs in the kitchen or sitting room.

Her heartbeat slowed down to normal and she went back to bed. She knew she would get into trouble if her father knew or suspected what was happening, and Philo would be banished from the house. She lay down beside Philo, wondering what had got into her; what force had driven them into doing what they did before that bang brought them to their senses. "I don't know who or what made that noise," she spoke in the dark, but she was sure Philo was wide awake. "Please, let's sleep now."

No word passed between them again until they drifted to sleep and woke early in the morning. Philomena helped Ginika to prepare breakfast. They did not discuss what had taken place during the night. In fact, Ginika was uncomfortable when the thought of it invaded her mind. During breakfast and after it, she looked covertly at everyone – excluding Philomena – to see if any of them gave her a strange look or stare, but she detected no such thing. She was almost convinced a rat had made the banging noise she and Philo heard. After breakfast, she escorted her guest to the main road and they stood there chatting until a vehicle stopped and whisked Philomena away.

Late in the afternoon, a young man brought two letters to the house: one was for Ginika and the other was for her father. She looked at it and recognised Nwakire's writing. Why did he write a letter instead of coming home, she thought, disappointed? She went into her room to read her letter. She tore open the envelope and read in silence. "My God," she cried, and dropped the letter, tears flooding her eyes.

She picked it up and started again to read from the beginning. "My dearest Gini," he wrote, "I have joined the army. I am training as an officer now. Forgive me for not telling you earlier, but I thought you might have tried to dissuade me; it would have been difficult to defy you. So, I did it secretly. Take care of yourself. I know we will be given a pass after the training; I will come and see you then. Goodbye for now. Yours affectionately, Nwakire."

Ginika folded the letter and gazed vacantly in front of her for some minutes. "Kire, my brother, why did you do this without letting us know? When will I see you again?" She spoke as if he was there with her, but she knew it would be long before she would see him again; if she would ever see him again. Ginika wept gently.

When Ginika heard her father's voice bellowing her name, she knew he too had read his letter and from it had learnt that Nwakire had defied him and joined the army. "Ginikanwa," he roared again.

She left her room and went to meet him in the sitting room. He was sitting in his favourite chair which no one else sat on except him. Immediately he saw her, he waved the letter before her and exploded. "Take it and read." She did not take the letter; her hands hung by her sides, without moving. He continued, "Your precious brother has joined the army without telling me." His voice broke and for a moment, Ginika thought he would break down and cry. She would hate to see that. So with eyes that exuded empathy, she appealed to him silently, asking him to be brave. But she did not think he understood. Perhaps he misinterpreted her non-verbalised gesture as pity or indifference, as his hostile words showed.

"You will not read it? You are both the same, are you not?" he sneered. "Tell me, was he right to treat me, his father, with such disrespect? Such callousness – how can one understand it? I do not know what I did to you two to deserve the way you treat me. Both of you have been rebellious time and time again. I do my best for you, but you hardly show appreciation. I am sure you knew he was going to do this, did you not? He could not have done it without telling you, could he?"

Ginika almost retorted, but checked herself. She knew he was terribly upset by Kire's action, as she was. He was venting his anger on her because she was there to receive it, and he wanted to hit as hard as he had been hit. Let him have his way, she thought. But he would not make her judge Kire or his decision to join the army, no matter what he said. After all, those people in the army and those who had been killed fighting were people's sons and husbands.

Ginika stood there, looking in the direction of the radiogram, thinking that she would not bring herself to play music now that Kire had gone away. Meanwhile, her father turned and left the room, taking the offending letter with him. She saw that he was heading for his bedroom. For a moment she stared into space.

Ginika returned to her room as a thought hammered in her head. Surely she would now leave Mbano for Ama-Oyi, as there was little to detain her here. She longed to see Auntie Chito and her family. Besides, she would make herself useful acting in the play written by Eloka Odunze to entertain Biafran soldiers. She might be lucky to stumble on Kire's future battalion during one of their performances.

Part Two

BEFORE THE
BEGINNING

8

Ginika woke up with a start, wondering if the alarm had sounded. The clock ticked *kim, kim, kim* on the small stool beside her bed. She stretched, certain it was the alarm clock that had startled her, but she soon realised that her bed was wet around the area where her buttocks rested. She gave a little cry as she felt her heart do a somersault. Her mouth filled with saliva. She had urinated on herself, on her bed, she thought. This was what woke her up, not the alarm clock. What would Auntie Lizzy say? How she would ridicule her! Ginika cringed from the jeers which she could already hear, "*Hmm*, wetting your bed at your age? Shame! Couldn't you get up to do the nonsense in the right place, foolish girl?" And Papa would stand there supporting her every word. She must get up and change into another night-dress, hide the soiled one and wash it later when she was alone in the house. What about the mattress and the sheets?

Ginika touched the wet area of her night dress; her fingers felt sticky. This could not be urine, she thought, feeling the clamminess again. She jumped out of bed and rushed to the switch on the wall nearest to the door; she flicked it on and all the lights flooded the room. She took a look at the bed, at herself and burst into tears, thinking she was hurt, that something terrible had happened to her. She tore at her dress and underwear, yanked them off and changed into fresh ones – all the time weeping. Should she tell her brother, Nwakire? He must be fast asleep, she thought. She ached for her mother and wished she had not died. She wished her father had not married Auntie Lizzy. Ginika glanced at the clock and saw it was three in the morning. She sat on the only chair in the room and cried her eyes out until dawn.

Her father, Ubaka, discovered her in this state at about six o'clock. Her eyes were red and puffy from hours of crying. He had received no response when he knocked, so he gave the door a shove and walked in. "Ginikanwa, what are you still doing in bed …?" he began, but halted when he saw her face. "What is the matter with you? You look terrible." He stood there waiting for her to answer his questions. "Did you not hear me? Have you forgotten we are leaving for Ama-Oyi at eight?"

Ginika's eyes sought her father's, but finding no sympathy there, looked away. More tears streamed down her face. Ubaka's heart softened a bit. He decided to go to her though he did not want to encourage her in what he termed her peevish ways, her resort to tantrums when it pleased her. "Tell me, what the matter is. Are you ill?"

The word 'ill' triggered a bout of weeping. "Yes, I'm ill. I hurt myself, but I don't know how I did it," she wailed.

"Tell me about it," Ubaka said gently, for he already suspected what the matter was. He glanced at the bed and saw she had stripped her mattress; there was no sheet on it. "Show me." When she still hesitated, he asked, "You are bleeding, are you not?"

Ginika nodded, wondering how he knew. She heard him say, "You are not ill. It's a normal experience for a thirteen-year-old girl like you. Do not cry anymore. Wait, just a minute." Ginika heard him call Auntie Lizzy. He came back and said, "She will explain it to you and tell you what to do." Ginika savoured the sweet thought that she was not ill, that there was nothing to worry about. She felt as if a big load had been lifted from her heart and looked forward to attending the Thanksgiving Service taking place at Ama-Oyi that Sunday, which she had earlier concluded she would miss.

IT WAS late afternoon before the sale of perishables was concluded in St Mark's Anglican Church, Ama-Oyi, after a Thanksgiving Service most people present thought was the best in the past five years. One of the salesmen shouted, "Our people, *ndewonu*, thank you for your patience." Ginika longed for some fresh air outside. The smell of sweat from so many bodies and the occasional fart released from an unidentified anus almost suffocated her. She knew there were other items still to be sold – electronic gadgets, electrical appliances, kitchen equipment such as mortars, pestles, brooms and livestock which people presented as *ihe onyinye*, thanksgiving offerings to God for blessing them and their families and also to ask for protection in the coming days and months. The salesman took a radio and held it up very high. "Whoever buys this will receive all the news about Nigeria in the privacy of his house; he will not bother with Radio Rumour." This remark drew much laughter from the crowd. Ginika got up and escaped without being noticed.

She sat on a stump not far from where they had parked, waiting for her father and Auntie Lizzy. She could see Nwakire talking to a girl wearing a skirt and blouse made from Dutch wax. Ginika looked down at her own dress – a loose red gown made from cotton material. She had decided to wear it in case it got soiled, but she was sure it would not, for Auntie Lizzy had taken adequate care of her and she felt quite protected. She felt self-conscious, though, wondering if anyone noticed the bulge in the back area, near her buttocks. Ginika smiled, as she remembered how she had agonised over her condition, in the morning, not knowing it was a good thing that had happened to her. She was astonished no one had told her about it before, not even in school. Was it because she was in Form One and was not expected to have started menstruating, as Auntie Lizzy implied? She had said, "I am surprised your period has started so early; I saw mine when I was fifteen. My mother told me her own started at sixteen. Yours came too early at thirteen." Ginika had said nothing; she had continued to clean herself and do as Auntie Lizzy instructed. She looked up and saw Nwakire and the girl laughing. What had he said that amused the girl so much, she wondered? Nwakire was in Form Three at Okrika Grammar School. He told her he could have a girlfriend if he wanted and there was nothing Papa could do about it. Did he ask the girl he was talking with to be his girlfriend? Was this why she was laughing like that?

"Hello," a voice greeted her, startling her. She looked up and saw a tall skinny boy smiling down at her. His teeth were evenly formed and very white. "My name is Eloka Odunze. I saw you sitting quietly and peacefully and decided to disturb you." He laughed. Ginika stared at him, and said nothing. Not wanting to talk to him, she wished he would go away. She felt uncomfortable with him, and attributed this feeling to her condition at the moment. And would her father not be angry if he saw her talking with him? Ginika remembered the time he had seized a letter a boy she knew in primary school had written to her. It was during the first term holiday and he had scolded her, angry that a boy should write her a letter barely three months into her secondary school education. "What will happen when you get to Form Four or Five?" he had raged. Ginika shuddered. And here was this skinny boy talking to her barely eight months after the other incident. She heard him sneer, "Can't you talk? Why don't you say something? For your information, I know your family. You live in Port Harcourt, don't you?"

Ginika was about to say something when she sighted her father and Auntie Lizzy striding towards her. From the dark look in his face, she knew he was angry. Two men followed them, carrying the things they had bought – yams, plantains, bananas and a basket of melon seeds.

Ginika stood up immediately. "Come on, get into the car," her father commanded. He gave the skinny boy a withering look and did not respond to his greeting. Ginika walked rapidly to the car, ahead of all of them. He opened the boot and the men stowed away the food items. "Where is Nwakire?" he demanded. Ginika pointed, but Nwakire had already seen them and ran forward to join them, the soles of his shoes making *kpo kpo kpo,* as they hit the ground.

They drove out of the church compound in silence. When they entered the tarred road, her father asked, "Ginikanwa, who is that boy you were talking to?"

"I was not talking to anyone," she protested.

"The boy I saw standing near you – who is he?"

"I don't know." She shrank to her corner, adjacent to Nwakire – far from her father and Auntie Lizzy who sat in front. Auntie Lizzy's elaborate headdress prevented Ginika from seeing what was in front as the car sped away.

"You said you do not know the boy?" he persisted.

"That was what I said, Papa. I don't know him," she replied in a slightly raised voice, annoyed with him and with the skinny boy who was the cause of her ordeal. She wished he would trust her, and not always think she wanted to do wrong, to disobey him.

"He is a total stranger and you were talking with him?" he barked. "Ginikanwa, how many times will I tell you to stay away from boys? You will only get hurt."

"Papa, I did not go to him; he came to me where I sat waiting for you and Auntie Lizzy. Should I have shooed him away?" She sighed and shut her eyes.

Lizzy turned sideways, grabbing her headdress which threatened to fall off its high perch. "Ginika, you are now a woman, do you know that? With what happened to you today, you have become a complete woman," she intoned. "So you must take care of yourself and keep the boys at bay. If you do anything with them, *afo ime achaala*, pregnancy will come."

Ginika squirmed in her seat, hating every word issuing from Auntie Lizzy's mouth, wondering why she and her father should pick on her in this cruel manner. Was this what every girl went through in her home? If her mother were alive, would she treat her the way Auntie Lizzy treated her? Ginika told herself that she was happier at school than at home, except when Nwakire was around, but he was not there most of the time.

"Gini, what happened to you?" Nwakire asked, turning to her.

She looked at him, shook her head. "Nothing," she whispered.

"Nothing?" he asked, staring at her, but when she winked at him, he smiled and said, "You'll tell me later then."

Ginika dreaded the few days left of the Third Term holiday, the Christmas season, knowing that there would be more criticisms from Auntie Lizzy and inevitable fault-finding from her father. She wondered if they derived any joy in making her and Nwakire uncomfortable. She knew, of course, that she was more the butt of their attack than Nwakire probably because she was a girl and he a boy. "Bend down properly to sweep, *ukwu ruo gi ala*, you hear?" Lizzy would scream. "Do you not know you are a girl and will one day do these chores in your husband's house? Who will you say trained you when they start to find fault with you? Not me-o!" Auntie Lizzy would stand behind Ginika as she swept the floor and press her back with her hands. Boarding school had become a perfect respite for her from her tormentors, though school had its own unpalatable aspects like waking up too early at five, scrubbing the discoloured cement toilets and bathrooms and washing the pots and tureens used in preparing and serving food to students.

Ginika sighed with relief when, two hours later, they arrived home in Port Harcourt where her father worked as a medical officer, one among six doctors, in the General Hospital. She liked the house in which they lived in the GRA – a rectangular bungalow with a large sitting room and three bedrooms, located in a tree-lined street called Park Avenue. This lovely house also held unpleasant memories for her. Her mother died there seven years ago while giving birth to a third child who also did not survive. Not that Mama died inside the house, Ginika reflected, but it was from the same house that she was taken to hospital. She had been only six years or slightly more then, but she remembered…

As soon as the car stopped, Ginika opened the door and walked rapidly towards the house.

"Ginikanwa, where are you hurrying to?" demanded her father. "Who will carry the things in the boot?"

"Don't mind her!" Auntie Lizzy spat, "Her servant will take them in."

Ginika turned and mumbled her apology. She was actually rushing off to the toilet to tidy herself up and had completely forgotten the food items in the boot. Assisting Nwakire, they carried the plantains, yams and basket of melon seeds into the house.

Nwakire found a folded note someone had pushed under the door. "For you," he said, giving it to Ginika. She looked at it and smiled. "Oh, it's from my friend, Tonye Efeturi." She announced to everyone's hearing, not wanting her father to have the wrong idea. She noted mentally that she must find time to visit Tonye; this was her third visit and each time Ginika had not been there to receive her friend.

9

Eloka watched the girl get into the car; he did not look away until her father had started the car and driven off. He hoped he had not got her into trouble, for he had seen the dark look in her father's eyes and the hostile stare the girl had given him as she obeyed her father. He shrugged and turned away. On impulse, he ran after the two men who had helped them take the items they had purchased to the car. His new shoes were making a squeaking sound as he ran and a group of little boys were pointing at him and laughing. He was embarrassed and stopped, but he still wanted to catch up with the men, so he increased his pace. "The man you helped is Dr Ubaka Ezeuko, is he not?" he asked in Ama-Oyi dialect.

"Yes, that is his name," one of the men replied, staring at him, noting his hard breathing after the exertion. The man was anxious to get back to the hall where the sales were still in progress. "Is something wrong?" he asked impatiently.

"No, nothing is wrong. I just wanted to ask after his daughter. Please, can you tell me her name?"

"Why do you want to know her name?" the man demanded. His eyes perched on Eloka's face and from there climbed down to his legs, resting on his black shoes. The second man, who had watched the scene silently, laughed and entered the hall. The man spoke again, his voice studded with scorn. "You students, your eyes are always in search of girls instead of reading your books. You are all *izizi-nso-agbogho*, womanizers."

Eloka scowled at him. "You insult me because I asked a simple question? Just go away." He hissed and turned away.

The man booed him. "*Anumanu*, beast. She is safe where she is; fly after her if you can." He laughed derisively and hurried into the hall.

Eloka was still fuming from what he termed the man's unprovoked aggression when he saw his parents emerge from the hall followed by three men lugging the things they had bought. His mother held a hefty hen which tried to free itself from her grip. Eloka hurried forward and took the hen from her.

"Thank you, *nna*," she said, inspecting his face, as if to reassure herself that he was happy, with nothing bothering him, for his comfort was her joy and she often acted as if she lived to dote on him. "You have been outside? Were you bored with the sales?" She stretched her right hand and pressed down the collar of his shirt. As he moved away, she stopped him. "Wait, let me do it properly." She lifted the entire collar and folded it afresh until it was even on both sides.

"Thank you," he said, striding after the three men carrying things, ranging from electrical appliances to household equipment.

"Did you want to buy everything, Onwaora?" Eloka heard her tease his father. He shrugged; he could not understand why his mother insisted on calling his father Onwaora – People's Moon – which was his *ozo* name and title. She used to call him Ofodum until he acquired this name after taking the title. She herself took the title Loolo, as the wife of a titled man. Eloka was relieved that his father did not call her by this title, but continued to call her Akunnaya. Even this name Akunnaya baffled Eloka; he wondered why parents would give their daughter such a name which actually meant 'her father's wealth'. It was obvious that the parents had, at the beginning of the child's life, decided that she was a source of wealth to her family and only a wealthy man would be allowed to marry her. And in his mother's case, the plan seemed to have worked, for his father was a rich man by Ama-Oyi standards, by any standards, in fact. He admired his father in some ways – he had always worked hard. He made his money in marketing palm produce before he branched out into farming. Eloka was sure his father had the biggest farm owned by an individual in Nigeria. But he had had other ambitions too, Eloka knew. He once contested for the mayoralty of the Port Harcourt Municipality and failed woefully. A more charismatic business mogul had won. Incidentally, the man's son was Eloka's close friend. Eloka had been upset with his mother when he found her crying because his father had lost the contest and she could not be mayoress – a position she had coveted for years.

"Let me do it," he said to the driver, as he struggled to force the items into the boot of the Mercedes. Eloka rearranged the load until they were all accommodated in the available space.

"*Nna*, this is why I always want you to pack my things when I am about to travel," Akunnaya enthused, her eyes full of admiration, of pride. "David, I hope you watched how he did it? Next time, he will not be there to rescue you." She stabbed the driver with a scornful stare.

"Yes, Madam," David replied.

Akunnaya retied the outer layer of her two-piece *intorica wrappa* and sat on the seat behind the driver. She patted her headdress and adjusted it at a slanting angle. She was strikingly beautiful and had been a celebrated beauty in her teenage years. Among all her many suitors, Chief Odunze won her love and led her to the altar a virgin. Eloka was proud of his mother and showed her off to his friends when she came to see him during the school's visiting day. She would bring food and fruits which he shared with his friends.

Eloka took the seat beside the driver and wound the window-glass down. Chief Ofodum Odunze squeezed himself into the car and took the seat beside his wife – *owner's corner*, as Ama-Oyi people would describe it. Eloka smiled to himself, remembering the day he sat in that position when he was a little boy of ten and his father had barked, "*Si ebe ahu puta*, come out from there! Wait until you buy your own." He had rushed out of the car. His father did not share that seat with anyone, not even his mother. If she were to be taken anywhere without him, he instructed the driver to take her in another car, never in the Mercedes. Eloka would wonder time and time again if his father's attitude to that corner seat in the Mercedes was driven by the same attitude to a certain small room in their house in Port Harcourt. The room was always under lock and key; its door was smaller than other doors in the house. No one knew what was inside, no one claimed to have ever entered it, except his father, of course. There were some things about his father he did not understand.

"In spite of the hardship in the land, many people brought valuable things for Thanksgiving," Chief Odunze observed. "The pastor was very happy." He addressed no one in particular. His wife responded, "I was not surprised. People wanted to show appreciation for what God had done for them. Our people say that if you thank someone for what he did for you, he will do more. I think it is the same with God. He blesses you more if you show appreciation for past blessings."

Eloka laughed. "It does not follow. How can we be sure God wants plantains, goats, yams and all the things people brought? What will he do with them?"

"You are talking like the small boy you are," Chief Odunze admonished. "It's there in the Bible; God expects us to give from what we have and what we produce."

When they got to Obigbo, they stopped to buy fuel. Chief Odunze alighted to urinate. One of the attendants directed him to a makeshift toilet behind the car-wash area of the petrol station. He came back and ordered the driver to move faster, as he needed to get home as quickly as possible to use a proper toilet.

"Onwaora, what happened?" Akunnaya asked. "You did not use the toilet in the petrol station?" She turned towards him.

"There is no toilet, except a roofless open enclosure." He shuddered. "If you see it, you will vomit whatever food you have in your belly, even the food you ate yesterday." He shook his head.

Akunnaya burst into laughter, throwing her head forward. Her headdress fell and landed at Chief Odunze's feet; she stooped and picked it up quickly and put it back on her head. "God forbid. Travellers suffer in this land; you cannot find a decent toilet anywhere when you are on the road. This is why I do not drink water when I travel so that I will not have the urge to pass water. I also do not eat food in case my stomach gets upset and compels me to look for where to offload."

Chief Odunze chuckled at the mention of the word 'offload'.

"This was why I wanted to get into the local government," he said. "I entered that contest because I wanted to be mayor to change things in Port Harcourt and its environs. But I lost. What is the new mayor doing? He has not achieved anything since he was elected, almost two years in office. He and his supporters are only good at throwing cocktail parties. So so enjoyment; nothing to show for the money they are collecting." He shrugged and pressed his back hard against his seat.

"The cocktail parties are nice, you must agree," said Akunnaya, with a gentle voice. "It is an important way of knowing who is new in town and what style is in vogue. Onwaora, you will agree you have met people there who have been useful to you in one way or another. It is also good for business. Remember, it was at a cocktail party you met the managers of some of the department stores that you supply goods to now."

They arrived home in silence. Eloka laughed as he watched his sisters jostling at the front door, each trying to jump out first to welcome him and the others. "Stop that! What is happening there?" Chief Odunze rebuked. "Do you want to hurt yourselves?"

Ijeamasi, the older girl, pulled through first, screaming with laughter. She ran forward and flew into Eloka's arms. "Eloka, welcome," she cried. "Papa, how was the journey?"

The defeated one, Ozioma, ran to her mother and embraced her. "Welcome, Mama," she greeted in a muted voice, still smarting from the pain of defeat. She was thin like Eloka, with an unformed body that proclaimed her twelve years of living on earth. She was dark-skinned like the rest of the family, but had inherited her father's round face.

"You are too old for this game, now," Chief Odunze reprimanded. "What will you say if you break your hand or leg?" he looked from one to the other. "Ijeamasi, you should know better. You are older." He turned away from them.

"Yes, Papa," Ijeamasi replied, still giggling.

"I hope there is food in the house? We are hungry." Akunnaya gave Ijeamasi an enquiring look.

"Yes, Monica finished cooking long ago." Ijeamasi had her mother's attractive features; she was sixteen but had the figure of an eighteen-year-old. Her breasts were well-formed and she had broad hips.

"Did you assist her, or you left her to do it alone?"

"We helped her." Ijeamasi linked her hand to Eloka's and pulled him towards the front door, as David opened the boot.

"Wait, let's bring out the things in the boot," Eloka said, gently extricating his hand. "Ijeamasi and Ozioma, come and help."

"Did Adaeze come to Ama-Oyi for the Thanksgiving?" Ozioma asked her mother, as she took from David the radio Chief Odunze had bought during the sales.

"Be careful with that radio," her mother cautioned, then answered her question. "No, Adaeze did not come; we learnt her baby is ill and she has taken him to hospital."

They had dinner in the spacious dining room, with a long table made from mahogany. The straight-back chairs were carved by a well-known carpenter in Aba. Eloka liked them. He had gone to Aba with his father to take delivery of the chairs, with their van. He remembered his father had been so pleased with them that he not only paid the man the agreed sum, but also gave him extra money.

Eloka watched Monica as she brought in more *oha* soup and pounded yam. She caught his eyes, smiled and asked. "Eloka, do you like the soup?" She had tiny teeth, with a gap in the middle of the upper row. The gap added to her attractive look when she smiled.

"Yes, I do," he beamed, raising his right hand in acknowledgement. "You are the best cook in Port Harcourt," he complimented, and he meant it. He was sure Monica cooked even better than his mother, though he would not admit it to anyone. "I am full," he admitted, "but I will eat more from the one you have just brought." Monica had been with the family since he was a little child. She was always there, stable and sweet-tempered. At school, when his geography teacher taught them about the Rock of Gibraltar, he thought that was a good expression to describe Monica's solid presence in his home.

"Make sure you eat enough, *Nna*," his mother advised. "I think they starve you at that Stella Maris College. See how thin you have grown. Go on, eat some more." She pushed a plate of meat towards him.

"You always go on about how thin I am, Mama." Eloka frowned. "We eat well in school; it's just that we work hard and run a marathon race every Friday. You cannot be fat if you do all that."

They all burst into laughter. "Make sure you do not run the race on an empty stomach," his father advised, picking his teeth and looking speculatively at Eloka.

"I will not." Eloka scooped more pounded yam into his plate. He took the soup plate and ladled the *oha* soup generously into his plate.

"Monica, give some food to David." Akunnaya instructed.

"Yes, ma, I have already done so."

After eating, Eloka washed his hands and watched Ijeamasi and Ozioma join Monica in clearing the table. He washed his hands with soap to ensure the oil from the soup was thoroughly removed. He enjoyed eating pounded yam or *garri* with his hand; it was a luxury he enjoyed at home, but was not allowed to indulge in at school. He hated eating *garri* with fork and knife, but that was exactly the way they had to eat it in the refectory.

"Onwaora, remember …" Akunnaya said to Chief Odunze, as she got up from her seat. "I want to have some rest now." She gave him a lingering look.

"Remember what?" he asked, washing his hands and wiping them on a napkin Monica presented to him.

"What we discussed last night," she reminded him. "Do you remember now?"

He nodded. "Yes, I have not forgotten." He waved her off.

Eloka could not help noticing how his father sometimes treated his mother like a child; sometimes in a rather avuncular, condescending way that hurt him whenever he saw it, as if he meant to say she was inferior to him. He did not say it in words, but Eloka saw it from time to time especially since he entered secondary school and developed a discerning mind, a mind of his own. He looked away from his father.

He was picking his teeth too when his father left the table. "Come and see me when you finish, Eloka. I want to talk to you," he said. Eloka wanted to ask his father where he wanted him to see him, but when he saw the heavy figure heading for the bedroom, he knew that was where he would see him. Eloka did not waste time, but followed his father immediately, wondering what he had to say that he couldn't say before his mother and sisters.

"Oh, you are here already?" His father looked up as soon as he entered. "Sit down. I will not detain you for long. I know you want to go and rest; we all want to rest after that journey." He glanced at his watch. "Seven o'clock. The day is gone and tomorrow is a busy day for me."

Eloka sat in an armchair and faced his father who lay propped up on three pillows in his spacious bedroom. His parents had always had separate rooms, Eloka thought, even when they were not well off and lived in a two-room accommodation. His father had one room and his mother shared the other with her four children – Adaeze, his eldest sister, himself, Ijeamasi and Baby Ozioma. The bed would take three people comfortably, even four, he thought. He had heard some of his classmates say that a couple that kept separate rooms were not in love with each other, that they were not close, for it was in the night when they lay together that a couple could discuss intimate and important issues.

"I received your report card on Friday," his father informed him, interrupting his thought. Eloka looked up quickly, his eyes trained on him enquiringly. "I will not say it is a bad result," he continued. "In fact, it is good, but it can be better. You came third in class. Good. But, I ask myself, what about the two boys who came first and second? Are they better than you? In what way are they better? Are their fathers richer than your father? Are their parents more intelligent than your parents? Do their fathers love them more than we love you or spend more money on their education than I spend on yours? Those are my questions and I want to know. What do you have to say?"

Eloka stared at his father, wondering why he was the way he was – always boastful. He knew his father came from a poor background and never went beyond primary four. He also knew he would rather die than admit this to his associates. He gave them and everyone the impression he had had a secondary education. It was Uncle Adiele, his father's elder brother that had unwittingly revealed one day that they had both stopped in primary four because their father could not pay their fees any longer. Eloka did not ask his father, as he would be deeply offended if he knew about it.

"Eloka, I'm waiting for your answer. Why can't you take the first position?"

"I did my best," he said sourly. "You say my best is not good enough, Papa? We are thirty in my class. What about the person who is at the bottom? What about the fourth, the tenth candidates, the twenty-seven students after me? What will their parents say to them?" Eloka gave his father a gaze full of challenge. He was not afraid; he had ceased to fear his father when he went into secondary school and met other boys from homes like his. But he would not be deliberately disrespectful.

"Eloka, you ask me questions instead of answering my questions?" Chief Odunze could not hide his astonishment, his annoyance. He shook his legs like someone suffering from *omandide*, a disease of the nervous system.

Eloka relented, though he would not allow his father to turn him into the creature he had fashioned in his heart. Eloka wanted to be himself. "All I am saying is that I did my best in all my subjects. Did I score less than seventy-five per cent in any of them? Take a look again, Papa. I assure you I will continue to work hard; I will not disappoint you or waste your money."

"That's what I want to hear, my son. Good." He stopped shaking his legs and sat bolt upright. "You will move into your final year in less than a month. Have you thought of what you want to do after secondary school?"

"Yes, I have." He looked his father in the eyes and said, "I want to proceed to Higher School and after that enter university to study engineering."

"I want you to read agriculture so that you take over the management of the farm when I am old or when I am no more. That is the course I want you to read, agriculture." He said it with so much glee that Eloka was amused. He thought his father sometimes acted like someone who had lost touch with reality. He simply smiled but said no more; what was the point arguing with his father in his present state of mind? He would not understand. He would lose his temper and the conversation would end in anger. He knew what he wanted to do with his life and meant to pursue the career he wanted. Even the subjects he had chosen for his final year tallied with his ambition, but his father was not learned enough to notice this. Eloka thought it best not to enlighten him.

"That is settled then," he intoned, and moved to a fresh subject. "Your mother and I think you should be on the lookout for a nice girl from a good family whom you will eventually marry. You are our only son for now. We are not sure whether another will come, so we are anxious about grandchildren. Do not get me wrong, we do not mean you will marry today or tomorrow, but just for you to have it in mind. You are eighteen, going to nineteen at the moment, but . . ." He inclined his head to the right; his eyes pleaded for understanding. One plump arm rested on his lap, the other gesticulated in the air as he marshalled his points.

But Eloka was already on his feet. "Please, don't raise this subject again or I will think that you and Mama are planning my downfall. How can you be thinking of marriage for me when I do not even have my school certificate yet? I refuse to listen to this type of talk." He turned to walk away.

"All right, my son," Chief Odunze conceded. "We will let the matter rest for now. But I want you to know your position in this house as our only son. You cannot escape getting involved in an early marriage; it is the tradition of our people. That is all."

WHEN THE time came for Eloka to go to university for his undergraduate studies, he did not hesitate to register as a student of electrical engineering. He did not tell his father the course for which he had registered. He did not inform him that he had not registered for agriculture. Chief Odunze did not ask him; he assumed Eloka had done as he had instructed the last time they had discussed the matter. Chief Odunze remained in this state of ignorance for nearly two years. Eloka felt fulfilled.

However, the political crisis in the country worried Eloka; he saw it as a threat to peace, and a threat to peace is a threat to education and development. He became more concerned as the killing of easterners intensified and got out of hand in northern cities, towns and villages. He watched as easterners, especially Igbo people, returned home in droves. What would happen to these people who abandoned their businesses, their work and education to escape death at the hands of people who were once their friends, colleagues and neighbours?

he wondered. Would they ever return to the places they ran from? How would they survive? Eloka watched the situation keenly to know in which way the pendulum of discussion and negotiation between the Federal Government and the Eastern Nigerian Government would swing. Meanwhile, he participated in rallies organised by Nsukka students on the crisis.

"We will immediately write a strongly-worded letter to the Federal Government to express our views on the crisis and the pogrom," the Student Union president had announced to students at a rally, in front of the union building. He gripped the loud speaker, as if he was in danger of losing it to another speaker without having had his say. He spoke for some time condemning the killing of innocent civilians and the general insecurity in the country. The crowd of students listened attentively, shouting slogans from time to time. "*Aluta continua*! Power to the people! Down with murderers! Enough is enough!" Some primary school pupils and secondary school students, who waited for their parents to close from work and take them home, rushed to the scene. Their voices rang out to increase the din. Eloka had looked at them and laughed. They had found a big distraction, he thought.

Eloka had raised his hand and, when he was permitted to speak, said, "I suggest we send a delegation to the Military Governor, Lieutenant Colonel Odumegwu Ojukwu, as a gesture of support. I also think the Students' Union should organise activities to raise funds to alleviate the suffering of the refugees from the North – the people who fled their homes and workplaces for security reasons as well as the wounded."

Many people had spoken and made suggestions as to what students could do. Eloka was pleased when his suggestions were implemented in the following months. But the situation had deteriorated and it seemed to him there could be no peaceful resolution to the crisis. And indeed he felt his fears had been justified when Eastern Nigeria was declared an independent state and Yakubu Gowon swore he would attack Biafra and crush what he described as a rebellion. As Eloka returned home for the long vacation, at the end of his second year examination, he knew that physical conflict would be the next stage in the crisis.

THREE DAYS after Eloka returned to Port Harcourt, Chief Odunze came home fuming. He was shouting Eloka's name and cursing him roundly in Ama-Oyi dialect. Everyone ran out to find out what was happening. Akunnaya cried, "Onwaora, what happened? Why are you cursing your son like that?" She tried to restrain him, just as Eloka approached from the back of the house. Chief Odunze pushed his wife aside and blustered into the sitting room, saliva foaming at the corners of his mouth. Akunnaya turned and walked out of the room. Her eyes were full of anger.

"Where is Eloka? Where is that headstrong boy who thinks he is *eze-onye-agwanam*, the one who knows it all?" he bellowed like a bull maddened by the bites of tsetse-flies. He swung his left arm and then the right to adjust his *agbada*. "I say where is that ingrate, who behaved like an overfed child that bit off his mother's nipples, forgetting that he would need to suckle again? *Ewo*, I have seen an abomination."

"Papa, what's the matter?" Eloka entered the sitting room just as his father was lowering his heavy body into a chair.

His calm and unperturbed demeanour seemed to infuriate his father the more.

"Eloka, what is this I heard from Osita, Chief Unegbu's son? When I visited his father this afternoon, Osita told me you are not studying agriculture but engineering. Is this true?" Chief Odunze fixed his gaze on Eloka's face, willing him to answer immediately.

Eloka stared back at his father and nodded. "Yes, I'm studying electrical engineering. I told you all along that I wanted to study engineering. I'm not interested in agriculture and I knew I would not do well if I registered for it."

"Eloka, was it not enough that I, your father who is training you and paying your school fees, wanted you to read agriculture? Should you not have respected my wish and registered for the course? What will happen to the farm now? Who will manage it after I am gone?" His eyes smoked; his legs shook, hitting against each other. "And for me to find out this wicked act of yours from an outsider breaks my heart."

Eloka shook his head, unsure how to address the issue. He knew his father's limited education would not allow him to understand that one did not just read a course because one's father wanted him to be in a certain profession. How could he explain to him that there were things like aptitude, ability, interest, vision and ambition and that they all had a role to play in what one ultimately decided to study in the university? He didn't think his father would understand, so he did not attempt to explain. Instead, he would apologise to him for the humiliation of getting the information from an outsider, his fellow student, Osita Unegbu. "I'm truly sorry, Papa; it was a mistake and an oversight not to have mentioned it to you."

Chief Odunze was somewhat mollified but knew it

would take him quite some time to recover from the shock that his son was not studying a course directly related to his investment, his business – the huge farm he hoped to leave him to manage some day. Eloka knew his father was a proud man.

Chief Odunze beckoned Eloka to a seat opposite him. As soon as Eloka sat down, his father declared, "The only thing that will make me forgive you this act of disobedience is if you promise to pay attention to the farm during the holiday and whenever you are in Port Harcourt. I want you to know everything you require to know about the farm. Do I need to tell you it will be yours and your children's one day? Are you with me? Do I have your word that you will do this?" His eyes had not left Eloka's for one moment.

Eloka smiled, shrugging. "That's all right. I'll do my best whenever I'm around."

"Well, we can begin today. I will go and change into work clothes and you can do the same, if you like; we will go on a tour of the farm and I will show you new things you did not see during your last holiday. Ask David to bring the pick-up to the front of the house." He lumbered to his feet and waddled to his room.

A few minutes later, Eloka and his father set out for the tour, with David driving the vehicle. They drove through the hectares of land which Eloka knew his father had paid a fortune to acquire mostly from the locals but some part of it from the government. There were a palm plantation and an orchard. Eloka often took walks in the plantation and the orchard. The cassava and yam sections were quite extensive. As they drove past, Eloka waved to Osondu and the other labourers sweating in the sun.

"We have started a piggery," Chief Odunze informed him. "That is what I wanted to show you. David, drive straight to the piggery."

Eloka turned to his father. "You started a piggery? What on earth for?" He was not sure that was a good idea. "How is it doing?" He turned, facing the road, as David negotiated a corner and headed for the house. "Is the piggery close to the house?" Eloka asked, astonished, wondering if it was a good idea to keep such dirty animals near the house.

"I decided to start a piggery because there is a growing market for it," Chief Odunze explained. He coughed to clear his throat and spat out the phlegm into the road. The muck did not go far, as the wind deflected it, causing it to land on the car window, close to where Eloka sat in the front seat. "Sorry, did that touch you?" Chief Odunze asked.

"Almost." Eloka used some tissue paper to wipe it off.

"It is the harmattan cold and dust; they give me catarrh. As I was saying, there is a steady but growing demand for pork, especially by white people. They seem to eat pork a lot. I want to meet this demand. That's business; you find out what people want and endeavour to satisfy their needs, their desires." He laughed.

David stopped a few metres to the house, nearer the labourers' quarters, though, and Eloka got out and waited for his father to lead the way. He could hear the pigs grunting; he found the noise repulsive. The sty was cemented all round, with holes to let in air, and the structure was roofed with corrugated iron sheets. Eloka looked in and saw the pigs rolling on the filthy ground; some buried their snouts in the muck. He counted twenty of them – twelve adults and eight piglets. He wondered if they were searching for food or simply enjoying the feel and smell of dirt. He watched the way they pushed their elongated and pointed mouths into anything they came across, the way they trotted about, grunting, as if they never settled down to rest as goats do when they chew the cud. "What's the other pig eating?" He pointed. "The fat one, she seems pregnant."

Chief Odunze laughed. "Human excreta: that is what she is eating. They enjoy it very much. Is that not so, David?"

"It is so, sir," David confirmed, bursting into laughter. "This is where we deposit our *nsi,* our wastes. Look at the *ngidi* where we sit to do it." He pointed, directing Eloka's gaze to a raised platform with a hole configured to perfectly accommodate human buttocks.

"My God! How horrible!" Eloka exclaimed, nauseated. He turned away from the fat pig and her companions. "Papa, there must be a better way of keeping these pigs. If people know you feed them excreta, do you think they will like to eat your products?" He did not think he would like to come back to this place again. "Let's leave this place before I throw up."

Chief Odunze stopped laughing. "You see what I mean? This is why I wanted you to study agriculture so that you can introduce modern farming here. You see now what you have done by refusing to do as I wanted? Whom do I have left to send to the university to learn farming techniques? You are my only son …"

Eloka sighed and without uttering another word, he walked towards the pick-up.

A few days after Eloka and his father toured the farm, the Federal Government declared war on Biafra. Though Yakubu Gowon had called it Police Action, Eloka knew it was nothing short of a full-scale war. He felt very sad because war would disrupt everything, including his education.

"It has happened!" Chief Odunze exclaimed, as the family sat in the sitting room listening to the news. "Gowon has attacked Biafra. We are now at war." He snapped his fingers with such ferocity that the noise produced sounded like oil-bean pods exploding in the harmattan.

"What did we do to these people that they won't even leave us alone after driving us away?" Akunnaya turned to stare at her husband's fingers snapping away.

"Eloka, you will not be able to return to Nsukka," said Ozioma who was now a young woman of seventeen. Her eyes were fixed on him. "What will you do? You think of nothing but your university."

"No one will be able to return to school, including you," Eloka retorted. "In any case, who is talking about school now? We should all be thinking of the war. No one knows how long it will last."

Each of them relapsed into thought. Silence dominated the atmosphere for a while. Chief Odunze had stopped snapping his fingers, and now stared in front of him. Eloka wondered if he was thinking of the farm and how the war would affect it.

The uncertainty of it all oppressed him and, for a moment, he wondered if he should join the army. He had heard that some of his classmates had done so even before Ojukwu declared Biafra's independence. He heard recruitment into the army and training were going on secretly; such moves had started when intelligence reports received indicated that Yakubu Gowon had all along planned to use force against the East. Eloka knew his father would object to his joining the army; it would be impossible to get him to give his blessing to such a decision.

Eloka got up and left the room.

10

Ginika, now in her fourth year at Elelenwa Girls' College, had recently celebrated her sixteenth birthday. She felt she was old enough to attend a dance taking place in Ugiri, one of the communities in Mbano. She was not new in Mbano – her family had been living there for one year since her father was transferred from Port Harcourt. She had made new friends in Mbano, though they hardly got close to each other, as they were all in boarding school. She valued the short periods she was able to see them during the holiday. She missed her best friend, Tonye Efeturi, who lived in Port Harcourt with her family. Each time her father was transferred, she lost friends – some she never met again. But she made new friends in the new location. Anna Nwoke was one of her new friends in Mbano. Ginika did not need much persuasion from her friend, Anna, the first daughter of one of the midwives in Mbano General Hospital, to take an interest in the forthcoming dance.

"Ginika, baby, it's going to be great fun," Anna cried, her face glowing with warmth. She sat in an armchair in Ginika's home, during her second visit that Easter holiday. A Form Four student of Ovim Girls' School, she was about the same age as Ginika though shorter and fatter. She had two horizontal facial marks her parents gave her at age five as part of the ritual to disconnect her from *ogbanje* children in the spirit world – her kindred spirits determined to draw her away from the world of the living. Ginika had told Anna that the marks were cute and made her look so pretty especially when she smiled.

"Yes, I know," Ginika replied wistfully. "I hear Seven-Seven Brothers Band and Royal Highlife Maestros will be supplying the music." She was not sure her father would let her go, but she would ask him.

"So you will go then?" Anna asked. "I haven't told my mother yet, but if she knows you'll be there, she will allow me to go." She shook her body in excitement.

"Don't rejoice yet," Ginika cautioned. "I haven't told my father; he might refuse to give me permission."

"You ask your father today and I'll ask my mother. Tomorrow we meet and compare notes." Anna looked at Ginika, expecting her to agree to this strategy.

"Why don't we do it this way?" said Ginika, clasping her knees. "I'll ask my father while you are here; he'll soon be home for lunch. Then tomorrow I come over to your house and we tackle your mother together. What do you think?"

"Brilliant! We'll do that; I know it will work." Anna beamed.

GINIKA AND Anna were playing Snakes and Ladders when her father arrived home for lunch. Anna got up to greet him; Ginika looked up and smiled at her father.

"Welcome, Papa. How is the hospital?" She greeted him sweetly, hoping that this would prepare him ahead of her request and put him in a good mood. She was determined to attend the dance at Ugiri and hoped her father would be reasonable. She wished Nwakire were around to lend his voice, but he had stayed back in school for continuation lessons his school had organised for the Fifth Form and the Upper Six students.

"Welcome, sir," greeted Anna, curtsying. She gave him her famous smile which illuminated her *ogbanje* mark.

He dropped his diary on the table, nodded to Ginika and turned to her friend. "Are you not the midwife's daughter?"

"I am, sir," replied Anna. "How's work, sir?" Anna sat down beside Ginika.

"Work is fine," he replied. "What are you two doing?"

"We're playing a game, Snakes and Ladders." Ginika got up to fetch his lunch.

"*Hmm*, you should play Scrabble," he advised. "Scrabble is better and will help you to build new words in English. If you play Scrabble, you not only entertain yourselves, but also learn."

Ginika, who had paused at the door to hear him out, nodded and then went out. Anna smiled and said, "Thank you, sir, for the advice."

They continued with the game while her father ate. Ginika looked up from time to time to check on her father's progress with his food. She gave him surreptitious glances; from his face, she saw he was pleased with the food. She and Auntie Lizzy had prepared it before Auntie Lizzy went out to plait her hair. He had always loved pounded yam and bitterleaf soup. Ginika rejoiced that this was the food he was enjoying now. Fate seemed to be working in her favour; today's lunch happened to be her father's favourite meal.

"How is your father?" he asked Anna. "I understand he lives in Umuahia. Do you hear from him?"

"Yes, sir, he is well. He comes to see us most weekends when he is free. He is with the Ministry of Works." She had suspended the game to respond to his question. Now she turned back to Ginika who had waited patiently for her to finish.

"Your turn," she reminded Anna, pleased with the way things were going. Somehow she felt her father would not be able to refuse her request with Anna's voice supporting hers, especially if she told him, as they had agreed, that her mother had given her permission to attend the dance.

As soon as her father began to wash his hands with the water in a basin Ginika had brought for him, she launched her campaign. "Papa, I have a request to make," she began. As he looked up, her eyes held his and she did not look away from that sombre face until she had had her say. "The Students and Teachers Association of Mbano is organising a dance next Saturday in Ugiri; they have invited all students from Mbano." She paused for breath, but only for a moment. She continued, "Many students plan to go from here and I want to go with them. May I?" There, she had blurted it out and now she would wait to hear his answer. Her heartbeat raced, as she perched on her chair. She had shifted to the edge of it to tense her body and thrust her head forward to be able to speak eloquently. She hoped this posture would give him the impression that she was serious about the request.

Her father picked up a napkin and wiped his hands. With a white handkerchief he fished out from his pocket, he cleaned his mouth. Ginika studied his every move, heart on fire. Anna stared in front, waiting for the right moment to come in.

"You said the dance would take place in Ugiri? That is far, at least four miles away. How will you get there?" He returned the handkerchief to his pocket.

"We are going in a group," Ginika explained, relaxing a little, but she knew the battle was not won yet. "Some of the male students have bicycles and some will borrow their fathers'. They will take us to the venue."

Her father gave a short laugh. "Bicycles? Can you sit on a bicycle from here to Ugiri?" His gaze was speculative, but it was not certain to Ginika whether he was agreeing or disagreeing to her request.

"Yes, I can. I will ride with Bobby, Dr Unogu's son." She hoped this information would help him make up his mind, positively. "The dance is in the afternoon, at two o'clock. We will be back before seven. They called it Tea-Time Dance; it will take place in the Ugiri Primary School building." Ginika did not know what Tea-Time Dance meant or why the organisers chose to describe the dance in this term, but from the posters and handbills she saw, it was an afternoon affair which should be over before the end of the evening.

Anna spoke quickly. "Sir, I am going too; my mother has given her permission. Please, give Ginika permission so that we can go together."

He asked, "Who will provide the music?" he reached for the packet of toothpicks; Anna dashed forward and gave it to him. "Thank you," he said.

"Seven-Seven Brothers Band and Royal Highlife Maestros are coming," Anna informed him.

"All right, you have my permission to go to the dance, but make sure you return in good time."

"Thank you, Papa." Ginika smiled broadly. She could hear her heart thumping with excitement.

"Thank you, sir," Anna said, curtsying again, as she had done when he entered the house.

He picked up his car keys and went out. Ginika and Anna waited until they heard the sound of the car driving out of the compound and gave a shout of jubilation. They fell into each other's arms and hugged, screaming with laughter all the time.

"We did it! We did it!" Anna cried.

"Yes, we did it!" Ginika shouted back. In celebration, Ginika played some Congo music and they danced *Cha-Cha-Cha* until they were tired.

SATURDAY, THE long-awaited day arrived. Ginika felt on top of the world – she was going to her first ball, her first public dance, with live bands performing. She gazed at the dress she had decided to wear and felt totally satisfied; it was the dress Auntie Chito had made for her last Christmas. It took time before she decided to wear it. She had debated with herself whether to wear it or the one her father had also bought on the same occasion – Christmas. He always gave her as well as Nwakire a new outfit every Christmas. Auntie Chito did the same, explaining that her sister – their mother – was not there to give them Christmas presents, so she had to do it on her behalf. Ginika would wear her dress afterwards, pretending it was from her mother. In the past, especially when she was little, she had wept, but she no longer wept now.

The dress she had chosen was pink and trimmed with white ribbons. It had a narrow bodice, a full skirt that flared out from below the waist; the style was called 'low waist'. She loved it; it emphasised her slim waist and gave her what she called a *fairy-queen* look. When Anna came for her at one o'clock, she was already dressed and waiting.

"You look absolutely stunning," Anna gushed, her eyes full of admiration.

"You too, Anna; you look gorgeous." Ginika looked approvingly at her friend's white top and midi skirt made from lace material. "*Igbujekwe*, you're going for the kill today," she teased, laughing.

Anna's laughter was hilarious. They trotted off to the rendezvous – the mango tree in front of the County Council Office – where four people were waiting for them. Bobby Unogu and two other boys had bicycles; a girl called Ngozika was with them. Ginika got on Bobby's bicycle while Anna and Ngozika rode with the other boys.

The hall was almost full when they got there after two o'clock. It was a long rectangular building with a platform which had been decorated and prepared to accommodate the bands. But by four the two bands had not arrived. The students waited another hour; still there was no sign of the bands.

"I'm worried." Ginika turned to Anna. "I told my father we would come back before seven, but look at the time; the bands are not even here yet, let alone the dance starting." She sighed. "This is not good enough."

"I wonder why the bands are not here. Is this the way these musicians behave? They don't know how to keep time." Anna hissed.

Royal Highlife Maestros arrived eventually at thirty minutes past five. The musicians hurriedly set up their equipment. Some students had left in annoyance but many were still there. Ginika found the music interesting and danced vigorously with different partners. She watched the musicians and thought they were good. Perhaps they wanted to make up for their lateness. Seven-Seven Brothers Band did not show up and Ginika wondered what would have happened if Royal Highlife Maestros had also failed to come. It would have been a total disaster, she thought. She looked at her watch and saw it was past seven.

She found Anna who was wiggling her hips to the rhythm of the music, in front of a boy with bushy hair. "Anna, we should be going," Ginika said. "It's past seven."

"Oh, let's stay a little longer; the dance has only just warmed up."

After fifteen minutes, Ginika went back to her and insisted, "We must go now. Let's find Bobby and the rest." Without waiting for Anna's response, she went off in search of Bobby and found him dancing with Ngozika. "Bobby, please, can we go now? I promised my father I would come home by seven." She had to shout into his ear because of the loud music. She could feel the bodies of the dancers brushing against hers in the crowded hall.

"But the dance has only just started," Bobby protested with a raised voice because of the blaring sound of the music. "It's not our fault the band came so late." He looked away to avoid Ginika's distressed expression and went on dancing. "Go back to Ken; he's waiting for you over there."

Ginika returned to Ken, but her mind was no longer in the dance. Ken held her waist and shook it. "Baby, come on, dance with me. Don't spoil the show." His breath smelt of alcohol. She thought he must have bought it at the makeshift bar set up outside the hall. She kept pestering Bobby and the others until they succumbed to her demand. It was well after eight before they left; she was anxious to get home quickly.

Ginika and Bobby rode in front, followed by Ngozika and Ken, Anna and Chide, the third boy. Ginika was grateful to the moon which lit up everywhere. The bicycles also had their own light and she was sure they would get home safely. She could hear Bobby breathing hard as he pedalled his bicycle up a small hill. "Are you okay?" she asked.

"Sure," he grunted, before the hard breathing started again. Ginika knew he would rather die than admit it was tough-going for him.

"Shit!" Ken cursed, as he battled to steady his bicycle. He and Ngozika crashed to the ground. "My mother-o!" Ngozika shouted.

"What's the matter?" Bobby asked, braking sharply. His long legs sought the ground and steadied the bicycle. As soon as Ginika's feet touched the ground, she hurried to Ngozika.

They discovered that a sharp object had ripped apart the tube and tyre of Ken's bicycle. There was nothing they could do but walk. Ginika, Anna and Ngozika walked in front and the boys came behind, pushing their bicycles. Ginika quickened her steps, forcing the others to do the same.

"What an adventure!" Anna giggled.

Ginika frowned at Anna's giggles, wondering what was funny about their situation. She felt as if a human hand had gripped her neck, choking her; she could not breathe normally. Her father would be mad, she knew; how he would express his anger worried her. Would he beat her? She shook her head; she was almost sure he would not allow her to attend a dance ever again.

"Please, shall we go to my house first?" she pleaded. "I want my father to see all of us together; then he will believe me when I tell him what happened." They had reached the County Council Office which was quite close to her house.

"That's all right," they chorused.

As soon as she knocked on the front door, her father opened the door and stood there staring at them. His eyes were full of anger as he stood there as threatening and infuriated as a vengeful god.

"Good evening, sir," five voices greeted him, in unison. Ginika said, "Good evening, Papa."

He did not respond to their greeting, but he checked the ferocious words that jostled to be let out from his slightly open mouth. "Get into the house," he ordered Ginika and shifted to let her in. She waved to her friends and walked past him, into the house. To the others, Ubaka said, furiously, "Now, go home immediately."

"Yes, sir." Again the chorus sounded as one voice. They turned and he watched them stride away into the night.

When Ginika walked in, Auntie Lizzy sat up and stared at her angrily. "Ginika, what were you doing outside till this time? Do you realise how worried we were? Twelve o'clock and you were not home." She raised her hands up in exasperation.

Ginika said nothing. Her father entered and bolted the door. He sat opposite his wife. "Ginikanwa, sit down and tell us why you are coming home at this late hour," he hissed.

After she told them what had happened, Ginika looked at their faces. She wondered if they believed her. Whether they did or not, she had told them the whole truth.

"Why did you not come home when the band did not show up as planned? Why wait for them till seven – the time

152

you were supposed to come home?" Lizzy asked, getting up. "Uba, I am going to bed. I am tired."

"Come to my room immediately," her father said, after Auntie Lizzy had left. Ginika trembled. What did he mean by asking her to follow him to his room? Was he going to flog her? She cringed; it was a long time since he had whipped her last. She remembered it was in her final year in primary school. He had not beaten her since she entered secondary school. Would he start again, now? She hesitated.

"Did you not hear me? I say go to my room at once."

She got up slowly and walked ahead while he came from behind. She stood near the door, watching his every move. She would run out if he tried to beat her. To her surprise, he locked the door. His next words took her by surprise.

"Did any of the boys touch you?"

"No," she replied, frowning.

"We shall see. Remove your underwear and lie down on the bed. I am going to examine you."

"No, Papa, please, no one did anything to me. We were in the hall all the time." She shrank further away from the bed and pressed her back against the wall.

"Look, Ginikanwa, do as I say; or do you want me to force you?" He glared at her.

"No, no, Papa, please."

"Get on with it!" he barked, moving threateningly towards her.

Slowly she pulled off her underwear. The examination was brief but thorough. Ginika lay on her back totally devastated. After he had finished, he told her to get up, and she could see he was more relaxed. "I was afraid those boys did something to you, but I am satisfied they did not. You can go to your room now, but remember, what happened today should not repeat itself. You are not allowed to keep late nights. I do not want any man around you until you finish your education and get married. Then someone else will be responsible for you."

Ginika picked up her underwear and left the room. She did not speak to her father for three days and three nights. During those days, she whispered several times, "I hate you!" She was sure she would never forgive him. She would remember this ugly incident all her life, this violation of her body.

11

Ginika lost interest in going home during the holidays. She would head for Enugu instead of Mbano to spend with Auntie Chito and her family the few weeks of holiday that came at the end of each term. Her father sent peremptory commands which were largely ignored. This was the situation for over a year.

During one such visit to Enugu, Ginika headed for Nwakire's hostel at medical school. She tapped the door and waited. When there was no response, she knocked loudly and heard, "Come in if you are good-looking"; she laughed and pushed the door open. Nwakire's eyes lit up and he got up from the bed where he lay reading *The Pilot*. "Here, at last, comes my beautiful sister," he beamed.

"Kire, *kedu*, how are you?" She walked into Nwakire's warm embrace. "I thought you had forgotten I was coming and gone out. Where are your fellow students? The hostel looks deserted." She held him at arm's length, looking at him, as if he was a painting to be inspected; she seemed satisfied with the way he looked. He wore brown shorts and a short-sleeved cotton shirt which was unbuttoned. The dark hair on his chest was quite visible.

155

"The students are in their rooms hibernating, as we all do on Sunday," he replied. "Come and sit down." He led her to the single chair in the small room he shared with another second year medical student.

"What are you reading?" She picked up the newspaper and scanned through the headlines.

"I was reading a feature article on the counter coup staged by northern officers and the kidnapping of General Aguiyi Ironsi and his host, Lieutenant Colonel Fajuyi. The situation is frightening. This country is in soup."

Ginika dropped the paper and faced Nwakire. "The coup is the talk of the town. Auntie Chito and Uncle Ray have talked about nothing else since I arrived in their house yesterday." She shook her head. "They said many officers from the East have been slaughtered like cattle and the coup plotters did not stop there; they have started killing people who are not soldiers."

"That is the worst part of it." Nwakire picked up the newspaper again. "Look at the pictures," he said, pointing. "You can see some of the people who managed to escape; they are returning to the East. Most of the people they are killing are Igbo. If the coup were an act of revenge, as the plotters claim, why are ordinary people being killed? Why are they killing innocent civilians who knew nothing about the January coup?"

"Uncle Ray asked the same question," Ginika said, looking at the pictures and expressing revulsion by wrinkling her face.

"How are they and their children?" Nwakire asked.

"Who?" Ginika asked absent-mindedly; her attention was still focused on the pictures in the newspaper.

"Uncle Ray and his family, of course. I haven't seen them for weeks; we've been busy with lectures and practicals. I didn't realise there would be so much to do in the second year."

She threw the paper to him and nodded. "They are fine and asked me to greet you. Do you know Auntie Chito complained they have not seen you for a long time?" She gave him a hard look, as if telling him that, since he lived in the same town as their aunt, he should pay her a visit oftener. "Perhaps you can come with me when I leave here and see them?"

"That's a good idea."

She kicked off her shoes and relaxed, her legs stretched and touching the end of the bed. "If Papa finds out I came to Enugu to spend the mid-term break, he will be mad." She laughed.

Nwakire stared at her. "You didn't tell him you would be coming to Enugu?"

She laughed again. "Why should I tell him? It's only four days – Friday to Monday; what's the point telling him. He would object if he knew anyway, so why should I bother? He would tell me to spend it in school as some of the girls do. How could I see you and Auntie Chito if I stayed in school?" She shook her legs in irritation; she was annoyed because she did not want to be criticised for her action.

"Even at the risk of his objecting and stopping you from coming, I think you should have told him." Nwakire's face was so serious Ginika stopped laughing. "Gini, your attitude to Papa borders on disrespect. I have wanted to speak to you about it. It's like a mini rebellion. May I know why?"

Ginika looked away from him and stared at the whitewashed ceiling. Why should Nwakire criticise her? After all he was often rebellious too. He had been a victim of their father's high-handedness as much as she had been. She remembered the day she had taken refuge in Nwakire's room during a thunderstorm. It was in the middle of the night and he had allowed her to sleep on his bed. Auntie Lizzy had found them in the morning and called out to their father, "Uba, come and see your children. Come and see." Her loud voice had woken them up and before they could react, their father descended on them, dragged her away and demanded to know why she had left her room for her brother's.

Ginika's mind returned to the incident after the ball in Ugiri and flinched. Two years after, it still hurt to think of what her father did to her in the name of protecting her. She had just completed her fourth year at Elelenwa Girls' College then. Now she was about to enter her second year in Higher School, but she had not forgotten. Would she ever forget? Since the incident took place, she had avoided her father whenever she could, travelling to Enugu to be with Auntie Chito at the slightest opportunity. A school friend had asked her once, "Why do you prefer to spend your holiday in Enugu instead of Mbano, where your family is?" She had replied, "I like being with my aunt and her family and feel at home with her more than with my father or my stepmother." This was not the whole truth, she knew, but it was true all the same.

When she looked down from the ceiling, she saw that Nwakire was watching her and waiting for her to answer his question. Should she tell him? She had never revealed her experience to any one. Should she remain silent now that Nwakire criticised her so pointedly in a matter of which he did not know the origin? Her acerbity had grown gradually over the years, right from her early teens, but, of course, it worsened following what transpired after the dance at Ugiri. Ginika smiled ruefully at the irony of the situation: the first time her father readily consented to her attending a social gathering alone ended in a fiasco – damaging the fragile bond that linked them as father and daughter.

"Gini, what's been happening to you recently? I feel you have been hiding something from me. What is it?" The ghost of suspicion which hovered over Nwakire's eyes decided for Ginika the course to take.

"Kire, you're right." She sighed, sat up and put on her shoes, as if what she was about to say did not only require absolute composure of the mind but also appropriate comportment of the body. "Something happened between Papa and me which I have kept from you."

As she focused her eyes on his, she noticed his dimmed slightly from anxiety. For a moment she wondered if telling him what their father did to her was the right thing to do. With a shrug, she told him what happened the time he had stayed in school for continuation class and she had attended a dance with other youths at Ugiri. All the time, she trained her gaze on him, willing him to hear her out, asking for his understanding, demanding that he took sides with her.

Nwakire listened attentively. His eyes focused on her face and did not deviate from it all the time even as the narration lengthened, for Ginika recounted the entire incident from the time they arrived in Ugiri for the dance until the time her father took her to his room. At first Nwakire's eyes only showed his eagerness to know what had happened to embitter Ginika so much that she hardly cloaked her antagonism towards their father, but as the narrative lengthened and climaxed, his eyes began to smoke until he exploded, "Gini, are you sure of what you are saying? Answer me! Papa did this to you?" Ginika nodded, wiping with her right hand the tears that had gathered in her eyes. "My God, I can't believe this." Nwakire stared at her but his eyes were so glazed Ginika knew his mind was far away, perhaps he was, like her, remembering the many frictions and conflicts they had had with their father and their stepmother over the years – the years following the death of their mother. Nwakire was older than her by three years and was, therefore, luckier to have known, enjoyed and appreciated their mother more than she who had been only six at the time she died.

"And you kept this knowledge from me for how long – almost two years? Ah, Gini, that was wrong; you should have told me and saved yourself the pain, the trauma of the ugly memory, a burden you have carried alone for so long. No wonder you have grown bitter and the bitterness has become so obvious." He shook his head.

Ginika felt something like a lump grow inside her and rise to her throat, choking her. She burst into tears, her shoulders shaking from the spasms of sorrow that overwhelmed her.

"It's okay, don't cry." Nwakire was by her side, comforting her. He held her close and said, "This will not happen again, I assure you."

WHEN GINIKA and Nwakire came home for Christmas holiday few months later, Nwakire confronted their father over what he called the immoral and tyrannical invasion of Ginika's privacy. He pursued him to his room one evening after supper and did not waste time in making his mission and his feelings known. "Papa, Ginika told me how you abused her two years ago, how you misused your power as a parent and as a medical doctor to inflict psychological and mental wounds on her."

When his father, who was sitting on a chair behind the table in his room, looked at Nwakire, he was shaken by the depth of hostility in his eyes. "Nwakire, have you lost your mind to speak to me like this? That you are in the university should not make you disrespect your father."

Nwakire stood in the middle of the room and glared at him. "You should not have done what you did; it was wrong, it was immoral and cruel. Your profession as a medical doctor and your position as her father were no justification for your conduct." He clenched and unclenched his fists.

"You have no right to judge me," his father said, in a stern voice. He removed his glasses and looked up at his son who stood before him, cutting the image of Amadioha, the god of thunder, himself. He must have thought Nwakire's anger would materialise into physical attack, for he drew back. The movement was slight, but Nwakire had noticed it and immediately allowed his hands to rest by his sides. "I was exercising my authority as a father to protect my daughter. I only acted as a medical doctor when I examined her physically to make sure she had not been violated. My action had no other meaning than what I have just explained to you." His gaze was both cold and disapproving, but this did not deter Nwakire from saying more.

"Your obsession with her chastity has gone too far. Do you think the way you are going about it is the best way to protect Ginika or to make her behave well? You are driving her to the wall and making her unhappy and angry with you. That's what you have succeeded in doing." Nwakire's voice was harsh. He did not realise that contempt had crept into it and he was guilty of the same misdemeanour he had charged against Ginika when they were in Enugu. "Anyway, what was done is past; but I want to ask you here and now not to do it ever again. It must not repeat itself. After all, you are a father, not a moral inquisitor or prosecutor." His eyes blazed like a forge.

His father stared aghast at him, devastated by the scorn in his voice and the disdain in his unnaturally bright eyes. "Nwakire, please, sit down." His voice was mellowed and conciliatory in a way that was new and strange, causing Nwakire to look into his eyes. "You misunderstand my motive; you do not understand what made me take that extreme step. Let me explain …"

Nwakire was surprised at the soft timbre of his father's voice, different from the impatient and brusque manner that had become second nature to him over the years. "Papa, let me call Ginika before you explain. I think she needs your explanation more than I do."

He nodded and Nwakire hurried out of the room. Soon he returned with her. Ginika looked with dread at her father. She thought he would be mad at her for telling Nwakire. But, to her astonishment, he was neither angry nor condemnatory.

"Sit down, both of you." He indicated the bed and they sat down, facing him. He stared into space for a full minute before he spoke again. "I have never questioned nor felt guilty about what I did on the night Ginika came home very late from the dance, for I did it to protect you." He paused and looked pointedly at Ginika.

He continued, "I still do not question my conduct because I am convinced I did the right thing at that point in time. You were much younger at the time and needed my protection perhaps more than you do today. This is not to say that I am no longer responsible for your protection; it is my conviction that a female child should be watched more closely in her relationship with the opposite sex than the male child. It is the female who usually gets hurt in any escapade between a man and a woman. I also think that it is the parents' responsibility to watch over their daughter until she gets married, and only then can her parents disengage from that responsibility. Unfortunately, in your case, your mother died and left the task to me alone. When I married your stepmother, she failed to play the role of a mother, as I had dreamed and hoped she would. I cannot say if I succeeded or failed as a father; sometimes I have my doubts."

Nwakire wanted to say something, but he continued, "I have never told you this, but I had a sister, much younger than I. When I was in the United Kingdom studying medicine, I dreamed of coming home after qualifying as a doctor and helping my family. My two brothers were apprenticed as traders after their primary education. There was nothing I could do about it, for I had no means of helping them. That I was able to study abroad was because I was awarded a scholarship by the colonial government. But my youngest and only sister was still quite small and I dreamed about how I would send her to a good secondary school and to the university after that. I came home after my studies to discover that my sister had been impregnated by her teacher in primary five and had died as he tried to assist her in aborting the pregnancy. It was the most shattering experience of my life at the time. You can imagine how I felt. She had died just before my ship docked at the Port Harcourt harbour. So the first social event I witnessed on my return from abroad was my sister's funeral. It was then I swore that such a thing would not happen to me again, and that I would take adequate steps to protect my female children or relations. This happened before I married your mother." He stopped and began to polish his glasses. He did not look at them.

Ginika did not know what to say after listening to her father. She was touched by his account, and could see how what happened to his sister had coloured her father's life and his conduct but she was still offended with him for what he had done to her. Should she commiserate with him or remain silent? Her mind was more inclined to do the latter. So she stared at the floor, saying nothing. She was hurt that her father did not see anything wrong in what he had done to her.

"That must have been tough for you, Papa," Nwakire said, shaking his head. "How come you never told us any of this?" He looked at Ginika briefly and returned his gaze to his father.

"I do not know; perhaps the pain throbbed for years, worsened by your mother's death at childbirth. I nursed all the hurt till it became a part of me, grafted to my skin. Thereafter, I could share it with no one, not even you, my children." His eyes were fixed on Ginika for some time. She stared back at him, without displaying any emotion; she thought she saw pain in his eyes. "You may go to bed now," he told them. "You have listened to some of my experience in life and I hope that explains my action to you." He picked up his glasses from the table and, as he was putting them on, Nwakire and Ginika got up to leave.

"Good night, Papa." Nwakire called from the doorway before he stepped into the corridor.

"Good night," Ginika said, without looking at her father.

"Good night," he replied, as he watched them leave.

GINIKA RETURNED to school early the following year. She found peace and joy in the beautiful compound. The school was surrounded by a thick forest which Ginika found enchanting because she thought it held secrets no human being could fathom. She liked the air of mystery that overshadowed this huge compound secluded from the prying eyes of neighbouring communities. She enjoyed the fresh air created by the natural environment and admired the different kinds of flowers that grew in the gardens in front of the hostels and classrooms.

The situation in the country had worsened; there was so much bickering between the Eastern Nigerian and Federal Governments over the killing of easterners, the issue of compensation and the security of easterners who lived and worked in the north and in Lagos. Ginika had become interested in politics like most students in her school. She listened to the news and kept in touch with Nwakire and Auntie Chito through the exchange of letters. Like most people, she was shocked when the Aburi Talks failed because Lieutenant Colonel Yakubu Gowon and his advisers failed to implement the decisions taken at Aburi. One of her teachers lamented as soon as he entered the class, "Girls, Aburi has failed. It is now 'To your tents, O Israel!' Nigeria is doomed." During that History period, Mr Ohanele did not teach the

Partition of Africa in 1884, which he had told them he would teach that day; instead he discussed with the class the tragedy unfolding in the country, the flight of peace and harmony in the relationship between the East and the rest of the country.

"Sir, why did Yakubu Gowon not implement the Aburi Accord?" asked one of the girls called Njide Igwe. She was bold and clever.

"The reason is not far to seek," Mr Ohanele pontificated, rubbing down the front of his pants. The girls giggled, as their eyes gravitated to his crotch. They knew he did this involuntarily but it never failed to make them titter. Ginika nudged Amina Yaro, the only Hausa student in the class whose father worked in Shell-BP. Amina shrank further into her chair, afraid to speak in class. Ever since the killing of easterners started in the north, Amina had lost her voice in class, had withdrawn from the hostel and came to school from home. Mr Ohanele continued, "The Permanent Secretaries in the various ministries, the professors in some of the universities and his British advisers warned Gowon about implementing the Aburi Accord as, according to them, it would amount to the disintegration of Nigeria. Yes, they told him that a united Nigeria ruled by a cabal at the centre was preferable to a Nigeria dismembered as a confederation." There was applause for the learned historian who was said to have studied at Makerere University in Uganda.

"Sir, what do you think Lieutenant Colonel Odumegwu Ojukwu will do? How will he react to the death of Aburi Accord?" Ginika asked.

"Thank you for that question, Ginika," Mr Ohanele said, scratching his head where the hair had receded. "Ojukwu has at least two options: go along with Gowon or pull the East out of the present federation of strange bedfellows and ultimately declare the East independent. It is not clear yet which of the options he will take, or whether he would take a totally different step." Again an ovation rang out for the learned teacher.

The Higher School students – as girls in Higher School were called in her school – were relatively freer than the students in Forms One to Five. Sometimes female teachers invited the senior girls to their houses and socialised with them. Ginika used such opportunities to listen to news about the situation in the country.

"Come over this evening and have boiled and roast maize with me," Miriam Taylor invited Ginika and four other girls in her literature class. She was about the most popular teacher in the school. She had shining blonde hair which she groomed meticulously and blue eyes that reminded Ginika of the sea at the Port Harcourt harbour each time she looked at her. Like the other ten missionary teachers, she wore her hair short. Ginika liked Miss Taylor and got on well with her. She found it easier to relate to Miss Taylor than any other teacher because she was the youngest and most pleasant among the missionary teachers in the school. Moreover, both of them had a passion for literature, especially plays and acting.

Miss Taylor's houseboy brought two trays containing boiled and roast maize. Ginika settled for boiled maize and followed Miss Taylor's example by smearing butter on it before biting into the cob. She watched the other girls make their choice. As they munched their maize, the girls gathered around the radio on a table in Miss Taylor's sparsely-furnished sitting room to listen to news. A gentle but very confident voice was analysing the killings of Igbo people going on in the North, in Lagos and some parts of the West and how it would affect the different groups in the country, how it had already polarised the people and destroyed the basis for trust and affection among the different ethnic groups.

"This programme is very good," Ginika said. "Is it aired every week?" She turned to Miss Taylor who sat in a cane chair, watching them indulgently. She shook her head. "Sorry, I haven't the remotest idea."

Ginika smiled, wondering how Miss Taylor spent her time when she was alone. Perhaps she spent a lot of time preparing and writing her lesson notes and reading books. Ginika was grateful for her friendship, remembering how she had written her father after her school certificate examination, advising him to allow Ginika to register for the Higher School class for she was a potential candidate for the university. Ginika remembered her exact words: "Your daughter, Ginika is university material." She was sure this recommendation had helped her father to take the decision to send her back to school for the Higher School course. Auntie Lizzy had suggested that a job should be found for her in a bank.

Belinda, a dark-skinned slender girl whose father worked in the Eastern Nigeria Broadcasting Corporation (ENBC) answered Ginika's question. "The programme is called News Reel. My father coordinates it."

Though Miss Taylor allowed the girls to listen and to discuss what was happening, she did not join them in the discussion. Ginika wondered if her position as a foreigner and as a missionary prevented her from discussing politics. She wanted to ask her, but changed her mind so as not to annoy or embarrass her.

They left after about three hours and returned to their rooms which were separate from the dormitories in which lived students in Forms One to Five. Ginika found her roommate, a science student, having her siesta when she arrived. She tiptoed to her section of the room, trying not to wake the girl.

THE HIGHER School students had their exeat – free day – once a month when they were permitted to go into town between eight in the morning and six in the evening. Ginika set out at nine with Tonye Efeturi who had been admitted to Elelenwa Girls' College the previous year into the Higher School class. Ginika had been overjoyed to be reunited with her friend – her *supe*, the shortened form of the word 'superior' which girls used to describe their close friends in the school – whom she had lost contact with after her father was transferred to Mbano.

"What's our programme like?" Ginika stared at the right side of Tonye's face that had an ugly scar which she said was from a deep cut she had when she fell down while playing netball in her former school. "I'm completely at your mercy and will go wherever you take me today." They walked side by side on the rough road that began at the school gate and ended at the junction where it joined the main road to Port Harcourt. Both wore their uniform – a yellow blouse carefully tucked into a knee-length green skirt and a green beret. They had their hair plaited neatly with black thread and pulled to the back – the way the school rules allowed the girls to dress their hair. The senior girls were also allowed to weave their hair;

Ginika preferred to plait hers with thread because she thought it made hair grow longer and faster than weaving did.

Ginika repeated her question, thinking Tonye had not heard her the first time. "What's our programme like today, Tonye?" Though she was on familiar ground, she had not visited the city centre since her family left Port Harcourt on transfer. They were on a bus and were approaching Diobu now.

"I heard you the first time but I didn't want to reply immediately because of the noise made by the traffic," Tonye said, as she got out of the bus. "This is your city as well as mine, so I cannot take you anywhere you are not familiar with." She was slight in stature and had a small face and very pointed jaw. "This way, please," Tonye added, taking Ginika's hand. They entered another bus which would take them to the city centre.

Ginika sat on a seat next to Tonye. "Really? Are you saying the town has not changed since I left it four years ago? *Hmm*, that can't be. What about all the people migrating here to establish businesses and those attracted by the growing presence of Shell-BP? And the thousands fleeing the north and Lagos and storming Port Harcourt, as ENBS announces on the radio? Have they not changed the face of the town?"

"Well, they have, if that is what you mean, but not much really. About our programme: first we'll go to my father's office so that I can collect some money from him. Then we walk over to the house and have pounded yam with peppery soup prepared with fresh fish and periwinkles. I assure you we'll have a good time before we go back to school." Tonye gave her a heart-warming smile.

"*Hmm*, I can't wait to get to your house to have a taste

of the famous periwinkles which I have not eaten since we moved to Mbano. Your mother used to prepare the soup so well." For a moment, Mrs Efeturi's face flashed into Ginika's memory: a smallish woman like her daughter who gave her fried fish and *guguru* when she visited Tonye. At such times, Ginika would remember the mother she lost too early and her heart would ache with longing for her.

"She still does," Tonye confirmed, with pride.

When they left the bus, they walked to the Nigeria Railways where Tonye's father worked. They were heading for his office when they saw him outside engaged in a heated conversation with two of his colleagues. He looked and saw them. He smiled a welcome. Tonye's father was such a cheerful man, Ginika thought, as she watched him and Tonye hug. He was a tall man and Tonye looked so small and fragile in his arms. Ginika could not remember ever having this kind of spontaneous and very warm hug with her father. How many times had they even hugged? she wondered. "Good morning, sir," she greeted Mr Efeturi, as her eyes briefly perched on his bushy hair which he had parted in the centre.

"Good afternoon, my dear girl. How are you? You came to visit us with your friend?" He laughed, extending his hand to Ginika. When she pushed hers forward, Mr Efeturi took it and shook it firmly.

"Papa, can I have some money, please? I need to buy some books and provisions." Tonye tugged at her father's hand to draw his attention, the way little children do.

"This daughter of mine will make me poor at the rate she harasses me about money," Mr Efeturi said with mock severity. He was laughing as he spoke and Tonye and Ginika joined him. He thrust his hand into his pocket and gave Tonye some money. He dipped his hand a second time and brought out one pound which he gave to Ginika. "This is for you, young lady."

Ginika smiled and took the money. "Thank you, sir."

On their way to Tonye's house – one of the buildings in the Railway Quarters close to the railway station – Ginika heard some people wailing loudly. "Tonye, can you hear that? The voices sound like those of people mourning."

"You're right." Tonye stopped to listen more. "It's coming from the Terminus, the area where trains stop. Let's find out what is happening."

Clutching her bag, Ginika ran behind Tonye who raced towards a train that had just arrived from the north. As they drew nearer the train the tumult increased and the cries sounded more like a dirge. Ginika could feel her heart beating fast, as if it would tear her chest and jump out through her throat. She could hear Tonye panting, but still running ahead of her.

"Tonye, please, wait for me." She was seized with panic, wondering what the noise was all about. She wanted to be with Tonye when they found out what was responsible for the noise.

Tonye stopped and waited for her. When she caught up with her, she saw how dilated her eyes had become. Ginika wondered why they looked like that, as if they were gorged with some shiny liquid. "What is it?" Ginika asked, her voice rising in a panic.

Like someone in a trance, Tonye said, as she pointed, "That woman walking away told me the train brought the wounded and the dead from the North. She said the sight is terrible. Ginika, I'm afraid to go there. I don't want to see it."

Even as Ginika hesitated, not knowing whether to go forward or backward, a force she could not resist pulled her towards the train whose rear she could now see clearly from where she stood. "Let's go forward and see," she whispered to Tonye. See, many people are rushing to the place. Come." She tugged at Tonye's left hand and as she tugged harder, Tonye's reluctant legs began to move. There was movement everywhere, as people came from all directions to see the train and its human cargo. Ginika felt her body jostled by people running past her and others running from the opposite direction. When they got close to the train, she saw a woman vomiting and crying at the same time. One woman held her head with two hands, screaming, as if she wanted to burst her eardrums and those of everyone else in the place.

On wobbly legs, Ginika inched her way forward; Tonye was right behind her, moving like a zombie. All Ginika could see at this point were people shouting, screaming and flagellating themselves, as if they wanted to die at their own hands. But there were those who made no noise at all but stood – dazed and looking hypnotized. The relentless force propelling Ginika pulled harder and she found herself pushing against other bodies in a mad effort to bypass them and look inside the train. She felt she possessed the strength of Dick Tiger the champion boxer, as she pushed and elbowed her way through the crowd. She glanced back and saw that Tonye was still behind her and was also pushing her way through. There was an unpleasant smell now.

Then she too saw what those who had come before her saw – an open carriage filled with human debris. Ginika saw severed hands and legs chopped, lying like pieces of wood on the floor of the carriage; there were dead bodies that were whole but with deep gashes in different places – the neck, chest and belly. Some of the bodies seemed to be covered with rust, but Ginika knew it was not rust but discoloured blood. Ginika began to tremble when her eyes caught the figure of a woman lying naked, disembowelled; a dead fetus was hanging from her abdomen, its umbilical cord still attached to its lifeless mother.

Ginika wrenched her eyes from the gory sight, shivering like a chick that had been pulled out of a pool. She felt tight in her chest and was aware of a searing pain emanating from that area of her body; her breathing became laboured. It was the feeling of suffocation that energised her into action and she struggled to get away from the sight. As she fought for a way out, she saw a gap in the crowd and stumbled towards it. She wriggled through, past dazed people with head injuries and machete cuts all over their bodies; a few of them had tourniquets on their bandaged arms. Ginika struggled her way to the open space. Then she flinched, for in the open space lay the headless torso of a huge man clad only in black trousers. In that brief moment, before she blacked out, Ginika's eyes dilated, as if they would pop, when she saw the corpse's mutilated legs and toes and the swollen neck around which blood had congealed. She lay a short distance from the bloated body.

Minutes later, when she came round, she found Tonye peering into her face and a few other people watching her. For a moment she was not sure where she was; when she remembered, she began to cry. Her body felt clammy and she touched herself; she was wet from the water they had poured on her in an effort to revive her. "Oh, Ginika, thank God you are all right," she heard Tonye breathe. The refrain was taken up by the bystanders. "Thank God-o. Take her away from here," they said to Tonye. Gingerly, Ginika got up, assisted by Tonye; she wondered how Tonye who had hardly supported herself was now the one supporting her. Deflated and struck dumb by what she had just witnessed, Ginika did not say a word until they reached Tonye's house; she was thankful Tonye was in a similar state of mind and did not try to talk.

Ginika could hardly eat the delicious meal Mrs Efeturi set before them. Each lump of pounded yam she swallowed stuck to her throat before going down; it was as if she was trying to swallow a pebble. She stopped after a few attempts. Even the sight of fresh fish and periwinkles that dominated the soup bowl did not tempt her nor whip up her appetite.

"Go on, Ginika, have some more," Mrs Efeturi coaxed.

She shook her head. "Thank you, ma, I cannot eat anymore."

"Tonye, have you finished eating? Have some more?"

"We are okay, Mama. What we saw stole our appetite. Next time Ginika comes here, I'm sure she will eat more." She turned to Ginika and smiled.

Ginika nodded. "Yes, thank you, ma, for the food." She remembered how much she had looked forward to coming into town. How could she have known what awaited them? She remembered the disembowelled woman and her dead foetus and trembled. But when the image of the headless body flashed in her mind, she began to shiver.

Mrs Efeturi, who was watching her, touched her gently and said, "Do not think about it anymore; try to blot it out from your memory."

Ginika nodded, but she knew she would not be able to do this, that the gory sight of those mutilated bodies would be an apparition that would haunt her all her life.

Mr Efeturi took them back to school in his Volvo. Ginika was grateful to him, for she thought that going back by public transport would have been traumatic for her and would have taken longer. She wanted to return quickly to the security of the school compound, surrounded by the warmth of her classmates, the calmness and efficiency of the missionaries and the law and order that imbued the school environment with serenity, with peace.

IN THE following weeks, though no more trainloads of dead and mutilated bodies of easterners arrived from the North, the chasm between the Federal Military Government and the Government of Eastern Nigeria had widened so much that there was no hope of peace and there was no indication that an amicable solution would be found to the crisis. The Eastern Nigerian Military Government published a small book *Pogrom 1966* which documented the massacre of easterners in the North and some parts of the West. The book was widely circulated in the East. Ginika saw a copy somebody had smuggled into her school. It reminded her of the dead and mutilated bodies she had seen at the railway station. She recognised the headless body she had seen which was pictured on the cover of the book.

She had become a radio addict, listening to news as often as she could in the company of other students. So when Yakubu Gowon announced the twelve new states he had carved out from the former four regions, Ginika was one of the students who ran round the school compound protesting the move. "We reject the twelve states!" the girls chanted.

They were later addressed by the principal, Miss Broomfield.

"We will not tolerate any acts of indiscipline in the school," the principal asserted, sounding as formal and dignified as she could. She was standing on the platform in front of the assembly hall. The girls stood in rows, according to their classes. All the teachers were present; they stood on the platform with the principal, as if to give her moral support, Ginika thought.

"You are students and you are here to learn. The aim of the school is to train you to become mature individuals who are able to remain calm even in the face of extreme provocation. You are not to take the law into your own hands. Those who break the school's rules and regulations will be punished accordingly." She went on for about fifteen minutes and told the girls to return to their dormitories and their rooms.

After the girls' demonstration, Amina Yaro stopped coming to school. Ginika was sorry that Amina had withdrawn from the school. She had wanted her to remain, as this would demonstrate the maturity of easterners who did not kill strangers in their midst as northerners did. She had heard on radio news that primary school pupils and secondary school and university students participated in the killing of easterners in the North.

A few days later, Chukwuemeka Odumegwu Ojukwu declared Eastern Nigeria a sovereign state. The new nation was called the Republic of Biafra. The jubilation all over the East echoed in Elelenwa Girls' School. Ginika joined her classmates in celebrating the new nation. In the evening, they carried the school's radiogram to the Domestic Science hall where they usually had their weekly get-together and danced away most of the hours of the night.

"Play *Adure*," cried Ebere Nkwocha, an Upper Six science student who was also the school's Senior Prefect.

"No, let's play music that will celebrate our new Biafra," Njide Igwe countered. "This is celebration time." She wiggled her big bottom.

"But do we have such music?" asked Tonye.

"Let's just play what is available and have a good time," Ginika suggested. The creation of Biafra, a country where the people of former Eastern Nigeria could live in safety, was worth celebrating, Ginika thought. The birth of Biafra helped her to deal with the depression caused by the sight of the trainload of mutilated and dead bodies.

Ginika crawled into bed at about three in the morning, tired and sleepy. The euphoria of celebration wore off, but hope was alive in Biafra. Ginika went about her studies with purpose. She would do well and qualify as a journalist, she told herself. She would like to work with Radio Biafra after she graduated. But that was a long time yet. Now she had to prepare for her Higher School Certificate examination which was expected to take place at the end of the year.

"Work hard," she said to Tonye. "We are the future hope of Biafra. We'll make her proud of us."

Tonye who had always told Ginika she wanted to study pharmacy laughed. "I'm doing my best. I want to be the best pharmacist in the world."

As the weeks flew past, Ginika followed the news closely. Since broadcasting was the profession she would love to enter after her education, she made it a point of duty to listen to broadcasters. Her school had no television, so she could not watch television to see the images of what she heard on radio, which she knew the television service highlighted and displayed visually. She was aware of the threat of war. It was the talk of the town and the radio. Even her classmates discussed it in the classroom.

One afternoon, Ginika was in the classroom with other girls when she heard the school bell ring. "What's happening?" she asked, looking up from Shakespeare's *Anthony and Cleopatra* which she was reading. "Who is ringing the tune for assembly at this odd time?"

"Something serious must have happened," Njide remarked. "The toad does not run for nothing in broad daylight." She laughed. She had the habit of using a proverb when she spoke, like an elder.

"Well, we can only find out by responding to the bell," another girl put in.

"Yes, let's go and find out what has happened." Ginika pulled up her skirt which she had unzipped to make herself more comfortable. She drew the zip up, picked up her book and dropped it in her school bag.

Outside, Ginika saw students spilling out from the classrooms. The Forms One to Five classroom blocks were located on the far side of the compound while the chapel and library building were near the main gate. More students trooped out from the fourteen hostels and hurried to the assembly hall. Ginika arrived in the company of three of her classmates. Miss Broomfield was already standing on the platform. Ginika thought this most unusual. The principal would normally wait for the girls and the members of staff to settle in the hall before walking in. Ginika searched the platform and saw Miss Taylor standing at the extreme right. Her eyes looked puffy, as if she had been sleeping when the assembly bell rang, but Ginika knew this couldn't have been the case, for Miss Broomfield would normally brief the teachers before calling an extraordinary assembly meeting like this one.

When there was silence all around, Miss Broomfield greeted, "Good evening, girls." Her face was sombre. Her eyes appeared wilted like banana leaves scorched by flames. Her usually well-groomed hair was somewhat dishevelled.

"Good evening, Miss Broomfield," the students chorused.

"You are all aware of the situation in the country, the crisis that rocked Nigeria and resulted in the creation of Biafra. We have tried to maintain our school with your cooperation in the face of difficulties. It has not been easy. We have worked in line with government's instructions all the time, conscious of our responsibility to you our students and the communities among whom we live…"

Ginika wondered if this was the only reason Miss Broomfield called this extraordinary assembly – to review the situation in the country. What she had said so far was common knowledge to everyone. Her ears caught the principal's next words and she listened attentively.

"I am sorry to tell you that we have been instructed to close the school until further notice. You will return to your hostels and rooms, pack your things, ready to leave the school compound tomorrow morning. Goodbye, girls." Miss Broomfield turned and walked out of the assembly hall.

Ginika did not realise that she had joined the other students to scream and protest. She did not want to go home. She had an important examination to take before the end of the year. If they left, when would they return? She knew no one could give her an answer to this question. She heard other girls screaming the same question. A junior girl standing in front was saying something Ginika could not hear because of the noise. She pulled the girl nearer. "What did you say?" she asked her.

"Miss Taylor asked me to call you. She is over there." The girl pointed.

Ginika looked up and saw Miss Taylor standing near the lawn in front of the assembly hall. Her blonde hair gleamed in the muted glare of the setting sun. She wore the blue flowered dress Ginika liked. She hurried to her.

"*Ginikar*," Miss Taylor called in that funny way she pronounced her name. "I'm sorry your education is being disrupted in this way, but don't worry. You'll return to school after the crisis blows over. Remember that and take care of yourself. You have great potential and it will be a pity to let it come to nothing. I hope to see you again when this is over. Goodbye."

Ginika wanted to ask her where she would be, whether she would return to England, but she could not bring herself to ask, probably because she did not want to hear that Miss Taylor might leave Biafra. Miss Taylor stretched her hand and Ginika did the same. They shook hands and looked into each other's eyes. She turned and walked away. The sight of her favourite teacher walking away from her perhaps for ever was distressing to Ginika, as if all she held dear was disappearing, as if her dreams were on the verge of collapse.

Blinded by unshed tears, Ginika stumbled to her room. She would miss her teachers, especially Miss Taylor, she would miss her friends and she would definitely miss the school where she felt so relaxed and complete. She did not know when she could return to school, but she told herself she would bear Miss Taylor's advice in mind. She would come back to finish her education no matter how long it took for the schools to be reopened. As she packed her things, she decided to head for Enugu to be with Auntie Chito and her family.

Part Three

THE MIDDLE

12

Ginika felt her heart leap with joy when she arrived in Ama-Oyi with her father that evening. It was windy and there were signs that rain would fall before it grew dark. Fascinated, she watched a gust of wind catch a dry leaf, blow it briefly upward, causing it to dance crazily before falling to the ground. She smiled because she remembered her physics lesson on gravity, in her fourth year at Elelenwa Girls' College. She saw the leaves of the coconut and *ube* trees at the back of the house swaying, as the wind wafted through them. She saw bunches of coconuts hanging down, ready to be harvested. She felt her mouth water; coconuts from that tree were usually delicious. She liked the big compound surrounded by fruit trees – orange, guava and avocado – which reminded her of the house in Mbano. They had not visited Ama-Oyi enough until after the war started. It had seemed that it took the war for them to realise that there was no place like home. She gazed at the storey building, eight years old and one of four such buildings in the whole of Ama-Oyi.

Taking her eyes away from the coconut and *ube* trees, and from the imposing house, she turned to stare at a small crowd that had formed in the veranda, watching her father as he parked the car. A fair-skinned woman and six young people, probably her children, were smiling at her and her father. Turning to her father she asked, in astonishment, "Papa, who are they, these people in our house?"

"Did I not tell you we have visitors in the house?"

"No, you didn't?"

"They are my friend, Ufo Ndefo's wife and children. They escaped from Enugu to Onitsha, their home town. They ran again when Nigerian soldiers started shelling Onitsha. They ended up staying in our house. Ufo Ndefo is a good friend and colleague. I had to allow them to live here when he requested it."

Ginika watched the woman as she waddled forward to greet her father. "Ubaka, welcome." They shook hands. She had a deep voice that sounded like a man's and Ginika liked her immediately. She was so fair-skinned, Ginika felt she was either an Afro- American or a West Indian or a half-caste. She had met quite a number of them in Port Harcourt, and most of her teachers were white people. So she was not intimidated by this woman's skin and voice.

The woman turned to Ginika. "Your daughter?"

"Yes," her father replied. "My daughter, Ginikanwa."

"How are you, my dear?" Mrs Ndefo asked. She shook Ginika's hand. Her hand was soft and sweaty, as if she had been working. Ginika looked at her and saw beads of perspiration on her face, though the evening was cool and it was threatening to rain. Ginika wondered how she felt after fleeing from enemy soldiers twice.

"I'm very well, Ma." Ginika withdrew her hand from the woman's and turned towards her children. The oldest, a girl, came forward and introduced herself. "I'm Amaka. Good to meet you, Ginika." Ginika smiled and thought Amaka couldn't be more than seventeen. The other five were boys between eight and fifteen. Amaka introduced her brothers and Ginika shook their hands, even the hand of Anayo, the youngest boy. She tried to remember all the names, but failed. Perhaps with time, she would match each name with the right face. They had a similar haircut. She thought they looked alike and since they did not look like their mother, they probably took after their father whom she had not met. It was through him her father had sent her the letter in Enugu but he had sent someone to deliver it.

"How are you, Carol? How are you coping with life in Ama-Oyi?" her father asked the woman, giving Ginika the key to the house. "Oh, our things have all been moved upstairs except the chairs and the bookcases in the sitting room downstairs."

Ginika heard her reply, "It's hard, but I'm trying to adapt to the situation. I can't complain; there's a war going on. I just can't imagine what we would have done without your help, Ubaka. We feel relatively safe in this place so far away from the sound of war. And thanks for the bunker behind the compound. There is no sign Ama-Oyi will ever be raided, but you never can tell, can you? It's comforting to know it's handy. Thanks so much." As Ginika listened to the husky voice, she was sure the woman was American, for she spoke like the two American Peace Corps teachers who had taught for a year in her school when she was in Form Five.

She heaved her suitcase on to the staircase. Amaka ran forward to assist her. Her brothers carried the rest of the things in the boot and they all trooped upstairs. Her father opened his door and the boys hesitated. "Bring the things inside," she

heard him say. "Leave the yams and plantain in the corridor."
Meanwhile, she and Amaka carried her suitcase into her room
which was next to Nwakire's.

"Is this your room?" Amaka asked. Ginika saw her face light
up.

"Yes, but I hardly use it; we come home only occasionally."

"Are you, like me, the only girl in the family?"

"Yes, but unlike you, I have only one brother."

"We are a crowd aren't we?" Amaka laughed. "People
always wondered how my mother – *Oyibo*, as she is called –
could have so many children. Sometimes I wondered too. I
guess she wanted another girl, but after she had five boys, she
gave up at last."

Ginika laughed. She liked Amaka's pleasant nature and
knew they would be friends. "How do you find Ama-Oyi?"
Ginika asked, as she dusted the table and chair in the room.
She turned and began to dust the bed which was made from
cast iron. She would have to sweep the room and later wash
the cement floor; it was coated with dust. They should come
home more often to keep the house clean.

Amaka dusted the wooden window. "I find it boring;
I don't have friends here as we have only been in Ama-Oyi
for two months. My brothers are luckier and keep each other
company. I keep myself busy with books. I read novels and
anything that I can lay my hands on. I have read some of your
books. I hope you don't mind?" She looked at Ginika briefly
and continued to dust the window.

"Not really. Thanks for helping. Now I have to see to
Papa's room and put the food-stuff away in the kitchen."

"Welcome. I'll see you sometime." Amaka dropped the
duster on the floor and walked out of the room.

Ginika knocked on her father's door and entered when he called out and told her to come in. "Can I dust your room?"

"No, I am not staying; I'm returning to Mbano immediately. I'll stop by briefly and greet my brother and his family and also Udo's mother. Take care of yourself. You are not alone in the house, so there is nothing to fear. You can join other students in the play production, but I hope you will behave yourself. Remember it was *your* decision to come in the first place. I would have preferred you to remain in Mbano with the rest of the family. I hope you realise what you are doing, but it is all right if you keep your senses about you and take good care of yourself."

"I'm all right, Papa," she assured him. "Nothing is going to happen to me. I'm here strictly for the play and can always return to Mbano after it if you want me. Remember, Auntie Chito and her family and my grandmother are in Ama-Oyi and so are Uncle Chima and his family as well as Udo's mother. I'm surrounded by all our relations. If I need anything I will go to them."

"Yes, I was coming to that. If you need anything or you have any problem, go to my brother and his wife; they will help you. I will come at the weekend to see you."

Ginika smiled sadly, wondering if he could ever trust her to do the right thing. He would always treat her like a child, hardly ever allowing her to use her initiative. "Thank you, Papa, for bringing me."

He shrugged and indicated the door. She walked out carrying his briefcase and he walked behind her. She watched him exchange a few words with Amaka's mother before walking to the car. "Can I follow you to greet Uncle Chima and his family?"

"Get into the car then; I have to hurry if I am to get to Mbano before dark."

"I want to close the gate after you have moved the car outside the compound."

"That is correct. I forgot," he said. He started the car and backed out of the gate. Ginika closed the gate and hopped into the car beside him.

Before the car stopped, Uncle Chima's wife and Ebube, her youngest child ran out to welcome them. "Ah, you have remembered us today," Uncle Chima's wife, Mama Nnukwu – as she was called to identify her as the most senior wife in the extended family – cried. "*Unu di agha*, how are you all?" she asked, pulling the car door wider open, so that Ginika could come out more easily. "How are you, *ada nma*, beautiful daughter?" she asked Ginika, touching her face and running her hand down her neck, bosom and belly. "*Idi nma nwam*, you are well, my child." Ginika laughed and said she was well. The main door leading into the four-room bungalow was wide open and Ginika could see the sitting room – a wide room with wooden chairs arranged in a semi-circle and a fairly tall table dominating the centre. The roof was of corrugated iron sheets which had turned rusty all over from years of bashing by the sun and rain.

Ginika returned her gaze to Mama Nnukwu who had turned to speak to her father. She wore a short blouse with long sleeves and tied a *wrappa* of the same material. Her hair was covered completely with a headdress of the same material. Her face was free of wrinkles, except for the few tiny lines under her eyes. Ginika wondered how she could remain so ageless at her age. She was sure Mama Nnukwu looked younger than Auntie Lizzy.

"How are your wife and son, Nwakire?" she asked, pulling her headdress further down to cover her ears.

"My wife is well; Nwakire has joined the army?"

"What? Are you sure of what you are saying?" she cried. Ginika marvelled at the perfect circle created by her mouth which she had opened wide, to show her disbelief and shock.

"Yes, it is the truth." He shrugged.

"And you allowed him? You permitted him to join the army? An only son?" She stood there staring at him. Ebube, her youngest child stood by her, listening and staring at Ginika's long earrings. Ginika beckoned to her and she moved towards her eagerly.

"I did not permit him; he joined without even consulting me." Her father shrugged again.

Mama Nnukwu shifted her eyes to Ginika, as if asking her if she was there when her only brother joined the army and did nothing to stop him. Ginika looked away, staring at the narrow footpath that separated Uncle Chima's house from Uncle Onagu's – Udo's father who was killed in Jos, during the massacre of easterners.

"When did your husband come home last?" he asked changing the subject. Ginika knew he did not like to discuss Nwakire, as it caused him much pain.

"He was here at the weekend. The other children are with him." She frowned. "I have asked them again and again what they are all doing in Aba. I am tired of asking and have shut my mouth. They say I talk like a woman. Well, I am a woman all right and must talk like one. But all I know is that there is no reason they should all be in Aba, with all the air raids I hear that take place there. If they all want to die at the same time, that is their problem. I have said; you are my witness."

"Do not worry, they will come home. I will contact Chima about it; some of the boys should come home and stay here with you."

"Let them not come." She hissed. "Let them leave Ebube and me in this house."

"Is Akueju in her house?" he asked.

"No, she went to market. She should be back soon."

He gave her some money and walked back to the car. "Ginikanwa, go back to the house at the end of your visit. I have to leave now." He gave her some money. "Give this to Akueju, Udo's mother. Tell her I came and that I asked after her and her children."

Ginika watched him drive off. She linked her hand to little Ebube's and followed Mama Nnukwu into the house.

13

On the day that Eloka heard that Ginika was in Ama-Oyi, he decided to pay her a visit. From what he heard, she had been in the town for three days. Was she here for a brief visit or to stay? Could it be that she had come to take part in the play? If the latter was the case, why did she not try to find out if rehearsals had started? He smiled. He had many questions, but no answers. Only one person could give answers to the questions and that person was Ginika, so he had to see her. He knew her house and had passed that way time and time again since he arrived in Ama-Oyi, hoping to see her. He knew every turn of the road to the house, every stump and every tree that lined the drive into their magnificent house. He always saw people – five boys – playing near the gate, but each time he asked them, they said no one called Ginika lived in the house. When he told them she was the daughter of the owner of the house, they replied that they had not met her yet.

His pilgrimage had continued. He did not know how to contact her. He desperately needed her to play the role of Mammy Wota in his play. He had even tried to audition someone else for the part. But each person he had tried failed to satisfy him. He was certain no one else would do. Apart from the play, he also wanted to see her again. He approached the house with a feeling of joy. He couldn't think of any reason he should feel this way. Could it be because the lead actor in his play was here at last? He smiled. Was this also the reason he had dressed carefully, putting on his favourite short-sleeved striped cotton shirt and his blue jeans which he knew fitted him so well? The five boys were there, playing.

"Hello, can you give a message to Ginika? She is here, isn't she?" He addressed one of the boys – the one he felt was the oldest. He was tall and skinny.

"Yes, she is. You are the man who was here asking for her last week?" He pulled one half of the gate open and allowed him to enter the compound.

"I am. Is she in?"

"Yes, I'll call her for you." He walked away, but turned back after a few paces. "Who should I say is looking for her?"

"Tell her Eloka Odunze."

He was standing in front of the veranda when he saw her. His eyes were fixed on her as she glided towards him and he said to himself, "Wow, she's even more beautiful than I can remember!" His pulse was racing when he shook the hand she extended to him. He admired the simple dress she wore, which fitted her like a mould.

"We meet again." She smiled and he found himself tingling all over with excitement. He hadn't realised how much he wanted to see her. He didn't think he would be filled with pleasure simply by being near her again.

"Please, come into the house. I've been busy all day sorting things out in the house, cleaning and washing things no one had touched for months. I was arranging my books and my brother's when Dozie told me you were here." He

194

followed her in and sat on a cushioned chair near the door. He saw two giant bookcases almost empty and many books scattered on the carpeted floor.

"No wonder you didn't have time to look around Ama-Oyi, to ask about the play and to find out how I was since you arrived."

She averted her eyes as he spoke. "Why should I find out how you were? Anyway, there is enough to keep me busy in this house at the moment. Look at our books. Even my father's medical books were not spared. The books were scattered everywhere and I have been trying to arrange them as they were before. Some are torn and a few have disappeared. I can't find *The Return of King Odysseus*, *Beyond Pardon* and *Oliver Twist*. These were books I enjoyed reading and wanted to keep forever."

"Who scattered them?" He picked up a medical journal and leafed through it before putting it down.

She looked at him. "Who else? The five adventurers in the house." She laughed. "At first I was angry, but you cannot be angry with them for long. They are so playful and friendly, but they are like a hurricane – always on the move, disorganising things and sometimes spoiling them."

"Who are they?"

"They are the family of my father's friend who was displaced. They came from Onitsha and are taking refuge here."

"How did they have access to your books? Was the door not locked?" He looked at the books she was showing him and was shocked at the degree of damage done by the boys.

"I think my father left the sitting room door open for them. They use the rooms on the ground floor. But the two bookcases were always locked; we never left them open. They broke it open to have access to the books; it's unbelievable, but they did. See where they broke the lock."

"Does your father know about this? He won't like it."

"No one will. It's a mess." She sighed. "I told their mother; I hope she will be able to restrain them. Anyway, they have apologised to me and I've forgiven them." She shrugged and he thought she must have been very upset when she discovered the books scattered. She was looking down and he could see the top of her head where her braided hair was gathered and piled up in a style called *boys follow me*. He knew because his sister Ijeamasi was fond of the style and made her hair that way.

"Ginika, when can you come for rehearsals?" he asked, changing the subject so that they could discuss the matter that had brought him to her house. "We've started, you know and we've been looking forward to your joining us. Your part is there waiting for you." He wanted her to look at him because he wanted to look into her eyes; so, he paused before he spoke again in a quieter voice, "Ginika, I'm glad you're here." She looked away from him, as if she was reluctant to meet his gaze.

Her eyes were fixed on one of the bookcases as she replied, "I'll like to start next week; will Monday be all right? I hope to complete the work I'm doing in the house by weekend." She glanced at him and he nodded.

"Monday's fine. We haven't really started serious rehearsals for *Mammy Wota*," he admitted. "We've been focusing on *Arms and the Man*."

She nodded again, clasped and unclasped her hands which had earlier rested on the arms of her chair.

"Is that your mother with your father?" he asked pointing.

His eyes had caught a framed wedding photograph hanging on the wall.

She looked at the photograph and smiled. "Yes, my mother and father on their wedding day." With the corner of her right eye, she saw another wedding picture – her father and stepmother's – and hoped he wouldn't notice it.

"It looks new; it's remarkably well preserved." He didn't want to leave yet, but he thought he should not stay too long. She had much work to do and might even have started wishing he were gone. He thought he saw a frown on her face. Her lips appeared to have a pout and he could only attribute it to discontent with his presence. It seemed this was her way of showing resentment. He had detected it on her face the time he visited her in Mbano. He got up. "See you on Monday in the primary school hall near the market; that's where we've been meeting."

He saw the frown and the pout disappear as she smiled and he thought she looked so pretty when she smiled or laughed. "I'm sorry I didn't offer you anything" she said. "Not that I forgot; it's just that there's nothing in the house to give a visitor."

"That's okay, some other time perhaps."

She saw him off and shut the gate.

THROUGHOUT THE evening, Eloka was in high spirits. He hummed a song as he worked in his rose garden, in front of his home. It was a much smaller garden than the one in Port Harcourt which he might never see again, now that the town had been evacuated. He wondered what was happening there;

had the Nigerian forces dug in? Was it a ghost town, as the two sides battled for control? Eloka was relieved his family escaped unhurt. No life was lost, only property, of course, which was a small thing in comparison with people's lives. His father and mother were heartbroken, though, because they had not been able to evacuate all the livestock and furniture. Still they had been able to bring back many of their things. The pigs were completely lost and so were the cassava and yam which were nearly ready for harvest. He was grateful to Osondu who had had the presence of mind to bring in the rabbits.

He straightened up and surveyed the rose bushes. He felt undiluted pleasure at the sight before him. The roses were safe because they were inside the walled compound. He knew if the garden was outside, people would cut the flowers to beautify their homes or just for the pleasure of holding and smelling them – rose lovers like himself. He was worried about the dry season which would come in a few months; if he did not water them every day, the roses would die then. At the moment, rain fell regularly, so they were all right. There were too many things to worry about these days. Fuel was one of them. For a moment he glanced at his father's Mercedes parked at the corner, under the orange tree, and covered with a tarpaulin. Could it ever leave that spot, he wondered? Where would the fuel to move it come from? Eloka was able to drive the estate car still because he had stored fuel in the garage as soon as he returned to Ama-Oyi, when petrol had not become a rare commodity. Now it could only be obtained at an exorbitant price in the black market. When the fuel he stored finished, the two cars in use in the family would be grounded.

"Eloka, come and eat." Ozioma watched him pruning the

roses, touching the rosebuds gently, as if the partly-opened flowers would disintegrate with the slightest pressure.

Eloka looked up briefly and saw her eyes glued to the pink roses. He knew she liked them best. He bent his head again and continued to prune the red roses. These were his favourite. He liked them better than the white, yellow and pink ones. A few more minutes and he would be done; then he would go in and eat. He realised he was hungry and had only had a bite at breakfast. His mother was sure to scold him again about what she called his poor eating habits. He shook his head; did she realise he was over twenty-five?

"You've been working in your garden all evening. You take care of those roses as if they are human beings."

"What's wrong with my working in the garden all evening?" Eloka asked, staring at her sulky face. "Does it disturb you?"

"You promised to mend the handle of my suitcase which got broken. You know it is tomorrow I'm going to Adaeze's house to stay for a while. What will I use to pack my things?"

He watched the way she twisted her lips and wrung her hands, and laughed. He understood the reason for her raillery. "Okay, I have heard you. It's not late yet; I'll mend it tonight."

"Thank you." She smiled. "Mama said I should tell you that your food is getting cold."

"Okay, I'll be there in a moment." He shook his head, irritated by his mother's undue concern for him. He thought she doted on him too much and he disdained it. When would she realise he was now a man? What would she do if he joined the army? That could happen any time; there was a war raging in the land, after all.

He pruned the last of the rose plants and straightened

himself up. He surveyed the garden and was happy with what he had done. He didn't know how long he could indulge in this pastime, but he would, as long as possible. Growing roses and rearing rabbits were his passion. He would want to go on doing both till there were no roses to grow, till there was no rabbit to rear.

HE ENTERED the house, a smaller version of the storey building in Port Harcourt – one of the four to be found in Ama-Oyi. His father and mother were having their dinner in the dining room. "*Nna*, your food will get cold. Come and eat now," his mother said. "Will you eat here or should I ask Ozioma to take it to your room?" They were eating rice and stew with goat meat. He didn't like rice and stew very much, but he was hungry and so would eat anything.

"I'll eat here," he replied. He sat at the other end of the table, opposite his father. He chewed slowly, his thoughts focused on Ginika. He saw her face in everything he did since their meeting. He just couldn't get the image of this reticent and detached young woman out of his head. He went over their meeting earlier in the day, analysed what they had said and reflected on her facial expressions at different points in their conversation. Eloka didn't realise he had smiled, until he heard his mother ask, "*Nna*, what is making you smile like that? It must be a happy thought because your face looks so happy." She gave him a tender look.

He frowned. His mother had never hidden the fact that she loved him more than her other children. Sometimes he wished she did not show it so openly; only God knew if his father and his sisters were jealous. He would not blame them if they were; his mother gave enough reason to be. "Mama, sometimes I think you see things that are not there," he rebuked. "Just let me be."

She laughed. If he thought he would make her stop teasing him by making such sharp remarks, he was wrong, as her next sentence showed.

"Onwaora, am I wrong?" she turned to his father. "Did he not smile?"

His father smiled. "He did; as a matter of fact, I saw it clearly. And from my experience, it is only when a man is excited about a woman that his face is blessed with such a happy smile. Eloka, may we know if this is a true observation in your case?"

They laughed. His mother swayed towards his father. "Onwaora, I hope the experience you are talking about is not with other women? Eh? I will cut off the ears of any woman who excites you."

"Look at the way two of you are going on when you know there is a war going on," Eloka said, not sure of how to respond to their coarse jokes.

"You are wrong," his father replied, still laughing. "There is no time love or passion thrives better than in wartime. People are more easily excited that way, I think, because of the danger that is visible everywhere, the threat to life. The fear of imminent death makes people want to love and enjoy themselves."

Eloka did not want to discuss this subject with his father. He was surprised at the way he was talking this evening. If it had happened in Port Harcourt, he would have thought he was drunk. But Ama-Oyi was not Port Harcourt, so his father couldn't be drunk. He shrugged and said, "I'm off to my room. Thanks for the food, Mama." He was on his feet when his father asked him to sit down. He wished his father would not go on raising the issue of his taking a wife. He was sure that was where their jokes were leading to. The last time his father brought up the subject, he had even asked if Eloka would like him to assist him to find a girl from a suitable home who would make him an excellent wife. His mother had added salt and pepper by mentioning the name of a girl from their in-law's lineage – a relation of Adaeze's husband. She had added that Adaeze was sure the girl was wife material – those were her words, *wife material*, as if the girl were an object up for sale.

Eloka sat down again, but on the edge of his chair. His body was stiff and his hands gripped his knees. He was ready to walk out on them if they raised that worn-out subject.

"I wanted to mention that one of my uncle's sons, Leonard, was chosen to represent our family in the recruitment of soldiers into the army; he was sent in your place. Of course, you know about the seasonal recruitments that have been going on since the war started. You need not worry about being recruited." His father had a look of satisfaction that infuriated Eloka, as if he was saying that he had done a great thing and Eloka should be pleased with him for protecting him from the obligation of fighting in the Biafran army.

"Why did you do that?" Eloka asked sharply. "If it is my turn to be recruited, why should you prevent me from going?" He tried to keep his voice down, but his father was trying his patience too much. He feared that one of these days, he would explode and surprise his father and would end up doing something that would hurt everyone.

"*Nna*, calm down; your father is only trying to protect you," his mother soothed his fears. "I want you to see everything he does in that light."

Eloka stared at her, angrier than before. "Protect me from what? What about those fighting, do they not have fathers? Are they not human beings? If everyone is protected and not allowed to enlist in the army, then who will fight this war? Look, I'm tired of your trying to protect me."

"*Nna*, you know our extended family looks up to you as a university student. They are hopeful that you will become somebody important in future, so they do not want anything to happen to you. Leonard was trading in crayfish in Lagos before he ran back home ..."

Horrified and chagrined about what he supposed his mother was going to say, Eloka interrupted her, "Mama, just listen to yourself! So Leonard is not important and does not have the prospect of becoming somebody to be reckoned with because he is not at the university? He is expendable, but I'm not? He's the one that can afford to get killed, not me?" Eloka stopped, wondering if he could ever see anything the way his parents saw it. He started growing away from his parents – especially his father – and their static ideas after his secondary school education. He began to see his father in a new light when he lost his bid to become the mayor of Port Harcourt. His father had not only vilified Nimrod, the winner of that election but had also thoroughly discredited other popular and astute politicians like Onwenu, Ihekwoaba and Akwiwu. Even the celebrated AC Nwapa in Aba did not escape his negative criticism. It was then that he knew his father was not a man who played fair.

"Look at the way you are talking," his father said in a

pained voice. "Our extended family knows my predicament. They know and understand that I have only one son. That is why they pick other people and hand them over each time the recruitment officers come. Families with many sons are obliged to donate a son to stand in for families with just one son. This is what has been happening in your case; you have been skipped each time. Instead of being grateful, you are barking at me."

Eloka shook his head and shouted, "Why should I be grateful? Grateful for what?" He felt he could no longer endure his father's meddlesomeness in his affairs, the way he treated him as if he were a child.

"*Nna*, calm down," his mother pleaded. "Please, do not upset your father; he meant well. He is doing all this for you, for all of us. Come back."

"You heard your son, didn't you?" his father roared, facing his mother. "I don't know what to do with him. He always wants to have his way. Only what he says or thinks or does makes sense to him. Is that the way to survive this war? Is that a way that will lead to a good life? I am fed up. If he wants to join the army and die, let him."

"Please, Onwaora, do not say such things. Do not say he should join the army and die. Do you want to kill me? Okay, two of you kill me and let me die so that you can do as you like." She started to cry.

Eloka hissed and walked out of the room.

14

Ginika went to see her aunt and her family after the visit of Eloka Odunze. It took her almost an hour to walk to the house located in another village in Ama-Oyi. She chose to walk along winding paths, away from the main roads, as the trees lining the paths provided some shade. It was a shorter way to get to her aunt's house, anyway, and she wanted to get there as quickly as possible to be able to return home the same day.

"Mama, Ginika is here," her aunt's eldest child, Obika, shouted as soon as she entered the compound. Instead of going to Ginika, he rushed into the house to his mother first.

Ginika laughed. Obika was just being the ten-year-old he was, she thought. "Obika, come back. Come and greet me," she called. She looked round the compound. Her eyes widened when she saw how fresh the bungalow looked; Uncle Ray must have had it repainted recently. But who would be repainting a house at this time of war? Perhaps he did it just before the war. His car was parked by the right, under a mango tree which she knew Uncle Ray planted the year Obika was born. It didn't seem he had used it recently. With the scarcity of fuel everywhere in Biafra, most people who still owned cars had parked them. Her father still drove his car because he was given a ration of fuel weekly on account of his profession. But how much longer would that privilege continue? She looked away from the car and, as her eyes roved, she observed the rows of bitter-leaf trees growing sturdily close to the wall, and thought she would ask her aunt to cut some of the leaves for her to take away.

"Ah, Ginika, when did you arrive in Ama-Oyi?" Her aunt stood at the door, beaming. Obika stood beside her, one hand holding his mother. But when Ginika walked into her aunt's outstretched arms, he stood aside, smiling. "Come in. *Ukwu gi amaka*, your legs are good; we are just about to have lunch."

"Lunch, at this time?" Ginika glanced at her watch. "Isn't it too early for lunch?" A feeling of joy spread all over her as she followed her Aunt into the sitting room which occupied a central position in the bungalow, with the other rooms branching off from it. Her aunt was dressed in an old maxi dress Ginika remembered and liked. She was with her when she bought it at Ogbete market in Enugu years back.

"It is early, I agree, but Ray and I did not have breakfast, so we decided to have an early lunch. We were working in our little cassava farm at the back of the compound. You know, everyone in Biafra who has land has been told to cultivate so that there will be plenty of food – even if it is only a small space. Do you know I have planted pepper and tomatoes in empty paint containers? Can you imagine, the tins which we left in the store after repainting the house last year have proved quite useful? That tells you nothing is useless." She laughed. "Sit down. Let me go and call Ray; I think he is in the backyard."

"Thank you, Auntie Chito." Ginika threw herself into a chair and shut her eyes. She was going to be happy in Ama-

Oyi in spite of the war. She was free to do what she wanted – act in Eloka Odunze's play, visit her aunt, go swimming in the Ngene River, sleep and discover what other girls were doing to support the war effort. Her mind dwelt on Eloka and she smiled. She liked him because he was gentle and considerate. She liked how he looked – his jet black skin, his big eyeballs, the type girls described as romantic eyes, at school. Her smile widened and turned into laughter when she heard Uncle Ray's voice. Her eyes flew open and she jumped to her feet.

"*Nwayi oma*, beautiful woman, how are you?" He chuckled, as she fell into his arms. He always called her *nwayi oma* and he said it slowly so she knew he meant it; he was not just flattering her. She often wondered if he had in mind beauty in the physical or spiritual sense, but she had never asked him. Behind him were their other three children – Ugo, Ona and Nonso aged nine, seven and five, respectively. "Auntie Ginika, welcome," they chorused, looking up into her eyes, smiling so warmly that her heart sang for joy.

She wriggled out of Uncle Ray's encircling arms and turned to the children. She hugged each of them, rubbed her cheek against theirs. "Obika, come, I want to hug you too," she said. "When did I see you last?" He came hesitantly, feeling self-conscious. "Hey, so you are now a man and too big to be hugged, eh?" she teased, drawing him into her arms.

"How is Nwakire?" her aunt asked.

"He joined the army."

"Really?"

Ginika shrugged. "Papa didn't like it. He was angry and upset."

"When did you arrive?" Uncle Ray asked, sitting next to her.

"Yesterday evening; my father dropped me and went back immediately." She looked at him and thought how relaxed and cheerful he looked in the midst of his family. Uncle Ray was her favourite uncle and she liked to chat with him. He made her laugh so much each time they talked. With his boyish looks, one would think he was Aunt Chito's younger brother, not her husband.

"Oh, wonders will never cease!" exclaimed her aunt. "Your father allowed you to come home and stay in the house alone? Well, I am pleasantly astonished. But are you not lonely in that big compound?"

"Not at all, the house is full. Some refugees from Onitsha, Papa's friend and his family occupy the whole ground floor of our house. The man has six children and there is a housegirl too. I'm not lonely at all."

"No wonder your father allowed you to come home alone," her aunt muttered. She ruffled Uncle Ray's hair – a gesture Ginika knew well which, however, never ceased to amaze her – and said, "Food is ready; let's eat it while it is hot." To the children, she instructed, "Obika take your sister and brothers to the kitchen and eat there; your food is on the table already."

After the children had trooped out, Uncle Ray asked, "Why are they not eating with us?"

Ginika had expected the children would eat with them as usual, as they did in Enugu. Uncle Ray enjoyed having the children around him; he played with them a lot. Ginika could picture him on the carpet, as they climbed all over him. One day she had laughed so much when she came into the house and found little Nonso perched on Uncle Ray's back as he assumed the position of a horse. Nonso had swayed his body forward and backward, riding his father and crying, "Oya, move! Carry me to the playground." Uncle Ray had neighed, pretending to be a horse, and Nonso had screamed with laughter.

"Their *wahala* is too much. Let them eat there today and let me enjoy my food, without shouting at anyone." She cut a generous amount of *fufu* and dropped it in the flat plate in front of Uncle Ray and put some in Ginika's plate before her own. She ladled out *egusi* soup into their bowls and served herself after they had started eating.

Uncle Ray laughed. "I know; they are quite a handful. When they get older, we will have more peace in the house. Their bickering and cries at each other will reduce."

"It's too much. Ona does not realize Obika is older then she is. She will tackle him and yell at him. She does not know she is a girl …"

"Should a girl not assert herself?" he asked. "What do you think, *nwayi oma*?" He was smiling at Ginika.

"I think she should. Anyone who feels like it should assert himself or herself."

"You two have a right to think what you like, but I would not like my daughter to be too forward," her aunt declared.

"Darling, this soup is very sweet," he said, changing the subject. "No woman cooks *egusi* soup like my wife. I am a very lucky man." He gave Auntie Chito a charming smile. Ginika turned to see how her aunt would take the compliment. He was always complimenting her, she thought. She was glad to see her aunt's eyes light up with pleasure.

"How many other women's *egusi* soup have you tasted?" she teased. "Let me not find out that you go about sampling other women's *egusi* soup."

They all burst into laughter.

"You know I do not do that and will never."

"Auntie Chito, the soup is really good. Thank you." Ginika washed her hands carefully to rid them of the smell of *fufu*. She enjoyed eating *fufu*, but its lasting smell on one's hand sometimes put her off.

"I am happy you like it. I will put some for you in a dish when you leave."

"That will be wonderful," she said, beaming. She would eat it tomorrow with *garri*. She gathered the plates and carried them to the kitchen. Her aunt asked her not to wash them because she had taught Obika, Ugo and Ona how to do the dishes and they did it well.

When Ginika came back, she said to Uncle Ray, "We were relieved when Nwakire came back with the message that you were safe after the evacuation of Enugu." Ginika remembered how worried she had been until Nwakire returned with the good news.

"We were luckier than many families," he replied, biting into a piece of stockfish. It was only property we lost, but even that is not a big deal, for we had furnished this house well before the war. We have most things we need to get by at a time like this. We are lucky Ama-Oyi is not near the war front, so we can hope to remain in our home till the war ends and we are able to cultivate the little piece of land that belongs to us." He pushed his plates away and drew the basin of water close to wash his hands.

"Things are not as good for Biafra as in the beginning. We have lost some of our territory, the push into Nigerian territory was repulsed and our forces were dislodged from the Midwest. We have lost quite a number of towns and Calabar and Onitsha are among the more recent ones, and there are too many refugees; I wonder where they will all live if Biafra continues to shrink …"

"*Haba*! Ray, the way you talk, one would think it is all bad news," her aunt put in. "But we have made some gains too. We are refining our own petrol; Biafran scientists in the Research and Production (RAP) unit are making us proud with the things they are producing. What of our *ogbunigwe* – the mass destruction mine? Some countries have recognised us – Tanzania, Zambia, Ivory Coast, Haiti and Gabon – and I heard that France is helping us and may soon recognise us."

Ginika had not been following the news as closely as she did in Mbano. She wished there was room for optimism as her aunt tried to indicate. She wondered if the recognition by these countries would make much difference. Nigeria was still pushing into Biafran territory and did not want to discuss peace, as the government felt they would soon win the war.

"Did your uncle tell you he would soon leave us?" her aunt asked mournfully.

Ginika looked up immediately. Was Uncle Ray going into the army? This was the hottest news in every community – the news about a number of young men joining the army to fight the vandals, as Nigerian soldiers were called, since they began to loot and sack any town or village they entered, since they started bombing markets and people's homes. "No, he hasn't told me?" She turned to him. "Uncle Ray, where are you going?"

"I have been home since we ran from Enugu. Isn't it time I got involved actively again in the war effort? I have been attending meetings in Ama-Oyi, but I need to do more than this." He seemed to be choosing his words carefully. Ginika watched him.

"Why are you going round and round; tell her where you are going." Aunt Chito spoke as if she was not happy that he was leaving home. Ginika could understand her worry though she did not yet know where he was going.

"Let me say it if you are finding it too heavy for your mouth." Her aunt glared at Uncle Ray, blinked and looked away.

Uncle Ray started to say something, stopped and shrugged.

Ginika understood that they had argued this matter over and over again. She could see how vexed her usually cheerful aunt was. She could see how drawn Uncle Ray's face had suddenly become. Uncle Ray who would deny her aunt nothing. He would even do her shopping for her and buy expensive gifts for her in spite of his modest teacher's salary. He would bathe the children if she asked him and whatever else she wanted. But this time he would not do what she wanted, it seemed.

"He is going to Ikot Ekpene to serve in the Directorate for Military Intelligence. That is where he is going. Tell me if he is qualified for this work – an ordinary school principal like him. Where did he learn military intelligence? Is he a soldier?"

Her aunt could be sarcastic if she wanted. Ginika felt the urge to laugh, but she knew it was not a laughing matter. Her aunt was distressed; she did not like where Uncle Ray was being sent. How was she going to comfort or console her?

"You go on and on, as if we are not going to be trained, as if there are no other civilians in the Directorate. I have explained everything to you many times, but you do not want to understand. I do not know what else to say or do." He looked at her appealingly, but she did not look at him.

"You will receive training?" Ginika asked.

"Yes, we will be trained for a month or so in Umuahia before our deployment. I am not even quite sure I will be deployed to Ikot Ekpene; it could be Aba."

"Auntie Chito, don't worry, he will be all right. We will keep praying for him." Ginika did not know what else to say. Since her brother joined the army, she understood that people took similar decisions and steps on a daily basis, in Biafra, especially men. It was so common that people took it for granted; it was only when it touched you directly that you felt devastated. Even now, she had not heard a word from Nwakire and was sure her father had not – whether he was dead or alive, no one in the family knew. All she had understood from his note was that he would be trained as an army officer at Bishop Shanahan College (BSC) in Orlu, where Biafran army officers were mostly trained. She had worried herself sick about it, until she decided not to. Instead she prayed for him whenever she could. She would do the same for Uncle Ray after he would have left.

"How long are you staying in Ama-Oyi?" Uncle Ray asked.

"I don't know yet. I came for the play we are staging to entertain our soldiers. I will join the other actors and actresses for rehearsals on Monday."

On her way home later in the evening, Ginika's heart was burdened with the knowledge that the wall of security surrounding her aunt had suffered a breach. For the first time since their marriage, they would be separated; they would live apart. She knew things would never be the same again for them.

GINIKA DISCOVERED Udo sitting on a metal chair in the veranda when she reached home.

He got up and moved forward to greet her. "Sister Ginika, good evening." He gave her a weak smile.

"Udo, when did you return?" she asked, astonished. She hoped nothing disastrous had happened. Nwakire, was he all right? she wondered. "Has something happened?" Her eyes searched his frantically.

"Uncle sent me. He said I should tell you he has been transferred to a hospital in Alaoma, so he would not be able to come as he told you. He is to report to the new hospital immediately."

"My God! Papa transferred at such short notice? I didn't know they transfer people in wartime. What is this? They just break families and move people at this uncertain time?"

Udo said nothing; he just looked at her.

"Udo, please, come in." She tried to control herself. Udo was tired and needed water to drink or food and she was keeping him standing outside, and asking him questions she was sure were beyond him. "Did you walk across to see your mother?"

"No, I thought I should see you first before going to our house." The way he looked at her gave her the impression he was asking if he did the right thing.

"Thank you for waiting. I hope you didn't wait for a long time? How long have you been waiting?"

"Not too long," he said. She knew it was long, that he lied to save her from either feeling guilty or feeling sorry for him. Her eyes turned to his shoes that were caked with dust and mud.

"How did you get here?" she asked, as they climbed the stairs. "By public transport?"

"Yes. Uncle dropped me at Anara and I took a bus that dropped me in front of Orieagu market, and from there I walked home."

"Put your things in that room with a red curtain and join me in the kitchen. I'm going to prepare something for you to eat. You're hungry, aren't you?"

He nodded. He grasped his bag and walked to the room.

"That looks quite heavy. It seems you brought all your things with you?"

"Yes, I won't go back to Mbano. Uncle told me to stay in Ama-Oyi, and that I should stay with you."

Ginika could not help wondering if her father had sent Udo to watch her and make sure she did not invite boys to the house. He had almost said as much before he left the other day. He had stressed she should behave herself. She unlocked the door of her room and went inside. After changing into a loose-fitting green dress, she went downstairs and unlocked the kitchen door. She greeted Mrs Ndefo who was cooking with her housegirl in the store which was converted as a kitchen for their use. "Good evening, ma. I can smell the *ukwa* you're cooking; the aroma is delicious." She smiled.

Mrs Ndefo nodded and smiled. "That's the only thing I eat now; I'm sick of it. You know, sometimes, I feel like throwing up. Grace tries to prepare it in various ways, but still it feels like medicine in my mouth."

Grace laughed. "Ma, I think you should try something else, like boiled green banana."

"*Hmm*, that's worse. I tried it in Onisha; I can't stand it."

Ginika brought a chair and placed it at the entrance to the

kitchen so that she could talk with Mrs Ndefo some more. She wondered why her meals were so limited. "Why don't you eat other things – yam, plantain, rice…?" She was cutting up yam into small pieces which she would boil for dinner. She had some stew to go with it, and she knew Udo would like it.

"I'm diabetic. You know what that means?" Mrs Ndefo looked at her.

Ginika shook her head; though she had heard of diabetes, she did not really know what the sufferer went through, ate or did not eat.

"Well, it means I cannot eat a lot of things. Breadfruit is about the only thing available to me in Ama-Oyi. The situation is appalling; we'll all die if the war does not end soon."

"Why are we all going to die?" Ginika heard a baritone voice ask humorously. She looked up and saw a wiry dark-skinned man probably of her father's age. Immediately, she knew he was Dr Ufo Ndefo. She saw his son's features in his face.

"Good evening, sir," she greeted.

"You must be Ubaka's daughter? We've never met, have we? The day I was to meet you in Enugu, an emergency case in hospital detained me and I had to send a driver to deliver the letter your father had asked me to take to you." He was smiling, appraising her, and seemed to admire what he saw. "You are beautiful like your mother."

"You knew my mother?" she asked with excitement. Here was someone who knew her mother as a young woman, she thought. She would give anything to hear him talk about her. Auntie Chito had told her things, but hardly enough. She was thirsty for knowledge of her mother, the woman whose head was eaten by a baby that did not want to stay, as Ama-Oyi people would say.

"We all did, all the friends of Ubaka. He was proud of her beauty and showed her off. We had all studied in the United Kingdom, but none of us got married until we returned home. Your father married before the other three of us, his friends."

Ginika was astonished that her father never mentioned all this to her and Nwakire. He hardly discussed their mother both in the past and now. She felt wonderful to hear that her father loved her mother and was proud of her beauty. What happened then? Why did he not love his children or demonstrate it? Why didn't he transfer that love to his and her children? Ginika wondered if his marriage to Auntie Lizzy was to blame.

Ginika looked up and saw Udo coming towards her. She remembered the news he had brought her. She turned to Dr Ndefo. "I have just heard that my father was transferred to Alaoma Hospital."

"He has been transferred?" Dr Ndefo and Mrs Ndefo exclaimed together.

"Oh, that's problematic for him," Dr Ndefo said. "Alaoma is not far from the war front. Who told you?"

Speechless, Ginika pointed to Udo.

"Well, not to worry." Dr Ndefo's voice was more pleasant now. Ginika was sure he had noticed her anxiety and wanted to cheer her up. So Alaoma was near the war front; and this was where they had transferred him. "I am also in a hospital near the front, in Nnewi. This is why my family is here. Don't worry. Your father will be okay in Alaoma."

Ginika nodded. She washed the pieces of yam and put them in a pot and over the stove to cook. She came back and sat down, staring in front of her.

"Is your father coming to Ama-Oyi this weekend?" he

asked. He was still standing where he had stood since he came out from his room, but now he was leaning against the back of the chair on which his wife sat.

"No, he sent a message that he wouldn't be able to come."

"I see. I had wanted to discuss something with him. It will have to be when next he comes." He bent down and kissed the top of his wife's thick hair which she had gathered together and held in braids with a brown band. "I'm returning to the room," he told her.

Ginika washed the knife she had used to cut the yam. She glanced up at Udo. "Please, go and get me more water from the tank, and after that we will fill the drum in the kitchen."

15

Early, the next day, Ginika took Udo to Orie market to buy the
food they needed in the house. They had set out early to beat
the sun and to arrive before the market became too crowded
for easy movement.

"Are you sure we are going in the right direction?" Udo
asked, puzzled. "This is not the way to the market."

"It is. The market was relocated because of air raids.
Though Ama-Oyi had never been raided, the town's
local council moved the market into the forested area as a
precautionary measure. We are going to the new area." She
had been there once since she arrived home and knew the way.
She was really pleased to have Udo around. It felt good to have
company – someone of her own. Though the house was full
of people, she realised she did not have a sense of family with
Mrs Ndefo and her children. She liked them quite all right
and got on well with Amaka, but it was not like having her
flesh and blood with her. Udo's coming home was a heaven-
sent opportunity.

"Sister Ginika, can we buy *akidi*, our local beans? I haven't
eaten them for ages."

She saw the appeal in his eyes. "Why not? We'll get some;

but just pray the money stretches far enough. Papa only gave me just a little money and promised more on his next visit, but the transfer has made it impossible for him to come at the weekend. We just have to manage until we see him." She gave him a sympathetic gaze.

"We can buy less meat and less fish and less everything," he suggested.

"*Hmm*, less meat and less fish," she mimicked. "Are you not in Biafra? How many people eat meat and fish in Ama-Oyi now? This is a poor community, you know. Most of the people are poor; even before the war few people here ate meat. The situation is worse now."

Udo shrugged and made no more suggestions. When they got to a place where the path was narrow, Ginika allowed him to go before her. He trotted ahead, kicking broken branches out of the way and swinging their shopping basket back and forth.

"Don't break the handle of the basket," she cautioned. She looked at his shorts which had pictures of zebras on the two sides of his buttocks. "Have you seen a live zebra before," she asked, laughing.

"No, I have not."

"Not even in a zoo?"

"No, I have never been to a zoo."

The path broadened and they walked side by side. "Don't they have a zoo in Jos?"

"I don't know," he replied, scratching his head.

"Didn't your father take you there?"

"No, Papa did not take us to such places," he said sheepishly. "He was always in the market selling rice with Mama. The only day he did not go to market was on Sunday when we went to church. After church he visited friends or attended the Ama-Oyi town's meeting."

Ginika reflected on the life led by her uncle, Onagu, and his family. It was as restricted as the life she was used to, but unlike Onagu, her father did not belong to Ama-Oyi town's union in the places they lived – Port Harcourt and Aba – where the union had branches. "You know, Papa did not take me to the zoo," she informed Udo, "it was my teacher who took other pupils and me to the Port Harcourt zoo when I was in Primary Six."

The buzzing noise of the market told them they were almost there. "Stay close to me all the time so that we don't lose each other," she advised. "In fact, I want you to walk in front so that I keep you in sight at all times. I don't want to start looking for you."

"I cannot get lost. I know how to get home if we lose each other." His voice sounded very confident.

She laughed. "Okay, still I don't want to lose you, as you are the one carrying the basket and I need to put the things I buy in it."

They were in a part of the thick forest called Oke-Ohia, Great Forest. Ginika only visited it once when she was a child and had gone to see her grandmother with Nwakire. A boy had taken them to Oke-Ohia to gather mushrooms. She had been frightened but the boy was confident and whistled merrily as they walked in the forest. "You will be surprised when you see the market," she said. "It is right inside the forest."

They broke through and Ginika could hear the sound as Udo drew in his breath and exclaimed, "What a big place!"

She smiled. "Yes, it hits you once you emerge from the forest and enter the clearing. I was astonished when I came here three days ago." She saw that the market was already in full session. It was a huge open space that accommodated hundreds of buyers and sellers of various articles and commodities. Each commodity had its reserved portion and Ginika already knew where to buy the things she wanted. She looked up and saw how clear the sky was, almost cloudless. It would be a very hot day, she thought. It was best for them to shop quickly and leave. In such weather, one sweated so much. The smell of sweat from people's bodies could be suffocating. And the noise was daunting; the buzz was so great she could hardly hear what Udo was saying. She could not hear herself either, so they stopped talking. She heard people around her shouting to be heard. Some people haggled; some laughed, raucously, as jokes hit and rebounded from their eardrums. Ginika shuddered. She skirted some parts of the market and was headed for the areas where she needed to buy things. She was surer of her movement today. The other day, she had come with Akueju, Udo's mother; she would have lost her way if she hadn't come with her. She bought yams and some garri. She bought some stockfish and smoked fish, bypassed the meat sellers and headed for the vegetable section to buy *akidi*.

"Sister Ginika, look at the *akidi* in that small basket," Udo pointed. "It looks so fresh."

Ginika followed his finger and saw the basket; the *akidi* was really fresh. "Yes, let's price it." She called the attention of the seller who was chatting with her neighbour. "How much is this one?" she asked, pointing. Then she heard a swishing sound and listened. "What was that noise," she asked, turning to Udo. Udo looked blank. It sounded like a plane, but the swishing sound was strange. The seller was talking to her but she was not listening. The sound was increasing, and there was indication other people had heard it too. She heard a loud voice crying, "Hey, it is enemy plane-o! Take cover!"

Ginika did not have time to think, but the training she had had as a special constable guided her action, as she grabbed Udo's hand and cried, "Follow me! Bend forward as you run!" They took off before the other people in the market who seemed mesmerized by the sound of the planes. Some of them stood in one spot, watching, as the first plane entered the space, in the sky, above the market. Ginika found the first tree at the edge of the forest and shouted to Udo, "Stop! Lie down beside me!" Even as she listened to the whooshing sound of the jet bombers, she heard the first explosion. The earth shook. Ginika flung one arm round the base of the tree and pressed her head to the ground; she could feel Udo's body pressed to her side. "Stay down! Keep your body flat!" she whispered fiercely. "Don't get up!" Was she trembling or was it Udo's body quivering and shaking hers?

She felt rather than saw legs running past, pounding the ground where they lay; she was grateful for the tree which acted as a buffer, shielding her and Udo. Without this protection, she knew they could easily be trampled to death. The explosions rocked the ground, assaulted the air again and again. Ginika heard anguished cries around her and held on to the tree. For a moment, she ventured to look up, and saw two jets turning directly overhead; they shone like silver, in the sun. In that instant, she saw one of them release some objects she could not identify; the objects fell from the rear end of the plane like the droppings of a goat. Could these be rockets or cannonballs? Soon after, before she lowered her head completely, she saw an arm and a leg fly past and land a little distance from her. She shuddered. People were still running past, crying out in their frenzy. As she pressed her head down once more, Ginika felt a human body land on top of her. She fainted.

She woke to the sound of weeping and lamentation. She twisted her body and the weight on top of her rolled off. She flinched at the sight before her – a thin woman with a battered head, still bleeding. Udo lay still. For a moment her heart stopped beating, as she thought he was dead. His body was spattered with blood. She shook him, and gave a little cry when he opened his eyes and fixed them on her. He seemed dazed, semi-conscious. "Udo, it's me. Wake up." When she read fear in his eyes, she knew he was conscious. To the left of Udo, Ginika saw the body of another victim lying across a severed leg. She was sure the man was dead because he lay perfectly still and his eyes looked glazed.

Slowly she got up and pulled Udo up. He had a wild look in his eyes which frightened Ginika the more. She wondered if her own eyes were like that. "Let's go," she whispered, and he complied mechanically. She grasped his hand and guided him through the carnage. There were craters here and there, and she avoided them. The dead and the wounded littered the ground. Many had died instantly and might not have suffered any pain, she thought. As she passed, one woman moaned, "Please, help me; it's my leg." Ginika looked and saw a bloodied leg, looking pulpy like a sponge. She averted her eyes. There was nothing she could do. She whimpered, and stumbled away, still clutching Udo's hand. There were howls here and groans there. All she wanted was to get far away from the gory scene. Further away, she saw limbs ripped off from their owners, and other body parts lying around as if they were for sale. Some of the bodies were trapped by chairs and stools people had brought to the market. As they stumbled to the side from which they had entered the market, Ginika cringed at the sight of blood spattered on trees, on the ground, on merchandise and on the dead bodies lying everywhere. She looked at Udo and, cradling him, she steered him towards the path that led to their home.

GINIKA AND Udo were almost at the gate when Amaka sighted them and gave a loud shout, "Ginika and Udo are back; they are safe." She ran forward to welcome them. Mrs Ndefo and her sons hurried out of their rooms and stood in the veranda.

"Oh, Ginika, thank God you're alive." Amaka threw her arms open and Ginika collapsed into them. Amaka had to spread her legs to stop two of them hurtling to the ground.

For the first time since the air raid, Ginika felt the urge to cry. She had walked home in a daze, following the path without really seeing it. The few people they met on the way were rushing to the market apparently to look for their relatives who had gone there to buy or sell. No one had asked her questions or stopped to help her. But she was conscious of the fact that the news of the bombing had travelled everywhere in Ama-Oyi. The comfort of Amaka's arms seemed to loosen the tight knot inside her, and freed her tear ducts. Ginika sobbed uncontrollably, as if crying could obliterate the images she saw at the market and blot out completely the memory of the nightmare. Involuntarily, she remembered the railway station in Port Harcourt and the mangled bodies she had seen in the carriage and the decapitated torso of the unidentifiable man. Fresh tears surged into her eyes and flowed down her face.

Amaka led her gently past the gate and into the house. Mrs Ndefo took over, pressed her to herself and comforted her. "Hush, my dear. It's okay. You'll be all right." She gave her a handkerchief to wipe her eyes and blow her nose.

Ginika nodded. "Thank you, ma," she said. "I'm okay. But it was horrible." She must not break down like this, she thought. Where was Udo? She turned her head and saw him, still not talking but he looked okay. His eyes were normal again.

It was Amaka that first saw her back and cried out. "Ginika, are you all right? Your dress is stained with blood at your back?"

She turned sharply, but she could not see her back, of course. She put her left hand behind her and tried to touch her back.

"The blood is dry," Amaka observed.

"Were you hurt?" Mrs Ndefo asked anxiously. "Do you feel pain at all in any part of your body?" She called out, "Dozie, run and bring me the First Aid Box."

"I was not hurt," Ginika said, worried about the blood, still feeling her back. "Oh, I remember now, one of the people wounded fell on top of me where I took cover. A woman. It must be her blood." She shuddered, as memories of the tragedy came flooding back. She looked down at her body and saw that her blouse was stained with mud and her shoes were discoloured and caked with red earth.

"Let's go into the sitting room so that I can help you remove the dirt in your hair," Amaka volunteered.

Perhaps I should just go and have a bath." She kicked off

her shoes. She and Udo were lucky to be alive, she thought, breathing normally again and feeling a little better.

"Let me remove the dirt first," Amaka insisted.

In the sitting room, Ginika sat on the first chair she saw and tilted her head toward Amaka who sat next to her.

"There, they are all gone." She showed her bits of dry leaves and twigs she had extracted from her thick long hair which she wore plaited, as usual. Mrs Ndefo sat opposite, and watched her. Before her on a side table was the First Aid Box Dozie had brought a few seconds earlier. Ginika was now sure she was not injured, either externally or internally. She knew they would like to know what had happened in the market, but were reluctant to ask, having witnessed her distress moments ago. Ginika looked out of the window and saw Udo laughing in the veranda and telling Dozie and his brothers about the air raid. She was amazed he had recovered quickly enough to laugh and narrate the experience with remarkable aplomb. She shook her head.

"We were so worried," Amaka said, looking into her eyes. "We saw the planes when they passed, before the raid and afterwards. We heard the explosions."

"We knew you had gone to the market with Udo," Mrs Ndefo put in. "It was such a relief when we saw both of you coming back."

"It seems you hadn't bought anything before the raid," Amaka remarked. "You had nothing with you."

Ginika groaned. She had forgotten all about the shopping basket with the things they bought. She didn't even remember exactly where they lost it. She shook her head and then stared at the ceiling.

"You left it in the market." Mrs Ndefo said matter-of-factly.

Ginika nodded. "Please, can we talk about it another time?" She shuddered again and shut her eyes.

"Of course, forgive us for keeping you here." Mrs Ndefo got up and asked Amaka to help Ginika upstairs and assist her in any way she wanted. "Don't worry about Udo; he seems all right. I'll take care of him. Just go up and rest and don't worry about lunch. You'll eat with us, or Amaka will bring it up if you prefer."

Ginika nodded her thanks. All she wanted at the moment was to get to her room. She was grateful Mrs Ndefo would look out for Udo, though he seemed to be all right. She could hear his voice describing the sound of the jets. "We heard *fiooo* . . . *fiooo* . . . *fiooo,* before the explosion. I think there were more than two planes," she heard him say. And Dozie's voice replied, "They were three; we saw them when they flew past." Undoubtedly, Udo was all right. Ginika allowed Amaka to walk her upstairs.

In the safety of her room, she undressed and lay down. Amaka left to boil water for her bath. When it was ready, Ginika went downstairs and had her bath. Back in her room, she lay on her bed, her eyes shut. Amaka left her to rest, and returned thirty minutes later to check if she was all right or needed anything. She found her lying perfectly still but wide awake and staring at the ceiling. She couldn't sleep. Amaka sat on the only chair in the room and both were silent till Mrs Ndefo sent Dozie to inform them that lunch was ready. Amaka went down but returned soon afterwards with her lunch and Ginika's. Udo helped her to bring the plates up.

Ginika ate very little though the food was delicious. She stared at the fried plantain and *jollof* rice which ordinarily she enjoyed very much. The thought of food brought up the images of arms torn, legs ripped off and heads smashed, robbing her of her appetite, nauseating her. She pushed the plate away.

"Sister Ginika, eat a little more," Udo coaxed. He stood in front of her, pleading with his eyes.

Ginika stared at him, resentfully, as if she disapproved of his acting normally and giving the impression that what had happened in the morning never took place. She nursed the thought that Udo considered her weak and spineless for feeling shattered over the morning's experience. Did everybody think she was being dramatic rather than courageous? Mrs Ndefo and Amaka had even expected her to talk about it, to tell them how it happened. Were they disappointed that she couldn't talk about it, that she couldn't deal with it? A weakling. Was that what Udo and the rest thought of her, she wondered? After all, this was one of the ugly faces of war, a consequence of war. "Take it away," she said in a raised voice, glaring at Udo. He looked at her, and she thought he was angry with her for raising her voice. She watched him take the plate and leave the room.

Ginika lay back on her bed, watching Amaka eat her food slowly. She watched her chew each mouthful and swallow. When she finished eating, Amaka got up and left the room, carrying the plate with her. Tears filled Ginika's eyes; she thought she had driven them away. They had done no wrong and were only trying to help her. She trembled at the thought that she had hurt them and had seemed ungrateful. Unchecked, her tears flowed freely, trickled down the sides of her face until they reached the pillow and wetted it. In spite of her misery, her feeling of abandonment and her remorse, Ginika was determined not to call out. She would lie awake all night. She would face anything that might happen to her. She would face her nightmares alone.

Hours later, she still lay on her back, staring at the ceiling, lost in her wretchedness. Her head was throbbing when Amaka returned with a small mattress – the type students used in secondary schools – and a lantern. Without saying a word, she placed the mattress on the ground, at the foot of Ginika's bed. She probably thought Ginika was already asleep. Ginika remained quiescent. Amaka wore a pink night-dress that reached down her ankles. She must have scrubbed her face. It shone in the pale light cast by the lantern. Her hair was covered with a black hair-net. She lay down and covered herself with a *wrappa*. Ginika watched her, fascinated by her calmness, the deliberateness of her actions and her stupendous equanimity. Suddenly a feeling of wellbeing, a sensation of relief overwhelmed her and she felt like singing for joy. She heard herself say, "Amaka, thank you."

Amaka lifted her head up long enough to reply, "You're welcome. Good night."

"Good night." For the first time since morning, Ginika smiled. She thought she would sleep well, without having any nightmare. She knew she was going to be all right.

16

Ginika stared at herself in the full-length mirror in her room. She ran a comb through her hair and, pulling it back, held it with a black band. She wore a pale-green dress. She had decided that it was going to be dark colours henceforth since Ama-Oyi had joined the list of towns targeted by enemy planes. She felt that bright colours were too visible, as they could attract the attention of bombers easily. She looked forward to joining Eloka Odunze and the rest of the cast for rehearsals at the primary school hall. She resolved not to allow the fear of air raids to keep her permanently indoors, as it had done to Mrs Ndefo, who stayed in her room all day, ready to run into the bunker at the slightest noise. Her fear had become so obsessive that she only came out of her room at night and left the preparation of meals solely to her housemaid and Amaka.

"Fear is destructive," she had said to Udo. "I won't allow the vandals to cripple me with fear." She had joined other people in calling the enemy vandals after witnessing the carnage at Orie market. Only vandals could kill innocent men and women in a market without a guilty conscience, she rationalised. Besides, if they called Biafran soldiers rebels, surely they deserved to be called vandals.

When she arrived at the venue, there were many people there already. She glanced at her watch and saw she was late by thirty minutes. The hall was a rectangular building with a platform at one end of it. Some people were on the platform rehearsing. The floor was rough and uneven and she wondered how the pupils and teachers had felt when they met in the assembly hall before schools closed. She searched for Eloka and saw him standing to the right and directing the play. He looked her way and waved. She nodded and smiled. He wore a white T-shirt and black trousers. As she looked at the different faces, she recognised Njide Igwe, her classmate and waved to her. Njide sat on an extra-long bench propped against the wall on the left of the hall. She waved back and beckoned to her to join them on the bench. There was just enough room for her to perch and lean her back against the wall, which was covered with drawings.

"When did you arrive?" Njide asked. "We've been waiting for you. Eloka mentioned that you would be here today."

Ginika looked at her face quickly and thought the way she called his name gave the impression he meant something to her. Were they friends, she wondered? She recalled Eloka had told her in Mbano that it was her classmate that told him to invite her to act the part of Mammy Wota. And the classmate in question was, of course, Njide. For a reason she did not understand, her heart palpitated.

"I came back a few days ago." She pointed to the platform. "I wasn't expecting the rehearsals would start so promptly. I'm glad it is not the play in which I'm involved."

"Eloka is a stickler for time," Njide replied, rather proudly, Ginika thought. "If you want to work with him, you have to keep to time. He insists on this."

"Do you have a role in any of the plays?" Ginika asked.

"No, I'm in charge of costumes and props," she said. "You are acting the lead role in *Mammy Wota*, aren't you? Have you learned your part? Rehearsals have also been going on, and someone has been playing your part. You'll take over now you're here." She flashed a smile, revealing the attractive gap in her front teeth.

There was no doubt that Njide was deeply involved in the plays – as deeply involved as Eloka himself. She talked with confidence and acted as if she was among the people that decided what happened in the Ama-Oyi Students' Association; yet she was no older than Ginika and was, like her, a Higher School student. Ginika wondered if there were no female university students in the association to lead the girls. Then she remembered she had heard that Ama-Oyi had not yet produced a female graduate, and none of her women was even an undergraduate. "I'll do my best," Ginika heard herself say.

"Have you learned your part?"

She hesitated before she replied. "Even if I have, it cannot come right until I have started rehearsing."

"That's true." Njide laughed and then grasped Ginika's hand, "*Shsss*, Eloka is looking at us. He is displeased that we're talking and distracting people's attention."

Ginika withdrew her hand. "Oh, I'm sorry." Her eyes focused on Eloka and the actors on the platform. It was easy for her to follow the action, for she had read the copy of *Arms and the Man* Eloka had given her. She watched him as he directed the play and was amazed at his skill, though he had received no training for it. She realised he was proficient in many things. He was good at mechanical things, and with gardening and farming and keeping rabbits, she thought, remembering their conversation in Mbano.

"Stop!" Ginika heard and stared. She was astonished, for Eloka was speaking rather too strongly to one of the actors, a girl. His eyes fumed. "Look, you just have to get it right! We've been on this long enough for you to know your part. We don't have the time to go on like this." He waved his hand in the air. Mortified, the girl bent her head. Ginika was sure that if she were close enough to the platform, she would see Eloka's short moustache twitch. She had observed it the time he came to Mbano and also the day he came to her house in Ama-Oyi. The twitching seemed to occur when he felt or spoke strongly about anything.

"Now, let's begin again," Eloka said in a softer voice. Ginika watched and saw him smile, flashing his white teeth – a sign that the girl had done well, that the scene was all right.

Eloka waved the actors away and, like birds freed from a cage, they jumped down from the platform, laughing, as their friends hailed them and paid them compliments. Eloka walked over to where Ginika sat next to Njide. "Hello," he said. "Glad to see you. I hope you're ready to start today?" He stood before her, his lips parted, his eyes shining and gazing into hers.

"Elo, well done," Njide greeted, trying to catch his eye, and frowning when she failed to achieve her aim. She stood up with force and almost upset the wobbly bench; Ginika and four other girls sitting on the bench got up quickly fearing the bench would collapse and throw them on the floor.

Eloka dashed forward to steady the bench, his body brushing briefly against Ginika's and sending sparks of excitement all over her body. It was the first time their bodies had come into close contact; the other times had been mere handshakes. "Be careful," he exclaimed, smiling down at Ginika's upturned face, which glowed so close to his.

"So sorry," cried Njide. "I forgot the bench is very shaky." She turned, looking anxiously at Ginika and the other girls.

"It's okay," Ginika said, standing aside and leaning sideways against the wall and laughing like the other girls.

"These benches are in very bad condition," remarked one of the girls called Eunice, who seemed to be the youngest in the hall. She could not be more than fifteen, Ginika thought. If people as young as this joined the association, then she would bring Udo the next time she came for rehearsals.

They had a short break. Some of the people went outside to relax; others chatted with their friends in the hall. Njide tried to drag Eloka away. "Elo, let's go over there; I brought some snacks, *ogbara otii*. I'm sure you'll like it." Njide noticed his reluctance to follow her and added, "Ginika, you can come too. Don't you like *ogbara otii*? It's so tasty." Her big bust quivered as she gesticulated.

She called him Elo, a shortened form of his name, Ginika mused, wondering if there was any relationship between them. She followed Njide and Eloka to the other end of the hall where she had left a bag on a desk. They pushed a bench close to the desk and sat down to enjoy the *ogbara otii*. Ginika thought it was truly delicious as she bit into the white spongy snacks made from crushed melon seeds, wondering whether Njide would have invited her if she had not been talking to Eloka at the time. The break was nearly over. *Mammy Wota* was next. She hoped she would play her role well.

"Where were you the other day when the market was raided?" Eloka asked Ginika.

"In the market."

"In the market?" Eloka was shocked. "You were there when it was raided? My God, it must have been terrible for you." He looked at her carefully, as if trying to read her thoughts to gauge the impact of the air raid on her.

"It was; even now I can hardly deal with it." She shook her head.

"Then, we won't talk about it unless you wish to do so."

"Thanks." Ginika did not wish to talk about the air raid, so they changed the subject.

"Are you ready to rehearse today? We don't have much time left before the performance. We already have a programme and our tour of military bases should start in three weeks. Can you cope?" He looked at her in a way that told her he was depending on her.

"I know the part already, but it is rehearsing with the entire cast that will determine how ready I am. But I know the words already; I have been studying the script." She looked at him and saw how pleased he was. She hoped she would not disappoint him.

"Eloka, how come you took away the two most beautiful girls in the hall?" a voice full of laughter exclaimed.

Ginika looked up to see a light-skinned man with a moustache similar to Eloka's standing before them with his hands in the pockets of his faded jeans. Eloka laughed. Njide giggled, pleased with the compliment. Ginika merely studied the man's face. She was sure Eloka would introduce him.

"Ginika, meet Tonna Egbunike, one of us and my friend." Turning to the man, he said, "She's Ginika Ezeuko."

"Ah, the lady we all have been waiting for is here at last," Tonna said, shaking her hand and keeping it in his for a while.

"You're playing the lead role in *Mammy Wota*, aren't you? You're even more beautiful than the water princess. It's my friend's first play and we're looking forward to its production. I can see why Njide recommended you and why Eloka approved the recommendation."

Ginika laughed, embarrassed, but pleased with the compliment. She had better perform well in the play. Everyone expected wonders from her. "Thanks, you're so kind. I'll do my best. I hope you won't be disappointed."

After the break, *Mammy Wota* was next and rehearsal started in earnest.

Ginika liked the plot of the play, the themes and the characters that made it such an evocative, action-packed and dynamic play. She was comfortable with the storyline – an allegory about the conflict between Nigeria and Biafra in which Mammy Wota arbitrated and victory ultimately went to Biafra.

At first she felt awkward as she tried to get into the rhythm of the rehearsal. The other actors had been rehearsing for weeks and were at home with their parts. However, the smiles and winks Eloka was sending her way assured her she was not doing badly, and he was not a director that was easily impressed, from the little she had seen of him the time the other play was being rehearsed. Even Njide was pleased with her effort, as she could see from the expression in her face. As for Tonna, he did not hide his feelings, his approval, in the least. So it was an encouraging first appearance for her.

"That was a good performance." Eloka winked at her. This was another habit she discovered he had – his winks which made him look like a mischievous teenager.

"Thank you."

"Ginika, bravo!" Tonna enthused. "That was excellent."

"Thanks, Tonna."

When the actors left the platform, all the girls mounted the stage to perform a dance. Ginika was taken unawares, for she had not been told the girls were practising a dance. She found herself the only female who sat among men in the hall.

"Join them." Eloka said and winked again, causing her heart to make such a dash.

"Make a fool of myself? Have I been practising with them?"

"They haven't gone far. They only started last week. They thought a dance would energise our performance and give our plays a boost, and I agree. Why don't you go and sit on the bench with the drummers for today and decide later if you want to dance, or drum or beat the *udu*."

Ginika went up the steps, back to the platform and sat next to the girl beating the *udu*. The music makers went on, as if their lives depended on what they were doing. A pulsating sound filled the hall, followed by the voice of the lead singer and then the rest of the dancers. The music was so captivating that Ginika discovered herself swaying to its rhythm. Eunice glided into the front of the stage and began to dance in a most alluring and graceful manner. So this was what Eunice was here for? Ginika's eyes were glued to Eunice's supple body which twisted and turned like lightning. After Eunice's demonstration, the other dancers formed a circle and danced with vigour. Ginika looked at Njide who was twisting and turning, her ample bosom rising and falling, her big round buttocks trembling. Her eyes travelled round the circle, noting the skilled and the not-so-skilled dancers. She was certain she wanted to be a dancer, not a drummer or an *udu* beater. She turned her head and saw Eloka watching her.

GINIKA STOOD outside the hall, ready to set out for home. She was pleased with the day's activities and would try to come early for the next day's rehearsal. She had negotiated with Eunice to teach her some of the dance steps in the morning before the rehearsal. It was a pleasant surprise for her to discover that Eunice's house was not far from hers and that they both came from the same village.

"Care for a lift home?" Eloka asked. "Jump in and let me drop you."

She turned and looked in the car. Tonna sat in front with him, and Njide and another girl sat at the back. When she got in, he drove off. "I come in the car sometimes to warm it or the battery will go bad," he said, briefly turning sideways.

Ginika said nothing. It seemed to her he was trying to justify his driving a car at a time most people in Biafra walked, a time petrol had become a rare commodity, owned by a few people who hoarded it or had access to the few people who had remained powerful in spite of everything, or were in the top ranks in the armed forces – the army, navy and air force. Tonna was the first to drop off.

Njide scrambled out and took the front seat. "We don't want you to become our professional driver, do we?" she said to Eloka, laughing.

"Bye, everyone. See you tomorrow." Tonna grinned and waved until the car started and zoomed off.

Eloka fished out some sweets and peppermint from the glove compartment of his car and distributed them to everyone. "Thanks," they chorused. Ginika wondered when last she had had sweets – these were luxuries the war had stolen from most people. She removed the thin covering, dropped the toffee in her mouth and savoured it. The car left the main road and struggled through a narrow sandy lane.

The girl in the middle, whose name Ginika had forgotten, got off at a junction where her house was hidden by tall trees. She thanked Eloka and wished Njide and Ginika a pleasant evening. They continued in silence. Ginika wondered who would go first, Njide or herself, and she spent the next few seconds considering if she should join Eloka in the front seat if Njide got off first. It would look odd indeed if she were to sit alone in the back, directly behind him where she was now, while he sat in front alone. She was still puzzling it over when Njide spoke in a voice that sounded as if she was disappointed, angry even. "Elo, are you dropping me first?"

"Yes."

The car stopped before a red bungalow in front of which towered an almond tree. Ginika had to tilt her head back to see its top. When she looked down, Njide had alighted and was about to shut the door.

"Thank you for the ride," she mumbled. "Till tomorrow."

"Okay," Eloka replied and drove off. After a short distance, he asked, "Don't you want to come over here and sit with me?"

Ginika laughed, thinking that he had made the decision for her. "Let me come to the front."

He stopped, leaned sideways and opened the door for her. She slid in, sat without looking at him, but very conscious of his nearness. She was surprised that the first thought that came to her mind was what her father would say if he were to see her now. She smiled at the thought. For the first time in her life she was doing exactly as she wanted, without hindrance.

She was frightened at the burden of freedom, the air of liberty she breathed in Ama-Oyi. For how long would it last?

"Can I share your thought? I saw you smile. What's funny?" His eyes were on her.

Ginika was afraid he might notice the way her heart lifted, as if it shifted from its accustomed position. She could not stop the warm sensation coursing through her body from her belly downwards, nor could she prevent her pulse from quickening. Above all, she could not trust that her voice would be normal if she were to say something. So she kept silent.

He did not speak to her again but concentrated on the road. When they got to her house in a few minutes, she got out and began to thank him, but he interrupted her. "Can I come in for a moment, please?"

"Aren't you hungry?" she asked. "You should go home and eat. I'm famished and will have to start cooking immediately, as there is no food in the house." She would not meet his eyes, though she desperately wanted to feed her eyes on his handsome face and have a glimpse of his sparkling teeth.

"Just a few minutes. You won't die of hunger, I'm sure."

She opened the gate and he drove in. She asked him to park next to Dr Ndefo's Mercedes which he had permanently parked in the compound. The car rested on blocks of wood, as the tyres had been removed and stowed in the boot. Eloka got out and followed her into the house. There seemed to be no one around and Ginika wondered where Amaka and the boys were. She was sure Mrs Ndefo was hiding in her room. The house looked strange now there was quiet everywhere.

"Come into the sitting room. At least, I can offer you some water."

As soon as they went in, Eloka pulled her close. The

pressure of his strong athletic body, the feel of his slender fingers holding her made her whole body tremble and catch fire, as if a light was lit inside her. She turned to look at him and the fire in his eyes matched and surpassed hers.

"Have you any idea how beautiful you are?" he whispered, gazing into her eyes.

Ginika was enchanted by the sweet words flowing from his lips. This morning and even at the rehearsal, she had not thought this possible, especially with Njide dancing around him so possessively. Yes, she would ask him what his relationship with her was, not now, later perhaps. She had never been held this close by any man, nor had she felt like this about anyone. But she was sure Eloka was all she wanted. She had not acknowledged this to herself before, but then she was not aware of this knowledge until now. Defenceless in his arms, she allowed him to touch her, to run his fingers down her face ever so gently. She lifted her arms and clasped them around his shoulders.

Eloka lifted his face and smiled reassuringly. She waited for him, her chest heaving. He kissed her lips. His breath was warm and tasted of peppermint and she was sure hers tasted of the toffee she had taken in the car. She shut her eyes, for it seemed to her that this was the appropriate thing to do to stop her heart from flying away completely from her chest, to shield her eyes from the consuming fire his had become. She sensed him drawing away long enough to search her face, but soon she felt his tongue all over her face and neck after which it sought her mouth again, kissing her, his tongue seeking hers and finding it as she yielded. She had never been kissed so deeply before and she wanted him to go on and never stop.

He drew away again and she heard him say, "I love you,

Ginika, more than you can ever know or imagine. I mustn't rush things, my darling, or take advantage of you. You're special."

Ginika laughed, her eyes sparkling, and reached for his lips, kissing him passionately. "Eloka, I love you too," she said. "I've never loved any man before."

He drew her to a settee and they sat down. "I'm so glad you feel the same way. I was afraid you did not care about me and I couldn't bear it any longer. That's why I had to ask you to allow me to come in to tell you how I feel. I know now that I've loved you since the first day I met you." He rubbed his face against her bosom, drew her close and kissed her. Ginika responded eagerly, not wanting him to stop, not caring who came in and saw them.

After he left, Ginika ran to her room, locked the door and danced around, as if there was soundless music playing for her. She said again and again, "Eloka Odunze loves me! It's me he loves and has ever loved! And I believe him!" The wonder of what happened filled her with awe. She was loved by a splendid and accomplished young man. She was sure he came from a good family – the type of family her father would approve of, though she doubted if he would approve of her taking a boyfriend. Eloka respected her and thought highly of her. He did not just want a plaything else he would have tried to do something she might have regretted. Now he was gone, she was grateful he had not gone further than he did. Could she have resisted him if he had tried? It would be her first time too. She wouldn't want any other person to do it anyway whenever it would be done. She burst into laughter. Oh, she forgot to ask about Njide. She would ask him when next they were together, which she hoped would be soon.

Ginika was in this state of ecstasy when Udo returned late in the evening from visiting his mother and sisters. He was surprised to see her in high spirits. "Sister Ginika, how did your rehearsal go?"

"Oh, it went very well," she said. "How are your mother and sisters? I'm sorry I haven't cooked anything yet. Are you very hungry?" She wasn't really hungry and would only cook if Udo wanted to eat.

"No, I've eaten. My mother gave me some food for you. You won't believe it, she cooked *akidi* and yam." His grin was so wide that Ginika could see all his teeth.

"Wow, and she gave you some for me?"

"Yes, let me go and bring it."

As Ginika waited for Udo, she heard shouts downstairs and knew Amaka and her brothers were back. Ordinarily, their screams would distract and irritate her but today she was too excited, too happy to be disturbed or annoyed.

17

Eloka smiled at Dozie who had become the regular gateman who let him in whenever he came to the house to see Ginika. "Thanks, Dozie," he said and was about to ask him if Ginika was in when he saw her standing at the front door. The smile on her face was so sunny that his body became hot and his heart melted like wax. He thought he had never seen such flawless, such glorious skin as Ginika was blessed with.

"My Mermaid," he whispered, as she effortlessly walked into his arms as soon as he stepped onto the veranda. Since after the performance of the play in which she had distinguished herself as a fine actress, he had renamed her Mermaid, for himself. It was his special name for her.

"Welcome." Ginika rested her head on Eloka's shoulders without caring who saw her. She looked at the parcel in his right hand. "What's that?"

He released her and followed her into the sitting room. "I'll show you in a moment." He was about to sit down when she suggested, "Shall we go upstairs to my room?"

Without waiting for an answer, she led the way up the flight of stairs and into her room. Eloka, who was entering the room for the first time, admired its neatness, the matching door and window curtains and the spotlessly white bed sheet. He understood immediately that she had spent time preparing the room to receive him, for it was obvious to him she had planned that they would be together in her room and not in the sitting room, as had been the case each time he came to see her in the past two weeks.

"Lovely room," he observed, dropping the parcel wrapped with an old newspaper on the bed, and drawing her into his arms. "I've wanted to do this since I left you yesterday." His face was buried in her hair, and the pleasant smell of the hair cream she used filled his nostrils. "Does this type of cream still exist in Biafra?" he asked, inhaling deeply. "It smells like perfume."

She laughed. "You won't believe it – I've had it for a long time, since before the war. I use it sparingly, only on special occasions, like this one."

He held her tight. She was so artless and innocent, he thought. She didn't hide her feelings, and she made you feel you could trust her. He tilted her head back and ran his tongue from her forehead to her neck before kissing her, his tongue probing, curling around and sucking hers. He could hear her sharp intake of breath, and felt her surrender to him before, in turn, seizing his tongue boldly and giving it a prolonged suck. Then she started to laugh and he laughed too. How wonderful to love and be loved, he thought. He released her and made her sit on the chair.

"Look what I brought you," he said, opening the parcel so tenderly, glancing at her face from time to time, and smiling because he could see she was wondering what it was that took him so long to unwrap. But he had to be careful so that his gift remained as perfect as it was when he wrapped it. Finally he lifted it up and showed her.

"Oh, what a lovely bunch of roses!" Ginika gazed at the reddest roses she had ever seen in her life. "Are these roses from your garden?"

"Yes, they are, specially tended for you these past few days." He extracted one of them – the freshest and the daintiest – and pinned it on her dress, above her left breast. "Red rose for my love."

Ginika's face was ecstatic. "Thank you, darling. I'll wear this all day," she said, fingering it, gently, "and the rest will go into a vase." She looked at him, her face suddenly serious. "Eloka, this is the best gift you will ever give me. It means so much to me, for I see it as a symbol of your love for me, and its redness reminds me of blood – the blood of our people that flowed in Nigeria before the war and is still flowing to this day. Red is a symbol of sacrifice, isn't it?"

"It is, my love. You sound so poetic. You have such talent, you know. I'm glad you like them; I took special care of the bed and the rose plants from which they came." He did not tell her that while waiting for the rosebuds to flower and blossom, he had guarded them against intruders, warning everyone in the house not to touch them, sometimes waking up in the night just to make sure they were there. He did not tell her that he had covered them with cellophane when it rained so that the wind and rain would not damage them, and also to protect them from dew. His efforts had paid off and yielded such an excellent result – wholesome blood red roses.

"They seem to have a personality of their own." Her voice was subdued, filled with awe, as she admired the roses which lay in the wrapping paper on her bed. "They are lovely, they sparkle."

Eloka was fascinated by the sharp contrast between the

redness of the roses and the whiteness of the bed sheet. "See how different they are," he told her, "the red rose and the white sheet."

"Yes, the contrast is so great; I didn't think of it."

Impulsively, he remarked, "Both remind me of your beauty, your innocence and your purity." He took the flowers and placed them on the table.

"Eloka, the things you say!" She bent down, as if to hide her face. He saw how self-conscious she was and laughed. "Am I not saying the truth?" He did not wait for her answer, but bent down and lifted her and put her gently on the bed.

"Mind my rose," she cried.

"Nothing will happen to it." He unpinned the rose and put it close to the ones on the table. "You can wear it later." He began to undress her, ritualistically, feeding his eyes on her superb body, marvelling at the beauty, the exquisiteness of every part of it – her firm rounded breasts, just enough without being superfluous; her taut and flat belly with a button of a navel; her velvety thighs; and her shins, ankles and feet that looked so smooth and delicate. With his mind inflamed by the sight, his male body hot like a forge and his heart beating hard, like the *ikoro* drum, Eloka was waging a losing battle against his vaunting desire. But, he had to do things right; he had to act in a manner that would never provoke regret or guilt. He had to be sure he was on the right course. Ginika lay quiescent, gazing into his eyes with all the love her soul had reserved for this man, and he knew she was ready to go all the way.

"Have you ever thought or dreamed of getting married? Have you ever desired to be yoked to a man for the rest of your life?" he asked as he bent over her and kissed her soft lips.

"Yes, I'll want to get married to the right man and have

children after graduating from the university – at least that was my dream before the war," she said. "I hoped one day I would marry a man I adore and have children." She shrugged, thinking about the war and wondering what would become of her dream of a good education and a family of her own, someday.

He lifted his head, and with her body stretched before him in all its glory, he said, "Can I fit into that dream? All I'm saying is I love you and want to be that man you adore. Mermaid, will you marry me?"

In that state of nudeness, and with her eyes shining, Ginika nodded. "Yes, I will marry you, Eloka. You're the only man I have ever loved. If you want to marry me today or tomorrow, I'm ready. You have the qualities I admire and want my man to have."

He paused. "What are these qualities?"

She laughed. "You're intelligent and confident and you are someone who can listen. I like your strength of character, your individualism; you are not worried about what people say or think."

He sighed, as joy flooded his heart. He felt like lifting her up and dancing round the room with her, but he thought better of it. His Mermaid was gazing at him, radiant and telling him things with her eyes. Her shyness had gone because she had surrendered her body to him just as he had surrendered his to her. His heart ached with love as he looked at her and saw the soft and artless expression in her eyes, which he could only interpret as deep and sincere affection for him. With his eyes still on her, he began to remove his clothes. He pulled down his pants and discarded his shirt, winking at her. He smiled because of the way she stared at him. From the expression of wonder in her eyes, he knew she had never seen the naked body of a man in her life. As he stood before her, completely nude, her eyes shifted upward and met his. Eloka laughed when he saw her eyes widen with an expression he thought was a mixture of astonishment, fascination and terror. He slipped into bed with her and with a movement that was almost rough he pulled her to him and held her close. She responded for a while and then tried to push him away.

"I'm afraid, Eloka. I have not done it before."

"I know, sweetheart. But there is no need to be afraid. I'll be gentle."

"How did you know I haven't done it before?"

He laughed. "Everything you've been doing betrays it. Even your eyes."

He put his mouth on hers to stop further speech from either of them. The kisses they gave each other ignited a flame that engulfed them. She panted and clung to him, even as his fevered and moist lips set out on a passionate journey from her mouth down the smooth road of her neck. Enticed by the firm swell of her breasts, his lips paid homage to each honeyed fruit from Nature's own garden. Her body swooned as his lips progressed to the flat terrain of her belly. Then he held her close and pledged to cherish and protect her. The climax was so intense and poignant that the wrench caused little or no anguish; her terror emptied in great delight.

As they lay in bed, she with her head on his shoulder, he knew he loved this woman, and his feeling for her was like a consuming fire, which would burn any obstacle in the way of his claiming and possessing her. At last, he thought, he had found his other half.

LATER, ELOKA took Ginika home to meet his family for the first time. Now that he was sure they loved each other, he was ready to introduce her to his parents. He had not introduced any woman to them before as his girlfriend, so he knew her presence would excite them and cause them to raise the issue of marriage again. Well, he had shifted ground and was prepared to listen to his father. He wanted to get married, as his parents had suggested, but for a different reason. They wanted grandchildren, but he did not want to have a child at this time. He was not going to marry her so that she could give him a baby now; perhaps after the war, they would start a family. He wanted to marry her because he loved her and wanted her for keeps. He wanted to share his life with her and to share hers. It was not his idea to use her and dump her, as many men were doing to women in Biafra. He didn't just want a win-the-war wife, as men flippantly referred to women they were sleeping with, without commitment. And many girls slept around with men out of frustration or need. She was too precious and besides, it was not his habit or style to treat a woman that way.

"What are you thinking about?" she asked, stroking his moustache.

They were walking down the main road that led to the Orie Market. Ama-Oyi had changed much since the air raid that caused the death of hundreds of people and the amputation of many limbs.

"I'm thinking of you. Is there any other thing I do from morning till night except to think of you? Maybe I should join the army to keep busy, now we are finished with the plays."

He turned and smiled down at her. She looked so pretty in her brown skirt and pink blouse. The red rose he had specially chosen for her was pinned to her blouse and looked a bit wilted. "What did you do with the rest of the roses?"

"I put them in a vase half-filled with water to keep them fresh for as long as possible. You were deep asleep and I let you have your beauty sleep. You didn't even know when I pulled the sheet from under you."

He had seen her removing the blood-stained sheet. "I knew when you removed it, but acted as if I was asleep." He smiled.

"Eh? You saw me and said nothing? Naughty man!" She averted her eyes, so that he did not see what lay in their depth.

"I saw it, Mermaid. You're so sweet and pure." He took her hand and lifted it to his lips. "What would I do if I left you and went into the army?"

"Don't talk of going into the army unless you want to kill me," she cried. "My brother is there and you want to leave me?"

"A man has to keep busy at this time. Biafra needs all her young men to defend her."

"There are other things you could do to serve Biafra."

"Like what?"

"You could work in the Refugee Office or the Procurement and Supply Unit. We could perform the play in other places, in other towns, not just in barracks; we can use it to raise money for the execution of the war."

"No, I think the time for acting plays is over. Don't you see things are changing and getting grimmer? How do you even get vehicles to take the cast to the towns or villages to perform? I'm glad we did well while it lasted. The performance at Eleven Division – 11 Div, as they call it – in Nnewi was very good. You were exceptional. I was afraid the Commander was going to take you away as his woman. He kept looking at you."

Ginika burst into laughter. "I would have resisted if he had tried."

"Would you have been able? You know they take any woman they want – that's what I heard."

"God forbid it! Is that what they do? It was good there. Our *Gbapee* Dance was so good. The music set the whole town on fire and people were running out to see us as we sang and beat our drums and *udu* in the military truck that drove us round the town to announce our presence. I think that was why we had such a big audience in the barracks and also in Nnewi Town Hall, don't you?" She broke into a song, dancing a few steps, with him laughing softly as he watched her.

> *Gbapee, gbapee, gbapee*
> *Onye obuna gbapere ayi uzo*
> *Na ayi na-abia – eee!*
> *Gbapee, gbapee, gbapee*
> *Gbapere ayi uzo*
> *Na ayi na-abia – eee!*
> [Open, open, open
> Everybody, open wide the door
> For we are coming – eee!
> Open, open, open
> Open wide the door
> For we are coming – eee!]

When she came to the end of the song, he clapped his hands and said, "Bravo! I agree completely with your observation.

Our performance at 11 Div raised the morale of the officers and men and helped them to destroy the large convoy of Nigerian soldiers at Abagana, the following week. I heard that the Abagana invasion was the most ambitious the vandals had undertaken since the war started. Had they succeeded, the war would have ended in a matter of days and they would have overrun our forces between Awka and Nnewi and connected with their forces at the western side of the River Niger. This would have meant the end of the war. 11 Div saved the day; they did wonders, and with little ammunition."

Ginika nodded. "It was reported that they captured a huge consignment of armament that would last till the end of the war, even if the war lasted another one or two years."

"Ha! I don't know about that, but I heard it was substantial. I'm glad we helped in a little way to motivate our soldiers." So many rumours flew around and one didn't know which was false and which was factual, he thought. Rumour mongering was part of the scourge of war affecting everyone.

"I think so," she agreed. "*Mammy Wota* is a good play with themes that are relevant to our situation in this war and this is why people like it so much. Eloka, you are a genius. Who, except those who know you, would believe you, an engineer, wrote the play and directed it?"

He laughed. "I'm not an engineer yet."

"Almost," she replied.

He smiled and returned to discussing their performance. "What do you think of the performance at the Air Force Base in Ekwulobia?"

"I think it was also good. I liked the Commanding Officer; his humour was infectious. And he looked so distinguished in his uniform. Why did they all wear uniform, even in the night?"

"I guess because they had to be ready in case of emergency or enemy attack. I think they wear it all the time. Didn't you hear that since the Uga Airstrip was constructed and the air base opened at Ekwulobia, this area has become a war front and a target for the enemy planes? We should expect more air raids in Ama-Oyi, which is not far from Ekwulobia."

"We were very lucky to stage the plays the time we did. Refugees from Awka occupied the entire primary school compound the week we finished our rehearsals, as if they were waiting for us. Where would we have had the rehearsals?"

"Ama-Oyi is now a major town in Biafra; as big towns are evacuated, small ones take their place. There are many refugees here; where will our people find food to feed them or sell to them? My father is the chairman of the Ama-Oyi Local Council and oversees the refugee camp and all matters pertaining to the war in the town. He was appointed to this position when he returned to Ama-Oyi after the fall of Port Harcourt."

"It cannot be an easy task."

He laughed. "For him it is. He likes to be in authority and to be busy. He was idle for a while after his return, but now he has some work to do."

"By the way, is it not the one people call 'Chop-and-go Council'? Mama Nnukwu, my uncle's wife, calls it *Olokara Kansul* because, according to her, members of the council embezzle funds meant for executing the war and steal relief materials meant for the refugees. I almost died of laughter when I first heard the phrase – *Olokara Kansul* – as if the councillors grasped and swallowed everything within their reach. Our people have a sense of humour, I tell you. But, do you think she is right?"

Eloka laughed. "People will say anything. I don't think she is right because I have not seen my father bringing in loads of relief material to the house. But whether other members of the council do it, I have no idea." He had heard such stories about people in authority stealing things entrusted to them. It's disheartening for ordinary people who suffer most in the war, he thought. He would mention it to his father for him to know what people were saying about his council.

They approached a checkpoint manned by three civil defence officials – a young woman and two men. One of the men stood near the heavy pole that formed a barrier before which every driver or cyclist had to stop and be questioned and searched. People walking past could also be halted and queried if they looked suspicious enough to be considered saboteurs. The woman and the second man sat on a bench, by the side of the road, chatting in a lively manner. Eloka and Ginika greeted them and passed.

"I was trained as a special constable in Mbano, you know, but have never put the skill to use except the short period I engaged in training others. I must find a way of being useful in Ama-Oyi now we have finished with the play."

He understood her point: they had to find ways to keep busy. It was embarrassing to think of those fighting in the various fronts while he was still at home doing little. The play had been a good excuse to remain in Ama-Oyi, but what would happen now that phase was past? However, a new phase of his life had just begun with her occupying his mind twenty-four hours a day in the past three weeks. He would think later, but for the moment he wanted to be enthralled by nothing outside her sweet embrace. "Mermaid, we'll think of things to do to keep busy, but let's enjoy each other's company now."

"Good talk: do I take it that I'll hear no more about someone going into the army?" she teased.

"Don't count on it." He laughed. "How is your father doing in his new hospital?" he asked, changing the subject.

"I don't know. He has not come home since his transfer. He sent Monday to bring some money to me the other day. But from what I heard, the hospital is not far from the war front."

"And your stepmother? Where is she?"

"I haven't the faintest idea. Nobody has told me anything. When Monday came, I wasn't at home, so I lost the opportunity to get information from him. It was Udo who received the money he had brought for me."

At a bend, they turned left and the road became wider and smoother. A double row of oil-bean trees, evenly spaced out, graced this portion of the road. At the end of the road was a storey building with a tall gate. A flower bed bloomed on either side of the gate.

"That's our house." He pointed. "I told you it is not far from yours."

"This distance is not far? We have been walking for nearly an hour." She glanced at her watch.

"It's because we were just strolling. We would have reached home long ago if we had walked faster."

"I hope your girlfriend is not there waiting for you? If she is, let me turn and go back home." Her expression was teasing and mocking all at once.

He turned quickly to look at her face, his teeth gleaming in the sun. "Who is my girlfriend?"

"Are you asking me?"

"Yes, you tell me since you know her." He grabbed her hand.

"You know her, Njide. The way she was acting throughout the rehearsals and performances as if she owned you."

"Did I respond as if she owned me?"

"Are you asking me? I want you to tell me what she is to you."

He detected some seriousness in her voice that demanded attention; he understood that he needed not only to reassure her, but also to let her know the truth. "There is nothing serious between Njide and me. We are just friends. I'm not in love with her; I treat her as I would any female acquaintance. I like her because she is committed to the Ama-Oyi Students' Association and was vital to the success of our drama project. I'm really grateful to her and for her contribution. She handled the costume and make-up aspects very well. But, that's all. It was nothing personal. Have I answered your question, Mermaid?" The relief he saw in her eyes assured him he had done the right thing, and that she was satisfied.

"Well, yes, but I just couldn't understand why she was so hostile to me. Remember we were classmates and had got on well at school. I noticed she countered whatever I said especially when I tried to contribute ideas about improving the dance. Eunice, the lead dancer taught me privately and I was able to catch up rapidly. It was Eunice who told me one evening when we were practising in our house that Njide said I stole her boyfriend from her. And I said to Eunice, 'How did I steal her boyfriend?' Eunice replied that Njide had complained that since I returned to Ama-Oyi, you had not looked at her nor visited her, that all your attention was focused on me."

Eloka shook his head and said nothing. She continued, "I avoided her thereafter, and would not allow her to make up my face before any performance, for I was afraid she might stab my eyes with the eye liner or mascara brush, and pretend it was an accident."

Eloka turned and gave her a wide look and then burst into laughter.

"You may laugh if you like, but I'm a woman and know what an angry and jealous woman can do." Her voice was cool. Then she too laughed.

"The gate is open," he said, steering her towards it. "Welcome to my home, Mermaid."

AFTER ELOKA had taken Ginika home, he returned to find his parents waiting eagerly for him in the sitting room. His father had a satisfied expression in his eyes. His bulky body which had lost some weight – though not enough to be noticed by anyone who did not know him before – since after the fall of Port Harcourt, shifted and turned to his only son. His mother's eyes shone, as if she had poured sparkling eye drops into them.

"*Nna*, welcome back. I'm glad you returned quickly because I am dying to tell you how happy I am." She followed him with her eyes as he entered and walked toward them.

"My son, you don't know how happy you have made us by introducing the girl you want to marry to us. Is this not what I have been long waiting for you to do or allow me to help you to do? I am happy you have made your choice yourself; it is better that way, I think. We will not waste time in approaching her family, I assure you. Before you know it, you two will be man and wife. War or no war." He beamed at him.

Eloka smiled, and continued towards the staircase with the intention to return to his room.

"Eloka, don't go yet; we want to have a few words with you," his father added.

"*Nna, cherenu*, wait; sit down a moment," his mother implored.

Without saying anything, Eloka sat down on a chair near the foot of the stairs.

His father smiled. "You chose well, my son. She is beautiful and young. I can see she has not been spoilt. When I see the way girls run after soldiers, especially officers, I cry in my heart. What will happen to them if this war lasts long? I wonder. I am happy our Ijeamasi is safely married now to the man from Ekwulobia. As for Ozioma, I am watching her. If I see her doing *fim*, I will marry her off too."

Eloka frowned and began to say something, but changed his mind.

"Yes, she seems a good girl. We will make enquiries to ensure she comes from a good family: the type of home we would want our daughter-in-law to come from."

"You can make enquiries, if you like," Eloka said, "but I would like to marry her as soon as possible."

"*Nna*, that is all right." His mother's eyes were soft and bright. "I agree the girl is very beautiful. I hope she is well mannered. *Agwa bu nma*, character is beauty. Let us hope she has a good character."

"Can I go now?" he asked. Sometimes he felt like walking out of his home and going somewhere else to live.

"Yes." His father waved a plump hand whose fingers sported two rings – one made of gold, the other silver.

18

Ginika was thankful to her *chi*, her guardian angel, for the wisdom in her request that Eloka should turn towards home at her gate and not follow her into the house. He had protested, arguing that he wanted to make sure she got into the house safely, but she had insisted on his not coming into the compound. They had reached a compromise; he stood in front of the gate, in the twilight, waiting until she had slipped into the compound and shut the gate before he waved to her and sauntered off. She had waved back, missing him already, and wishing they were already married so that they could be together always. Then she froze. In the corner of the wall, very close to Dr Ndefo's immobilised Mercedes, stood her father's white Peugeot 403. Ginika trembled. Her father was home.

As she moved forward, her astonishment increased when she saw a van parked by the left side of the compound, under the orange tree. She wondered if the rest of the family had returned with him – Auntie Lizzy and Monday.

"Sister Ginika, welcome. Uncle is here with the others." Udo gave her a knowing look, which she understood meant that her father was angry with her for not being at home. "He asked where you went to, but I said I didn't know." He walked to the van and lifted out something that looked like a heavy suitcase in the poor light; she couldn't see it clearly. So they had come home for good, she thought? They had brought their things in the van. She hoped they had brought the few things she had left in Mbano – her books in particular.

"Monday, what are you doing? Have all the loads been brought from the car and the van?" Ginika heard Auntie Lizzy's voice, as garrulous as ever. She shivered. Irritating days were coming, she thought.

"Welcome, Auntie Lizzy," she greeted, as her stepmother emerged from the house and entered the veranda.

"Ginika, where have you been? Can you please assist? The luggage has to be moved into the house. The driver insists on returning to Oko this night."

Ginika looked at her and nodded. Auntie Lizzy looked rather unkempt. She was a caricature of her usual well-manicured and neatly-dressed self. "What's happened, Auntie Lizzy? You look tired."

"You are asking me what has happened. You should thank God your father and I escaped with our lives. The enemy entered Alaoma this morning, and we had to run for our lives. They shelled the town for hours before they moved in, but we left immediately the shells began to land. The hospital moved to Oko. It was a miracle we were able to find fuel to bring the car and the van here, at a high cost, of course. We bought the fuel and stored it when we suspected the enemy would strike soon." She shook her head. "But, why am I talking to you about this now? Please, join Monday, Udo and the driver to clear the van."

"Is it not better that I leave them to clear the van, then I could get some food ready for you and Papa? Aren't you hungry?"

Auntie Lizzy grimaced. "Ah, did we have time to think of food? We were more concerned with our safety. Okay, go and prepare something for us. Where are the lanterns? Light them and bring one here. Your father will need one upstairs." As Ginika hurried away to comply, she called her back. "What do you have in the house? What do you want to cook?"

Ginika hesitated, remembering there was not much food left. They had been managing on as little as a tuber of yam and sometimes ate in Mama Nnukwu's or Akueju's house. "We have some yams and beans."

"We brought some rice. Take some of it and prepare jollof rice. We also brought some tomatoes and fish; take some of that too." She then went into the sitting room and lowered her bulky frame into a chair.

Ginika was thankful that neither her father nor Auntie Lizzy saw Eloka. They would surely meet him soon, but she would not have liked it if they had met him this night. Her father was talking to Mrs Ndefo in front of her room, close to the door that led to the kitchen, when Ginika reached there.

As soon as he saw her, he turned squarely, facing her. "Ginikanwa, where are you coming from at this time?"

"Welcome, Papa. I went to see a friend."

"Who is the friend?" His face was completely bereft of the smile it had donned when he was speaking to Mrs Ndefo.

Ginika wished he would not start his inquisition this day of all days when she was so happy. He wouldn't even respond to her greeting, and she had wanted to tell him how pleased she was to see him safe, after escaping from Alaoma with his life, the car and the other things they had brought in the van.

"Papa, you have not met the person." She looked at his face, pouting.

"Does the person not have a name?" he asked, irritated.

"Ubaka, why are you insisting?" Mrs Ndefo laughed, throwing back her shaggy head. Her hair was not pulled back and confined at the nape of her neck with a band, as was her custom. She looked bigger than she was in the bulky housecoat she wore and stood outside her door while Ubaka leaned on the wall opposite. "Let her go, please, and continue with your story, which is so interesting. What happened to the refugees in Alaoma? Do you know where they moved to? One of Ufo's two sisters was sheltering there with her children. I wonder where next they'll find shelter at the rate Biafra is shrinking."

Ginika saw her father's anger evaporate, as he turned back to Mrs Ndefo. She breathed her gratitude to her for coming to the rescue and dashed into the kitchen.

THE NEXT day, Ginika woke up early and prepared breakfast for everyone. Monday and Udo helped her. She was pleased to see Monday again and was cheered by his infectious humour.

"*Daa* Ginika, you did not ask me about my *capenta* work?" He grinned from ear to ear. He was mixing *akamu* in a big bowl.

Udo, who was slicing yam and ripe plantain, stopped and looked at Monday, and then began to laugh. "You are talking of carpentry work, Monday. Wait until the army boys see you. They will conscript you and you will go to the front to do carpentry work. Maybe you will make coffins for them there."

"*Chei*, hear what this small boy is saying," Monday cried. "I was not even talking to him."

"Udo, shut your mouth. How can you make such jokes?

Look at you. You think boys of fourteen like you cannot fight in the army?" Ginika glared at him. She was frying some of the pieces of plantain Udo had already cut. The plantain sizzled in the hot oil and exuded a delicious smell.

"Sorry, Sister Ginika."

"It's Monday you should apologise to, not me."

"Sorry, Monday." Udo started to slice the plantain again.

"Monday, tell me, what happened to your carpentry work?" she asked softly.

Monday hesitated before answering. "I wanted to tell you I was able to complete the training before *Oga* was transferred from Mbano. I am now a whole *capenta*," he announced with pride, turning to Udo, as if challenging him to jeer if he dared.

"Well done, Monday. That's good. You may use your skill even in this wartime, who knows? I am sure there are chairs in the house you can help us to mend. You may even charge people in Ama-Oyi to repair things for them and make some money."

He smiled. "After the war, I will open my own *capenta* workshop."

They had set the table when her father came down with Auntie Lizzy. Ginika greeted them. "Good morning, Papa. Auntie Lizzy, good morning. I hope you slept well?"

"As well as anyone could at this terrible time," her father replied, taking his usual seat at the head of the table.

Auntie Lizzy sat at the other end of the long table. She was still in her night-dress, but wore a dressing-gown over it. "Good morning. The food smells nice. It is good to be home; I hope I will not have to move again before the war ends. I am tired of moving from one town to another." She poured some *akamu* into her plate and helped herself from the plates containing fried yam and plantain.

Ginika and Udo waited until her father and Auntie Lizzy had served themselves, before they took their own food. Monday had either disappeared to the small room near the store where he slept to have his own breakfast or he was eating it in the kitchen.

"Udo, when you finish, get water ready for my bath," Auntie Lizzy instructed, as she got up to return to her room. "I feel lazy this morning and will have a long rest in bed after my bath."

Her father nodded, and wiped his mouth with a table napkin. Ginika felt her family was blessed to still live in their home – and what a comfortable home – when many people had lost their homes and were living in refugee camps. Ama-Oyi people were lucky that their homeland was in the heartland of Biafra, she reflected, chewing her fried plantain slowly and savouring the *akamu*, which she spooned into her mouth from time to time. Though there was no sugar to sweeten it, it was delicious all the same, especially as it was taken with fried plantain, which was so sweet. She glanced at her father and saw that he was in a good mood. Should she speak to him about Eloka and their plan to get married? Eloka had asked her to let him know as soon as her father came to Ama-Oyi. He said he would like to speak with him on the issue of marriage, and that his people would come to see her people as soon as her father was around. How would he take it? Whatever his reaction, she needed to let him know before Eloka came to see him to save him the shock of hearing it for the first time from him.

As soon as her father climbed the stairs to his room, she pursued him there. She knocked.

"Enter, the door is open," he said, and when she was inside, "Ginikanwa, what is it?"

Her courage almost failed her, but she was not going to return downstairs or go to her room without having her say. "Papa, there is something I want to discuss with you," she blurted out, her pulse racing.

"Sit down." When she was seated, her hands folded and resting on her knees, her face glued to his, in his spacious bedroom, "What is it?" in a voice that was not altogether abrasive, but not cordial either. A voice that was even and flat, like the bottom of a valley.

He sat on the bed, his face expressionless.

"Papa, I want to get married." She saw him flinch, as if she had struck his face, and continued immediately, "A man from Ama-Oyi has proposed to me and I want to marry him…"

He allowed her to go no further. "Are you out of your mind, Ginikanwa? Who is this man? Have you forgotten your education, and will you not return to school when the war ends?"

"But when will the war end? No one knows? So how can one wait for something one doesn't even know when it will end or if it will end at all? But, even if the war ends, there will be no problem, for two of us have agreed that we'll both return to school." Her gaze was bold, unwavering. She could see he was surprised at what he might consider her boldness or forwardness.

"I will not like you to get married at this time. Think of your life – what this disruption will mean to you in the next few years. No, I cannot support you in this madness. Who is the man, anyway?"

"Eloka Odunze, the son of Chief Ofodum Odunze."

"The name rings a bell. Where did I hear this name?" He was puzzled.

"He is the president of Ama-Oyi Students' Association and was studying engineering at Nsukka before the war."

"You want to marry a student? Can he take care of you? How old is he anyway to want to get married?"

"He's about twenty-five."

"Ginikanwa, you should forget this so-called marriage and keep yourself busy until the war ends, and you return to school. This is all I want to say on the matter."

They sat for a while in silence. She knew he expected her to accept his words as final and leave his room, but she had not finished yet. "Papa, I have made up my mind to marry him. I love him very much. Please, do not stop me. If anything happens, you should not blame me." She observed his face twitch, as a gust of anxiety blew over his eyes, clouding them.

"What do you mean? Has he touched you?" His voice was ominous.

She stared at him. "Yes, he has touched me, but he did not force me."

She watched his face collapse like a mud wall sodden with many years' rain. For a moment, he battled with his emotion. When he lifted his face, his eyes were still like a stagnant pond, like something dead. "Only a few weeks you were left alone and you messed yourself up, Ginikanwa. How can you explain this unforgivable act? After all I did to keep you upright. You have disappointed me."

She was touched by the degree and depth of his devastation, and wondered if she had done right in telling him what she had done. Should she have kept that aspect a secret only known to her and Eloka? It was too late to withdraw it. "Papa, I'm sorry if I disappointed you, but you have nothing to fear. Eloka and I love each other very much. All we want is your blessing."

"*Si ebea puo*, leave my room." His words, spoken in Ama-Oyi dialect, sounded so final that she got up immediately to take her leave. She heard a slight noise from Auntie Lizzy's room which adjoined her father's and was connected to it by a narrow door. She was almost certain Auntie Lizzy had been eavesdropping. She hesitated, then turned and left the room.

But her feet froze on the threshold, as raised voices assaulted the air on the ground floor. Ginika could hear Auntie Lizzy's harsh voice shouting and Mrs Ndefo's quieter voice responding in strong terms. She knew then it was not Auntie Lizzy who had made the sound she heard earlier; it was someone else in her room who had eavesdropped – perhaps Udo or Monday – but it didn't matter anyway. The shouting downstairs seemed to be getting out of hand; she hurried away.

"If you cannot manage, then leave," Auntie Lizzy raged. "Imagine, I should not say what should happen in my own house? Who are you? *Esi be gi eje b'onye?* Whose house does your house lead to? Whether you are from America or from London, you cannot do as you like in this house. And let me tell you: you had better make your children behave well. Did you give them any training at all? They are rude, forward and lazy."

As Ginika ran down the stairs, she heard Mrs Ndefo reply indignantly, "You can't talk to me like this; you insult me. Is it because I live in your house? I can't exchange words with you – you're shameless. I don't blame you. You talk to me because you find me in your house in this godforsaken village."

"Why do you not return to your home? What are you doing here? Others like you are in refugee camps. Are you not grateful to live in a house like this? Do not allow me to open my mouth."

Ginika was shocked to see the hate in Auntie Lizzy's face as she stood in the space between the kitchen and the door leading into the house. Her face looked distorted and grim as words flew out of her mouth like a palm kernel cracking machine in full motion. Mrs Ndefo stood outside her door, as if she would scurry back into the room where she burrowed all day, like a squirrel. Two of her children flanked her, the other four stood outside, not far from Auntie Lizzy.

"Please, don't speak to my mom like that," Amaka said, her eyes blazing. "Is it because you don't have children of your own that you abuse us?"

Auntie Lizzy trembled, her chest heaving; she had a *wrappa* tied above her breasts and a towel draped across her shoulders. It seemed she had come out of the bathroom before the argument developed. She lunged forward to slap Amaka, but Ginika grabbed her around the waist.

"Auntie Lizzy, please, calm down." Ginika clung to her.

"Leave me, Ginika. Get your hands off me. Did you hear what this *ochicha*, this cockroach said? I'm going to teach her a lesson."

Ginika sighed as her father arrived and roared. "What is happening here? What is the matter?" Silence reigned, dominated the air. "Lizzy, what is the problem? Why are you shouting?"

Mrs Ndefo broke down and wept. "Ubaka, your wife has said terrible things to me. No one has spoken to me like this all my life."

"Carol, please, calm down. I will handle this. I am really sorry that you have had to go through this." He touched her shoulder and patted it.

Ginika watched her father comfort the distraught woman,

and was pleased he did not support Auntie Lizzy; no matter what Mrs Ndefo had done, it was wrong to speak to her like that. She glanced at Auntie Lizzy who hissed and stormed into the house, straight up the stairs and into her room.

Mrs Ndefo wiped her eyes with the handkerchief Amaka gave her. She tried to explain. "She was angry with the children and said they were wasting the water in the tank." Her voice was steadier now. "I heard her voice and came out to find out what the matter was. She was fuming and asked if we thought the water in the underground tank was tap water that ran without stopping, and was this why we used water as if it would not finish. She said from today my children should go to the stream to fetch water. She was going to lock the tank and not allow us to use it. As I tried to calm her down, she told me my children have no manners, that they dirty the house and make noise all the time. She said so many things I don't remember. That's all." She blew her nose noisily into the handkerchief.

"I'm sorry about what happened. I will talk to Lizzy, but you might also get the children to make less noise."

Mrs Ndefo nodded. "Thanks, Ubaka." She turned and entered her prison, as Ginika referred to Mrs Ndefo's room whenever she discussed the family with Eloka.

GINIKA WENT up to her room to reflect on her encounter with her father. She wanted to be alone. What was she going to do? She would have to tell Eloka and they would plan together how to get round the obstacle that was her father. She lay on her back across her bed, staring at the ceiling. Her frenetic mind settled next on her teacher, Miriam Taylor. What would she think if she heard that she wanted to get married? Would she approve? She had asked her the last time they met each other always to think of finishing her education no matter how long the war lasted.

But marrying Eloka would not stop her education; in fact, it would aid it. Eloka had promised they would not have children until after the war. He also said that when the war ended she could take the qualifying exam and go straight to Nsukka because Nsukka had a programme that admitted candidates with O' Level subjects, unlike the other universities which admitted only candidates with A' Levels. And if she was admitted to Nsukka, then they would be together as they studied. What could be better than this – they would be happily married now and if they survived the war, they would still be together? She couldn't understand why her father would want to oppose such a good thing.

A cry reached her from downstairs and she thought Auntie Lizzy was angry with somebody again. But, the cry sounded like jubilation and it was Udo's voice, not Auntie Lizzy's. Ginika heard the sound of feet running upstairs; it was Udo, taking the steps two at a time. "Brother Nwakire is here! Brother Nwakire is here! Brother Nwakire has come home!"

Ginika yanked her door open and raced downstairs with the speed of wind. She met him at the foot of the stairs, about to mount them. She hurtled into his arms and he had to exert all his energy to break the impact of her cannonball of a body.

"Oh, Kire, my darling brother, I'm so happy to see you alive." She laughed, shouted, wept and danced. She was beside herself with joy. She pulled back, examined him from his head to his feet, as if to make sure he was the one and that he had no wound or disfigurement in his body. He wore a camouflage uniform, the type most army officers wore, and he looked so striking and handsome. The 'Rising Sun' symbol was embossed on his uniform, on his shoulder, and his rank was prominently displayed also on each shoulder, close to the symbol. "The sign of the rising sun," she murmured, touching the bright yellow symbol. "Biafra is our rising sun, the newest nation on earth." Her voice was reverential. With eyes that sparkled, she gazed at his new beard. "Wow, you have grown a beard, like His Excellency?" She laughed.

"Well, I admire him, but the beard grew because I didn't have time to shave."

"Eh, are you so busy you cannot shave?" she asked incredulously. "Do you see His Excellency often?"

"No. There is no way he can visit all the soldiers, but I have seen him twice. First, when we passed out, after our training, he was there. I remember his words as he challenged us to give our very best and as he tried to stir us to fight well because most of us were going straight into battle from training. He said, 'Everything we do in life echoes in eternity. The evil men do lives after them, as Shakespeare said. But I tell you, fellow Biafrans, the good work men do lives after them too. Do your best and forever be remembered by our people.' The second time, he came to thank us after a major battle in which we were successful. Among other things, he said, 'I would like to say thank you to all of you, officers and men. I'm proud of you.' We were touched. His humility and sense of duty are admired by many people in the armed forces. He has a capacity to motivate and encourage people."

"I'm so glad you got a pass to come home," she said; there

was a soft light in her eyes, as she continued to look at him.

"Ginika, I have prayed for this day." His voice was laden with emotion.

"Yes, me too." She hugged him again. "Oh, Kire, welcome home. These my eyes that have seen you again will never go blind. But, why do I keep you here standing?"

She looked up the stairs and saw her father coming down slowly, staring at Nwakire, as if he were a ghost. She understood he had thought Nwakire was dead and might have agonised over it, but, as always, he had not breathed his thoughts or fears to anyone and carried the burden all alone.

"Nwakire," he called. "This is you?"

"Papa, it's me. I've come home to visit you. I was given a pass and I'm here at last." He laughed. They embraced.

Ginika could hardly hide her astonishment. Was it her father embracing Nwakire? He must have missed him, terribly, she thought. She looked away from them and looked round. Udo stood by the corner, smiling, while Monday had a cherubic expression on his face. Mrs Ndefo and her children hovered at the entrance to their rooms, still cowed by Auntie Lizzy's attack.

"Carol, this is Nwakire, my son, who is in the army," her father said, turning to Mrs Ndefo.

"Welcome," she murmured, smiling broadly, but when she saw Auntie Lizzy coming down the stairs, she withdrew into her room, like a snail that sensed the presence of its enemy.

"Nwakire, welcome," Auntie Lizzy cried, embracing him. "He is an officer now." She laughed.

They all trooped into the sitting room to hear his story. Auntie Lizzy asked Monday to go and prepare some food for him. Ginika saw how crestfallen Monday was, and knew he wanted to hang around and listen to Nwakire talk about his experience in the army.

LATER, AFTER everyone had gone to bed, Ginika knocked on Nwakire's door and waited. As soon as she heard "Come in" she turned the door handle and went in. He was expecting her. His room had been swept and a fresh sheet spread on the bed.

"How wonderful it is to be home and to lie on a decent and comfortable bed! Gini, thanks for making my room beautiful."

"You deserve to be pampered," she murmured. "When last did we see you? And you said you're here for only three days?" When he nodded, she continued, "Then we must do all in our power to make you happy, to make the three days memorable. I hope you'll be able to see Auntie Chito. She'll be angry and hurt if you don't visit her before you go back. And Nne, our grandmother, will be so pleased to see you; she asks after you each time I go to see her. She's been staying with Auntie Chito since Uncle Ray left home. You must see them."

"I'll definitely see them before I leave. But where did Uncle Ray go? You said he left home."

"Auntie Chito is lonely and worried because Uncle Ray went away to work in the Directorate of Military Intelligence. I think he's in Ikot Ekpene or Abak or somewhere near there. I go to keep her company whenever I can."

He lay on the bed. She saw his uniform folded and placed on the table. She sat on a chair which she had pulled close to the bed to be near him. She smiled painfully, as she remembered the times Auntie Lizzy pulled her away from Nwakire's room when they were growing up, shouting, "You silly girl, you are too close to this your brother. Stay in your room. I don't want to find you always in his room, either sitting on the chair or lying on his bed. Okay?" Ginika would recoil, and scream as Auntie Lizzy dragged her away. It went on until she entered secondary school at twelve.

"Where did you do your training as an officer?" she asked, gazing at him.

"We were trained in Orlu. The training camp is at Bishop Shanahan College (BSC)."

"Were you many? And how long did the training last?"

"Why do you want to know all this? Do you want to join the army too? If you do, Papa will have a heart attack."

They roared with laughter.

"Kire, I'm serious. I want to know."

"Okay, Your Majesty," he teased, "but if you want to know our secrets, you will get nothing from me concerning that."

"Oh, no, not secrets, just information about life in the army."

"Okay. We were many and were trained for three months before we passed out and got commissioned. I started as a Second Lieutenant, but now I'm a Lieutenant."

"Was the training difficult? Did they drive you hard?"

"Very difficult; we were driven too hard. Sometimes one felt like running away, but one had to endure. We were put through many endurance tests and exercises. I survived. I'm in Mgbirichi now, but my battalion could move from there any time. You're not sure of anything; you obey orders." He laughed. "Now tell me about yourself; what has been happening to you?" he gazed at her. "You look well; in fact, you are blooming. What's the secret? I hope my little sister has not been swept off her feet by a Prince Charming?" He was teasing her outrageously, but she enjoyed it. She thought she would give anything to see him periodically like this to know he was all right.

"What a magician you are!" she said softly. "Or is it a wizard?" She gazed into his eyes. "Kire, you are right. I'm in love and want to get married."

"What? Are you serious? Who is this man who has captured the heart of my sister? He must be special." He sat up, looking steadily at her.

"Indeed, he is. You may even know him; he's Eloka Odunze, who was studying engineering at Nsukka before the war. He's about twenty-five. Kire, I want you to give us your support. Papa objects to my marrying him."

"What's his reason?" he asked carefully.

"He said I should wait for the war to end and finish my education."

"He's right, Gini. Marriage is a very serious matter and demands commitment. Do you realise this? Don't you think you should wait? If he loves you, he'll wait till the war ends and finish his studies before marrying you." He watched her.

She was silent for a while. Was Nwakire also going to refuse to give his approval? she wondered. She would be shattered if he objected. What he was doing at the moment was to caution and advise her; he was not objecting categorically. Perhaps if he saw how resolute she was, he would give his blessing. What he thought about the issue mattered to her so much.

"Kire, I have made up my mind; I'm already committed

in some special ways and we love each other very much. There is no going back." She shrugged.

For a moment he looked worried. "You're not pregnant, are you?"

"Oh, no, that's not what I mean," she said, shaking her head. She thought she would not give him the impression that they had gone all the way. She still remembered her father's reaction; she couldn't bear to have Nwakire judge her, as her father did.

"Let's end the matter for now. I hope to meet this man before I leave, then I'll give you my final answer. Okay?"

"Yes, I'm sure you'll like him." She glowed.

THREE DAYS after Nwakire returned to Mgbirichi, Monday disappeared. At first, they thought he had gone for a walk, though it was unlike him to go anywhere without telling someone in the house. Ginika needed him to help her to pound *fufu* for lunch, but when he did not come back, she asked Udo to do it.

Auntie Lizzy was upset and said she would deal with him whenever he returned or send him back to wherever he had been. Ginika knew she did not mean what she said because Auntie Lizzy depended on Monday to do so many things for her – wash her clothes, buy things from the market, split fire wood and cook. She could not afford to send him away. But by evening he was not back.

Everyone's annoyance turned to anxiety. Ginika sat with Udo in the veranda, as they watched out for Monday. "I hope he has not been conscripted into the army?" she said. "Every day soldiers visit Ama-Oyi to look for men to conscript. I see them when I'm out." She remembered teasing Eloka the other day when he hurried into the bush as he saw people that looked like soldiers approaching. She would surely go insane if Eloka was conscripted.

"Do you think he went to see his people?" Udo asked. "He could be missing them."

"I don't think so. Mbawsi is very far from here, and it wouldn't be easy for him to get there. There is hardly any transport on the roads."

"Uncle is coming home." Udo pointed, and she turned and saw her father riding an old bicycle into the compound. He had bought it from a bicycle repairer who had a workshop near the market.

Ginika shook her head, as she watched him struggle to negotiate the part of the drive that was covered in loose soil, before he reached the gate. Life had taken a turn for the worse for the family. Unable to find fuel for his car, her father now went to work with a rusty and wobbly bicycle. He had to ride ten kilometres to Oko five days in the week to attend to his medical duties. How long could he sustain this effort? For how long too would he go on? He was not a young man any longer. Ginika sighed.

"Udo, take the bicycle from him into the house." As Udo ran forward, she stood up and waited for her father to enter the house. She shuddered to see the grim look on his face, the sweat-soaked shirt that clung to his body. How haggard he looked, she thought. He had aged rapidly and she blamed the war. It must have been a difficult journey for him with all that sweat, on a cool evening like this.

"Papa, welcome," she greeted, taking his bag in which he

kept some of the vital instruments he always carried with him when he went to work.

"Good afternoon."

She could hear his laboured breathing. She climbed the stairs and he followed her slowly. She had dropped the bag on the table and was leaving his room when he came in.

"Ginikanwa, wait." He opened the bag and took out a brown envelope that looked a bit squeezed. "Read it." he said, stretching his hand towards her.

Her heart missed a beat and she wondered what devastating news the envelope had brought. Her father's countenance warned her that the news was cheerless, though she couldn't be sure as he hardly ever rejoiced visibly or openly when something joyful occurred. With some trepidation, she pulled out the sheet inside and saw it was a leaf from an old exercise book, which had turned brown. She unfolded it and examined it before reading. It was a letter from Monday, written in a smattering of English. Ginika read the letter.

> "*Oga, sir,*
> *I beg you forgive me, but I go join army to follow my mate fight the war. I hope you tell my madam and Daa Ginika that I go fight war. I hope we go meet again after the war. If I die, it is well. If I no die, I thank God. Goodbye, Oga. From your servant. Monday.*"

Ginika slowly put the letter in the envelope and returned it to her father.

"Put it on the table," he said, looking up from the book he was reading.

"Papa, when did you receive the letter? Did he give it to someone to take to you?"

"No, he put it in my bag. He must have put it there last night. I saw it hidden among my papers when I opened my bag this morning, in the hospital." As she turned to leave, he added, "Young people, they are difficult to understand."

Unable to find an appropriate response to his remark, she walked out of the room and went in search of Udo. She found him chatting with Dozie. "Udo, come with me." She took him to the deserted veranda and broke the news to him. "Monday has gone to join the army." She remembered Udo taunting Monday and wondered if this was responsible for his action.

"Monday has gone to join the army?" Udo's voice was subdued. "How did you find out?"

"He wrote a letter and put it in Papa's bag before he left the house. Papa saw it when he got to the hospital this morning. Monday has gone, and he didn't say where."

Ginika was sure he too remembered his remark that had hurt Monday so much as to make him complain about it. Udo's eyes were filled with tears, but he made no sound.

"Why are you crying?" she asked. "It's not your fault. It's his decision. It's okay."

Udo nodded, as a tear dropped on his right cheek and rolled down to the corner of his mouth.

Auntie Lizzy who went to see a friend came upon them in this mood. She stared at Udo first then looked at Ginika. "What has happened? Is Udo crying? What's the matter with him?

When Ginika could put in a word, she replied, "It's Monday; he's gone and joined the army." She watched Auntie Lizzy.

"What are you saying? How did you find out?" She stood

with one leg on the first step and the other leg on the second leading up to the veranda.

"He wrote a letter to Papa."

"*Nwa torotoro*, turkey! He left without even telling me after all I did for him. Imagine that! He has forgotten that I sent him to learn carpentry. What an ingrate. Let him go and join the army. He will die there. Idiot!" She walked past them without another word.

Ginika heard the sound of her heavy steps, as she climbed the stairs.

19

Ama-Oyi was bombed again, but this time only one person was killed. Ginika heard a loud explosion in the night and ran downstairs. She was followed by Udo, her father and Auntie Lizzy.

"Everyone come out and run to the bunker," her father cried. "Carol, are you awake? Bring your children to the bunker."

Mrs Ndefo and her children were already ahead, racing to the bunker at the back of the compound. "We're out already," she called out. Amaka was fumbling with the back door. Udo pushed her aside gently and opened it. The moon was shining faintly, but it provided enough light for them to stumble out.

Ginika heard a scraping sound as someone – was it Udo? – dragged away the iron sheet that was used to cover the entrance to the bunker to prevent snakes from crawling inside. It was not easy to get into the bunker, with everyone bumping into everyone else. They were afraid to light a lamp because they thought the plane would see the light and drop a bomb on them.

Ginika heard the sound of a plane receding in the distance until it petered out. She was trembling.

"I think they have gone," her father said, "Let us return to the house."

"So it's going to be night raids now? O Lord, what kind of life is this? I'm tired. I'm fed up!" Ginika started to sob.

As her voice rose hysterically, Ginika shuddered. What was the pilot looking for in Ama-Oyi to warrant his coming to drop bombs in the town in the middle of the night? She got the answer to the puzzle in the morning when she went with Udo, Amaka and Dozie to fetch water from the Otaru River. On their way back, she heard two women discussing the previous night's raid. She increased her pace so that she could hear them.

"Did you hear that loud noise that woke everyone up last night?" one asked.

"Yes, my sister. It was terrible, and I could not sleep again until morning. I thought Ama-Oyi was being invaded by the enemy."

The second woman was short and plump. Her large water pot pressed down her neck, and Ginika thought her neck would have become shorter by the time she got home.

"It was a Nigerian plane that bombed Ejike Okoro's house," continued the first woman who was tall and fair-skinned. "The man was carrying *npanaka*, an oil lamp, when the plane flew past. I was told the man flying the plane turned back and dropped the bomb, thinking it was a military camp. The bomb dug a big whole in Ejike's house and he was killed on the spot. Luckily, his wife and children were spared. The house was not touched, but Ekenma is now a widow and her children have become fatherless overnight."

"*Hei, o di egwu*, it is terrible," the second woman cried. "These people are wicked. They are hard-hearted."

As soon as Ginika got home and emptied her tin of water in the huge water pot in which drinking water was stored, she went upstairs to tell her father what she had heard. It was Saturday when he did not go to the hospital. He was shaken by the news. That very day, he hired three workmen to cover with palm fronds the top of the 403, Dr Ndefo's Mercedes and the entire roof of the house, so that enemy planes flying past would not see them. Ginika had noticed that Eloka's father had done a similar job in his compound the last time she visited Eloka. Dr Ndefo's car was filled with some of their things that could not be brought into the house for lack of space – clothes, crockery, books and few electrical gadgets.

Ginika knew the men were not from Ama-Oyi, for they spoke a dialect that was different from that of her town. She asked them and they told her they were refugees. They worked till late afternoon and were given roast yam which they ate with palm oil. Everyone was satisfied with the work they did, and her father paid them good money for their effort. Ginika thought the house and the cars were safe from attack. She felt more secure and would no longer panic and quake whenever a plane flew past.

WHEN GINIKA chatted with Amaka later that evening, after her father and Auntie Lizzy had gone out to see Uncle Chima and his family, she noticed Anayo, Amaka's youngest brother, playing football with a premature coconut that had fallen from the tree at the back of the compound. "Anayo, don't break your toes with that coconut. It's too hard to serve as a football."

The eight-year-old laughed and continued to kick the

coconut. "Anayo, didn't you hear what she said? Do you want to hurt yourself? Come on, let me have that coconut."

Anayo picked up the coconut and gave it to Amaka. "Come and sit by me, darling," Amaka said softly. "Don't worry, you'll soon have as many footballs as you want."

Anayo smiled and sat close to his big and only sister who spoilt him all the time. Ginika had scolded Amaka lightly more than once for spoiling the boy, and Amaka had replied, "He's the baby of the family and everyone spoils him."

Anayo stood up and looked at Ginika. "Uncle Eloka was here this morning when you went to the river. See what he gave me." He took something from his pocket and displayed it proudly. It was a miniature image of a dog carved from wood.

"It's beautiful, Anayo," Ginika enthused. "Can I look at it?" He gave it to her. "Did you say Uncle Eloka was here this morning?"

Anayo nodded.

"Did you see where he went when he didn't see me? Did he go home?" She was cautious with her questions.

"He spoke with your dad."

"With my father? How did you know?"

"Because I saw them. Your dad came downstairs and they talked in the sitting room."

"You saw them talking? For a long time?"

"I don't know. I left when my mom called me."

"Thanks, Anayo, you're a very good boy."

Anayo nodded and ran to the back of the house when he heard one of his brothers calling his name.

Ginika was astonished as well as mortified. Eloka came to the house and spoke with her father, yet he had not mentioned it all day. He did not mention it when she went up to tell him about the bomb that killed the man called Ejike Okoro last night. He said nothing to her all day when the workmen were in the house. And now he had gone with Auntie Lizzy to see Uncle Chima, but had said nothing to her. But, wait a minute: could it be because of Eloka's visit that her father had gone to see Uncle Chima? Her heart gave a jolt, and she became excited. Had her father changed his mind?

"I have something to tell you, but do not mention it to anyone yet," Ginika heard Amaka say.

She looked at her friend's face and saw a big smile there. "I'm all ears."

"My dad has succeeded at last to persuade the government to allow my mom to travel out to get proper medical attention. She'll take us with her to America. We'll leave in a few days. I just couldn't keep it from you any longer. But please, don't tell anyone. Mom and dad want it that way. I think it's because of your stepmother, whom they don't trust. Dad said he'll let your dad know a day to our departure. Can I trust you to keep it to yourself?"

"Yes, you can. No one will hear it until your family reveals it."

"Thanks, I know I can trust you."

"I'm happy for your mother who will be returning to her family, but are all of you going?'

"Yes, but dad isn't coming with us. He'll remain here. Mom's health has got worse, and there are no drugs for her diabetes. Dad fears what may happen to her if the war is prolonged."

"How do you go?"

"Dad has made all the arrangements. A vehicle will come for us in the evening and we travel to Uli airport in the night.

We'll fly out of Biafra in one of the planes that bring relief materials. From there, we'll find our way to America. Among my brothers, only Dozie knows."

"Good luck, Amaka," Ginika breathed.

"Thanks. We'll be back as soon as the war ends."

Ginika wondered if that would be possible. Amaka and her brothers would continue their education in America and, by the time the war ended, might not want to come back.

IN THE morning, Ginika woke up early as usual. She was sweeping the compound when she saw that one of the windows of Dr Ndefo's Mercedes was broken. Surprised and intrigued, she drew closer to have a good look. She shouted when she saw that a lot of things had indeed been removed from the car. Most of the clothes and the crockery she used to see there as she passed were gone. She circled the car and noticed the boot was partially open, the lock damaged.

"Who did this?" she cried.

It was too early for any of them to have risen from bed, but those who heard her voice came out to see what the matter was. Udo, Amaka and Dozie stood, gaping at the vandalised car.

"Who has done this?" Amaka asked, turning to Ginika.

"I don't know. Thieves, I think. They came in the night when we were all sleeping. How terrible!" She stared at Amaka. "I'm sorry about this." She couldn't think of who could have done such a thing, not only stealing things but also damaging the car. Then she remembered the three workmen – the three refugees – and wondered if they did it. They had seen the Mercedes and the things stored in it and apparently could not resist the temptation to raid it in spite of the fact that they were paid well and even given food where food was scarce. She looked at the low compound wall and knew the thief or thieves had climbed it to have access to the car.

"I have to tell my mom what happened." Amaka shrugged. "She'll be upset when she hears about it."

Ginika watched her go, and thought how relieved Mrs Ndefo would be when she finally flew out of the country. She bent down and continued sweeping. She would have to report the theft to her father as soon as he woke up, and that would be much later because he did not wake up early on Sunday mornings.

TWO DAYS after Amaka told Ginika about her family's plan to leave the country, it became a reality. It was late evening and Ginika had just returned from visiting Eloka, though she had told her father she was going to see Auntie Chito. She did visit her aunt but it was in Eloka's house she spent most of the time. He walked her home and stopped before they got to the gate.

"Be careful on your way home," she told him, "I don't want you to be conscripted by the soldiers roaming in Ama-Oyi and looking for young men to capture."

He laughed. "If they catch me, I'll follow them. They'll save me much anxiety, and I'll stop looking over my shoulders all the time I'm outside my home."

"Do you know what you're saying?" she teased. "There'll be no husband and no wedding if they catch you."

"Okay, let me go before they come." With a chuckle he took off.

Ginika was laughing softly as she entered the compound. Her father and Auntie Lizzy sat on the balcony upstairs, leaning on the railing. Ginika looked away, wondering if they had seen her with Eloka. Though her father had still not mentioned his discussion with Eloka to her, she had heard Eloka's version of what took place. Eloka seemed quite sure her father had shifted ground. She was still waiting to hear from her father. Meanwhile she would continue to see her beloved Eloka.

It was when she turned away that she saw it – a small bus, the type that carried fourteen people – parked to the left of the compound, near the underground tank. Amaka and her brothers were dressed up and were putting their things into the bus. As they grinned at Ginika excitedly, their father emerged and came towards them. He had a small suitcase in his hands.

"How are you, my dear," he said when Ginika greeted him. "You and your friend will miss each other, won't you?"

Ginika and Amaka nodded simultaneously.

"I'll drop my handbag and come down to assist." As she started walking away, she saw Udo carrying a bag and moving to the bus, and she was glad he was helping them. She was sure he would miss Dozie his friend, just as she would miss Amaka. She would have to find someone else to plait her hair. Amaka had done it for her since she returned to Ama-Oyi, and she had also plaited hers.

After putting her handbag in her room, she went to the balcony to greet her father and stepmother.

"The Ndefos are moving out," her father said.

"Yes, they said they're leaving the country," she replied, non-committally.

"They did not even have the decency to let us know until this afternoon," Auntie Lizzy spat. "Let them run away to America and leave us to swim or sink here. When things were good they stayed, but now things are bad, they run away. Let them go. Who cares?"

Ginika understood Auntie Lizzy was piqued that she was disregarded by Mrs Ndefo, but what did she expect? She was hostile to the woman and her family. Though their stay in the house was a big challenge and tried one's patience sometimes, they were nice people, Ginika thought. The boys were just behaving like most boys their age, and one needed to be patient with them, and if they were corrected, they listened. Ginika liked that about them.

"Ginika, so you have nothing to say? Did they do well? Did your friend tell you she was leaving?"

"Lizzy, what is it?" her father asked. "Let the matter rest. Does it matter when they told us? It is possible they did not even know when exactly they were to leave. Much of the decision was not theirs. Dr Ndefo told me he had to wait for government to give him clearance."

Ginika relaxed, for she hadn't been sure how to deal with Auntie Lizzy's frantic questions. "I want to go down and help them," she said and hurried away.

She met them trying to tidy up the rooms. Amaka was sweeping her mother's room and Dozie was sweeping the ones used by the boys. "Don't worry about the rooms," Ginika said. "Udo and I will tidy them up later."

"Bless you, Ginika." Mrs Ndefo smiled at her. She was dressed in a long black dress that reached to her ankles. Her hair was neatly pulled back and held with a large hairpin.

"Are we ready?" Dr Ndefo asked jovially.

The boys chorused, "Yes."

Mrs Ndefo nodded, taking a last look to ensure she had forgotten nothing. She checked her handbag and smiled. "My American passport – I have to make sure it's with me."

"Driver, get in the bus and turn it to face the gate," Dr Ndefo instructed. To Ginika he said, "Can you tell your father we're about to leave?"

Ginika went up again and returned immediately with her father. Auntie Lizzy hissed, and did not get up.

"Uba, we're about to set out. I'll take them to Uli and stay with them till they leave. I'm not sure I'll be allowed to get to where the plane is, but it doesn't matter so long as they get there. As we agreed, some of our things will be here. We moved them into a corner of the room at the back of the house, as you suggested. The Mercedes will remain where it is. Thanks for your help and support." They shook hands.

"Well, safe journey. Carol, take care." Her father also shook hands with Mrs Ndefo, and patted the boys' shoulders.

"Ubaka, thanks," Mrs Ndefo said. "I appreciate all you did to help us." She turned to Ginika and hugged her. "Take care of yourself." She smiled. "And you too, Udo."

"Goodbye." Ginika hugged Amaka.

"Goodbye." Udo waved to Dozie and his brothers.

The sound of "goodbye" filled the air as they got into the bus. Dr Ndefo sat in front with the driver.

It was twilight by the time the bus drove out of the compound. Udo closed the gate. As Ginika, her father and Udo walked towards the veranda, the house was quiet and seemed deserted.

20

Ginika was in the kitchen preparing breakfast with Ozioma, in Eloka's home. Sitting on a low chair, her body slightly bent forward, she pounded beans in a mortar. She had made friends with Ozioma, Eloka's youngest sister since she became Eloka's wife. Being a wife was a new experience and she was trying to deal with it. So far she was succeeding and enjoying it. Getting up in the morning – she was doing that in her former home – and sweeping the rooms and preparing breakfast, assisted by Ozioma, preparing other meals at appropriate times and enjoying her husband. The past two weeks were like a dream to her. She had never thought her life would change in such a short time.

She had moved into the Odunze family home as Eloka's wife a week after Amaka and her family left Ama-Oyi. Once the two families agreed to the marriage between their children, the process leading to their formal and legal union moved rapidly. For Ginika, the week had seemed too long. Not only did she want to become Eloka's wife as quickly as possible, but also she wanted to escape from her home which had become quite cheerless after Nwakire returned to his battalion, and after Monday ran away to join the army, and after Mrs Ndefo flew to America with her children, taking Amaka away. Living with Auntie Lizzy became too much of a strain and watching her father descend more and more into gloom sapped her energy and cast a shadow on her happiness.

Auntie Lizzy would nag, "Ginika, where did you go? Has the time for lunch not passed or you want me to prepare it?" Sometimes, it was, "You will go to Orie market to buy the things we need; I'm too tired to go today," or "Why do you allow that man, Eloka, to visit so often, and to take you to his house? You are not yet married, you know."

Her father buried himself in his room when he was not at work, almost as Mrs Ndefo had done. It seemed to Ginika that he had inherited the habit of solitude, in the negative sense, from the woman. If he spoke to anyone, it was in monosyllables. "Udo, run off now"; "Ginikanwa, just watch it! Get out! Have you no shame?"; "Lizzy, stop! Enough!" Such peremptory instruction, censure or declamation was all that came from him. He had hurt her feeling by not discussing his intentions with her before receiving his prospective in-laws. It was the very day Eloka and his people came for the coconut ceremony that her father mentioned it, in passing, "Your future husband and his people are coming here today; I expect you know already." She was aghast. If Eloka had not told her, she would be hearing it for the first time and in such a manner. She had long given up the hope that she would ever understand what drove her father's mind and actions.

Ginika wanted to escape. Udo was the only light in the house, but often he was not there, as he had to walk across to his home to be with his mother and sisters.

Ginika remembered that she had been astonished as well as overjoyed that everything worked out as she and Eloka had hoped and planned. His father and his *umunna* had come for the *iku-aka*, 'the knocking on the door' – the coconut ceremony, as it is called – to announce their intention to take her as a wife into their family for their son. She had frowned when Eloka's father intoned, "There is a flower we saw in this house which we have come to pluck," – as if she were something delicate and transient as a flower. Ginika had laughed when she observed the formal and solemn atmosphere invoked and maintained during the enactment of all the rituals. But at every stage, humour broke loose to temper the serious undertone of the ceremonies. She understood that she, as well as Eloka, was more or less an onlooker until each was called upon to do one thing or the other at appropriate times, before the union was sealed and they could begin to live as man and wife.

The traditional aspects had been greatly played down because of the war and the terror, the anxiety and the sadness it generated in the community and in the communal life of Ama-Oyi. Only three days earlier, one of the high-ranking army officers – a native of Ama-Oyi – had been brought home and buried in his family compound with a 21-gun salute. He was a colonel, and had been an officer in the Nigerian army before the crisis that led to war. People said he was an experienced and disciplined officer. There was much wailing that day in Ama-Oyi. The war was beginning to wear everyone down, she thought.

After the *iku-aka*, the rest of the ceremonies which should have taken weeks or even months were compressed into just one visit to her home, on a Friday. She had worn a new navy blue dress Auntie Chito gave her – only God knew where she got it. Eloka had put on a local dress known as Biafran suit – a shirt and a pair of trousers of the same grey fabric. The shirt had short sleeves and six medium-sized buttons; and the loose trousers fitted him well.

"Ginikanwa, come here," her father had called. She was hovering behind the door and went into the room where he sat with all the in-laws on one side, and their own *umunna* on the opposite side. They had all assembled for the paying of the bride price and the wine-carrying ceremony. Smiling shyly, she had looked round the sitting room. She could recognise some of the people, but not everyone. Eloka sat between his father and mother while his sister, Adaeze, sat near their mother. There were three other people from his family but she did not know them then. Oh, there was Tonna, sitting in the corner. He had smiled and nodded, as she smiled back.

On the other side were her father, Uncle Chima, and three other male relatives. No woman from her family was there, for they were sweating it out at the back of the house, putting finishing touches to the food they would serve later, after all the rituals had been completed. She knew her father and Uncle Chima had already received the bride price, and her father had called her in because she was required to accept a cup of palm wine, drink half of it and then give the other half to the man she had chosen to be her husband. She was aware that this final act on her part would seal the marriage after Eloka had accepted the cup and drained it.

"Take this cup of wine, and give it to your husband after you have drunk from it," Uncle Chima had intoned. "*Matakwa*, know that we are ignorant of who he is until you show him to us by kneeling before him to give him the wine. Whoever takes the cup from you and drinks the wine is henceforth to be known as your husband, as far as we are concerned. Daughter, is this clear?" He had looked at her solemnly.

Nodding, she had taken the cup from his hand and moved slowly towards Eloka who was smiling gently. One of the men from his *umunna* stretched his hand to take the cup, but she drew away from him. Tonna made a similar gesture, and she shook her head and moved away. She approached Eloka and knelt down. She drank some of the wine which was neither sweet nor sour and gave him the cup. He drank the wine, and everyone laughed and some clapped their hands in delight.

Afterwards, the women entered, carrying bowls of food, kegs of palm wine and jugs filled with drinking water. Mama Nnukwu had said, "Our in-laws, we greet you. *Unu abia*, welcome." Ginika knew that if her mother were alive, she would be the one to welcome the in-laws at this stage. She had wondered where Auntie Lizzy was. Wasn't she the one who should play the role of her mother? Later, in the evening, she had taken her things, and her family had said their goodbyes.

"Goodbye, Sister Ginika," Udo had said, as his eyes misted over. "I'll come and see you."

Her father, Auntie Lizzy, Mama Nnukwu and Uncle Chima had hugged her. Tears stung her eyes, but she held them back. The other relatives shook her hand and wished her well. She saw Akueju hurrying forward and waited to hug her. She gave Ginika a lovely enamel dish. "Use this to serve soup to your husband." She was profoundly touched and gave Akueju another hug. "Thank you," she had whispered. And surrounded by her new family, she had moved to her new home.

The following day, Saturday, the pastor in charge of St Mark's Anglican Church, came to the house at the invitation of her father-in-law and, at a simple service witnessed by few members from the two families, they were married in the spacious sitting room.

Ginika had not forgotten how happy she was that day she went home finally with Eloka to be his wife in every respect. The memory would ever be fresh though other happy days had followed. Now she had settled down to what she believed would be a blissful married life in spite of the war raging and claiming more lives and territories, in spite of the sorrow and misery spreading all over the land like an epidemic.

Ginika finished pounding the beans and stoked the fire to heat palm oil in a frying pan. Ozioma had mixed the *akamu* with water and waited for the kettle to boil. She was using a kerosene stove. Ozioma watched her sister-in-law, happy that her brother married such a beautiful and cheerful girl.

"When this gallon of kerosene finishes, we'll have to use only firewood. I hate the smoke it spreads everywhere."

Ginika laughed. "Few people use kerosene now. When I was in my other home, we used firewood or *ichere*, palm kernel shells."

"I know. I don't know where Papa got the kerosene. We have been using it for more than two months. This is the last gallon."

Ginika wondered if he took it from the ration given to refugees, remembering how she had heard that members of the Ama-Oyi Local Council misappropriated materials meant for refugees. But she did not express her thoughts to Ozioma. She started to fry the beans, scooping the creamy mixture with a wooden spoon and dropping it in the hot oil.

"Ginika, the *akara* looks and smells so nice. Where did you learn to fry *akara* like this? You must teach me the secret," Ozioma said admiringly.

Ginika smiled as she removed the golden bean cakes from the frying pan and put them in a large sieve. "There is no secret. It's practice; just watch me and you'll learn."

Eloka stood at the kitchen door, watching them. Ginika did not know he was standing there. "Mermaid, what are you cooking that smells so delicious?" He wrapped his arms around her.

Ginika laughed. "Darling, don't do that unless you want me to pour hot oil on myself. See the oil; I'm so close to it."

"I can't keep my hands away from you, my bewitching Mermaid."

"And you, Little Sister, what are you doing? Helping your *wife*?" he teased Ozioma.

"I'm not *Little Sister*; I'm almost the same age as your wife, you know. I'm a big girl now. When will you realise it?"

"Never, you'll always be my little sister." He bent down and laughed in her face.

She pushed his face away playfully and said, as she made the *akamu* with the boiling water, "Okay, you will get tired one day and start calling me by my name."

"Mermaid, I've swept our room and tidied it. You'll like it when you see it. Am I a good husband or not?"

Ginika and Ozioma laughed.

"Thanks, darling," Ginika purred. "You're the best husband in the whole world."

"Just being useful, you know." He stared at nothing in particular, and his eyes had a dull sheen. Ginika hoped he was not in that sad mood he slipped into once in a while. She supposed it was the effect the war had on people. She too felt that way sometimes, in spite of her new life that brought her closer to the man she loved and married.

"Mama will have a fit if she hears you swept your room," Ozioma said. "Don't let her hear you. She will say you're spoiling your wife."

Ginika looked up quickly to see Eloka's face, and waited to hear what he would say.

Eloka did not respond to his sister's statements. He went back to the main house, calling to Ginika, "See you soon, Mermaid."

AFTER BREAKFAST, her father-in-law went off to the refugee camp to see the warden. Ginika heard him tell her mother-in-law where he was going and when he would return. She was surprised, for her father did not always say where he was going. He would just pick up his car key and walk out of the house. But, she couldn't really be sure; perhaps he told Auntie Lizzy when they were alone. She wondered how they were coping with hardly anyone to help out in the house, except Udo. But Udo had told her when he visited her that he stayed more with his mother and sisters since she left. How was Auntie Lizzy coping with house chores which she hated and would always depend on Monday to do? When Ginika was around, Auntie Lizzy would expect her to help out and she did so gladly.

Ginika and Ozioma were clearing the table when Eloka called her. "Come to the room," he said.

"I'm busy clearing the table, and will come as soon as I finish."

"Leave it to Ozioma and come."

Ginika looked appealingly to Ozioma, as if asking her to excuse her.

"Go, I'll do the rest and wash up."

He was lying in bed and leafing through an old magazine.

He dropped it as soon as she entered. "I want my wife here with me; this is where you belong, by my side."

"Is that all?" She laughed. "Is that why you called me away when you knew I was working?" She gazed at him, her heart twitching at the sight of his moustache, his strong chest which she could see because his shirt was not buttoned, and his legs which were more attractive than any legs she had seen.

"Isn't it enough that I want to be with you? Isn't it enough reason to make you leave what you are doing and hasten to me? Our honeymoon is not over, you know. If there were no war, we would celebrate our marriage differently. At this moment, the only important thing is to be with my wife." He winked at her and she knew he was joking. He was teasing her; above all, he had unpleasant news for her.

She had come to know him a little better since she started living with him. She now knew that if he wanted to give her bad news, he first tried to make her laugh, to create fun around, before dropping his bombshell. He was not the kind of man who was frivolous about serious matters, especially concerning the war. But he would clip the claws of bad news with humour before unleashing it on her. Her greatest fear was that he would one day get up and tell her he was off to join the army.

She was wondering what his news was when he reached out and grabbed her around the waist. He fell back on the bed with her on top of him. With a little cry, she said, "You want the bed to break?"

"The bed is strong and cannot break because we fell on it. Come, Mermaid, let's be happy."

She drew away and looked into his eyes. "Now, what news is oppressing you? I'm sure you have something to say to me?"

He laughed. "What makes you think I have something to tell you? You witch of a mermaid." He caressed her cheeks.

"Am I not your wife? I know a lot that will surprise you." Struggling with him, she added, "I haven't had my bath yet."

"Who cares?"

"I do."

"You're always clean to me whether you take a bath or not. Have you ever heard the phrase *oma uma aghu ahu*, one who is always clean? One of my father's friends took that as his *ozo* title name."

They roared with laughter. Ginika laughed so much that tears flowed from her eyes. He was still laughing as he began to undress her, and it was very easy because she did not have much on. She too began to undress him, having become bolder since she became his and he hers. Within a few seconds they were naked and intertwined like yam tendrils. As their hands worked on each other, as his lips caressed her breasts, she moaned with her eyes shut. But only for a brief moment, for she was now loving him in a special way. Like a doe she roved boldly and frolicked around the verdant land of his body while he murmured again and again, "Mermaid, I love you, I adore you. Oh, how I love you." He pulled her up tenderly and they looked into each other's face.

She saw how his face shone and she was sure hers glowed, for the two faces must be reflecting each other like mirrors. She was delirious with joy because she knew he loved her as much as she loved him, and she thought she must protect this precious feeling they shared, even with her life. She was aware of the palpitations of her heart and feared it might pack up. But in a moment, she was not thinking of her heart any longer, as she felt his strong arms around her. She responded with vigour. He held her tight, bruising her delicate skin against his muscular frame. She could feel the fire of his love, the force of it and she felt more secure than she had ever felt before in her life. The wonders of loving and being loved, she marvelled. Love found her and she found love, she thought. At the height of their loving, she cried out, and he did the same, their voices mingling, fusing into one indistinguishable sound.

They swooned into each other's arms and lay quiescent, completely satisfied.

GINIKA WOKE up hours later and sat up. She glanced at her watch which was on the table. It was past the hour for lunch. She gave a short cry and hoped Ozioma and Michael, the houseboy, prepared lunch. She shook Eloka.

"Darling, do you know what time it is? Wake up."

Eloka stretched, and drew her close. "What time is it?" he murmured, his eyes still heavy with sleep.

"It's past two o'clock."

"That's okay. Are you going somewhere?"

"No, but I was thinking about lunch. Let me see if Ozioma and Michael have cooked lunch. You're hungry, aren't you?"

"Not really; you've fed me with love."

"Be serious." She pulled his moustache and he cried out. "Why did you cry out? Was that little tug painful?"

He groaned: "Some wives are cruel."

Laughing, she got up and started to tidy herself and put on her clothes. He watched her for a while and did the same. "Mermaid, sit down. I have some news."

She sat down on the bed, her heart racing, and he sat next to her. She knew all along that he had something to say and she only hoped it was not very bad news.

"Tonna has gone off and joined the army. He sent me a note this morning. I was shaken and felt bad when I read the note, for we were together the other day and he didn't mention it. Why should my best friend not tell me after he had made such a serious decision? I don't understand it."

Her heart beat rapidly. Was this a sign of things to follow? Would he also decide to do the same? Ginika knew that Eloka and Tonna were quite close and had no secrets between them. Why did he leave without telling his friend what he was about doing?

"Perhaps, he didn't want you to persuade him not to go into the army," she suggested. "He didn't want to bear the burden of your objection which he would disregard." She put her hand into his.

He pulled his hand away, and she was taken aback at his reaction, as if he hated what she had said.

"What makes you think I would object to his joining the army? Why should I? He or I or any young man can join the army at any time." His eyes were as hard as nuts.

She was seeing another side of him. She was learning more about him, and it was good, she thought. She got up and was walking out of the room, when he said softly, "Mermaid, come back, I have not given you all the news."

Without saying anything, she sat down again by his side.

"Do you remember the couple whose wedding ceremony pastor had said he would perform after ours?"

Ginika thought for a moment and then remembered the pastor saying he had another wedding to perform the following Saturday or so at St Mark's Church. He had said something like "This is a season of weddings."

"Yes, I remember. What about the man?" she asked.

"Well, the bridegroom was not as lucky as I am. He was

304

conscripted into the army as he and his wife were walking back home after their wedding in the church. I was lucky because my father had used his influence to make the pastor solemnise our wedding at home. The poor chap had no one to do this for him, so he was caught by conscripting soldiers. I heard he is an only son like me." His voice was awash with sarcasm and his laughter was harsh and mirthless.

Ginika stared at him in horror. "Are you blaming yourself or your father for what happened, for the man's conscription? Darling, you shouldn't. It's neither your fault nor your father's, believe me."

He shrugged and lay back on the bed, staring at the ceiling.

Ginika felt her heart go cold. She had meant to tell him a story she had heard the day before, but decided she was never going to tell him, considering his reaction to the conscription of the newly-wed man. She had heard that last week, an *nmonwu*, a masked spirit, was conscripted by a group of soldiers. His followers had scattered and disappeared, but the masked ancestral spirit had not moved fast enough and they grabbed him. She was told that the soldiers took the *nmonwu* away, and that one of them had said, "Boys are fighting in the war front and you are masquerading about in your village."

"I want to check on lunch," she told him, hurrying out of the room. She was sure he would get over the shock of Tonna's action and the feeling of guilt he seemed to have about the conscription of the unfortunate bridegroom. Her heart went out to the bride who would be languishing in misery now. Ginika knew that she, too, was vulnerable – Eloka might get conscripted if he was not careful. She sighed: she could feel the young bride's agony though she did not know who she was.

21

Ginika was in bed with Eloka after they had lunch. It was hot and the wind seemed to have deserted Ama-Oyi. Everywhere was still and stale.

"The war has taken everything from us. I hope it has not taken wind and fresh air away too," Eloka said, chuckling. He lay on his back, listening to the love songs Ginika sang from her *Record Songs Book*. He did not particularly relish listening to such songs but gave in to her wishes to humour her.

"It's the weather," she replied. "Though it rains occasionally, it is the dry season still. It will not get cooler for two or three months." She went back to the book of love songs – one of the things she made sure she took with her when she moved to her new home – and searched for a song to sing to him. She was determined to make him like it, for it was a hobby she had always enjoyed. She loved singing and acting – they often go together. She remembered that there were a lot of songs in *Mammy Water* and she had loved it. Her interest in singing had started at an early age as a member of the choir at St Cyprian's Church, Port Harcourt. But her love of acting began when she acted the role of an angel in her school's Nativity Play when she was about nine. Acting was in her family: she recalled, at age six, her pregnant mother acting a lazy wife and mother in a play called *Eko Madam* on Mothers' Day. It was one of the few images of her mother that would never be wiped off from her memory. It was indelible. Her mother was pregnant with the child she died giving birth to. "Let me sing Elvis Presley's 'Lucky Lips' and then Cliff Richard's 'Bachelor Boy' to remind you of your bachelor days," she said, freeing herself from the grip of memory.

Eloka smiled. "Go on as you wish."

"I like the words of Elvis's song. We sang it a lot in school. Every girl knew the song and when one person started it, everyone would join in." She didn't sing from the book this time, as she had learnt it by heart. When she came to the part she liked best, she pressed her face to his as she sang.

'You got lucky lips
Lucky lips are always kissing
Lucky lips are never blue
Lucky lips will always find
Someone new to love and kiss
You may not be good-looking
And you may not be so rich
But you'll never ever be alone
'Cause you got lucky lips.'

She stopped because she was not sure she got the words right. She hadn't sung it for a long time. As she turned the covers of the book to check, she heard Ozioma calling her name.

"Ginika, Udo is here to see you."

"Thanks, tell him I'll be with him soon." She stroked Eloka's moustache. "Darling, I'll sing the other one later." She jumped out of bed and went to see her cousin.

SHE FOUND Udo in the sitting room where Ozioma had asked him to wait. As soon as he saw her, he got up. She hugged him. "Is there any problem? I hope you come in peace?"

Udo laughed. "Sister Ginika, you always ask me this question each time I come to see you. What are you afraid of?" His red shirt was unbuttoned because of the heat and her eyes perched on a scar on his stomach, and she was surprised she had not noticed it before; she touched it. "I got the scar when my appendix was taken out just before the war," he said.

She withdrew from him and waved him to the chair from which he had got up to greet her. She was ready to respond to his question. "Listen to the type of question you are asking me – what I'm afraid of? Is this not war? Are we not all afraid of one thing or another? Is anyone sure of his or her life?"

"Oh, I understand now what you mean. There is no problem at home except that life is becoming impossible. Food is getting scarcer. Do you know that many Ama-Oyi people queue up at the relief centres to beg for the food – corn meal, salted stockfish, corned beef, tinned fish, dried milk and rice – planes fly into the country?"

"Ah, who does not know?" She sighed. "We eat some of those here too but we don't have to queue because my father-in-law brings them home. I think he gets a ration because of his position as the chairman of Ama-Oyi Local Council." Ginika grimaced when she remembered how members of the council were vilified and labelled *Olokara Kansul*.

"The other day, Auntie Lizzy sent me to Caritas' storehouse to queue for stockfish and salt. Some people there asked me if I was a Roman Catholic. They told me and some other people who were not of their denomination to go away and look for the World Council of Churches – WCC – centre and queue up there. Can you imagine? Religion has come into getting relief material."

Ginika was dumbfounded. "What did you do?"

"I did not do anything; I continued to wait. The WCC has no store in Ama-Oyi, so I could not go to them. The nearest of their stores is in Ihioma, isn't it?" He looked at Ginika who sat opposite him.

"I don't know. But did you get food after waiting?"

"I waited for over three hours then one man came out and asked us to go, claiming that there was nothing in the store. He said we could try the following week."

She laughed. "They always say that to get rid of people because they are worried that enemy planes would strike if people gather in front of the store. This is what somebody told me; I have never gone to beg for relief material to find out what happens."

Changing the subject, she asked, "What about your mother and sisters? I hope they are all right?"

Udo shook his head. "Things are not easy for them. Mama can hardly find enough food for my sisters and herself. Their main food now is the cassava husk which she soaks in water and dries before grinding it to make *fufu* or mixing it with vegetables to make *achicha*. Sometimes, I take my food to my sisters."

Ginika shuddered. Things had not gotten that bad where she was, the place she called home now, though they no longer ate meat and fish as they did when she moved in newly. She knew things would get worse if the war did not end soon. "How is Papa? Does he still go to work with that *alikirija* bicycle?"

"So you didn't know? He stopped going to work because there were no drugs in the hospital. You know there was no proper hospital in the first place, as they were using a temporary place, hoping to go back to Ogidi where the hospital was originally located. But our soldiers have not been able to recapture the area. Uncle said they were not receiving drugs anymore and he had to stop going there."

"Is that so? God, what will he do now?" She pictured her father cooped up all day in the house, like Mrs Ndefo. She was sure he would become depressed soon if nothing happened to distract him. She shook her head several times.

"But, I overheard him telling Auntie Lizzy that he hopes to start work in the dispensary at Ekwulobia which has been turned into an emergency hospital. He said they had drugs there and even admitted a few sick people in the former maternity wards adjacent to the dispensary."

"It will be better for him if this plan works out, as Ekwulobia is not as far from Ama-Oyi as the other place," she said, her spirit lifting. "It's very hot in here. Shall we go out and sit under one of the trees in front of the house?"

They had hardly settled down under an orange tree when Eunice arrived. As soon as Ginika saw her, she cried, "Eunice, the great dancer, where have you been? I haven't seen you in ages." She gave Eunice a glowing smile.

"You didn't bother to look for me." Eunice sat on the chair Udo had run into the house and brought for her. "Ginika, you didn't treat me well, did you? You got married and didn't invite me and you ask where I've been. I have been here all along."

The smile had not left Ginika's face. "Sorry about that, but it was a very private wedding. We did not invite anyone except a few members of the two families. It was not possible to celebrate the wedding because of the war. We plan to have a big party when the war ends." She thought Eunice had put on weight and it suited her. Who could eat well enough in this war to put on weight, she wondered?

"How is Eloka, your husband? I didn't know you two were that serious about each other to want to get married at this time." She was smiling now.

Ginika laughed. "I love him and he loves me, so we got married. How did you know?"

"Njide told me."

"Njide? Is she in Ama-Oyi?"

No, she went into the Red Cross."

Ginika's eyes widened. "Red Cross? But there is no Red Cross office in Ama-Oyi. How did she get involved?" She could not hide her astonishment and her admiration for Njide's capacity to serve, remembering her commitment during the performance of their play.

"I don't know exactly where she is, but when I saw her she told me they are close to the war front and move with the soldiers – at the rear."

Ginika shrugged, staring far ahead. "Well, she's very brave, isn't she? I don't think I'll like to be near the war front; I fear the vandals. The sound of shelling is enough to make me faint." She returned her gaze to Eunice. "What about you? Are you at home? Or are you planning to join the Red Cross too?" She laughed. "As for me, you can see I'm a housewife."

"I work at the officers' mess at the Air Force Base in Ekwulobia. I've been there for about three months."

"What do you do? You serve them food or what?" She could understand why Eunice had added weight – she and the other girls must be eating well there. She had matured too; her breasts were definitely fuller.

"We are about six girls; we cook their breakfast and dinner, but their own men serve them. We never go to the mess. I came home because of the air raid last week. The air base was bombed and the mess is one of the buildings affected, so we were asked to go home until the commanding officer sends for us."

"Will you go back if he sends for you? With the air raids and the bombs?" She looked hard at Eunice, amazed that she was not frightened; that she put her life deliberately at risk; that she was able to convince her parents to allow her to work in such a place at her age. She couldn't be more than sixteen, could she? She was the youngest girl during their play and dance performance.

"I'm not sure yet. I'd like to go back, but I don't know what my parents will say. I'll discuss with them if the commander sends for me and the other girls. I don't want to be idle; I want to do something to help."

Eloka came out of the house, walked over and stood beside Ginika. He wore a black shirt which he neatly tucked into his jeans. She stretched her arm and encircled one of his legs. "Darling, see who has come to see us."

Eloka grinned. "Eunice, how are you? You've added some weight."

"Good evening, Eloka. Congratulations; you married the most beautiful girl among us." Eunice shook hands with him.

Eloka and Ginika laughed. Udo who had remained silent all this while also laughed.

"She's lovely, isn't she?" Eloka bent down and caressed Ginika's cheek. She was thrilled by his voice which vibrated with pride.

"I'm going out to stretch my legs." Eloka rubbed Ginika's shoulder. "I'm tired of staying indoors."

She wanted to tell him to remember that soldiers from the recruiting station were milling around, looking for men, but decided against it, knowing how he hated to be reminded of the need to lie low. She nodded and removed her arm from around his leg.

Then, a few minutes later, Ginika went to see Eunice off, Udo got up and walked about the compound admiring the trees and the birds that flitted from tree to tree, chirruping. Ginika found him watching a bird which Eloka told her was called *okiri*.

"I often stand and watch those birds too," she said. "They are so free and apparently unaware that there is a war raging in the country."

Udo laughed. "Are you sure? It's possible they sense and know a lot of things like human beings; the difference is that they don't talk like we do."

"You may be right. Perhaps they have a language we don't understand."

They were engrossed with the bird when Eloka raced into the compound and sprinted into the house. For a second, Ginika had seen his face and the fear written all over it. She froze and stared at Udo. Before she could move, a man in military uniform ran through the gate and halted when he saw Ginika and Udo. She looked at him and saw the three bars on his shoulder which told her he was a sergeant.

"Where is the man who ran into this house just now?" he asked Ginika, breathing fast. "Show me where he is if you don't want trouble."

"Which man are you talking about? I didn't see any man." It dawned on her that the soldier was after Eloka to conscript him. As she watched, three other men in plain clothes walked in and she understood they were with the sergeant. She had heard that most soldiers on conscription exercise didn't wear uniform any longer, so that the people they targeted, who naturally were none the wiser, could be more easily caught.

The sergeant glared at Ginika, ready to harangue her again, but Chief Odunze, who had heard voices, came out and the man turned towards him and greeted him.

"Sergeant, what is the matter? Why is your voice raised?" Ginika heard her father-in-law's authoritative voice demand.

The sergeant looked at him and his stern look softened as he replied, "A young man ran into this house and we are here to get him, sir. We need soldiers to fight the war."

"And you think it is in my house you will find the soldiers to fight the war. All right, take me with you to the front. Do you have no respect for age? Why don't you go and conscript your father?"

The sergeant stared at him, frowning.

Ginika could see he was angry but he tried to control himself, as he did not yet know who was talking to him. Ginika pinched Udo and whispered to him to get into the house.

"Do you know how many members of my family are fighting in the various fronts?" her father-in-law asked. "Do you know what I go through every day as the chairman of Ama-Oyi Local Council and the chief refugee officer in this area? You are from 11 Div, are you not? Go and ask your commander about Chief Odunze."

"I'm not from 11 Div," the man said.

"Then you are from the Awka Sector? I know your commander and he will not be pleased to hear you came here threatening me in my own house. You may go now and don't enter this house again if you know what is right for you."

Ginika breathed more easily when she saw the sergeant and his men turn and leave the compound. She sighed, as relief washed over her. She saw her father-in-law in a new light. The sergeant carried a gun and looked quite strong, but he had treated her father-in-law with respect, maybe not exactly respect but caution.

"Our wife, *kedu*, where is your husband?"

"In the house," she replied. "Papa, thank you very much. Thank God you are at home today. I don't know what that sergeant would have done if you hadn't been here. He pursued Eloka into the house, and he had only gone outside for a few minutes to stretch his legs."

He frowned. "I have told Eloka not to go out except in the night. If he is not careful, they will catch him one of these days and I will not be there to protect him."

Ginika saw Eloka approaching behind his father but the next moment he turned and walked away. She was sure he overheard what his father said and was angered by it, so she decided to go in and comfort him. She saw Udo in the sitting room. "Udo, wait, don't go yet until it is dark. These soldiers are so desperate they will conscript even small boys."

In their room, she found him brooding. He sat on a chair behind the table where some of his books and hers were stacked. His hands rested on the part of the table that had no books on it. She went to him immediately and stood by his side. Bending over him, she said. "My darling, don't let what happened this evening upset you, please…"

Eloka flinched and frowned. Ginika was taken aback by his reaction. He raised his right hand and said, "I'm all right. I just want to be left alone for a while."

"You want me to leave the room?"

"Yes, please." And when she stood there hesitating, uncertain about what to do – go or insist on staying – he pleaded, "Mermaid, please."

"All right, I'll go."

ELOKA REFUSED to join the family at table and Ginika decided to take his food and hers to the room. She knew he was displeased with his father and was not ready to listen to him discuss the evening's encounter while they were having dinner. He would start lecturing him again on the wisdom in not going out at all during the day until they had found something he could do which would have the power to protect him from the harassment of conscription.

She had planned it so that the food he liked was cooked for dinner. When she set the plates on the table, after he had helped by clearing the books away, she could see he was genuinely delighted. She was happy to see him regain his good cheer. She had had to drag an extra chair into the room.

"Mermaid, this is good food by war standards," he enthused, as he spooned jollof rice into his mouth and followed it up with a piece of fried plantain.

"I'm glad you like it. The plantain is from here – we harvested it from the small plantation behind the compound. How blessed we are still to enjoy the fruit of our soil when most people have fled their homes. Our God and our ancestors are wide awake and have continued to protect Ama-Oyi from the ravages of war."

"And may the protection continue until the war ends." He picked a piece of fish with his fork and gave it to her. He smiled, as she opened her mouth wide and the fish disappeared into it.

"My turn to feed you." She put a piece of plantain in

her mouth and allowed a portion of it to jut out. She leaned forward and invited him to take it with his mouth. He did and they laughed. Ginika told herself that she would love this man till death did them part, as she had vowed the day the pastor came to this very house and joined them as husband and wife.

After they had eaten and listened to news on Radio Biafra, they decided to retire early to bed. There was no striking news. From the broadcast, they understood that Biafra had neither lost more territories nor regained any of the lost ones. There was, however, a news item about the effort being made by mediators to get the two sides to a peace talk somewhere in East Africa, but the broadcaster said Nigeria was making impossible demands and Biafra preferred to continue fighting rather than renounce her independence as Nigeria stipulated.

"How do they expect us to renounce our independence after coming this far?" Ginika asked indignantly.

Eloka put his finger across her mouth and pulled her to him. Immediately, she responded to him and they clung to each other as if something was about to tear them apart. "I love you, my Mermaid." His lips were pressed to hers.

"I love you too, my darling." Her heart ached for love of him and she wondered if this was a good sign. It seemed to her that pain and pleasure, sorrow and joy were an indistinguishable part of their love. Was the war responsible for this paradox? The feeling haunted her and eroded the perfect outline of her happiness.

Cocooned in Eloka's arms, she fell asleep and did not wake up until he shook her gently early the next morning.

"Good morning, Mermaid. You slept like a baby," he whispered in her ears. She turned round, facing him. Looking at her, he added, "You're lovelier this morning than you've ever been."

Ginika smiled and hugged him. "My darling, you say such nice things that will make me become conceited if I'm not careful." She threw a leg over one of his. "I hope you had a good night's sleep yourself?"

"I did, but I also spent part of the night thinking and have arrived at a decision."

Ginika looked at his face, as her heart lurched, like a drunkard. "What decision?" she heard herself ask in a voice that sounded strange even to her.

"Mermaid, you must take this with courage, I have decided to join the army." He said it so matter-of-factly, as if he was asking her and himself why he had delayed so long to reach it. She couldn't bear to see the glint of satisfaction in his eyes, the type one experienced if one had peace of mind.

Ginika burst into tears.

"Why are you crying?" he asked gently, stroking her long hair. "Do you want me to be conscripted and taken away like a criminal, when I'm qualified to train as an officer? Should I continue to live like a rat – hiding in the day and scuttling about in the night? Is this the life you want for your husband? You'll be safe here; my father and mother will take care of you for me. And Ozioma is your sister-in-law as well as your friend. She loves you, I know."

She gazed at him and her tears flowed faster.

"You're the first to know, my love," he said softly. "I will inform my father and mother later." His face was set in a new mould that terrified her.

Ginika understood that nothing she did or said would stop Eloka from enlisting in the army. But this knowledge rather than pacify her brought her more anguish.

22

The following morning after Eloka had left home to enlist in the army, Ginika and her father-in-law went to the refugee camp where she was to start work as assistant warden. Eloka had asked his father to find work for her in the camp to keep her busy. As she trudged behind her father-in-law, Ginika remembered the scene earlier that morning.

The family had been unusually quiet at breakfast. Everyone missed Eloka. From time to time, Ginika's eyes kept glancing at the seat he normally occupied at meals. Tears threatened to overwhelm her but she managed to keep them at bay. Her mother-in-law's eyes occasionally also swept Eloka's seat. Unlike Ginika, who bore her suffering patiently, Eloka's mother groaned more than once.

"Oh, Eloka, my son, may God protect you."

"Mama, it is enough. Don't worry. Just pray for him." Ozioma had said soothingly.

Ginika increased her pace to catch up with her father-in-law. For a man of his age and build, he was agile enough. She believed he was older than her father, though she couldn't be so sure. Slim people often looked younger than fat people who were of a similar age, she thought.

319

She was grateful that she wouldn't have to be idle if she started working in the refugee camp. She had never worked in her life, but there was a beginning to everything, she surmised. This was going to be her first working experience and she looked forward to it. Her eyes roamed far and wide, and observed passersby and those far ahead of them – women going to work, children trotting about, running errands for parents or older siblings, especially young men hiding away from conscripting officers. She was somewhat relieved her Eloka was free from such hibernation. Ginika sighed wearily.

"We are almost there," she heard her father-in-law say.

"Yes, I know the place." They were now walking side by side as the path widened.

"You have been to the camp?" He turned to look at her.

"Not exactly. I have passed this way several times on my way to visit my aunt though I have never entered the camp. It was here Eloka and I and other students rehearsed the plays we staged in Nnewi and at Ekwulobia." She hoped he knew about the plays, which unfortunately they were not able to perform in Ama-Oyi before they disbanded.

"Yes, Eloka mentioned the plays." He turned, looking forward. "Here we are. We will go and see the warden and I will introduce you to the other workers and the refugees."

The primary school compound was completely taken over by the refugees; even the teachers' quarters were occupied. The buildings were draped with palm fronds and assorted leaves as camouflage. Ginika saw women engaged in one task or the other – washing clothes in metal buckets, gathering wood under trees, playing with emaciated children and babies, and sweeping the surroundings. Some sat under the trees chatting quietly, while others lay spreadeagled on threadbare mats, staring vacantly into space. She noticed that there were no young or able-bodied men in the camp, only old men, old women, younger women and children.

Her father-in-law took her to the office, a whitewashed bungalow with a peaked and rusty roof. "As you can see, the headmaster's office has been turned into the refugee office. This is where all the workers stay from eight in the morning to four o'clock in the evening when they close, and you will join them there." He smiled.

The warden stood up as soon as they entered. "Good morning, Chief," he said, as his eyes perched on her father-in-law briefly before travelling to Ginika's face.

"Good morning, Asiobi. How is the camp? No problem, I hope?"

"None, sir. We have just received some relief materials and will distribute them to the refugees soon. The consignment came from the WCC."

"Good." He touched Ginika's shoulder and said, "This is Ginika, my daughter-in-law, who will work with you as your assistant. Where are the other workers? I want to introduce her to them, too."

Mr Asiobi smiled and shook her hand before calling out, "Janet, where are you?"

A pretty young woman emerged from an inner room, carrying an exercise book with a red cover. "Sir...," she began and stopped when she saw Chief Odunze. "Good morning, Chief," she greeted, curtseying. "Welcome, sir." She looked at Ginika, assessing her dress and her body, critically, before turning her eyes again to Chief Odunze.

"Janet, how are you? Meet my daughter-in-law who will work here with you all." To Ginika, "Janet Nsoh is the camp secretary, though there is very little secretarial work needed here." He laughed.

Ginika observed that Janet didn't laugh; instead she turned and said, "Nice to meet you, Ginika."

As they shook hands, Ginika smiled. "I'm pleased to meet you, Janet." She felt elated that someone of about her own age worked in the camp.

"Emma and Inno are with the refugees now," Janet said.

"You will meet them later." Mr Asiobi smiled again.

After her father-in-law had left, they walked across to the area where most of the refugees lived and Mr Asiobi introduced her to the other two workers, Emma and Inno, before also presenting her to the refugees. The two men were walking towards them apparently returning to the office.

Ginika shook hands with Emma, a knock-kneed man of about forty-five and Inno who, though younger and stronger, was a halfwit with two fingers missing from his right hand. She thought these two would be free from conscription; even in a desperate situation, she didn't think anyone would conscript them, for they didn't look as if they would make good soldiers.

When Inno caught Ginika looking at his deformed hand, he babbled, "You have seen my hand, eh? I lost two fingers at a saw mill before the war. The machine cut the fingers *wham, wham*, like this." He demonstrated, contorting his face to show the degree of pain he experienced at the time. Ginika battled to contain the laughter that shook her, but when she heard Janet laughing heartily, she threw her head back and gurgled with laughter.

Mr Asiobi led the way to the refugees. Ginika was pulled back and detained briefly by Janet who whispered, "Prepare yourself for a shock." Ginika looked at her quickly, wondering what she meant. She had never visited a refugee camp, so she could not begin to imagine what shock awaited her. Well, she would soon find out.

Ginika stilled her body for whatever lay ahead. But she was not prepared for the sight before her in the various rooms – former classrooms and assembly hall – occupied by the refugees as their living quarters. The first thing that struck her even while they were still some metres away was the pungent odour oozing from that direction. Mr Asiobi entered the hall and Ginika could hardly recognise it as the same place where they had rehearsed the plays. A sea of heads confronted her and as she drew closer to the human scarecrows, she almost cried out at the image presented by some of them.

"*Geenu nti*, listen, all of you," Mr Asiobi announced with a loud voice, "We have a new person who will work here with us and help you. Her name is Mrs Ginika Odunze, Chief's daughter-in-law."

Ginika stepped forward to be seen properly. She smiled, her eyes darting from one part of the hall to the other. She was struck by the indifference in most of their eyes, as if they were asking what difference it made to their situation if another worker joined the staff. She overheard a very dark-skinned woman with exposed breasts, who sat close to where she stood, whisper to her neighbour, "One more person to steal our stockfish and corn meal." Ginika was shocked, but pretended she had not heard what was said.

As they proceeded to greet the refugees, she was shocked by their state of permanent depression. "Miss, how are you?" asked an old man who lay on a torn mat. "You are beautiful, my daughter, and you remind me of a daughter I had before this terrible war. I don't know where she, her two brothers and my wife are now. We ran in different directions when the enemy entered our town." His eyes were glazed with boredom and grief. And Ginika wondered if he would survive the war even if it were to end soon. The man looked so emaciated and weak.

"Papa, be patient," she consoled him, touching his scraggy leg. "You will find your family when the war ends."

He nodded, but Ginika knew he did not believe her, for his eyes remained dead, grey and hopeless. She felt like fleeing from the camp, wondering if she would be able to work here, in the midst of so much woe and suffering. Again, she thought of how lucky Ama-Oyi people were to live in their own town, till their soil and harvest food crops no matter how poor the harvest was, no matter that sometimes the crops were stolen, by refugees and local thieves, before they matured.

When they moved to another room, Janet whispered, "This is where *kwashiorkor* victims are. The Red Cross set up a kitchen for them where special meals are prepared for them, but many of them will not survive because it's too late." She pointed to a little girl who was struggling to sit up. "That girl over there is ten years old. Look at her."

Ginika went to the girl. "Can I help you?" she asked gently, tears struggling free from her eyes. The girl stopped, looked at her and nodded. Her eyes were like *umi*, shallow wells filled with muddy water. Her head had a few tufts of hair which ironically had the colour of gold. With her jutting wrinkled forehead, sallow skin, sunken cheeks and emaciated body, she looked more like a wizened old woman than the child of ten that she was.

As Ginika lifted the child, her tears splashed on the balding head. "Oh, God," she moaned, as if she were in pain.

"Thank you," she heard the girl say, and her tears ran down her cheeks, each drop chasing the one before it. "I can't bear this," she murmured to herself, wiping her eyes with the back of her hand. She wanted to run away, but did not. As she moved the child, she noticed she had soiled her clothes. She turned to Janet. "What do I do? See, she passed excreta on herself."

"Are you going to use your hands or clothes to clean her up? There are two women who look after them. They will soon be here. Let's go, the warden is waiting for us."

Ginika cast sympathetic glances at the child and laid her back on the smelly mat. "They will change your dress and clean you up when they come," she whispered to the child. As she walked away, she saw the child's eyes following her, pursuing her, and she knew those eyes would haunt her for the rest of her life. She fled the room, away from the house of horror – she had counted twenty children, in the room, in various stages of dehumanization. She knew some of them would be dead before long.

"One more section to see," Mr Asiobi hinted, leading the way.

As they were about to enter another room, Janet whispered, "We enter the place we call 'Room without Hope' – where we keep those about to die."

Ginika stared, dreading going in. Could she face the inhabitants of 'Room without Hope'? She hesitated. Janet gave her hand a tug.

The unpleasant odour hit her before she was smack in the darkened room. Why was the room dark at noon, she wondered? Then she discovered that brown paper covered the gaps between the roof and the walls.

"You have come to see if I am dead," a feeble voice cried out in the extreme corner of the room. "I am not dead yet."

"What does that mean?" Ginika asked Janet.

"His name is Matthew. He is seriously ill. We call him 'The Singer' because he likes to sing or chat all the time. Initially, he sang only war songs, but when his condition deteriorated, or worsened considerably, he changed to gospel songs."

Matthew lay on his back, his rigid head facing up. He broke into a song.

"Into you have I run, O Jehovah
Do not allow me to be shamed
Do not allow me to be shamed
Jehovah, let me not be shamed
Youths, come and sing with me
Let me not be shamed forever."

The song pierced Ginika's heart, drawing her to the side of the singer and sufferer. Though there were ten others in this pathetic situation, her attention was focused solely on Matthew. He lay on a makeshift bed with a tattered and grimy sheet. She could smell him a short distance away. As she approached, he swivelled around to look at her, his sunken eyes glued to her face.

"You are new here?" he asked and a weak spark lit his opaque eyes.

She nodded, her eyes brimming with tears.

"Don't cry for me," he told her. "Cry for Biafra. I didn't go to war, but war found me here and finished me."

"Hush, don't say that." Ginika bent towards him gently,

observing his bare torso and worn trousers. She was surprised to see he was a young man. "How are you today, Matthew?"

"Help me and turn me over to face the wall. My back is sore," he pleaded.

He was a veritable bag of bones; all flesh had vacated his body, turning him into a living skeleton. She looked at Janet, who shrugged, as if telling her that the choice to oblige Matthew was hers. She gripped a bony arm and a scraggy leg and half-lifted him before turning him. Ginika went rigid, stifling a scream, for Matthew's back and buttocks were covered with sores. She stared at the raw, reddened skin.

"Bed sores," Janet whispered. "Let's go," she said mechanically.

As she stumbled after Janet, Ginika refused to look at the other inmates who lay motionless, as if they were already dead. Their state of half-life not only frightened her but also made her feel guilty to be alive and well. She wanted to escape to the fresh air outside.

As she gulped fresher air outside, she asked Mr Asiobi, "Who takes care of them? I mean the ones who are ill?" Ginika shuddered.

"There are women who are paid to take care of the bad cases, like the children we saw earlier and the people in the last room we inspected. The other refugees take care of themselves. They get relief materials when they are available – they are not always available – and prepare food for themselves." He shrugged. "There is very little we can do for them here. We supervise them, report when they are sick and organise their burial when they die. Many have died."

"Every week, someone dies in this camp." Janet shook her head. "A dead body means nothing to me now. Before the war, I don't know how many dead bodies I had seen. Now I see at least one every week. If I have a choice, I'll leave this work. It breaks my heart."

"You seem used to the terrible situation here," Ginika put in. "You're not from Ama-Oyi, are you?"

"No, I'm a refugee myself, from Nenwe. I ran first from Enugu, then from Awka and ended here. I was a Grade II teacher in a primary school before the war. This is where I ended."

"Janet, don't complain," Mr Asiobi stingingly rebuked. "You should be grateful to be alive after all you went through."

Janet laughed. "I am, believe me."

"I hope Chief told you we are paid with relief material?" Mr Asiobi asked, turning to Ginika. "We are not paid cash here. We are volunteers more or less and receive a ration of relief when and if it is available.

"That's all right." Her father-in-law had not told her this, but it didn't matter because she was not there to earn money. She wanted to be useful.

"We can return to the office now. You can see the other rooms some other time." He waved to Ginika and Janet to walk before him.

"Sir, go ahead, I want to show Ginika something first." Janet took hold of Ginika's hand. When Mr Asiobi was out of earshot, Janet said, "Look at those houses," pointing, "Wealthier and more influential refugees live in those. They were formerly teachers' quarters, but are now occupied by 'lucky people'." Pointing to another building, she continued, "I live in one of the rooms in that long building. Can you see the house over there? That used to be the headmaster's quarters, I was told, but it is now occupied by a rich businessman from

Awka. You may wonder how somebody like me managed to get a room there to myself." Without waiting for Ginika's reply, she added, "An air force officer who is my friend helped me. I hope you'll come to see where I'm ensconced one day?" She laughed.

"Yes, I will come one day, not today though."

"See the other house," she pointed again. "I learnt it used to be the second master's house, the man next to the headmaster. Do you know who lives there even now?" There was a mischievous glint in her eyes that Ginika could not help noticing. She became curious, wondering who it was, but when Janet told her, she gave a little cry because she wouldn't have guessed right even if Janet had given her a hundred chances to guess who it was.

"Chief's lover lives there with her two young children. He visits her regularly and I see him because my room faces the house. She is from Awka and her name is Nwoyibo Moneke. You will meet her today when she comes for her share of the relief material we shall distribute this afternoon."

Ginika had heard enough. She was not prepared to discuss her father-in-law with Janet who was a total stranger she had just met. However, her heart was thumping with excitement as she reflected on the information. How could her father-in-law do this? Wouldn't his wife be furious if she found out? Didn't he consider the family before taking a mistress and giving her one of the choicest living quarters in the compound? What a scandal! She blinked her eyes in sheer distaste and disgust.

"Let's get back to the office before Mr Asiobi gets annoyed with us," she said.

Janet stared at her. "You're not offended by what I told you about your father-in-law, are you?"

"Of course, I'm not." She shook her head. "I'm only surprised because I didn't expect it."

"Anyway, you would have found out soon even if I had not told you. Chief hardly hides his interest in Nwoyibo."

How come her mother-in-law had not found out then? Ginika thought.

⁂

AT NOON, Mr Asiobi sent word round, asking the refugees to assemble for their relief materials. Emma and Inno brought the bags, cartons and tins out and placed them under the trees where they would be shared. This was a part of the compound where a cluster of trees formed a dense canopy that hid it from the view of any enemy plane that flew past.

"Let's take some chairs out there," Janet said.

"Okay. How many?"

"You carry two and I'll bring two also."

Janet and Ginika carried chairs to the shade for Mr Asiobi and the rest of the workers to sit during the exercise. Inno brought a table and placed it in front of Mr Asiobi.

"Use your sense, move the table to the other side," he chided.

Inno laughed sheepishly, obeying him at once. "Sorry, sir," he stuttered, lifting the table expertly in spite of his deformed hand.

From his enthusiasm, Ginika could see he loved his job. But who in his position wouldn't, considering that the job brought him valuable rewards in the form of relief materials. Ginika knew that many people in Ama-Oyi would jubilate if they had Inno's job. She was not sure if what she heard was true, but Janet had jokingly informed her that Inno had a pretty girlfriend and that it was the gift of food that attracted the girl to him.

Many of the refugees were there already, smiles pasted on their grim faces, as they rejoiced. It was over three weeks since the last supply, Janet told Ginika.

Mr Asiobi sat behind the table and the other workers sat next to him except Inno who walked about to keep order. The refugees formed a long line and waited patiently for their turn. Ginika knew that they were quiet and did not jostle because they were sure to get their share no matter how small the supply. Janet told her that the sharing was done equitably and what the first person got was what the last person received. Sharing was done according to individuals and not family, so that a family of five would get more than a family of two. A person alone got just one person's share. Janet told her she got her share as a refugee as well as a worker; at the end of the month, she received her payment in form of relief material. Ginika could see why she looked strong, healthy and well-groomed. Or was there another source of income for Janet? Ginika wondered. She prepared to assist in the sharing, but sat down when she heard Mr Asiobi's stentorian voice.

"Where are the sharers?" bellowed Mr Asiobi. "Start the sharing immediately, so that we get done as soon as possible."

Five women detached themselves from the crowd and came forward. Janet told Ginika the women were officially selected to help in sharing items and they were rewarded modestly after their task.

"Quickly, please." Mr Asiobi prodded in a hectoring tone of voice. "Nkonyelu get on with it. And you, Grace, start with stockfish."

Nkonyelu, light-skinned, with a pleasantly rounded figure responded immediately, scooping up corn meal into the bowls presented to her on the queue. Grace was podgy and sour-faced, but she complied with instructions readily enough. She gave each person one full length of stockfish. Soon each of the five women was busy giving out an item of relief.

Fascinated, Ginika watched as their hands moved like lightning. She was sure she could not have done so well if it had been left to her to perform the task. These women were experts, she thought.

"I wonder what they did for a living before the war drove them away from their homes," Ginika said to Janet.

"Oh, they were carefully chosen to do this work – because of their age and their trades. They were all traders at Eke Awka, before they were displaced. Nkonyelu told me she sold rice and beans, and Grace sold melon seed and *ogbono*." She laughed. "They make our work easier; I would hate to do this." She waved her hand towards the women. "I'm a trained teacher, not a trader."

"They certainly seem happy to do it." Ginika turned her eyes again to the women.

In less than an hour all the materials had been shared among the refugees. The workers' share was set apart. Ginika was impressed – and said as much to Janet – that there had been no rancour of any sort and the exercise had gone through peacefully.

"Well, yes, but it is not always this peaceful, though. The other day, two women quarrelled and abused each other roundly. But it is generally peaceful here. If you go to the relief centres at any Caritas or WCC, you will see people struggling and pushing. There, it's a free-for-all."

"That's what I hear," Ginika agreed. She heard the woman called Nkonyelu ask Mr Asiobi, "Sir, do you want us to share your own for you?" She pointed to the workers' share.

"Thank you, but don't bother. We will share ours later."

"You didn't even ask me to show you Chief's lover," Janet remarked, nudging Ginika. "*Hmm*, you are not curious. If it was me, I would not rest until I have found out."

Ginika turned to her. "Okay, show her to me."

"Don't look in that direction until I finish with the description, or she'll know I'm talking about her. Her eyes are directed this way. She is wearing a green blouse and a flowing yellow skirt. She is neither fat nor thin – somewhere in between. Finally, she has glossy dark skin and a nose as straight and pointed as that of a maiden mask. Now search for her by Mr Asiobi's left. I'm not looking at her any longer."

"I hope I remember all your description. It was too detailed and I've forgotten half of it already," Ginika said, looking up and directing her eyes towards Mr Asiobi's left.

"At least you remember she is wearing a green blouse and a yellow skirt," Janet reminded her.

Ginika saw her after a brief search – a strikingly beautiful woman, almost regal in carriage. She was indeed looking their way, but because Ginika was not staring, she was sure the lovely creature was none the wiser. She was also looking in her direction and Ginika suspected someone who was there earlier in the day when Mr Asiobi introduced her must have told her that she was Chief Odunze's daughter-in-law. Ginika wondered what the woman was thinking. Would she feel endangered with her lover's relation working at the camp? Was she worried Ginika might find out about her affair with her father-in-law and report the matter to her mother-in-law, Chief Odunze's wife?

Ginika continued to cast sly glances at the woman who now stooped down to lift a basin in which she had put all the items she got. She straightened up and walked away towards the second master's house which now belonged to her. Her two little children, a boy and a girl trotted behind her. Ginika guessed the boy could be six and his sister four. She was basing her estimation on her aunt's children.

"She's beautiful," she stated. "Is she not married? Where is the father of her children?" She thought, however, that her mother-in-law was more beautiful than the woman though she was a lot older. The refugee woman's skin glowed and her face was without any wrinkles, not even around her eyes or at the corners of her mouth. Perhaps she was not up to thirty, Ginika thought.

"Some people say he's in the army, but no one knows. He has never visited her, to my knowledge."

Ginika shrugged. "Perhaps, she's a widow."

She decided to leave her share of the relief material in the office until she contacted Udo to pick up the pack and take it to his mother. She believed they needed the items more than her new family did.

GINIKA GOT home at about five o'clock and went to Eloka's rose garden where she pottered about for some twenty minutes, tending the roses, lifting fallen stems and weeding. She knew she was not good at gardening and had detested it at school when they had to work in the garden every Tuesday. Osondu was not looking after the garden well, she thought, saddened by the sight of blighted leaves and wilting and fading blossoms. Only Eloka could prune the roses properly and bring them to life. He had green fingers. She smiled at the thought. Osondu hid all day in the house to avoid being conscripted. The other day she had heard him bleat, "*Chinekem*, my God, my body will go mouldy from hiding all day in this house." And Ozioma had laughed and scoffed, "You coward, go and sit down!" When Eloka returned home, he would be disappointed to see the state of his garden and his roses, she thought. But when would that be? When would he come home?

Ginika picked a red rose – one of the very few left in the garden – and pressed it to her nose, inhaling deeply, thinking of Eloka and longing to have him back. She returned to the house and joined Ozioma who was already preparing dinner. She was cooking *ndudu* and maize which would later be blended in hot palm oil mixed with red pepper, *uziza* and salt. Her father-in-law loved the dish.

"*Umu agbogho*, young ladies, well done," her mother-in-law greeted, as she came into the house and walked straight to the kitchen. "What is producing this delicious smell?" Ginika wondered where she was coming from; she looked beautiful in her *wrappa* and white blouse made from lace material.

"We are cooking *ndudu* and maize," Ozioma announced.

"Is your father home?" She looked at Ozioma.

"No, he went for a council meeting. He said I should tell you not to wait for him for dinner, that he would have his whenever he returned."

"All right, we will dine without him."

As she walked away, Ginika felt sorry for her, thinking how ignorant she was of her husband's philandering, wondering what she would do if she found out. She was sad about the whole thing, but decided not to tell her. She didn't know what her father-in-law would do to her if she exposed him and if he found out she had done it. And she was certain her mother-in-law would tell him how she got to know, so she was determined to keep her lips sealed. From the little interaction she had had with her mother-in-law, she knew she was the type of woman who could not keep a secret. She would see nothing wrong in telling him how she found out, without considering the repercussions on her informant.

As Ginika poured some palm oil into a sauce pan to heat it, her mother-in-law called her. She found her in the sitting room, holding up her headdress which she had unwound and tried to straighten with her hands. As she folded it, she said, "I will like to talk to you in my room after we have had dinner." She smiled, as if to tell her there was nothing to worry about, that she only wanted to chat with her and to get to know her better.

Ginika nodded, feeling a little uneasy. She had to admit that sometimes she felt intimidated before her mother-in-law especially since Eloka left home. He had been a buffer between her and his family, making sure they treated her well. Not that she had anything to complain about really, but sometimes she felt Eloka's mother resented her. Perhaps she had had someone else in mind for him. Eloka told her jokingly once that Adaeze, his sister, had found him a wife; so desperate were they to get him married off. He had said, "I beat them to it by choosing a wife for myself; not that I would have succumbed to them even if I didn't have you."

She rejoined Ozioma who looked up quickly, staring at her for a while. "Why is your face like that? Is something wrong?"

When she shook her head, Ozioma added, "Don't worry about Mama. Sometimes she likes to make sure everyone does as she wishes, even Papa. But we all know how to wriggle out of her schemes and outwit her." She laughed. "She doesn't think as fast as she acts, remember that."

Ginika stared at her, not knowing what to think or say.

"Ah, you look so serious. Relax. Remember, you have a friend here, me," pointing to her chest. "Don't forget that Eloka asked me to take good care of you. And I will."

"He said that?" Ginika laughed. "Did he forget I'm older than you and should be the one to look after you?" She was grateful to have Ozioma around, someone whose age was close to hers. She didn't know how she could have managed if she had been left alone with her parents-in-law.

AFTER DINNER she waited for her mother-in-law to retire and followed soon. Ozioma had said she and Osondu would clear the table and wash the dishes, so she was free to see her mother-in-law and retire to her room afterwards – her room now that Eloka was away.

She knocked gently and waited. "Come in, the door is open." She remembered that Eloka had told her no door in the house had a lock except the front and back doors. The bunch of keys to all the rooms had been taken away and they never found out who did it. His father changed the front and back doors and had new locks fixed, but he did not come round to doing the same for the other doors until the war started. When she and Eloka wanted privacy, they would simply push the table against the door to bar or block it.

Ginika pushed the door and stood at the entrance. This was the second time she had entered the room since she started living in the house. Ozioma usually swept the room in the morning.

"Sit down, Ginika." She pointed to a chair opposite the armchair in which she sat. She had changed into a loose gown that gave even more bulk to her plump body. She waited for her to sit down before speaking again. "You miss your husband, don't you?" She smiled.

Ginika nodded, and laughed. "Yes, I miss him very much."

"We all do."

She looked up and saw her mother-in-law watching her closely. "Tell me, are you pregnant?"

Ginika flinched. She stared at her mother-in-law, scandalised almost. She frowned, wondering why she should ask her such a question. She said nothing.

"Didn't you hear me? I asked if you are pregnant. Is it wrong for me to ask my son's wife if she is pregnant?"

Ginika thought about it and decided to respond and politely, too, as she did not want any conflict to develop between her and her mother-in-law. It was unnecessary. It was important to maintain a friendly relationship especially as Eloka was not around. They needed to have peace, so that their prayer for his safety would be answered.

"No, I'm not pregnant."

Silence.

Her mother-in-law sighed heavily. "You're not pregnant?"

"I said I'm not." She looked at her.

"You allowed your husband to leave you, to join the army without making sure you are pregnant!" She did not try to hide her exasperation, her scorn.

Ginika was angry and disappointed in her mother-in-law, but she tried not to show any such sign. "Eloka said he didn't want us to have a baby during the war, that we should wait for it to end and finish our education."

"He said this to you? And you agreed?"

"Yes, I believe he's right. I quite agree."

"*Hei*, you quite agree, eh? *Lekwenu muo*, look at me-o! Why do people get married? Is it not to have children? Ginika, answer me now? So you married Eloka without intending to have children, to give him children and grandchildren to me and my husband? *Chei!* So we came to your father's house to marry you for you to come here and be staring us in the face? So you want to move about in the house empty, *ina ekpokoghari ebea*? God forbid a bad thing!" She snapped her fingers repeatedly.

Ginika began to say something, but refrained, biting her tongue. Her mother-in-law stared in front of her, with pursed lips.

"Mama, can I go now?" she asked, with the triumphant feeling that she had taken her mother-in-law's verbal attack without losing her temper or speaking to her in similar terms.

"Go. But I want you to know that I'm displeased with you. I know Eloka is partly to blame, but it is the duty of a wife to make sure her husband plays his role properly, especially in the matter of getting her pregnant."

23

Her work done, her hair washed and plaited, Ginika decided to spend her free time visiting friends and relations. She wore a loose black and white dress which she thought suitable for a long walk, for she planned to traverse the town to see everyone she had in mind to visit that day – her father and Auntie Lizzy, Uncle Chima and his family, Udo's mother and her children, Eunice, Janet and, lastly but most importantly, Auntie Chito and her children as well as Nne, her grandmother, who now lived with her aunt. It was a lot of ground to cover, but she was determined to accomplish her aim.

It was a cool Saturday afternoon and she did not have to go to work, but she was going to the refugee camp anyway to visit Janet who was now her friend. Ginika knew that ordinarily Janet would not have been her type, but the war had brought them together and forged a close friendship between them. She admitted to herself that sometimes she was shocked at Janet's brazen behaviour and calculating disposition in which she exploited every situation to her advantage, but there were other sides of her Ginika admired – her cheerfulness, her kindness and her independent spirit which made her fearless.

Her first destination was Eunice's house, but she didn't even sit down before leaving the place.

"Eunice is not at home," her mother replied to Ginika's enquiry.

"Thank you, ma. Please, tell her I was here."

"I will, my daughter. Go well."

She headed for the refugee camp, swinging her hand to the tune of one of the songs she had learnt and sung during the performance of *Mammy Water*. As she hummed the song, she thought of Eloka, wondering if he was in the battlefield or in the house where he lived. He had written her a note which an army officer who said Eloka was his mate in the training camp had brought to her. He wrote that they had finished their training and he was now in Etiti as an officer in 7 Commando Engineers. She hid the note under her pillow and read and re-read it every day. She wondered about the word, commando. Was this not the arm of the army called Suicide Squad? And this was the battalion in which her Eloka was serving. She breathed a prayer to God on his behalf.

Janet was cooking when Ginika arrived. A little girl pointed when she asked for Janet and she followed the direction of the pointing finger. She found her washing rice in a bowl, in a small kitchen at the back of the long building.

"Ha, madam, you've come to see me," Janet cried, beaming.

Ginika laughed. Janet called her madam when she wanted to tease her. "You're cooking? This small portion? Will it feed a lizard, not to talk of a human being?"

"It's only me. Am I cooking for a family?" The way she looked at her dress, Ginika knew she liked it. "You have such lovely dresses," she murmured.

"Yes, because I still have most of my dresses unlike you who lost most of yours when you ran from Enugu and Nenwe."

"It's true, but I must say I didn't have many nice clothes even before the war. My parents were poor – how I wish I knew where they are – and as a teacher, I didn't earn much."

"I hope they are safe where they are," Ginika remarked sympathetically.

"That is my prayer." Janet poured the rice in a pot containing some water and placed it over the fire she had built at the base of a tripod stand made of mud blocks. "Let's go into the room."

"Won't the rice burn? Who will watch it?"

"No problem, I will come out to check it from time to time."

"This small kitchen is for all of you living in this long building?"

"Yes, my sister. You need to see how people quarrel over little things here. I always stay away and come here to cook after they have all cooked and left. I hate to quarrel with any of them. They would seize the opportunity to abuse you and say things that will break your heart." She sighed.

Ginika understood well what she meant. She remembered the time she had gone to spend her holiday with Uncle Chima and his family in Aba. They lived in a typical face-me-I-face-you house. There were quarrels all the time with neighbours over everything – the kitchen, the toilets, the well and the line where clothes were spread to dry. She was frightened to use the half-filled and fetid bucket toilet, for someone was sure to be waiting outside and would bang on the disintegrating wooden door and shout, even before she had started, "Who is in there? Are you having a baby there or just shitting? Come out and let me use the toilet." Whatever was coming out would draw back into her body and she would hurry out to allow the impatient tenant to use the toilet.

"Where is your toilet?" she asked.

"Over there. It's a pit latrine." Janet pointed before pushing open the back door to her room. She went in and Ginika followed her.

"Is it clean?" Ginika asked as she sat down on a chair Janet pushed towards her. This was her first visit to Janet. She was impressed with the neatness she saw in the small room. There were pictures from old magazines pinned to the wall probably to hide the cracks that abounded in the walls. The ceiling was of bamboo but it was in good condition. A narrow cast iron bed meant for just one person hugged the wall. The mattress sagged a little, but the white sheet was clean. Under the bed were pots and plates and a big bag which Ginika guessed contained Janet's clothes and other possessions.

Janet rummaged in a small chop box and took what she wanted, before replying to her question. "The latrine is as clean as can be expected. We take turns to clean it." She emptied some *chinchin* into a plate. "Have some *chinchin* and tell me what you think about it. I made if from the flour and dried egg yolk given to us last week."

"It tastes nice." Ginika ate some more. "I'm going to try to make it at home. Did you use sugar?"

"No. Where can one find sugar? I put some salt."

Suddenly, Ginika started laughing and Janet looked up, wondering what was so funny.

"You know, that pit latrine reminded me of an experience I had when I was in primary school. For a year, my father worked in a hospital in a rural area, and we attended school there – my brother and I. The headmaster and his wife were friends of my family. He caned me and another girl because we had fought during recess in spite of the fact that he knew it was the other girl who started the fight. In fact, my punishment was more severe. I was displeased with him and nursed my pain and anger. A few days later, Auntie Lizzy gave me a parcel of smoked fish to give to the headmaster's wife. I threw it into one of the pit toilets. I didn't ever find out if Auntie Lizzy found out her friend did not receive the gift, but no one asked me about the fish. I felt satisfied that the headmaster was denied the pleasure of enjoying the fish."

Janet burst into laughter. "I didn't know you could do a thing like that."

"Well, I did." She changed the subject. "Can you come to our house tomorrow?"

"Sorry, I can't. I'm visiting my boyfriend in Nkwere."

"How many boyfriends do you have?" Ginika eyed her with disapproval.

Janet laughed. "Just three and they help me in different ways. The squadron leader in the air force base in Ekwulobia gives me soap, cream and hair thread from Lisbon; the captain in 11 Div in Nnewi gives me money to purchase what I need; and there's the major in Nkwerre whom I love most and whose company makes the war bearable. If he asks me to marry him, I will."

Ginika shook her head. "Keep the major and let the others go. Is it every man that talks to you that you become friends with?"

"No. If I did, then I would be friends with Mr Asiobi who has been harassing me since he started working in this camp."

So Mr Asiobi had approached Janet and she had rejected him? Ginika understood why he often found fault with Janet. "Janet, think about my suggestion. Be friends with the major and drop the others."

Janet pouted. "The rice must be ready now. Let me bring it in." She left the room and soon returned, carrying the pot. "Well-timed," she announced, smiling. "I was there just in time. We can eat now; I made the stew in the morning."

"I'll leave you to enjoy your meal," Ginika announced. "I must go now and see my father and stepmother."

"Stay and eat. The food is enough for two."

"Thanks, but I had lunch before I left home."

Janet covered the pot and prepared to see her off. She searched for her sandals. "Let's go."

Ginika who went out first, turned back in haste and almost crashed into Janet. "My father-in-law," she breathed.

Janet pushed past her and looked out cautiously in time to see Chief Odunze entering Nwoyibo's house. She pulled in and laughed. "I told you. As the saying goes 'to see is to believe'. Do you believe me now?"

Dazed, Ginika sat down. "Won't they see me if I leave now?" Her voice sounded anxious.

Janet laughed. "They should be hiding, not you? So why feel embarrassed or afraid if they see you?"

Ginika glared at her. "Janet, be serious for once! That man in that woman's house is the father of my husband!"

Janet nodded. "Let's go out through the back door. It's a good thing this building is not walled like the headmaster's and the second master's houses." She took Ginika's hand and led her out of the room.

"Will you tell your mother-in-law?"

"Never."

GINIKA STAYED only a few minutes in Uncle Chima's house, long enough to see that they were well though there were visible signs that they did not eat enough and that the war was taking its toll on him and Mama Nnukwu. Mercifully Ebube, their little girl, looked well.

"Uncle Chima, what about Bartie, Belu and Nwonu? Did they go out?"

"Ah, they did what other young men had done. Bartie joined the army last month; Belu went off with the intention to join, as he told me, the Biafran Organisation of Freedom Fighters – BOFF. Yes, two of them have gone. Our people say it is the dance that comes out in one's own time that he or she dances. They are dancing the dance of their youth – two of my sons are fighting in the war."

"What of Nwonu?" Ginika asked, saddened by the news she had just received.

"Nwonu is at home. He is hiding in the roof like most young men who refuse to join the army." He shook his head. "This war has taught us many things."

"Will you not sit down?" asked Mama Nnukwu, who sat on a mat, shelling melon seeds. "How is your husband? We heard he went into the army. Have you heard anything?"

"Yes, he wrote me a letter. He is well."

"God be praised. Our hope is in God." She sighed.

"Let me go," Ginika said after a brief pause. "I want to see my father."

"Go well, daughter," Uncle Chima said. "We are sorry we have nothing to give you."

"It's all right."

"Greet our in-laws." Mama Nnukwu returned to the melon seeds.

"I will. Stay well." Ginika turned to Ebube, her little cousin, and rubbed her head. "Bye, one day you will come and visit me."

Ebube nodded and laughed.

It took Ginika less than three minutes to walk across to her home. She was mollified as she entered the compound through the back door – the door they used when they visited Uncle Chima because it was just a stone's throw to his house. It was also the door through which they had run to the bunker the night a bomb exploded and killed Ejike Okoro. She looked round fondly, thinking that this was her first home before the one she now called home.

"Anyone home?" she called in a loud voice. When she heard nothing, she walked to the front of the house and stepped onto the veranda. She wondered how her father and Auntie Lizzy could leave the back door open when they went out. Thieves could enter and take things away. She would mention this when next she saw them. She was already turning away when she heard her father's voice.

"Who is there?" he asked, descending the stairs.

She noted how heavy his steps sounded. He asked who was there. Could he have forgotten her voice so quickly? she wondered.

"It's Ginika." She waited for him to open the front door.

"Ginikanwa, it is you. Welcome."

"Papa, good afternoon. I was almost leaving, thinking no one was home." She stared at him. "How are you?" He looked so ordinary in his rumpled shirt and baggy trousers – a far cry from the spruced up, immaculately dressed doctor she knew in her childhood.

"We are well. Come inside. I was sleeping; your stepmother went to plait her hair in her friend's house."

"Let's sit in the veranda. It's more airy than the sitting room."

"How are your people? Have you heard from your husband?"

"Yes, he gave someone a letter to deliver to me. He is in the commando battalion." Her eyes roamed everywhere within their reach. She saw that the compound was not as clean as it used to be. She would remind Udo to sweep it oftener.

They did not have much to say to each other, so she got up to go. "Papa, I've seen you. Let me go now." She took a small package from her handbag and gave it to him. "Give this packet of salt to Auntie Lizzy."

"Thank you. She will be happy when she sees it. She told me yesterday she could not afford the market price of a cup of salt."

Ginika smiled. "It was given to me in the refugee camp where I work." She felt sad that her father and aunt could not afford a cup of salt. Was he no longer paid for his job? But, did he even have a job now? She could not bring herself to ask.

UDO AND his mother were grating cassava when she entered their house. His two sisters were asleep on a mat.

"Sister Ginika is here," Udo cried, starting to his feet. He stood waiting for her to join them, looking at his hands covered with cassava pulp and knowing he could not hug her.

Ginika beamed at them. She stood, looking at the small basin half-filled with peeled cassava. "You are working?"

"Yes, but you can go off with Udo if you like. There is

very little left and I can finish it in no time," Udo's mother said.

"Did you buy it from the market yesterday?" Ginika asked, pleased that Udo and his family had good food to eat. She had been worried when he told her they ate cassava husks and had given them a part of the relief material she received.

"Ha! Who can afford to pay for this quantity of cassava?" Udo's mother laughed. "No, I did not buy it. My brother gave it to me this morning when I went to my paternal home. We have been dancing since I came back. We'll eat proper *fufu* for some days."

They laughed.

"I have nothing to offer you, nothing at all, in this house. This war is cruel. It will not stop until it has swallowed everyone." She shook her head.

"Mama, don't say that." Udo frowned. "Are you trying to bring us bad luck?"

"It will not last forever," Ginika murmured. "It will stop some day, sooner or later." She felt sad that Udo's mother had lost her husband, Onagu Ezeuko, at such a young age.

"We are in it already." Udo's mother shrugged. "We cannot run away."

Ginika waited for them to finish and for Udo to take a quick bath before taking her leave. Udo said he would go with her.

"Go?" his mother said, laughing. "Whenever you see her, you behave like someone who has seen his or her guardian angel."

Again they all laughed.

"Sister Ginika, are you not my guardian angel?" He gazed at her.

CHATTING ALONG the way, they headed for Auntie Chito's house, some two or three kilometres away. They passed a checkpoint and found two women and a militia man on duty. After walking for another kilometre, they saw another checkpoint.

"There are so many checkpoints in Ama-Oyi." Udo said after they had walked past the two people manning it.

"There is a rumour that some vandals and some saboteurs infiltrated into Biafran lines and are scattered all over the place. I think the checkpoints are meant to help track them down." Ginika did not believe this rumour. She thought people who spread it wanted to use it to explain the losses Biafra had suffered in recent times and to shift the blame to saboteurs. She had learned that some people had been arrested and charged with sabotage.

When they entered Auntie Chito's house, Ginika was surprised to find it quiet. Strange. The compound was usually noisy at this time of the day; the children would shriek with laughter as they ran about, playing.

"Where is everyone?" she called out loudly. She looked back and said to Udo, "Shut the gate."

She walked into the house ahead of him because the front door was wide open. In the sitting room she found all of them. She froze. Auntie Chito was weeping calmly, her face lathered with tears which she did not attempt to wipe off. She was surrounded by her four children. Anayo the youngest sat on her knees, gazing into her face as if this had the power to make her stop or drive away whatever caused her misery.

Ginika sensed Udo walk in. Finding her voice at last, she

asked. "Auntie, what is the matter? Why are you crying like this?"

"Ginika, my child, come and sit down." It was Nne's voice. Ginika hadn't realised she was in the room, as her attention had been focused on her aunt.

"Nne, good afternoon. What is wrong with her?" She sat by her aunt, waving Udo to a chair in the corner. "Please, Auntie, tell me."

"It's Ray. He's missing. No one knows where he is." She picked up the tail of her top *wrappa* and wiped her eyes and face.

"Chito, my daughter," her mother said, "I have told you not to cry. You are not sure your husband is missing; we only heard that Ikot Ekpene was evacuated and some towns and villages were cut off, but does that mean my in-law is missing? And when he came home last time, did he not say he would move to Abak? I don't know why you are making yourself unhappy when we are not sure of anything yet. He may well be safe where he is and you are here crying your eyes out. See your children looking at you. What do you want them to do? Be patient. Let us stare back at the thing that is staring us in the face."

Her grandmother's last statement amused Ginika but she knew this was not the time to laugh at her witty sayings or idiomatic expressions. Her aunt was unhappy. In a voice full of tenderness, she said, "Auntie, if what Nne said is true, then you shouldn't worry or cry. I'm sure Uncle Ray is safe and will return home safe and sound. God will protect him, for he is a good man." She put her arm round her aunt's shoulder.

Her aunt shook her head, as if she disagreed with Ginika's opinion. "Bad things happen to good people all the time without good reasons."

Ginika sat in silence, as she had no words to counter her aunt's assertion. It was not possible for one to understand life completely, she thought. In a way, her aunt was right to say that bad things happened to good people, but she did not agree that it was so all the time.

"Good evening, ma." Udo who had kept quiet since he came in thought it was the right time to establish his presence.

"Good evening Udo. I didn't know you had come with Ginika. How are your mother and sisters?"

"They are well, ma."

Ginika had hoped to have a good time with her aunt and her family and to listen to her grandmother's jokes and proverbs, but the gloom in the room and her aunt's cloudy face discouraged such light-heartedness. She had wanted to tell her aunt of the conversation between her and her mother-in-law, but she decided against it.

"I brought you some salt." She gave her a small packet similar to the one she gave her father.

"Thank you." Her aunt managed to smile, but it was not her usual sunny smile.

"How are the people you live with?" her grandmother asked in Ama-Oyi dialect. "Have you received any message from your husband? Are you expecting him?"

"Everyone is well. My husband wrote me a letter which a soldier brought to me. He said he would come whenever he obtained a security pass."

She did not stay as long as she would have loved to, if conditions were normal. She got up and hugged her grandmother before stepping outside, followed by Udo. Her aunt saw her to the door.

"Obika and Ugo, see her off to the end of the road

and return immediately," her aunt instructed her two eldest children. "I don't want you to linger outside. Come back here before I count five or I will beat you."

Ginika laughed as the two boys ran outside eager to see her off before rushing back home, so that their mother would have no cause to carry out her threat.

AFTER OBIKA and Ugo had raced back home, Ginika and Udo quickened their steps, as the sun had gone down and darkness was threatening to fall in an hour or two. "How do we go?" Ginika asked. "Do we part here and go our various ways, or what?"

"I'll walk you home and then find my way," Udo volunteered.

"That's my gallant one," she purred, stroking his head. "Thanks."

"Don't mention it." Udo laughed. "That's the way senior boys talk in school and we junior boys imitate them. "Don't mention."

Ginika laughed. "It's the same in my school."

They walked in silence for a while then she said in a subdued voice, "We have lost many towns and villages in this war. Did you hear what my aunt said? Ikot Ekpene was evacuated recently and many places were cut off. That was why she was afraid. Abak where Uncle Ray is has been cut off. But you know sometimes it's quite safe to be in such places, behind enemy lines, they call it."

"I wouldn't like to be in a town or village that is cut off. I wouldn't want to be behind enemy lines," Udo said with a shudder. "I have heard terrible stories of what happens to people caught in crossfire."

Ginika laughed. "What is crossfire? You are talking as if you are a soldier and know about these terms. But you are a bloody civilian like me," she teased.

Udo laughed. "I listen to people talk, and learn from them."

They were about to cross over to the road that led to her house, when a man who had been hiding in a little bush by the roadside dashed forward and grabbed Udo's arm. "What did you do that for?" Ginika was annoyed. "Leave him alone."

"Shut up, woman," the man barked. "You bloody civilian, move forward. You are going to fight the vandals."

Ginika shook like a dry leaf blown by harmattan wind. She realised he was a soldier in mufti, and on a conscription mission. The first thing that came to her mind was to beg the man to let Udo go. She wished she and Udo had the courage to overpower the man and run off, but that would be dangerous. He could kill one of them. Soon she realised that it would have been a foolhardy and futile move, for ahead of them were three other soldiers dragging other young men towards them. To the rear was a man in military uniform.

Ginika kept pleading with the man holding Udo to release him, but he grew angry and ordered her to go away. "I beg you in the name of your mother to let him go. He's only a small boy and too young to fight."

When the other group came closer, she was surprised to see that the man in uniform was an officer, unlike the sergeant that had pursued Eloka to the house.

"Sir, please, let my brother go," she pleaded. "He's only a boy."

The second lieutenant glared at her and asked her to go away before he got annoyed. Ginika looked at Udo who was helplessly being dragged all the way to join the others. She wondered if they had a vehicle waiting to take them away. What would she say to Udo's mother? Tears filled her eyes, but she knew this was not the time to cry. She had to think fast of a way to help Udo. A thought struck her and she started running, heading for home.

In less than ten minutes she was back, clutching a purse. The officer and his men were now rounding up their captives who were ten in number. Ginika saw that two were much older than the others, but they were not old. The rest – except Udo – were probably in their twenties.

As she drew near to the officer, his face darkened and she knew he thought she was coming to bribe him with money.

"What are you trying to do?" he barked.

She opened the purse and brought out two photographs. "Sir, please, take a look at these two photographs. See my brother who is a lieutenant in the army in full uniform. This one is my husband, also an officer in the army. Do you want to take my little brother away too? He is only fourteen, look at him well. Please, don't take him away."

The officer looked at the two photographs for some time.

Ginika shouted to Udo, "Quick, remove your shirt. What are you waiting for? Do it!" She screamed at him. Udo removed his shirt.

"Sir, recently he had his appendix taken out. The doctor said he should not do any hard work for now. If you take him away, you will kill him. He is too young to fight and he is not in good health to fight even if you think he is not too young."

As the officer looked from the photographs to Udo's

scarred belly, he hesitated. Ginika fell at his feet and wrapped her arms around one leg, weeping. "Sir, you're from 11 Div in Nnewi, aren't you? I recognise the emblem on your uniform. Do you remember the group who performed the play *Mammy Wota*?" She looked up and fixed her eyes on his face. "I played Mermaid and my husband wrote and directed the play. He has since joined the army. We are true Biafrans. Please, have mercy on my little brother."

The officer's face softened. He bent down, but Ginika drew away, not sure what he wanted to do. He smiled and pulled her up gently and returned the photographs to her. "That was a damn good play," he said, his smile broadening. "We enjoyed it. Take your brother away and keep him safe." He turned to his men and commanded, "Release the boy and let him go with his sister."

"Oh, thank you very much, sir." Ginika wiped her eyes and then put the photographs back in her purse. Udo came over to where she was and together, hand in hand, they walked to the house which was quite close.

"Thank you, Sister Ginika," Udo breathed again.

Both of them smiled as she said, "Don't mention it."

MUCH LATER, in the night, Ginika and Osondu took Udo home. Udo was quiet. He could hardly utter a word, for the experience had shaken him up more than anything in his life.

Ginika consoled him. "You're okay, but you must be careful from now onwards. You can see that you are not free anymore. No more walking about the town. If your mother cannot hide you, please, come here and hide with Osondu."

Osondu laughed heartily. "Soldier don get new style to catch people. Me, I will get new style to hide. I will never join the army. I dey ready to die than carry gun. *Na* so I tell Brother Eloka."

Ginika laughed for the first time since her encounter with the soldiers earlier in the evening.

24

On her way to work on Monday morning, Ginika was full of cheer. Her thoughts were filled with Udo and his lucky escape from the clutches of the soldiers who almost conscripted him.

As soon as she entered the compound, she knew something had gone wrong. There were no children playing about or doing one thing or the other for their mothers. The few people she saw looked at her mournfully. Mr Asiobi's face was grim and he did not respond to her "Good morning"; instead he turned to give instructions to two men who were in his office. She left them and walked into the narrow room she shared with Janet.

"Ginika, welcome. I came to pick up something before returning to the horrible scene."

"Janet, good morning. What are you talking about? What horrible scene? What has happened?" Ginika sensed something terrible must have happened to wipe the smile off Janet's face. She could not remember any time a smile did not lurk around Janet's eyes since she started working in the camp.

"My dear, there is nothing good about this morning, at all," Janet said brusquely. "Let's go; I'll tell you on the way."

When they entered Mr Asiobi's office, Ginika saw that he

had left it probably with the two men in his company when she came in. She followed Janet who was ahead, her trim figure encased in a tight-fitting blue dress swaying attractively as she walked. Ginika caught up with her.

"Can you please let me know what is happening?" The suspense almost choked her.

"Two children died this morning, a boy of seven and his sister aged five. It's so bad because they were two of the healthiest and liveliest of the kids. Their mother is called Mgboli. You know her, don't you?"

"Yes, I know Mgboli, a pleasant and friendly woman who lives in the big hall. What happened to those two beautiful children?"

"The story is that Mgboli bought cassava in Orie Market and thinking it was the type you just boil and eat, she cooked it and fed it to her children yesterday. Unfortunately, it was the poisonous variety and the poor children died before dawn. I heard her screaming this morning when I woke up. Then Mr Asiobi arrived and took over."

Ginika halted to digest the shock. She shook her head several times.

"Come on. Let's get there before Mr Asiobi gets angry."

"How sad!" Ginika knew how poisonous the variety of cassava grown in Ama-Oyi was. One of Mama Nnukwu's three goats died last month from eating from a basket of cassava left in the house. "Our cassava is very poisonous," she told Janet. "The type that is not poisonous is rare here, though one sees it occasionally; our people call it *okotorogbo*. Very few people grow it because it is not good for *fufu* and you know Ama-Oyi people love *fufu*. They wouldn't grow cassava that is not good for *fufu*."

"Mgboli miscalculated and unwittingly poisoned her own children. It's heartbreaking." Janet sighed. You know there were other deaths – Matthew is gone and so is the old man who said you were like his daughter. Do you remember him?"

"Of course, I remember him and went to see him several times to cheer him up. His name was Ndulue. *Hei!* When did they die?"

"Last night. This morning their bodies were stiff and cold."

"Poor Matthew and Ndulue," Ginika murmured. "At least, they're out of pain now and can rest at last. May their souls rest in peace."

As they approached the area where the refugees lived, Ginika heard someone screaming and knew it was Mgboli. In the far corner, to the right, she saw three men digging.

Inside the hall, the refugees sat or stood in groups; some were with Mgboli. Ginika saw a bowl containing some palm oil which the women had forced down the throats of the sick children to counter the effect of the poison. Near the bowl were coconut shells and she understood the women had opened the coconuts to get their sap to feed the children. But their efforts had failed to save Mgboli's children.

The bereaved woman lay on the ground weeping, calling on God and her ancestors to take her life so that she could be with her children.

"What am I living for?" she wailed. "What's the use of my life now? I have lost the two people whose existence compelled me to struggle on, to try to come to terms with a war that has stripped me of my possessions. *Ewo . . . Ewo . . . Chi m egbue mu-o*, my *Chi* has killed me!" She rolled about on the floor.

Ginika turned away, unable to bear the sight of Mgboli's anguish.

The women who tried to restrain her could not control her. They allowed her to have her way. *Gbagidigim, gbagidigim, gbadigim* – her body shuttled forwards and backwards, until Mr Asiobi and Inno grabbed her and held her down firmly. She struggled to free herself.

Nkonyelu and another woman cleaned the bodies of the two children in preparation for burial. They held them lovingly, as if they were alive, and dressed them in their best clothes. As Ginika stared at them, they seemed to have life in them still, giving the impression that they were only asleep and would wake up the next minute to reassure their mother.

Then the reverend father in charge of St Peter's Catholic Church arrived. He was tall, thin and dark-skinned and wore a surplice. As soon as Mgboli saw him, she quietened down a bit, but was still weeping.

"Father, I'm dead," she cried. "I'm lost. My children have left me." Her *wrappa* and blouse were stained and dusty. Her body was covered in sweat and her face wet with tears.

He came to her and, bending down, consoled her with gentle and encouraging words. He straightened and beckoned to Mr Asiobi. The two corpses were lifted and put in two coffins made from fragile wood hurriedly knocked together. Looking at the roughness of the coffins, Ginika thought it was the work of an amateur carpenter, just as the image of Monday entered her memory. For a moment, she wondered where he was, but her attention returned to the present when she heard Mr Asiobi instructing the two men carrying the coffins to take them to the newly-dug graves.

Supported by two women, Mgboli staggered to the

grave to watch the interment of her children. Some women whispered that she should not go to the grave, but she shook her head violently and insisted. They let her have her way. One of the women said, "Let her go; war is a terrible thing and many abominations have already taken place."

Ginika and Janet joined the throng of refugees to the graveside. She was surprised to see two bundles wrapped in two new mats, near the grave.

"The remains of Matthew and Ndulue," Janet intoned. "They're to be given a collective burial."

Ginika was shocked. So Matthew and Ndulue would be buried without coffins, she thought. Aloud, she asked, "But why all of them in one grave?"

"Do you consider what will happen if everyone that dies in this camp or in any other crowded place in Biafra was buried individually?" she asked softly. "There won't be enough space left that is not a graveyard."

Ginika shuddered. So they would be buried without coffins, she thought. She watched as the reverend father performed solemnly the burial rites. The bodies were lowered one after the other.

After the burial the refugees returned to their various quarters while Ginika and the other workers returned to the office.

MR ASIOBI left for the Zonal Refugee Office in Ekwulobia to report the day's tragic incident and the burial, leaving Ginika and Janet in the office. Emma and Inno stayed in the store when they were not needed.

Janet was her cheerful self again. "Whenever Mr Asiobi is not in the office, I feel more relaxed. That man gives me the creeps." She hissed. "And I'm stuck with him here. I wish he would be transferred to another camp."

Ginika stared at her. She sat on one side of the desk they shared as a table. The bench on which both of them sat was old and the edges had been devoured by termites, making the bench narrower than it should be. Even though both of them were slender, their buttocks still jutted out, and this made them uncomfortable. Ginika would get up regularly to minimise the strain on this part of her body.

"Are things that bad? Poor you, working with a man you detest! By the way, why do we sit on this uncomfortable bench when there are four single chairs in Mr Asiobi's office?" Ginika pointed and continued, "Just see where we sit and work. Let's ask him to give us two chairs. Will that be asking too much?"

Janet sneered. "I did, but he told me he had to keep the chairs in his office because of the important visitors that come to the camp – the Administrator of Awka Province, the Chief Refugee Officer, council members like your father-in-law and others. I gave up. So my buttocks and back suffer."

"Maybe I should ask him. I'm tired of this bench, before it injures my backside."

Janet waved her hand disdainfully. "Forget Mr Asiobi. I've been dying to tell you what happened here on Sunday evening. This was, of course, before Mgboli's children died and before Matthew and Ndulue died. Isn't it terrible how disasters follow one another?"

"What are you talking about?" Ginika gave Janet a curious stare, annoyed that she had a way of deliberately delaying giving information after whetting one's appetite. "Tell me before you kill me with suspense."

Janet laughed. "Wait for it, okay?"

Ginika hissed and ignored her, feigning indifference.

"Just listen. *Nne di gi*, your mother-in-law, was here with one man and they beat up Nwoyibo. It was terrible. They gave her a black eye and tore her dress. When some women heard her screams and went to investigate, they found her almost naked. Her blouse was torn and her *wrappa* wrenched off her waist and they left her with just her panties."

Ginika stared at Janet, mouth open, eyes popping out and hands clasping her robust bosom. "What! Are you sure of what you're saying?"

"I'm not saying I heard, I'm telling you I saw with my two naked eyes." Janet placed her two forefingers just below her eyes and pressed downwards so that her eyes were wide open. "With these two eyes, I saw them."

"This is terrible!" Ginika groaned.

"Your mother-in-law was wild with rage. I wouldn't want to cross that woman. She told the women who tried to intervene that if Nwoyibo did not leave her husband alone, she would kill her the next time she came to the camp. I was frightened, though I was not the person she threatened. Her eyes flashed like lightning."

"I don't know how my father-in-law will take this disgrace." Ginika shook her head.

"If it wasn't for the man who had come with her, Nwoyibo would have beaten her senseless. But that man just went to work, hitting her as if she were a bag of sand on which to practise boxing. Nwoyibo's children were screaming and I had to take them away. I did not know how it ended because when I brought back the children, the two had left and Nwoyibo lay on her bed sobbing."

"How did the man look?" Ginika wondered whom her mother-in-law had used to do the dirty job. Was it Osondu or Michael?

"He is tall and has a scar on his right cheek."

Ginika understood that it was Michael who had come with her mother-in-law. She remembered how Osondu hid all day in the house and knew her mother-in-law couldn't have brought Osondu, as she would have been afraid he would bungle the job in his anxiety to return home and go back into hiding. She was sure the fear of soldiers would incapacitate Osondu and prevent him from striking Nwoyibo.

Ginika heard Janet ask, "Did you tell her? How did she find out?"

"No, I didn't. I don't know how she found out. I wish I knew." As a thought came to her mind, she turned to Janet. "What about Nwoyibo? Is she all right?"

"She was badly bruised. Did you see her at the burial this morning? She must have been in her house. Nwoyibo wouldn't have been absent if it hadn't been for the attack she suffered. She and Mgboli come from Awka town."

"I see. I hope she was not badly hurt?"

Janet shook her head. "I don't think so. She must be in her room. I heard this morning that she plans to move to another camp, in another town. Some people say Ogboji. I don't know."

WHEN GINIKA arrived home from work, she sensed immediately that her father-in-law knew about his wife's attack on his lover. His face wore a sombre look and he sat in the sitting room shaking his legs: *tam tam tam*. He only mumbled and stared when she greeted him "Good evening".

"Papa, how was your day? How did the council meeting go?" she asked, cheerfully.

He had nodded and said nothing. Not even a ghost of a smile on his fleshy face. In the past, he would have responded cheerfully to her greeting and asked how the day had gone. She was worried because she was sure he thought she had told her mother-in-law of his relationship with Nwoyibo. As she went to her room, she wished he would call her and ask her point-blank if she had or hadn't, thus giving her an opportunity to exonerate herself. Now he was angry with her, thinking she was her mother-in-law's informant.

She changed her dress and joined Ozioma and Michael in the kitchen in cooking dinner. She looked at Michael who was pounding *fufu*, but there was nothing in his scarred face to show he had beaten up a woman the previous day. If anything he looked more cheerful than usual and Ginika thought he must have enjoyed doing what he did. Suddenly anger welled up in her against this coward of a man who, instead of going to the war front to fight the enemy, went to beat up a defenceless woman in a refugee camp. What a shame! Not that she supported Nwoyibo's behaviour, but she felt it was wrong to beat her up as her mother-in-law and Michael had done. Her mother-in-law should have confronted her husband before taking further action.

Ginika didn't say much at first to either Ozioma or Michael, for her mind still chewed over what Janet had told her and her father-in-law's disposition, but when Ozioma asked her about her day in the office, she couldn't avoid telling her what had happened in the camp that day.

"It was a sad day in the camp . . ." she began and paused when she saw the way Michael immediately stopped pounding and stared at her face, as if expecting to hear about the woman beaten up on Sunday evening. She continued because Ozioma was looking at her expectantly. "Four people died in the camp yesterday." Ginika saw Michael flinch, and understood he thought the woman he had beaten up had died. She enjoyed watching his twitching facial muscles, as fear filled his eyes. But she continued, "Two children – brother and sister – and two men died last night and were all buried today." Ginika hissed, as Michael took up the pounding again. She saw his face relax, as relief washed over him.

"That's terrible! What killed the children?" Ozioma cried. She was turning with a big spoon, the bitterleaf soup she was cooking. Her eyes were full of pity. "I'm sorry for their mother. How did they die?"

"Cassava poison: they ate cooked cassava their mother gave them."

Her mother-in-law came out from her room and stood at the kitchen door, watching them for a while. Ginika noticed how drawn she looked; she seemed to have aged overnight. "Is the food not ready yet? I am hungry."

"It needs a little more time," Ozioma answered. "It will soon be ready."

"Good evening, ma," Ginika greeted, looking up at her.

"Good evening," her mother-in-law replied. "How was work today?" Her eyes were glued to Ginika's, as though trying to read her mind.

Ginika wondered if she expected her to talk about what had happened to Nwoyibo. Her mother-in-law wouldn't be that thoughtless, would she? She was determined to disappoint her if this was what she expected to hear. "Two men and two children died in the camp last night and were buried this morning."

Her mother-in-law turned away. "Bring the food as soon as it is ready," she called out.

Dinner was served at exactly seven o'clock. The atmosphere was dismal. Her father-in-law said little unlike the way he would make everyone laugh in the past. Ginika stole a look at Ozioma, wondering if she noticed the rift between her father and mother. If she did, Ozioma did not show it. She ate her food with her usual commitment, as was her style, picking out fish bones, moulding her *fufu* carefully before dipping it in the soup and sipping her cup of water at intervals. She talked little when she ate, but would listen attentively to her parents' witticisms.

Ginika watched her father-in-law chew his meat slowly and indifferently, as if it were *achicha*, the dried slices of cassava he disliked so much. This evening there was no demonstration of wit. Her mother-in-law tried to draw him out, but he rebuffed her with silence. He only ate a little food and soon stood up to leave.

"Onwaora, have you finished? You didn't touch the food." She stared at him.

He nodded and walked out.

Ginika looked away as her mother-in-law turned her eyes towards her.

"Mama, what is wrong with Papa today? He's been acting strange since he came back this evening," Ozioma said, chewing a mouthful of stockfish. When her mother said nothing, she continued, "This stockfish is quite salty. I don't like it. Do you, Ginika?"

368

"No, I don't," Ginika said.

"Ginika, see me later," her mother-in-law said, as she left the table and went to her room.

Thirty minutes later, Ginika knocked and waited. When she heard "Come in", she gave the door a push and walked in. Her mother-in-law was lying in bed and sat up as soon as Ginika sat down.

With a stare that didn't deviate from Ginika's face, she said, "Why didn't you tell me that Eloka's father kept a woman in the refugee camp?"

Ginika stared back at her mother-in-law, wondering how to respond to her question, which sounded more like an accusation than a query. She remembered Ozioma's remark that everyone in the house knew how to get round this woman who did as she liked without considering the repercussion. She had said that they knew how to deal with her. Ginika thought that the best way to deal with her now was to lie to her.

With feigned surprise, she replied, "Mama, what are you talking about? Which woman? I'm not aware that Papa kept a woman in the camp. Did someone tell you this? The person could be a mischief-maker."

"So you have not seen Eloka's father enter one of the houses in the camp? If you have not seen him with your own eyes, has no one told you he comes there to visit a refugee woman with two children?" Her eyes were two powerful torches whose lights streamed into Ginika's eyes.

"No, Mama," she lied. "You know none of them would tell me such a thing even if it were true because they would think I would inform you as soon as I heard." Ginika stared at her mother-in-law steadily.

"Did you hear that a woman was beaten up in the camp last night?"

"Not at all," she lied again. "Four people died in the camp last night and that was all everybody talked about. They were buried today and that was what took up our time all day."

Her mother-in-law sighed. She lay back on her bed and waved her hand. "You can go now. Good night."

"Good night, Mama. Sleep well."

She heard her mother-in-law muttering to herself, but did not wait, as she believed the words were not meant for her ears. But just before she stepped out, Ginika heard her say, "This is what women suffer from ungrateful men after we have given them our all. But we must protect our territorial integrity. That is all."

25

When they entered Ama-Oyi, Eloka's heart leaped for joy. He would soon be in his home and set his eyes on his Mermaid again. He would also see his parents and his sister Ozioma as well as other relations. Time does fly indeed, he thought. The training had gone well and he had done well in the battlefield, so far.

Eloka smiled. He was not expected. This would make the reunion sweeter. "Sir, my house is very close now," he said to Major Joe Ekudu, in whose official car they had travelled. "Just round the corner."

"*Aroja*. Give the driver the direction," Major Ekudu said jovially.

Eloka smiled, wondering at the word '*Aroja*' which the major pronounced each time he agreed with anything or anyone. He'd heard him use it countless times. Was it someone's name or just a meaningless expression?

"Turn left," Eloka directed the driver with whom he sat in front. "Head for that storey building at the end of the road: that's my home."

"Okay, sir." The driver turned left and cruised towards the house.

"So be ready by eight o'clock on Thursday morning, Lieutenant Odunze. We'll pick you up then. Have a good time with your wife and family."

"I will, sir," Eloka agreed. "Safe journey to your home, and greet your family, sir."

"*Aroja*."

Eloka alighted and lifted his holdall. He saluted, his right hand touching briefly the tip of his cap. "Bye, sir."

Captain Pius Diala, the man who sat beside Major Ekudu and who had so far said nothing, now looked at Eloka and smiled. "Bye, Lieutenant Odunze."

"Goodbye, sir," Eloka saluted again.

He was grateful to Major Ekudu for the ride, which had made such a difference. It wouldn't have been easy hitching rides on the way especially as few vehicles were on the road. How wonderful that the major would pick him up three days later when his pass would expire and they would travel back to base together!

Hoisting his holdall on to his shoulder, he sauntered into the compound, whistling one of the popular war songs he learnt during his training.

Ozioma, who was reading a romantic paperback in the sitting room, saw him first, as she raised her eyes from the book and looked out of the window. She squinted, and looked again. When she was sure it was him, she threw down the book and ran out. Then she screamed in a loud voice.

"Everyone, come out and see-o! It's Eloka who has come back from the army!"

Eloka knew that she would come to him with the speed of a hurricane, so he prepared himself for the impact. When it came, it was mightier than he had expected and he found himself staggering backwards. What saved both of them from crashing to the ground was that he had the presence of mind to throw down his holdall and spread his two feet before planting them on the ground again, and there they remained like taproots until Ozioma was tired of hugging him.

"Eloka, *nwannem*, my brother, welcome home!" she shouted again and again.

Eloka laughed and held her at arm's length, examining her. "My beautiful sister, you're now a big girl and I don't think I'll call you 'little sister' any longer."

Ozioma laughed heartily. "So the army has opened your eyes to see your sister, at last."

His eyes were searching for other faces. He was looking over her shoulders, and moving towards the front door.

"I know whom your eyes are searching for," Ozioma teased.

He laughed. "Is she not at home?"

"No, she went to work."

"Oh, I forgot about that. She works in the refugee camp?"

"Yes, I will run there now and call her."

As she ran out of the gate, Eloka saw his mother hurrying towards him and he strode forward to meet her. She waited until he had stepped onto the platform that led to the ground floor.

"*Nna*, welcome," she cried, hugging him. "God in Heaven, I thank you."

He saw the shadows under her eyes and observed that her lower eye lids were puffy. "Are you all right, Mama," he asked anxiously.

"Yes, I was sleeping. I heard the scream and thought I was dreaming, but when I heard voices, I came out to investigate.

Come into the house. It's just like Ozioma to keep you outside instead of allowing you to come into the house before harassing you with her violent hugs."

Eloka laughed. He followed her into the sitting room and put down his bag. "She almost pushed me down."

"I know." Her voice was soft and almost indulgent. "She is like that when she is excited. Last week, when Ijeamasi's husband came to tell us that she had given birth to a male child, Ozioma almost threw him down in her excitement."

"Ijeamasi had a baby? That's good news."

"Yes, it is very good news." She paused, and then asked, as she gazed at him, "*Nna*, when shall we see your own baby?"

"After the war. Haven't I said this before?" He avoided her eyes. He did not want her to start on this subject now when he had just arrived home or she would get both of them upset. He rose to his feet. "How is Papa? Let me drop my bag in the room before Ozioma returns with my wife. I'll be back soon." He walked out, carrying his bag. He could hear his mother sigh and then hiss loudly, in her frustration.

ELOKA WAS back in the sitting room in time to watch Ginika and Ozioma jolt into the compound. He had not removed his uniform because he wanted her to see him in it. She was in front of Ozioma. He watched her as she ran into the house and got up to meet her.

Ginika threw down her handbag and fell into his arms. She didn't say a word at first; she just clung to him, a big smile on her face. Then she burst out laughing and crying at the same time. He held her close, and kissed her. His mother stared at them, disapproving this show of affection in public. Eloka laughed when he saw his mother's frowning face.

"Mama, what is it?" he asked, still laughing.

His mother laughed, too. "Two of you are behaving like children in front of everybody."

"Who is everybody, you and Ozioma?" Eloka led Ginika to a chair and they sat in it, holding hands.

"Eloka, you should have seen your wife when I told her you were in the house," Ozioma said, looking at Ginika.

"What did she do?" Eloka asked, with his eyes still fixed on Ginika.

"She screamed and ran out without taking permission from the man in charge. I called her back, but she refused to stop. I had to run after her and we didn't stop running until we reached home."

Ginika smiled, neither agreeing nor disagreeing with Ozioma's report. She stared at Eloka's uniform, touched and admired his epaulettes.

"It doesn't matter," Eloka said. "If they sack her, she'll come back to the house."

The three of them laughed.

"*Nna*, I am sure you're hungry?" his mother asked. "Ozioma, what are we going to cook for your brother?"

"I'll eat anything in the house, but I'm not hungry yet. Where is Papa? "

He saw his mother hesitate before answering, "He may have gone for a meeting, but I am sure he will be back before long."

Eloka was surprised she didn't know where he was, for he hardly ever went out without saying where he was going, or so he thought. "Let's go to the room," he said to Ginika. "I'll see

Papa when he comes back, and later I will have a look at the garden and go out to see some of our relations." He wanted to be alone with Ginika before people started coming to see him. He knew as soon as they heard he was home, relations would come to greet him.

As they were about to escape to their room, Osondu and Michael walked in.

"Brother Eloka," Osondu cried. "Welcome. You are officer now. So you don fire gun?"

"Yes. And I will take you with me when I am going back."

"*Chineke mee*, my God! No, no, no. I will not enter army, instead make I die." Osondu shook his head vehemently.

Eloka laughed, remembering how Osondu swore even before the fall of Port Harcourt when things were still fairly normal that he would never join the army or fire a gun. He could see that Osondu had not changed his mind.

"Coward! Stay here and eat *fufu* when your age mates are in the front fighting!" Ozioma hissed.

"Ozioma, it is enough," her mother said. "Is it everyone who will become a soldier?"

"Welcome, sir," Michael greeted, his voice husky, his eyes admiring. "You fine for uniform, sir."

"Thanks, Michael."

Eloka looked out of the window and saw his father enter the compound. "Papa is back." He got up and went to meet him at the door.

His father's face creased in a wide smile, as they hugged. "Eloka, how good to see you, my son. Welcome."

"Onwaora, welcome home," his wife greeted him.

"Ah, Akunnaya, our son is back." The smile his father gave his mother allayed Eloka's worry that something was amiss when she had earlier told him she didn't know where his father was.

Eloka sat down again. He knew that he and Ginika couldn't escape so easily now his father was back. He would have questions to ask Eloka and would want to chat about many things. It was all right, really, Eloka thought. He pulled Ginika down to the chair beside him. There was no hurry, he thought. They had three days to be together.

IN THE evening Eloka took Ginika with him to visit his uncle, Adiele, whose son, Leonard, had joined the army before him. He knocked on the outer wooden door and they went in without waiting for an answer. The compound looked deserted. "I'm not sure anyone is here."

"Let's try the backyard," Ginika suggested. She looked quite elegant in a brown A-Line dress, a popular style with girls in Biafra. Eloka had complimented her on it.

They turned right and walked to the back of the square white-washed bungalow where they found his uncle bent over a round stone placed on the ground, near the back wall. He looked up when he heard the sound of their footsteps.

"Eloka, is this you?" Adiele cried. He was sharpening the machete he was going to use to cut down a bunch of bananas behind his house. He straightened up, a man of slight frame so different from his tall and fleshy brother. He thrust his hand forward and Eloka shook it, smiling.

"Uncle, how are you and my aunt? Is she not at home?"

His uncle scratched his graying hair. "We are well. Your aunt went to visit her daughter who had a baby." He shrugged.

"Even with this terrible war on, women get pregnant and have babies. There must be a way to replace the thousands who die every day. The world has broken to pieces and scattered on our heads." His eyes focused on Eloka. "You look well. Soldiering suits you."

Eloka laughed. "I don't know about that, but we do our best. What about Leonard? Did you see him recently?"

Adiele frowned. "Leonard came home once. We haven't seen him again. He did not look well at all; he looked starved when we saw him. But we have not seen him for over six months and we don't know whether he is dead or alive. Our eyes stare at the gate all the time, hoping he will come home for a visit."

"He will come when he gets a pass, as I have done. Don't worry about him. What about Udim? Where is he?"

"Udim works with the World Council of Churches – WCC. We see him occasionally. He's our only hope now and brings us relief materials when he can. We have joined those who eat salty stockfish and that chaff they call corn meal. I cannot stand the yellow powdery one they call egg yolk or something that sounds like that. That is life."

They all laughed.

"Come into the house and sit down. I was going to cut that bunch of bananas," he pointed, "I will not be long."

"But the bunch does not seem ready? Are you sure it is ripe?" Eloka looked at the bunch hanging from a healthy-looking banana tree.

"I think it is ready enough," his uncle replied. "People, especially the refugees, steal anything they see. If I leave the bunch for another day, it will disappear. The way it is, they steal from you what you have in your hands; *o di egwu*, it is frightening. The other day, I saw a stranger up that *udara* tree, harvesting the fruit. I shouted at him. You know it is an abomination in Ama-Oyi to harvest *udara* in that manner. Our people wait for the *udara* to fall down, before picking it up. As you know, we never pluck it from the tree. But the war has brought many bad things."

"You are right," Eloka said, thoughtfully.

"I'll be back soon." He picked up the machete.

"No, we have many places to go. We have seen you and you are well, so we can go now. Greet my aunt when she returns."

"All right, if you must go. When are you going back? I will send some of the bananas to you."

"In three days."

"Good. You will be here for a while." He turned to Ginika. "You are happy to see your husband, are you not?" He smiled at her, exposing teeth stained by the tobacco he rubbed into his gum to prevent toothache.

Giggling, Ginika answered, "Yes, Uncle Adiele, I am very happy to see him."

ELOKA SHUT the outer door and then glanced at his watch. There was time for them to see more people before evening. Major Ekudu's 403 Peugeot estate car had covered the distance between Etiti and Ama-Oyi in less than two hours and he had arrived home earlier than anticipated. He was pleased, as this had given him more time to see people this first day of his official leave.

"Mermaid, where do we go next? Choose." He tickled her waist and she tittered.

"Ha, don't do that here or people will stare." Her voice was playful.

"Let them stare if they wish. I'm with my wife."

They strolled down the road that led to their house. He observed that his father had maintained it in spite of the war going on. Many other roads in Ama-Oyi were overgrown with weeds because most of the young men who maintained them had either gone into the army or were in hiding. Some had joined essential services or become workers in offices that were still able to give minimal service to people, like banks, post offices and the internal revenue office.

"Where shall we go next or are you tired?" he asked, looking at her shoes which were covered with dust like his. "Are your shoes comfortable? Do you want us to go home?" Her mind seemed preoccupied with something, he thought. He would have a heart-to-heart talk with her before he left for his battalion, just to make sure everything was all right.

She glanced at her shoes made from disused vehicle tyres. "My shoes are comfortable enough. I bought them from Orie market last month. This is what everyone wears now – slippers or sandals made from car tyres."

"And they look quite nice," he remarked, admiringly. "Our people are quite resourceful and are producing many things that were imported before."

"Some people call the locally made products *panya* or Igbo-made." She laughed. "They look down on them, admiring the few things that are brought in from Lisbon by the few people who are privileged to leave the country, or by relief planes."

"Inferiority complex or colonial mentality, isn't that what it is, eh? But, seriously, our scientists and artisans are doing well under the circumstances. We have been effectively blockaded by our enemy, but we are thriving."

"I agree with you. When I have money, I buy things made here. I like them."

"Hey, we are walking aimlessly," he said, chuckling. "Let's go visit my father-in-law. What do you say – or should we go tomorrow?"

"Let's go today and from there visit my aunt. She's unhappy at the moment because her husband is missing. Nothing has been heard of him since he left for Abak and that's long. When Ikot Ekpene was evacuated, Abak was cut off, we learnt."

"I'm sorry to hear this, but he could be safe on the other side, behind the enemy lines." He kicked away a stone lying in the middle of the road. "Okay, let's go and see your father and your aunt."

His strides were moderate, so she was able to keep up with him. The roads were virtually empty, as people preferred to stay indoors during the day to avoid being hit by cannonball or shrapnel if there was an air raid. The airstrip in Uga and the air force base in Ekwulobia attracted regular air raids and Ama-Oyi was near these two places and got its own share of air strikes. But he was pleased to walk about in his hometown again and enjoy the air – which was crisp and refreshing – especially as he did not have to look behind his shoulders for fear of conscription. He loved to be in Ama-Oyi even at the time his family lived in Port Harcourt. He came to Ama-Oyi as often as he could. He loved the tall trees especially those found near the shrines of the many *arusi* still worshipped by many in the town, the *ahaba* bushes in which he played as a boy and the townsmen and women dressed in modest and cheap clothes, going about their normal business. The war had not completely changed the people's habits.

"Mermaid, do you recall how I was hiding away, afraid even of my own shadow?" He shook his head.

Ginika laughed. "Now you walk about freely."

"Yes, with my pass safe in my pocket." He patted his trousers. "Even if a military policeman appears now, I'll look him boldly in the face and go my way."

They laughed so heartily that passers-by stopped to look at them.

They found the gate firmly locked when they got to her father's house. "It seems Papa and my stepmother have gone out," she observed. "The gate is locked from outside."

"Let's go and come back some other time. I'd like to see them before I leave. Let's go to your aunt's home then; I'm dying to be alone with you, my love." He gave her that special wink that had a way of making her heart race.

GINIKA'S AUNT was in a happier mood than the last time she had visited the family. Seven-year-old Ona announced their presence and her brothers ran out to welcome the visitors. Ginika beamed at them, patting each head fondly. After greeting her and Eloka, they ran off to play.

Auntie Chito stood at the door, waiting for them to come in. "Eloka, welcome!" she greeted. "Ginika, you're blooming, aren't you? Your husband has returned home."

Ginika smiled, hugging her. "Yes, but he leaves again in three days."

"Well, that's something. Make the most of it." She turned to Eloka.

He shook her hand and they followed her into the sitting room.

"Whose voice is that?" a voice called from one of the rooms. "Is that Ginika, my child?"

"Nne, it's me." Ginika called out, heading for the room. "I came with my husband to see you."

When she returned to the sitting room with her grandmother, Eloka stood up to greet the old woman. "My son, how are you?" She squinted at him. "You look well though you are thinner. Oh, the army decided to release you so that you can see your wife and your family again? We thank them. They did well." She shook his hand.

"Nne, thank you," Eloka replied, still standing while she found a chair and sat down slowly and carefully. Then he sat down. "How are you?"

"I am breathing, as you can see. The war has driven us into ourselves and into the house. We live day by day, from one day to the next, but no one knows what tomorrow will bring. We look to God." She blew her nose into a brown piece of cloth which she put back in the folds of her *wrappa*.

"All will be well," Eloka consoled her. "Be patient."

"If you say so, it is well. Where are you fighting? These people who are fighting us, are they human beings? They are pursuing us and killing us like chickens."

They laughed though the old woman did not laugh. Eloka understood that she was voicing her fears, re-living the nightmare that was the lot of most people in Biafra at present.

She blew her nose again and continued, "The other time they came with those things that fly like hawk and killed almost all the people in Orie market. I was not there – arthritis will not allow me to go far anymore – but I was told dead bodies lay in the market like dry leaves in a forest."

"Nne, that is what war means," Ginika explained. "Every side fights with what they have. Our enemy has war planes and uses them effectively though cruelly and immorally. They shouldn't bomb markets but they do. Apart from our Orie market, they bombed Afo Umuru market and others."

"What did market women do to be killed like *ehi Awusa*, Fulani cattle? That is what I want to know." She clapped her hands and puckered her face to show her disgust.

"They want everyone to feel the war – both those who fight and those who don't," Auntie Chito put in.

"Oh, I hope we do not all die before it ends." She hissed.

"I have fried *ukwa*, can I offer you some, Eloka?" Auntie Chito asked. "There's coconut to go with it."

"I'd love that. It's been long since I ate it."

When she brought it in a flat plate, she placed the plate on a small stool and put it before him. "I brought enough for two of you. Ginika, you'll have some, won't you?"

"Yes, of course, thanks, Auntie. I can never say no to fried *ukwa* and coconut." She lifted the plate and passed it to Eloka, before dipping her hand to take some.

"I heard your husband has not come home for some time?" Eloka asked.

Auntie Chito nodded. "Yes, they were cut off in Abak. We have not heard a word from him."

"I don't think you should worry at this time. People behind the enemy lines are often quite safe."

"That's our hope. We wait and pray." She paused and then asked. "So you're going to be here for three days? And where will you be going when you leave?"

"That's the question." He laughed. "You're not always sure where next you'll be. But at the moment, I'm with the commando in Etiti. When I get back, I'll know my next assignment." He knew one could be sent to another command any time. Major Ekudu had hinted that some changes might occur in their battalion, but nothing was certain yet.

When it was time for them to go, Auntie Chito hugged Ginika and then Eloka. He was quite tall and she had to look up to see his face. "Thanks for coming to see us, and thanks for returning to her," she pointed to Ginika. "We hear what many officers do with women, but we trust you're different. Take care of yourself and fight with wisdom and caution. We want you alive when the war ends."

"Thank you," Eloka said with all his heart. "I'll remember and treasure your words and your advice." He nodded towards Ginika and added, "Please, take care of her and comfort her when she is a bit down."

She smiled. "I'll do my best."

26

After dinner, on the eve of his departure to Etiti, Eloka and Ginika retired before the rest of the family to the comfort and privacy of their room. He pulled her to him and held her for a long time, standing in the dim light provided by a lantern.

"It's wonderful to be home, to spend time again with you, Mermaid."

"Did you miss me?" she asked, with her head tilted back.

"Very much. I missed you so much and looked forward to this visit which, sadly, ends tonight, for I'll leave early tomorrow morning as you know."

"You couldn't have missed me as much as I missed you. I'm sure when you were in the war front, you didn't think of me or anything else for that matter except the fight before you."

He laughed. There was a lot of common sense in what she said and he did not contest it. He held her tighter and then bent down to kiss her lips which were already parted, waiting for him.

"Shall we sit down?" he asked, leading her to the table where two chairs stood. "We have a lot to talk about this last night we'll be together until when no one knows."

She nodded as she sat facing him. "But, darling, can't I visit you where you are? Not all the time, but once in a while? Is it not allowed?"

He hesitated before he replied. "The issue is not whether it is allowed or not, it's not ideal. It's too dangerous at the front." The expression on her face told him she didn't agree with him, but he certainly had no intention of taking her with him. She would have to stay in his home till the war ended. That was the safest place for her to be, as there was every indication that Ama-Oyi would not become a war front. It was within the area called the heartland of the country.

"What are the other things you said we would discuss?"

"First, I want to know how you are. You haven't told me much, have you, sweetheart? Is everything okay? How is life with my parents? I hope they treat you well? I know Ozioma likes you, and I'm sure she's no problem to you, is she?"

She shook her head. "There is no problem except that Mama isn't happy that I'm not pregnant."

His face hardened. "She pestered me with this same issue of having a baby before I left home and even mentioned it the day I arrived home. So, in spite of all I had said, she asked if you were pregnant. Anyway I talked to her yesterday and made her understand there will be no baby until we are ready."

She nodded. "But if the war lasted five years, are we going to wait that long before starting a family?"

He laughed. "The war will not last five years. In fact, I think it will not last longer than a year or two from this time."

Her eyes grew wide. "What! How do you know?"

"I just feel it intuitively."

"And which side will win?" she asked, laughing.

"Our side, of course."

"Suppose we don't win? What happens?"

"We have to win," he said fiercely. "But if we lose then life won't be worth living."

She stared at him, frightened by the fire in his eyes and the pitch of his voice which seemed to say that was his final opinion on the matter.

"Any other problem?" He took her hand which lay on the table. He couldn't be sure, but she seemed to have something on her mind, but was reluctant to say it.

"Well, it isn't a problem, but I just want to tell you that I was twenty recently." She smiled. "Older by a year."

"Oh, yes, I remembered it but didn't have the means to send a message. Did you have a good time? Did you celebrate it?"

"No. But I sang songs from my *Records Song Book* and felt generally happy throughout the day. It was a Saturday and I didn't have to go to work. I stayed indoors, feeling good and thinking of you."

"Let's hope we'll celebrate the next one in a free country, at peace with her neighbour."

They laughed.

"One more thing," he began, "There's a small bag in the cupboard over there where I've left some money for you. Use it as you like; it's yours. And I've allotted some money to you monthly. Papa will give it to you at the end of every month after he has collected the money. You will be able to use it to buy some of the things you need."

"What does this mean?" she asked, mystified.

"Let me explain. Members of the armed forces are allowed to make allowances from their pay to their dependants. As your husband, I'm giving you this allowance."

"I didn't know this before," she cried. "My brother didn't mention such a thing when he came home. Thanks for the allowance." She took his hand and rubbed it against her face.

She got up and went to the cupboard to look for the money. "Darling, all this money for me!" she exclaimed, as she opened the bag. She touched the bundle of crisp notes, fresh from the mint. "You are too good to me. I love you so much. Do you know what people call this new money? *Nmege* – that's what they call it."

They laughed. She put away the bag and returned to him.

"Any other thing?" He stroked her hair. "Ask all your questions now because you won't see me after tomorrow for a while."

"I want to ask you a favour." She looked down on her hand which lay beneath his. "Can you take my cousin, Udo, to be your batman – is that what you call it in the army? I'm afraid they'll conscript him and take him away. He's not yet fifteen and they are already harassing him. The other day, they caught him and I had to plead before they released him. Please, darling, take him with you. He's good and dependable and will not give you any trouble."

He was thoughtful for a while before he responded. He would like to oblige her, but he was not sure Major Ekudu would be pleased if he brought someone. The man had agreed to give him a lift but there was no discussion about bringing a second person.

"I would like to take him if it's your wish and he's willing to come, but you know I came in another person's car – an officer senior to me – so I don't know if it will be convenient for Major Ekudu." He saw the disappointment on her face and continued, "I'll ask him when he comes tomorrow, but if it is not possible, I'll make arrangements to have him brought when I return to my base."

She gave a cry and jumped to her feet. Before he knew what she was up to, she fell into his arms and kissed him. "Thank you very much. Thank you, my darling. You don't know how happy you've made me."

"Don't rejoice yet until it has worked out."

"I know it will work out. The little voice that tells me things has whispered in my ear that it will work." She laughed and sat on his knees.

"I didn't know you have supernatural powers." He stroked her back. "But, how will you inform him to get ready? It's late and there'll be no time tomorrow. Major Ekudu will be here first thing in the morning."

"Don't worry. Udo is in this house and will pass the night with Osondu and Michael. He's ready." She winked at him the way he usually winked at her.

"What! You had it all planned already? Mermaid, you're something else." He stared at her, his mouth open.

She giggled and put her hand over his mouth. "I didn't want to take any chances."

"You remind me of the pranks I played when I was growing up in Port Harcourt. It was a different experience altogether, but what you and Udo schemed this evening reminds me of my boyhood." He laughed.

"Tell me about it. I'm listening." She turned to him eagerly.

"I used to go off with my classmates to play football during the holiday. Sometimes I would be out all day, playing with other football addicts. When it was evening, I would rush to the waterside and try to catch a fish or two to placate my mother, for I knew she would be angry with me. And as I entered the house, fish in hand, she would forget that I had been out all day and thank me for not only fishing for her but also for actually bringing fish home."

"I didn't know you were so naughty. Tell me more about your boyhood. You've hardly told me anything about your school days. You attended Stella Maris College, didn't you?"

"Yes. There were times I was out all day bird-watching while my mother would look for me everywhere or send Adaeze to search for me. I got to know many birds, their names and habits. *Okiri* and *Oridide* were my favourites; both are grey in colour. *Oridide* hovers near residential areas where it catches earthworms while *okiri* is found in *ahaba* bushes."

"Why didn't you tell me about birds before – you know I love them and their music? Please, go on." Her voice vibrated with admiration.

"Well, if you want me to go on, I will. Do you know the one called *ugeloma*? It flies high in the sky, in a group, but not as high as *ugo*, the eagle. There is another bird you need to know; it's called *apia* – a slender bird that flies very fast."

"After the war, we must go bird-watching as often as we can," she declared. "I love birds."

He caught hold of her hand and planted a kiss on her palm. "Let's go to bed. It's past nine. Remember I'll have to wake up early. I hope I won't oversleep."

"You won't. I have an alarm clock in my head which wakes me up at five every morning. Or is five not okay?"

"Five will be fine," he agreed, lifting her gently, and getting up.

For a while she watched him undress and then began to remove her own clothes. He was already in bed while she was still busy with her bedtime beauty rituals – gathering her braids and imprisoning them in a hairnet, rubbing off *otangele* eyeliner from her eyelashes with some sweet-smelling oil and finally using Vaseline to remove the dark lines drawn by the eye pencil she had used to tint her eyebrows.

Lying on his back, he watched her, thinking how different women were from men, how they meticulously maintained their beauty routine in spite of the war. He had observed this even in women who were close to war fronts and those that came looking for officers in the military base. They all tried to look beautiful with the cosmetics available to them. He learned that many who could not afford the imported cosmetics prepared their own concoctions sometimes with disastrous consequences – burns, rashes or patches on the face or body.

She slipped into bed and lay beside him. "Hold me, please. I'm afraid to let you go tomorrow."

"There's nothing to be afraid of, Mermaid. I know we'll survive this war." He turned and clasped her in his arms, pressing her so hard against his muscular body that she cried out. "Am I hurting you?" He reduced the pressure but still held her.

He released her, got out of bed and turned down the wick of the lantern. When he went back to bed, she had pulled off her nightdress. With a deft movement he divested his body of his pyjamas. They clung together, listening to each other breathe. He kissed her forehead, her eyes and her lips. She responded with equal ardour. Then, she began to cry.

"Mermaid, why are you crying? Don't spoil this perfect night?" She continued to sob and he began to sing one of the hilarious and erotic songs soldiers sang in the front, in the training camps and in trenches.

Agawalam ikwa ngbo, Baby m ana-ebe
Si ngbo atukwalam n'isi
Agawalam ikwa ngbo, Baby m ana-ebe
Si ngbo atukwalam n'anya
Agawalam ikwa ngbo, Baby m ana-ebe
Si ngbo atukwalam n'ikpu
Baby, isi m gbalaga
Onye ga-akwadi ngbo ma mgbalaga?

[I'm on my way to the battlefield
But my girl is afraid a bullet will hit my *head*
I'm on the way to the battlefield
But my girl is afraid a bullet will hit my *eye*
I'm on the way to the battlefield
But my girl is afraid a bullet will hit my *crotch*
Dear girl, if you ask me not to fight
Who then will fight in this war?]

He sang the song several times by substituting different parts of the body that could be hit by a bullet, but when he substituted *crotch*, Ginika laughed. He was pleased because he had succeeded in making her laugh. He wiped away her tears with his hand and gave her a long and passionate kiss. He felt her body tremble and his heart began to flutter, as his body hardened.

Reassured and comforted, Ginika let him into the core of her womanhood and anchored him.

27

Ginika was about to change into her nightdress when her mother-in-law called her to her room. A few minutes earlier, she had tidied the table where they had dinner, which was served later than usual because her father-in-law had returned late from where he had gone. She had wondered if he still saw Nwoyibo, for he often came home late since the refugee woman had moved away from Ama-Oyi with her children. If she was indeed in Ogboji – as people said in the camp – then she was not far away, as Ogboji was close to Ama-Oyi. Her father-in-law could go there to see her if he wished.

"Sit down," her mother-in-law said. She was sitting on the armchair in front of her dressing table and chewing a stick.

Ginika sat on a sofa which was pushed against the wall opposite the door and waited. Her mother-in-law scrubbed her teeth with the long chewing-stick and intermittently opened her mouth wide to gaze at her teeth in the mirror. She grimaced. "This war is terrible; one can't find a tube of toothpaste anywhere to buy. I'm tired of it all."

Ginika shook her head to show her empathy, but did not speak.

"Did you and Ozioma tidy the kitchen?" her mother-in-law asked, looking at her for the first time since she came in.

"We did, though Michael is still there doing the dishes."

"It is now three months since Eloka returned to his battalion, is it not?"

"Yes, it is." Ginika wondered what she was getting at.

"I'm sure you know why I called you?" Her mother-in-law glanced at her before putting her chewing-stick on a saucer placed on the dressing table.

"No. I have no idea why you sent for me."

Her mother-in-law gave a mirthless laugh. "I asked you this question before and I want to ask you again because of Eloka's visit home. Are you pregnant? Did you do what I advised you to do when I talked to you on this matter?"

"I'm not pregnant." Ginika felt anger rising inside her but she didn't want to give it room to grow. "Mama, I thought you and Eloka discussed this matter when he was here? Why do you bring it up again?"

"You are asking me why I bring it up, eh? My daughter-in-law asks me why I want to know if she is pregnant. *Aru*, abomination! Why do you think we married you – to come here and stare at us in the face?"

"Mama, I'm going to bed. Good night." She got up to leave.

"Sit down. I have not finished with you. You have not tried to see things from my point of view, have you? You listen to Eloka and allow him to have his way in this matter. He is a man: what does a man know in a matter like this? I'm amazed at your lack of common sense – a woman who is not anxious to have a child for a husband who is a soldier! Do you know tomorrow? Do you know what can happen even in the next minute? And you allow Eloka to go away again without at least attempting to get you pregnant."

Ginika was very angry and knew she would lose her temper if she did not leave the room immediately. Without another word, she walked out.

"You have no sense," her mother-in-law's angry voice pursued her. "You want to make me childless. I will show you, *anu ohia*, bush animal. You will see something in this house."

Ginika paused long enough at the door to hear her shout, "I said it when I first saw you that your beauty is skin-deep, *ocha ka omaka*. If only Eloka had agreed to marry the girl Adaeze found for him, I would not have been put in this condition." Her mother-in-law began to sob.

Ginika ran to her room, sat on the bed, thinking. What was she going to do? She felt like running away from the house, but where would she run to? Her father and stepmother would not receive her. He would blame her for disregarding his advice against getting married. Going to Eloka was not an option, as he had expressly said she should stay with his parents. She couldn't go to her aunt who was weighed down by her own worries and found it difficult to feed her family. Ginika would be another mouth to feed. How would she be able to continue to live with her mother-in-law who now regarded her as an enemy? She was no better off with her father-in-law. He had not been the same since his wife attacked Nwoyibo and ran her out of Ama-Oyi. She was aware their relationship had suffered a fatal blow with that incident. Ginika was amazed at the way they managed to fool Eloka, who did not notice they were estranged during the three days he was at home. They had played perfectly their part as a contented couple. But as soon as Eloka left, they returned to their state of forced civility.

What worried Ginika most was the knowledge that Ozioma would leave home for a month to help her elder sister, Ijeamasi, who had had a baby recently.

"I'm sure you can manage," Ozioma had said when Ginika cried out in dismay when she first told her about it.

"No, I can't manage." Ginika had wailed. "How can I be here alone with Mama and Papa?"

Apparently thinking Ginika was anxious about housework and running errands for her parents, Ozioma had added, "You are not alone – Osondu and Michael are here to help, so make sure you tell them what to do in case they forget. Don't allow Osondu to hide in that dark hole all day. Give him work to do in the house. And you will be at work in the refugee camp during the day anyway, so you won't be bored."

Ginika had wished she could breathe her fears to Ozioma who still appeared ignorant of her mother's action which had caused disaffection between her and her husband. This disaffection had affected everyone, especially herself, Ginika had thought, wondering how Ozioma could remain blissfully ignorant of the situation all this while. Or was she acting, like everyone else?

As these thoughts churned in her mind, Ginika understood that things could only get worse in the house. Ozioma would leave for Ijeamasi's house in a day or two. Ginika knew her mother-in-law was intensely unhappy about the breach of relations between her and Eloka's father. Ginika feared she would take it out on her though she had nothing to do with it. The situation was similar in the case of her father-in-law. She wished she could go to him and say, "Papa, I know you think I betrayed you and told Mama about you and Nwoyibo, but you're wrong, I didn't. I wasn't the one who told her."

She undressed and went to bed, but it took a while before she fell asleep.

TWO WEEKS later, Ginika was on her way to work when she saw Eunice coming from the opposite direction. She waited for her. Her face was clouded and Ginika wondered what was wrong.

"Eunice, what's the matter? You look ill." Ginika was surprised to see Eunice's untidy look – her hair was held back carelessly with a ribbon, as if she had dressed in a hurry. She wore a shapeless black dress.

"Ginika, something terrible has happened. I'm just coming from Njide's funeral." She began to sob.

"What are you talking about?" Ginika threw her handbag on the ground in confusion. "Whose funeral?"

"Njide's." Eunice wiped her tears away with the back of her hand. "The Red Cross brought her to her home very early this morning and buried her in a simple ceremony. They left immediately in the van."

"What happened?"

"I was able to be there because we heard a loud cry from her house – which you know is near mine – and went to investigate. I saw her mother rolling on the ground and weeping. I learned that she was hit by a bullet, as they followed behind our troops who were fighting."

"This is terrible. So Njide is dead?" Ginika shook her head, remembering the girl that had seen her as a rival. Her classmate at Elelenwa Girls' College who was so lively and active. Njide liked to get involved in anything that gave her an opportunity to serve. Now she was dead.

"You know I saw her ten days ago when she visited home briefly to see her parents," Eunice said. "She told me she was one of three girls selected by the Red Cross to accompany some children to Gabon next month to look after them there. She said they were some of the worst kwashiorkor cases. I remember telling her she was lucky to be selected. Now she is dead."

They walked in silence until they separated at a junction – Eunice heading for home and Ginika for the refugee camp.

THOUGH GINIKA could not describe herself as Njide's friend, she felt dejected after hearing of her death. Her thoughts were full of her and this made her absent-minded that morning. Janet noticed and, after a while, could not keep quiet about it anymore.

"What's the matter with you?" she asked. "I have had to repeat everything I say two or three times before you get it. Are you having problems at home?"

Ginika looked at her. Janet wore a green blouse and had tied a yellow *wrappa* over it. Ginika thought this was the first time she had seen her dressed this way. She looked lovely in the attire.

"A girl who was my classmate was shot at the war front."

"Eh? What was she doing at the war front?"

"She was a member of the Red Cross."

"The war has taken so many people." Janet's voice was solemn. "This is why I try to be happy whenever I can. I don't know when I will die. At least let me enjoy my life before I go."

Ginika said nothing.

"Would you like to attend a dance taking place in the

military base at Nkwerre next weekend? I won't miss it for anything." Janet was cheerful and excited. "Let's go and dance away our sorrows." She laughed.

Ginika marvelled at Janet's capacity to feel solemn one moment and cheerful the next. Nothing ever got her down. "No, I can't go to a dance. I can't even mention such a thing to my husband's parents. They'll think I'm out of my mind."

"Do you know who will be performing?" Janet asked, staring at her.

Ginika shook her head. "Who is it?"

"Celestine Ukwu will be there. I think there is another band, but I've forgotten what it's called. You still don't want to come with me?"

"No, where will I say I'm going? It is at night, isn't it?"

"Of course, it's at night. What about your aunt? You can tell them you'll spend the night in your aunt's house. We'll be back early the next day and you can return home and they will be none the wiser."

Ginika thought about it for a while. She thought it was impossible and shook her head again. "No, thanks. Enjoy yourself."

"Okay, but if you change your mind, let me know. Today is Monday; you have plenty of time to think about it – more than ten days."

"By the way, how will you get to Nkwerre? It's not exactly next-door you know."

"Transport is no problem. My air force boyfriend has agreed to provide the vehicle to take us there – I told him I'm going with a friend – but will not be bringing us back…"

"So how do you intend to come back?"

"You remember the major I told you about? The dance takes place in his base. He'll bring us back."

"You have it all planned," Ginika said, admiring Janet's resourcefulness, but thinking that it was not always directed to public good like Njide's, for instance. "Enjoy yourself. Count me out."

GINIKA DID most of the cooking in the house, as Ozioma was not there to assist. She prepared breakfast and served it before going to work. In the evening she cooked dinner. Her mother-in-law devised ways of making sure she did the work alone. She kept Osondu and Michael busy doing other things in the compound, so that they were not able to help her in the kitchen. Neither of them pounded *fufu* anymore, as Ginika did it, as well as cook the soup that went with it. On Friday, she was getting ready for work when her mother-in-law came into her room.

"You will not go to work today, as I want to send you to Orie market to buy what we need in the house."

"I didn't tell Mr Asiobi that I won't come to work today," she said, rubbing white powder on her face.

"Who is Mr Asiobi? Is he not the one Onwaora made the camp warden? He cannot do anything if we decide to stop you going to work any day. When you see him on Monday, tell him I sent you to the market. If he makes trouble, let me know."

Ginika said nothing. She was displeased, for she had wrapped some *akara* in banana leaves she wanted to take to Janet, Emma and Inno. She had done it in the past and they appreciated it. So she was going to give them what was left after breakfast. What would she do with it now? It would go bad by evening. She decided to go by her aunt's house on her way to the market and give the *akara* to her children. Her house was close to the road that led to Orie market.

The following day, there was much work to do in the house. Her mother-in-law insisted that all the rooms in the house had to be cleaned. Ginika was in the kitchen when she came in.

"Ginika, you will clean my room as well as Onwaora's, in addition to yours, Ozioma's and the kitchen. Osondu and Michael will clean the rest. Remember you will prepare steamed cocoyam for dinner – that's what I want Onwaora to eat – so you have to work fast."

"I can clean my room and Ozioma's another time…" she began.

"Why can't you clean them today?" She glared at her. "If you can't give me a child, you can at least keep the house clean."

Ginika flinched. "Mama, I don't like the way you treat me these days." She blinked several times. "What have I done to deserve it?"

"You are not pregnant and you are not nursing a baby, why should you not work in the house? It is only a corpse that lies idle."

Ginika looked at her face and was shocked by the dislike and scorn written all over it. "You know I'm not idle," she said. "I do my best in the house."

"Then go and work." Her mother-in-law hissed and went back to her room.

Ginika stood transfixed for a full minute before she began to scrub the floor of the kitchen. She boiled up inside her. With her hands shaking and her eyes flashing, she spat, "I'm not a slave or prisoner in this house and no one can make me one. I'm going to the dance with Janet. And no one can stop me." She hissed loudly and flung the scrubbing brush away from her and it hit the wall with a thud.

THE FOLLOWING Saturday, Ginika hid her party dress and shoes in a bag and went to meet Janet in the refugee camp. She felt her heart thumping and thought it would explode, but this did not make her change her mind. She was determined to go to the dance. She remembered the dance in Ugiri many years in the past which had earned her father's ire, leading to his abusing her body. But she was sure this dance would be different – it was organised by soldiers and she was sure they would do much better than secondary school students who had organised the dance in Ugiri. Besides, no one knew she was going to the dance except Janet. By Sunday morning they would be back and she would slip back into the house. She felt she just had to leave that house for a while before she lost her head and told her mother-in-law off.

"Welcome," Janet greeted, opening the door wider to let her in. "Flight-lieutenant Ohaeri assured me the vehicle will be here at six. We'll get there in less than two hours. Let me see your dress."

Ginika brought it out from the bag and showed her. "It's lovely and your hair is beautiful. Who did it for you?"

"A friend; her name is Eunice."

The car came exactly at six. The orderly knocked and Janet called out that they would soon join him and the driver. Ginika was impressed. Men in the armed forces kept to time, she thought, remembering Major Ekudu who had come punctually to pick up Eloka on the day he travelled back to his battalion.

"I told you they'll be here and on time too." Janet gloated. "Flight-lieutenant Ohaeri is a perfect gentleman. And so is Major Okon. You'll see my point when we get to Nkwerre."

Ginika said nothing. She had finished dressing up and was applying *otangele* to her eyelashes. Her dress was red on top and black from the waist downwards – a gift from Eloka after their marriage. She wished they would wait till it grew dark before setting out, but Janet said they would be late if they didn't leave early enough. Besides, the driver and the orderly would have to return to the air force base in Ekwulobia after dropping them off.

"I'm ready," Janet announced, preening herself in front of a cracked but long mirror she had bought second-hand from Orie market the week she arrived in Ama-Oyi. "What do you think of my dress?"

"It's beautiful." Ginika admired the navy blue dress with a tight bodice that emphasised Janet's slim waist and accentuated her breasts, making them look fuller. "Tell me, Janet, how did you persuade your boyfriend to give you a vehicle to take you to a dance in another military camp? Is he so broad-minded, not jealous at all?"

Janet laughed, as she patted her braids. "Do you take me for a fool? I didn't tell him we're going to a dance. He thinks we're going to see my mother who I told him lives in a refugee camp in Nkwerre. We'll ask the driver to drop us of, in front of a house I know well, and from there we'll walk into the army camp. It's not far."

Ginika stood before the mirror and gazed at her reflection. She began to rearrange her braids, hoping that this would keep her in the room a little longer. It should be dark soon, she thought. However, Janet was anxious to leave immediately. But before they stepped out of the room, a thought struck her and she drew back. "Ginika, I think we should take our dresses in a bag and wear them later when we get to Major Okon's house. I didn't think of it before, but the orderly might tell Flight-lieutenant Ohaeri that we are dressed up and he will become suspicious. Sorry about the delay."

Ginika smiled because she liked the delay; it helped her to buy time. They undressed quickly and dressed again. Ginika wore the dress she had come in earlier. It was already dark by the time they got into the vehicle.

"Good evening," Ginika greeted as she settled in the car.

"Good evening," the driver replied.

"*Oga* say make we return quick," the orderly said, frowning.

"No problem, Samson," Janet cooed. "As soon as you drop us, you start coming back. We will not delay you."

Ginika saw that he was not happy with them. It was past seven and they had sat in the car waiting for an hour. The orderly sat in front with the driver while Janet and Ginika sat at the back. Ginika stared at the man's head and thought it had the shape of a coconut.

Janet was right about the distance, Ginika thought, for they were there a little after eight o'clock. It took them about an hour. Janet directed the driver to stop in front of a bungalow in front of which stood a tall almond tree.

"Thank you. Here is all right for us. I want to see my aunt who lives here before going to see my mother in the refugee camp," Janet explained.

"Are you sure?" Samson asked. "*Oga* go ask if I take you safe reach your mama place."

"Yes, it's okay. The refugee camp is not far from here. Besides, you have to start going back or he will worry about you and the vehicle. Please, drive carefully. If you hear the sound of a plane, stop and switch off the headlamp."

They waited until the car disappeared from their view. Janet laughed. "Let's go. The military camp is over there, not far at all. The place was a secondary school. Major Okon lives in the principal's house which he shares with some other officers. Accommodation is very tight there."

As they approached the storey building, a voice shouted, "Who goes there? Stand to be recognised!"

Ginika trembled. This was her first visit to army officers' quarters. Though she had gone with Eloka and others to 11 Div to stage a play for soldiers, they did not go to where the officers lived or where the other ranks lived, for that matter.

"Don't be afraid," Janet whispered. "It is the routine here. It's the man on sentry duty that shouted."

A soldier in uniform came out and directed the light of his torch to their faces. It seemed to Ginika that he recognised Janet, as his facial muscles relaxed.

"We have come to see Major Okon," Janet announced.

"Proceed." He turned and went back to his post.

"Everywhere is so quiet," Ginika observed. "It's not as busy as it should be if there's a dance going on."

"This is what I'm thinking too," Janet agreed. "Well, let's find out. I didn't want to ask the soldier at the gate." She increased her pace and Ginika did the same.

When Janet knocked on the door, a young man in mufti opened it. When Janet told him she wanted to see Major Okon, he said, "Come inside," and then went away after they had sat down in the sitting room.

"My Janet, how are you?" a voice said behind Ginika and she swivelled her head in time to see a light-skinned man probably in his twenties climbing down the stairs. In a second Janet was in his arms, kissing him and being kissed.

Ginika looked away, waiting to be introduced. She was surprised to see that Major Okon was dressed in a casual dress, not at all like someone preparing for a dance. Had Janet deceived her? Or could it be she had miscalculated and confused dates?

"Honey, what about the dance?" Janet asked. Her arms circled his shoulders and he held her around the waist.

"Oh, you're here for the dance?" he asked. "My God, I forgot to send you a message. It was cancelled because the main band we were all hoping to see would not be able to make it. The band leader is ill. So we cancelled it for today. It'll take place as soon as the man is well."

Ginika felt as if she had been dealt a heavy blow. Her hope of having an exciting evening listening to her favourite band led by Celestine Ukwu plummeted and she felt like crying. Did all musicians always disappoint their fans and the people who engaged them? She recalled the Ugiri experience and sighed.

"And who is this lovely damsel who came with you?" He looked at Ginika admiringly. He was amused to see the wedding ring on her fourth finger. "What's that ring doing on that finger? To deceive the hawks in the camp?" He laughed and Janet joined him, but Ginika's unsmiling face watched him warily.

Janet said, "Honey, meet my friend, Ginika. Stay clear of her, she is hooked already, as you can see."

"Really? Whoever he is, he's a lucky chap," Major Okon

said. "Well, now you are here, I'll make it up to you to douse your feeling of disappointment. Let's go to the mess and have a drink. Afterwards, your friend can sleep in one of the spare rooms and first thing tomorrow morning I'll send you home. Okay?"

"Okay," Janet enthused, turning enquiringly towards Ginika.

She shrugged and nodded without enthusiasm.

Major Okon went up, changed and rejoined them. They got into his car and drove out of the gate. They met some other officers in the mess. Ginika stuck to Janet and Major Okon, refusing to be drawn into conversation with any of the officers. One particular officer who introduced himself kept pestering her and asking her questions. He was tall, dark and good-looking, but she hated the way he leered at her.

"What would you ladies drink?" Major Okon asked.

"Gin and lime," Janet said. "The same for my friend; I'm sure you'll like it." She turned to Ginika.

"Can I have something soft?" Ginika asked.

"Lieutenant Ugoro, could you please arrange to have our drinks brought to us? Gin and lime for Janet, soft drink for her friend and whisky for me."

"Yes, sir," the officer harassing Ginika went off to get the drinks.

It took him a while before he returned and during that time, Major Okon told them that the man had a room in the house where he lived. He was one of the brightest of the younger officers and was popular with the rank and file.

Lieutenant Ugoro returned with the bar attendant who brought the drinks on a tray. Lieutenant Ugoro distributed the drinks, apologising to Ginika because there was no soft drink left and he had brought her gin and lime like her friend.

Ginika looked at the drink. "Okay, thanks. I'll have this." She saw the man's face light up, but looked away quickly. She told herself it was not much, so it shouldn't get her drunk.

Ginika saw Janet asking for more and still more. She had not yet finished hers but she felt funny. She blinked her eyes and swallowed hard continuously for a minute, but the feeling persisted – as if she was going to throw up. She also felt dizzy. Am I going to disgrace myself before all these officers? she thought. But when she couldn't endure it anymore, she whispered to Janet, "I feel as if I'm going to be sick. Please, take me outside." She started to her feet, and Lieutenant Ugoro jumped up to assist her. "Don't touch me," she cried in a rasping voice. But before Janet could respond to her request, Ginika began vomiting and then slumped against the table.

Janet gave a cry and held her. Abandoning their drinks, Major Okon and Janet helped Ginika to the car. Major Okon sat in front with the driver while Janet sat in the back, supporting her. No word passed their lips until they had taken her to the room Major Okon had earmarked for her – a room his guests used.

IN THE morning, Ginika was sitting on the bed, crying softly when Janet came into the room. Her body was partially covered with the bedspread.

"Ginika, thank God you're all right . . ." Janet began but stopped when she saw her face. "Why are you crying? Are you still ill? It was only a little drink you had."

"Janet, I'm done for," Ginika cried. "I'm finished."

"What is it?" Janet stared at her.

The panic in her voice made Ginika say more: "I can't explain it but I think someone had sex with me." She started trembling.

"How can you say this? Who could have done that? Didn't you lock the door?" Then remembering, Janet said, "Oh, you couldn't have locked the door, as you were fast asleep when I left you. But what makes you think someone had sex with you?"

Ginika invited her to look at her crotch and thighs which had a man's fluid on them and showed her also patches of semen on the bed sheet. "I don't recollect exactly what happened," she said, as tears flowed down her face unchecked.

"Let's talk about this carefully." Janet sat down next to her and put her right hand around Ginika's shoulders. "When we took you into this room, Major Okon went to his room. I stayed here for an hour to make sure you were all right. You were sleeping peacefully and I thought you had recovered from the effect of the alcohol. I went to Major Okon's room and stayed with him till morning. Then I came to see you and found you like this. I can swear that Major Okon did not leave his room all the time I was with him. That's all I know." Janet shook her head.

"Did you undress me? Did you remove my panties?" Her eyes were glued to Janet's.

"No, I didn't. You were fully dressed and I allowed you to sleep like that. But what are you saying? Your clothes were removed?" Janet was horrified.

Ginika cried harder. "When I woke up, my panties and my clothes were lying on the table exactly where they are now. I haven't touched them yet. I was naked."

"Do you remember nothing at all?" Janet asked baffled.

410

"Very little. I only have flashes of memory. I recall someone having sex with me but I thought I was dreaming – I've had such dreams occasionally since Eloka left home."

"Who could have done this?" Janet stared at her. "Could it be that your drink was drugged last night? I can't think of any other explanation for what happened to you last night – the way you slumped and became unconscious at the mess."

Ginika remembered. "Can it be that lieutenant? What's his name?" She broke down and wept.

Janet ran out to tell Major Okon what had happened. He followed her to the room, looking deeply concerned.

"I'm very sorry to hear what happened. I have checked Lieutenant Ugoro's room but he is not there. The sentry told me he left the house quite early.

Ginika and Janet looked at each other when Major Okon said the lieutenant had left the house early. Ginika was sure he did it.

"Let me assure you that the matter will be investigated," Major Okon added.

28

Eloka received the news of his promotion to captain with little or no enthusiasm. He was not a career officer, he told himself, and therefore, was not bothered about rising high in the army. He knew why he joined the army – to fight and fight with commitment until victory was won. He believed unflinchingly that his people had no other option than to stand and defend themselves from annihilation. Not only were they driven away from the places they called home, but they were also forced to return to their homeland in the east and take up arms in self-defence.

He was not foolhardy when he found himself at the war front. He was cautious and careful and when it was necessary to retreat, he did because he believed it was better to run than to die unnecessarily. If you ran, you lived to fight again. He obeyed orders as a soldier but sometimes he used his initiative. This had not only saved his life, but also the lives of his soldiers and superior officers. He knew that was how the promotions came – he was lucky to take the right step at the right time. For a man who had not been in the army for longer than a year, he could be described as fast in his rise to the rank of captain.

The last operation that earned him his promotion was remarkable in a number of ways. The order had been clear:

dislodge the enemy and occupy their position. As usual they had very little ammunition and it was hoped they would augment what they had with what they would capture from the enemy.

"Lieutenant Odunze, what a night!" his company commander, Captain Osisioma, had whispered fiercely, as they crouched in the jungle, waiting for the zero hour when the attack would commence. "I feel like telling His Excellency to give me a break – I haven't seen my family for many months."

Eloka grimaced, but since it was dark, his commander did not see it. He hated being distracted at a time like this and wished the captain would shut up.

"Do you have a cigarette on you?" Captain Osisioma asked.

"It would be most unwise to smoke now, sir," Eloka said, cursing under his breath. As second-in-command – 2I/C – he knew his limitations and could only advise his superior officer.

"I know. I was just teasing you. I could do with a smoke, though."

Eloka cradled his Madison like a baby. He smiled to himself, for only recently, he had been cradling his Mermaid to his heart. For a moment he thought of her and felt happy. He was fighting for his country to make it safe for his wife and children – yes *children*. They would have them after the war.

There was a noise to his left, as if someone's boots had stepped on a dry stick and it splintered. He lay quietly, listening. He could hear the soldier to his left breathing. Was he asthmatic? Eloka wondered. His breathing was somewhat laboured.

When would the attack begin? The situation report had been encouraging. The enemy was not expecting to be attacked. Their location was vulnerable enough and could be easily assailed. They were well armed but combat weary and, therefore, could easily be dislodged and, above all, they were not too many.

The night had been bitterly cold; the harmattan was in the air. Eloka could hear the rustle of dry leaves as some of the soldiers lying around him fidgeted. Were they impatient for action to begin or were they afraid? It was not possible to know. Each person nursed his thoughts. Captain Osisioma did not speak again and Eloka was grateful for it.

"Attack!" The order was given and the battle had begun. "Attack, dislodge and dig in!" Eloka charged forward in the darkness, his head bent as he ran. There was a burst of small arms fire and the chatter and clatter of machine guns. The cry of the wounded filled the air, as bullets flew past like shooting stars, causing a victim to cry out when it came in contact with his body.

It got to a stage it was no longer possible to know who was who – friend or foe. As confusion reigned supreme, the enemy seemed to have regrouped and returned in a deadlier manner, unleashing mayhem on their attackers. It was obvious they had gained the upper hand, and after waiting in vain for Captain Osisioma to give the order, Eloka had to take the initiative and the command.

"Retreat!" he yelled. "Return to base, with immediate effect!"

The soldiers began a disorganised retreat, panic taking over completely. Eloka could hear the sound of mortar released by the enemy as it lit up the sky and exploded. Heavy gun fire and artillery boomed a tuneful dirge that haunted the spirit. The soldiers suddenly grew wings and fled to base, their brows lathered by the sweat of terror. They crawled back into the trenches they had deserted earlier in the day.

There was no sign of Captain Osisioma. Eloka was in despair. He wondered if he had been shot. There was only one way to find out. No one wanted to return to that hell fire except Eloka.

"Sir, it's too dangerous," cautioned the platoon commander, a quiet but brave soldier. "It's not safe. The enemy will be waiting."

"If they already have him, it is no use going in search of him," a second lieutenant opined.

Eloka smiled wanly and nodded. At dawn he left, his gun in his hand. He was determined to find Captain Osisioma and bring him back to camp dead or alive. As he neared the scene of battle, he lay flat on the ground and began to crawl slowly, cradling his gun. The harmattan haze was like a mantle cast by a magician to confuse onlookers. But he was not deterred by it. Daylight had broken in the horizon like a flower unfurling its enchanting petals. Eloka pressed on, his arms scratched by brambles and all kinds of thorns.

His eyes moved like a camera as he surveyed the area where he suspected the captain was, either dead or half dead. His gamble paid off, for a little distance from where he crouched, he saw him lying, as if he was dead. As he drew near, the captain waited, sensing that help was near. He was already putting away his cyanide-tipped needle when Eloka placed a gentle hand on his body.

"I'm here, sir," Eloka whispered.

"Thanks, I've been waiting for one of you to find me," he replied weakly.

There was blood on his uniform but Eloka did not know where exactly the injury lay, but that did not bother him at that point. He had to get both of them safely back to base. He lifted the captain and heard his suppressed cry. He gave him a piggyback ride and began the dangerous journey back because now he did not have the luxury of crawling on the ground, burdened as he was with the captain. He could hear the shouts of the enemy, in their location, apparently celebrating their victory. He strained himself to move swiftly, but carefully, his gun strapped to his body in front while the captain rode on his back. What he feared most was a sniper, but so far none seemed to be anywhere in sight. He inched forward, praying inwardly for luck until he was sighted by his men who ran forward to assist him.

Eloka smiled at Captain Osisioma as he lowered him to the ground with the help of soldiers. "Happy survival, sir," he said and saluted. "How do you feel?"

The captain nodded. "It's all thanks to you, lieutenant." He winced. "I think they shot my leg and something seems to be wrong with my back too."

While they waited for him to be evacuated from the front to hospital, Eloka asked, "Were you really going to kill yourself."

He nodded. "I told myself that if the enemy found me first, I would puncture my skin with the needle and that would be it."

"You're right, sir." Eloka murmured, "It's far better to kill oneself than fall into the hands of the vandals."

Men from the medical unit came and took Captain Osisioma away.

❧ ✿ ☙

HIS EXPLOIT in saving Captain Osisioma's life had reached the ears of the bosses at the headquarters. He was immediately promoted to captain and automatically became the officer commanding – OC – the company. He was now engaged in planning a new offensive, the initial one having ended in a fiasco. He would have to do his best to raise the morale of the soldiers.

As the harmattan wind buffeted the trees and spread cold air everywhere, Eloka looked up and could hardly see the sky because a dust haze covered everything in sight. He was thinking of the next battle. The soldiers had had a good meal earlier in the day – that was a good way to begin to rouse them to action. There was even a good supply of Mars cigarettes and some drinks – the things the enemy took for granted and got in large quantities.

"Sergeant Ugbugba, are the boys ready for action?" Eloka asked with a smile. He liked the sergeant very much and found him dependable and full of initiative.

"Yes, sir," Sergeant Ugbugba replied, saluting. He was standing in front of one of the trenches.

"It's rather quiet this evening. The harmattan haze is bothering the enemy perhaps." He chuckled when he heard Sergeant Ugbugba laugh.

It seemed as if the enemy heard him for there was a rattling noise approaching very fast and Eloka yelled, "Take cover!" The sergeant had barely dashed into a trench when an enemy air force plane came streaking in, dropping bombs in what Eloka knew was the first air raid since they dug into the area. The sound of an explosion rent the air, sending shivers down the spine of the soldiers lying in the trenches. But little or no harm was done, as the bombs landed beyond their positions. Not even one of the bombs landed on their emplacement, but Eloka was shaken. Something had to be done fast to recover their initiative in the sector.

"I wish they would send in reinforcements fast enough," he said.

"Yes, sir," Sergeant Ugbugba replied laconically.

As soon as the droning sound of the plane receded, that of shells took over. Eloka heard the swishing shells fly past, and he recognised them as the 105 millimetre howitzer, in action. "These people are certainly well armed," he muttered to himself.

The artillery fire continued till late evening. Eloka was not worried because he knew the enemy did not know their exact location. The shells had overshot their position and exploded, wreaking havoc on the vegetation but not on his men. He was almost lulled to sleep by the rhythm of explosion which seemed to him to beat a tattoo of discordant music.

The night was quiet and serene. And soon the awaited reinforcements of men and ammunition arrived to his great delight. The recce report was encouraging – the enemy was certainly not expecting them to attack, believing they had been totally annihilated after the last encounter, and that the air raid and shells had completed the task. He felt quite confident that his men were ready and strong for the looming battle which would begin at dawn.

He had the final consultation with his 2I/C and the platoon commanders.

"Lieutenant Ogan, what do you think of the boys' mood?"

"They are combat ready, sir," replied Lieutenant Ogan. "Don't worry, sir. The boys are determined to win this time and dislodge the enemy."

"Right. Remember the order. We dislodge the enemy and occupy their position and capture their weapons and ammunition."

"Instructions noted, sir."

Eloka went round, encouraging the officers and men. He was impressed by their determination, toughness, flexibility, and fighting spirit, spiced with good humour – qualities commandos were known for in this war.

He could feel the tension in the air, as he slapped this soldier on the back and patted another on the shoulder.

In the middle of the night, the movement began and when they got closer to the enemy, they started crawling along on their bellies. Eloka hoped that venomous snakes were not coiled up in the grass, in the area. Did any of the soldiers come from there, from Ozara? He should have tried to find out and would have been able to do so if it had occurred to him earlier. Now it was too late. They just had to crawl on. Suddenly, he felt a wetness around his chest and knew he had crawled into a swamp or wet ground. But he kept moving on.

Soon, they stopped and then took up their position, a few metres from the enemy trenches. Eloka could hear the sound of their movements – a kind of mock celebration was going on: no doubt, of their previous victory. Dawn was not far away. They waited, silent, unmoving. Eloka grinned with delight and prayed for a stroke of luck. He and his fighting men were now battle-ready and about to storm an enemy location with little or nothing – no armoured car, no artillery fire, no planes to clear the way with bombs or rockets or cannon-balls. Foolhardy? He chuckled at the seeming impudence. But they would dare, for fortune favours the bold.

At zero hour, he gave the order and the soldiers charged at the enemy like rampaging monsters. Their strongest ally in this fight to finish was the land mine, *ogbunigwe* – the mass killer, as it was called – and it came to the rescue. *Kagbim, kagbim,*

kagbim . . . Gbim, gbim, gbim! The noise was ear-splitting and utterly maddening. The enemy was confused. They panicked. The fierce-looking commandos who had tucked leaves into their clothes and helmets pursued them, opening fire. Bullets flew in the air like confetti and a swarm of bees. Machine guns barked and chattered like weaver-birds. The deadly Madisons played a tattoo of guitar music with bullets.

Taken unawares, the enemy put up a rather feeble resistance before retreating, abandoning their arms and ammunition and other equipment as they fled. Eloka and his men then dug in and took over their artillery weapons. An armoured vehicle, abandoned during the rout, still crouched in a corner like a giant crab. Steel helmets lay close to the trenches and cans of beer and soft drinks littered the area. There were leftovers of food which the fleeing soldiers had been feasting on, but now abandoned. A few dead bodies lay in awkward positions near the trenches. Here and there were the fresh ditches excavated by *ogbunigwe*.

Eloka was jubilant at the indomitable firepower of his commandos, a group of dedicated men outnumbered two or three times by the enemy they had succeeded in dislodging. Later, at a count, he discovered he had lost less than ten men.

"We did it!" shouted Sergeant Ugbugba.

"Well done," Eloka shouted to his men. He hugged Lieutenants Ogan and Inyang.

"This is victory worth celebrating," Lieutenant Ogan remarked, beaming at Eloka.

On the horizon, a young sun had risen from the east and was smiling at them.

29

When Udo arrived at 7 Commando Unit in Etiti, he was shown a small room at the back of the house where he put his holdall. The main house was a four-room bungalow with a sitting room in the centre. Udo discovered that Brother Eloka used two rooms while another officer, Lieutenant Ofoka, had the other two, but they shared the sitting room. Udo also discovered that the huge compound was a former secondary school which the commando battalion appropriated. Udo had arrived before noon and as soon as he had put away his things, Eloka sat him down and talked to him. "Don't wander about in the camp. Stay in the house for now unless I send you somewhere." Udo had replied, "Yes, sir."

He had learned to call him 'oga' or simply 'sir' like other officers' servants who had teased him for calling him Brother Eloka. One of them had laughed at him and said, "You don't know that in the army we never call anybody 'brother'. You are either superior or junior to the next person. Seniority matters here, and to anyone superior to you, you answer 'sir' or 'oga'. You should address Lieutenant Odunze in those terms." It was hard for Udo but he was learning fast.

He was excited to see so many soldiers in uniform,

moving in and out of the camp every day and conveyed in army trucks. He was astonished to see how huge the trucks were and how strong they looked. He came out in front of the house to look at the soldiers, or stood at the sitting room window to observe them. He admired their steel helmets, but their unsmiling faces frightened him. He watched them jump into the trucks with their guns and from his vantage position stared at the trucks as they trundled out of the camp.

A week later, Udo stood in front of the house, gazing at two trucks which had just parked some distance away. Presently, he saw soldiers in camouflage uniform climb in, one after the other. The first truck filled to capacity quickly, and the soldiers started getting into the second one. They all packed together like sardines, Udo thought.

"Where are they going?" he asked Caleb, a boy of his age who lived with Lieutenant Ofoka.

"Ha, you are just an ignoramus," Caleb replied scornfully. He was a skinny light-skinned youth with bow legs. "You see soldiers getting into vehicles and you ask where they are going?"

"Shut up, you foolish boy that walks like a duck," Udo said angrily. "Is it because I asked you a question that you call me an ignoramus?"

"Yes, because you asked a stupid question." Caleb's eyes flashed. "And don't ever call me a duck again or I will cut off your ears. Bloody civilian like you."

Udo laughed. "Okay, I'm sorry. I won't say it again. But you have not answered my question."

"They are going to the war front," Caleb explained. His tone was normal again.

"Eh, war front? Is the front near here?"

"When a war front is near you, nobody will tell you." Caleb laughed. "The noise of battle and the sound of shells exploding will tell you."

"I have never been near a war front." Udo shook his head.

"So you have not undergone training?" Caleb stared at him disdainfully. "And you are in commando battalion. Don't you know this is a battalion of strong men – the most powerful and respected battalion in the whole armed forces? Whenever something goes wrong on any front, the commando boys go there and the situation changes at once. They are the best fighters Biafra has. Everybody knows it."

"Have you been to the war front before?" Udo asked. "Have you fought before?"

Caleb hesitated before replying. "Yes, I have seen battle twice," he boasted, hitting his thin chest.

Udo doubted him but played along because he wanted to know more about 7 Commando. He knew he would not have the courage to ask Brother Eloka – as he called him in Ama-Oyi, though now in Etiti he called him *oga* – about the battalion or the fighting at the war front. Caleb was a good informant and should, therefore, be humoured. He had to remember not to call him a duck again if he wanted to keep his friendship; he had seen how enraged Caleb was when he did.

"Ah, you have fought in two battles!" Udo's voice was flattering. "At your age, you have done so well."

Caleb smiled and nodded. He adjusted the collar of his uniform – a green shirt and trousers – which he wore during the day while working in the house, though at night he would change into mufti before going to bed.

"When will you go to the front again?" Udo asked.

"I don't know. But if I am asked, I will go at once. I'm not afraid to fight." He turned his attention elsewhere.

"Is Lieutenant Ofoka your brother?" Udo didn't think so but he had to ask to know the relationship between Caleb and the lieutenant whom he was serving.

"Sort of, he is the first son of my uncle."

"Your cousin – that is what the English people call it." Udo smiled triumphantly. This was something the boastful and confident Caleb didn't know and had to be taught.

"What of you? Is Lieutenant Odunze your brother?" Caleb stared at him.

"No, he's my sister's husband. My sister asked him to take me with him and I am now his batman."

"Nonsense, how can you be a batman without military training? You are not his batman. You are only his houseboy – ordinary houseboy – that is what you are. If you call yourself his batman, what will you call Uzo?"

"Uzo is his orderly and I'm his batman – that's what Uzo told me."

Caleb roared with laughter and sat down on one of the steps that led into the veranda. He always managed to make Udo feel inferior and irritated in spite of his bow legs and skinny body. Udo thought that if anyone should feel less confident and inferior, it ought to be Caleb. He was sure Caleb had not been a secondary school student like him, yet he was so arrogant and conceited.

Udo dusted the steps with his palm before sitting down next to Caleb. He had washed the clothes Uzo asked him to, and was free to relax with his new friend, as he considered Caleb, though they argued all the time and quarrelled a lot. "What about you? What do you call yourself?" Udo sneered.

"I'm a batman – original batman, with training," Caleb bragged. "So your *oga* is married? My *oga* is not married yet.

No wonder I have not seen Lieutenant Odunze with a woman. He's about the only officer who does not bring girls to his house. Even married officers bring girls to their houses."

"Does Lieutenant Ofoka bring girls to this house?" Udo asked, disappointed.

Caleb laughed. "Wait and see. They all do it anyway."

"But how can they fight if they bring girls to the camps? How can they concentrate in the war? And you say they are the best soldiers in Biafra."

Caleb laughed again. "They even take girls to the war front. Some of them take their girlfriends into the trenches and you are talking about their houses. That one is a small thing."

"*Chineke m*, my God," Udo cried, with his mouth agape. "They take their girlfriends into the trenches! What of the girls? Are they not afraid? What if the vandals attack them, what will happen?"

"You haven't seen anything. Are you in this country at all?" Caleb laughed again. "You were hiding in your bush village. Now you have come out, your eyes will open."

"I was not hiding . . ." he stopped, remembering how he was almost conscripted by soldiers. He knew he had been hiding until Brother Eloka – his *oga* – took him away. If he had remained in Ama-Oyi, he would have continued to clamber up the roof of his house, battling with rats and spiders; sneaking out and in at night like a thief.

"I bet you were, with conscription widespread everywhere. No hiding place any longer for lazy civilians." Caleb threw him a look full of challenge, as if he was asking him to deny it or tell him to his face that he was wrong.

"Who is the officer in charge of this battalion?" Udo asked, changing the subject.

"It used to be a white man, Colonel Frank Stanton, but when he annoyed the authorities, he was sent packing and another person took over."

"Who took over?" Udo was grateful to Caleb for all the information he was giving him. He had tried to talk to Uzo but he had asked him to leave him alone.

"Colonel Atuegwu. He is a very brave soldier. When he took over, the commando unit was reorganised." Caleb smiled expansively, stroking his chin which was as smooth as a pebble. "Colonel Atuegwu is bearded like His Excellency."

"How come you know so much?"

"Because you see me cooking in the kitchen and talking with you, you think I'm nothing?" Caleb asked severely. "Did you not hear me say I have tasted battle? I'm a combatant. A combatant, you hear – which you will never be."

Before Udo could respond, a vehicle stopped, and his *oga* alighted. Udo stood up immediately.

"Good afternoon, sir," he greeted. He looked at his face closely – he always did this whenever he returned to the house after each day's outing. Was he hoping to read from his *oga's* face where he had been or what he had done in the day, since he told him nothing? Udo was a bit anxious about his vulnerable position in the commando unit as an untrained soldier. He had started feeling that way the first time Caleb called him idle civilian.

"Welcome, sir," Udo said, moving away from the step on which he was sitting.

His *oga* nodded and walked into the house and Udo followed him.

"Udo, I want you to get ready for military training. I'm sending you tomorrow morning to the place recruits are trained. But you'll return here after your training. Is that all right?"

"Yes, sir. I'm ready to go any time you want me to." Udo was so overjoyed that he jumped up, clapping his hands. At last he would be trained as a soldier. Caleb would not be able to insult him again. He wondered where the training camp was. Could it be the same camp in Orlu where he heard officers were trained? It didn't matter so long as he would be trained as a soldier. A commando too – the most dreaded and respected type of soldier in Biafra. "Thank you, sir," he said.

Udo saw his *oga's* facial muscles relax and soften.

THE PASSING-OUT ceremony took place after one month and Udo felt fulfilled. He was disappointed they were not given camouflage uniform but he was comforted by the fact that he was a trained soldier and knew so many things he hadn't known before about the army and about warfare. He knew Brother Eloka was to come for him, so his eyes searched the galaxy of officers who had come to witness the passing-out ceremony. He saw Brother Eloka, his *oga* – he must not forget he was his *oga* and not Brother Eloka anymore – talking to another officer and walked towards him. He stopped a short distance away, where he was sure his *oga* would see him and waited.

"Udo, congratulations!" His *oga* smiled and beckoned to him. Udo was delighted when he shook his hand and the other officer, a captain, did the same.

"Thank you, sir." Udo saluted, as they were taught in camp. He was glad at the opportunity to put into practice what he had learned. Of course, he had saluted the commander at the passing-out parade, but now he had his first opportunity to salute his *oga*, Brother Eloka, as he used to call him in Ama-Oyi, before he enlisted in the army.

"Go over there and wait for me," his *oga* pointed. "You'll find Uzo and Adim in the car."

"Yes, sir." Udo saluted again and marched off to find Uzo and Adim, the driver. He broke into a run, avoiding soldiers who were heading for the hostels, as they joked and laughed with their friends. He heard them discussing their experience during the training. Udo knew that soon the soldiers would be sent to the different war fronts as reinforcement. But he would be returning with his *oga* to Etiti. Would he have liked to be sent to the war front? No – capital NO! He didn't want to go to the front. He remembered that Sister Ginika had expressly told him to stay in the rear as Brother Eloka's – his *oga*'s – batman and not go to the war front with him. She had also asked Brother Eloka, now his *oga*, to ensure that he was not sent to the front because, as she put it, he was too young to fight.

Udo stopped running when he saw Uzo and Adim leaning on the vehicle. "Soldier man!" Uzo quipped, as Udo joined them. "You are now a proper soldier, Udo." He shook Udo's hand.

Adim also shook his hand, but with less enthusiasm. "Udo, you are now a soldier, eh?" He was middle-aged and had been a taxi driver in Enugu before the war. Udo had heard him say once that he joined the army as a driver because he would probably have been conscripted and trained as an infantryman. He also said that the army had commandeered his 403 Peugeot estate car which he had used as taxi, and he decided to become a driver in the army so that he could drive his car himself, because he could not bear to have another person do it. Now he was Captain Eloka's driver but if the car were assigned to another officer, he would drive the new officer and would still be close to his car.

"*Oga* said I should wait for him here," Udo announced. "He will be here soon." He sat on the bonnet of the car.

"Come down from there." Adim glared at him. "Do you want to damage the car?"

Udo jumped down. "Damage the car merely by sitting on the bonnet?" He laughed.

"This training camp is big," Adim observed, looking from one side to the other. "And well protected too. See how they camouflaged everything with palm leaves. See the big trees surrounding the place."

"They chose this place, I think, because they thought the vandals would not find it easy to raid." Udo sat on the grass.

"You can sit in the car," Adim said, opening the door.

"No, thank you. Let me sit here till *oga* comes."

"The time we did our training, we were given a pair of uniforms and boots for the passing-out parade. That time the army had everything it needed." Uzo looked disdainfully at Udo and other soldiers who had just passed out.

"Times have changed and things are worse," Adim remarked, staring at Udo's dirty canvas shoes which he had worn for the parade.

Udo noticed and patted his shoes, saying, "I'm lucky to have these. Some soldiers have no shoes at all."

"How did the training go?" Adim asked.

"It was hard," Udo replied, remembering the tough time he had in the camp. "But we learned a lot. It lasted only one month, so that the soldiers could be sent to the war fronts and the training of another batch could begin immediately. We were trained by officers and non-officers. Corporals handled mainly weapons and parade while sergeants are responsible for disciplining trainees as well as overseeing parade."

"What about officers? Did they not take part in training recruits?" Adim enquired, flicking away a grasshopper which had landed on his shirt.

Udo wondered why Adim, who had said so many times he would never carry a gun, was interested in military training. He looked up and saw Adim staring at him. Udo understood that he would not give up until he had received an answer to his question.

"So you didn't hear when I said we were trained by officers and non-officers? Officers from the rank of second lieutenant to major took part in the training. They handled everything else including war strategies. Of all we did, the endurance exercises were the hardest for me." Udo recalled all the difficult tasks they had to do like climbing ropes, scaling walls, marathon race. But he had enjoyed the parade, especially when they marched to the villages very early in the morning singing war songs. He liked the way the villagers came out to watch them pass and waved to them. Some of the women wept and shouted words of encouragement to them. "I performed well in parade and marathon race," he told Adim.

Udo saw Uzo scowling and concluded that Uzo was bored with what he was explaining to Adim. He wanted to sing his favourite war song, but desisted because he did not want Uzo to ridicule him. Some other time perhaps he would be able to sing it to Adim when they were alone. He stared ahead to see if his *oga* was coming.

"Did you hear that the vandals have taken Owerri?" Uzo turned to him. "We also heard Umuahia is threatened. I heard *oga* say that the vandals bomb Umuahia two or three times a day. In the daytime, people leave the town for the bush, or troop to the surrounding villages and return home in the night." He shook his head. "Things are really bad."

"No, I didn't hear." Udo stared at him, shocked. "They hardly gave us any information about the war except the few times they brought news of victories won by our soldiers in some war fronts."

"We heard that fierce fighting is going on in the Owerri sector, as our troops try to recapture the town," Uzo added.

"What about Etiti?" Udo wondered if life would be the same there when he went back. Was Etiti a war front? It wasn't far from Umuahia, or was it? He couldn't be sure. He turned to Uzo to enlighten him.

Uzo laughed. "You are talking of Etiti? So you don't know? We left Etiti three weeks ago."

"What, you don't live in Etiti anymore? Where are you now?" He was astonished and did not know whether to be sad or happy with such news. He would never see Caleb again and he had been looking forward so much to bragging before him about his accomplishments in the training camp. He had been looking forward to displaying his new status as a properly trained soldier before the arrogant Caleb.

"We are in Umuoku." Uzo clapped him on the shoulder. "*Oga* is now a captain and is commanding officer of a company. He was promoted after you left for training."

Udo was delighted to hear his *oga* was a captain, but was still saddened about the loss of Caleb. To whom would he feed the interesting news of camp life? There was no one now to impress with the military jargon he had learnt while the training lasted – such as Sit Rep: situation report; Recce: reconnaissance; AWOL: absent without leave. He had longed to return home to give Caleb the correct information about the difference between military formations – regiment, division, brigade, battalion, company and platoon. He was sure Caleb did not know. In fact, from the training he had just had, he knew that Caleb was a big liar – he had never had military training as he claimed. Much of the information he fed Udo was wrong or distorted, judging from what he now knew. But, there was no Caleb to unmask. Udo would not see him to call his bluff and puncture his pride.

Udo was agonising over what he considered his pain and loss when his *oga* approached with another officer. Udo squeezed himself into the front seat with Uzo. He was sandwiched between Uzo and Adim. As soon as his *oga* and the other officer had settled in the car, Adim drove out of the training camp and headed for Umuoku. Udo glanced at the officer's shoulder and saw he was a lieutenant.

"To reverse the downward trend is crucial," Udo heard his *oga* say to the lieutenant sitting beside him in the speeding estate car and knew they had been having a serious conversation before they came into the car. "Only a significant victory can raise the morale of our troops now. The loss of Owerri was a stunning blow to everyone and continues to erode our morale like a hemorrhage." His voice was forceful and Udo was alarmed, for when his *oga* spoke in this way, he knew things were very bad. He was not a man who lost his temper easily or made decisions frivolously, but once he had taken a decision, it was irrevocable.

"Nothing short of a miracle can change the situation, it

seems." Lieutenant Ana's voice was full of pain. Udo shivered, wondering who would perform the miracle. Was it God? He knew the vandals were also praying for a miracle, so that the war could end quickly.

"Don't be despondent. There is still hope, especially if the equipment and arms expected arrive in time. Our greatest handicap is not having the arms and the hardware to execute the war."

Udo was astonished that his *oga* said so much, knowing that he, Uzo and Adim, were listening. He wouldn't have done this in the past. Udo wondered if it was because he had undergone military training and was now a full-fledged soldier that his *oga* spoke so openly about military matters in his presence.

"The attitude of some of the officers is disappointing and inappropriate, sir," Lieutenant Ana said. His voice was low. Udo strained his ears to catch the officer's next words. "Many are *chasing* women more than they are chasing vandals. I worry to see the rate at which girls flood officers' homes and even follow them to the trenches. It's shocking."

Udo regretted that he was sitting in the front seat and so could not see his *oga*'s reaction, though he could hear the anger in his voice. "Yes, the shameful acts many of the officers indulge in at this time cannot be counted. And from the stories one hears, it seems the most senior officers are even guiltier of such profligacy."

Udo didn't know the meaning of 'profligacy', but he was sure it was very bad behaviour on the part of officers. How disappointing! If the big *ogas* were doing bad things, what did they expect the recruits and the other ranks to do?

"You remember, sir, how the entire brigade in Umuobiri was destroyed by a different kind of evil?"

Lieutenant Ana's voice was barely audible to Udo, and he threw his head backwards and inclined his ear slightly in the direction of the driver, with the hope of hearing him better.

The lieutenant continued, "The religious charlatan, who called himself Jesus of Umuobiri, claimed he had divine power to provide security to officers, save them from death in the war front and give them foreknowledge of any evil that could overtake them. He actually gave them charms and amulets to wear around their necks or waists and many believed these could give them protection."

Udo heard his *oga* laugh. He too laughed, for he was astonished that the false prophet was able to hoodwink the officers into believing he could save their lives.

His *oga* spoke again. "It is amazing that people believed such nonsense and entrusted their fate and their lives to such a charlatan who was said to have ripped them off. I heard he became wealthy with what he got from the officers. It was good the division was disbanded and reorganised. Only such a surgical operation could clean up the mess the brigade commander and the other officers created."

Udo was so engrossed with listening to his *oga* and Lieutenant Ana that he did not have time to look around and see where the vehicle was taking them, so he was surprised when Uzo nudged him and announced that they had reached Umuoka.

30

Two months after the ugly experience she had had in Nkwerre, Ginika headed for her aunt's house. She had not seen her and her family for more than two months. Apart from going to work, she had stayed at home most of the time, feeling depressed and irritable. Even her mother-in-law had sensed her mood and left her mostly to herself. Ozioma was still in Ijeamasi's house. Ginika found ways to scourge herself over what had happened – starving herself, dressing in drab clothes and working herself to the bone, scrubbing, sweeping, dusting and washing when she was not at work. She was thinner and her skin had lost some of its glow. She blamed no one but herself for what had happened to her. She couldn't forgive herself for going to Nkwerre with Janet.

She was surprised when she got to her aunt's house – almost by reflex, as she had not paid attention to where she was going. So engrossed was she with her thoughts that she didn't know when she passed the *iroko* tree which always hinted to her that she was close to her aunt's. She slipped in through the gate and knocked on the front door.

"Ginika, is this you?" her aunt cried, as she opened the door. She hugged her. "But, what's the matter? You don't look yourself." Her aunt stared at her before leading her to the sitting room.

"Auntie, please, can we go to your room? I want us to be alone."

"All right, come." Her aunt caught her *wrappa* which had come loose and retied it securely around her waist before heading for her room. Ginika followed her.

As soon as they entered the room, Ginika fell on the bed and began to weep. Her shoulders shook violently like those of a person suffering from malaria.

"Ginika, what is the matter? Why are you crying like this?" When she said nothing but kept crying, her aunt took her in her arms and comforted her. She allowed her to cry for a while before asking her again why she was crying.

Ginika clung to her, her face pressed to her aunt's bosom. When she raised her head at last, her aunt's blouse was soaked with her tears. "I'm sorry, Auntie," she whispered. She sat on the bed again and blew her nose with a handkerchief she took from her handbag.

"Now, tell me why you are upsetting yourself in this terrible way." She looked at her carefully. "My God, you have lost weight. Ginika, what is the matter?"

"Auntie, I want to die. Yes, yes, I want to die." Tears filled her eyes again.

"God forbid! What type of foolish talk is this? Is this what you came here to tell me?" Her aunt frowned.

"Auntie, I think I'm pregnant. I have not seen my period for two months." She dabbed her eyes and whimpered like a wounded puppy.

Shocked, her aunt could only bring herself to say, "Two months?"

She nodded.

"Keep calm and tell me what happened." Her aunt's face was now expressionless.

Encouraged by her calmness, Ginika started from the beginning and told her what had happened in Nkwerre. Her voice was tremulous but she was now in control of herself. After narrating her story, she bowed her head, waiting for her aunt to blame or rebuke her. She was surprised her aunt did neither.

"Nne and the children are sleeping. Let's go and see Madam Mgboji, the midwife at Ama-Oyi Maternity Home. She will confirm if you are pregnant or not. Even the way you have starved yourself could make your period cease. Let's go now."

Ginika felt relief wash over her – her aunt was kind and sympathetic. She had expected her to abuse her and call her names, but instead, she had taken the initiative in a positive way.

"Wait for me on the veranda," her aunt said. "I want to tell Nne I am going out, so that she can take care of the house. I don't want her to know you are here, as she will want to see you and ask where two of us are going."

Madam Mgboji's house was not far and they found her at home when they entered the compound. When they told her why they came, she asked Ginika some questions, and then examined her.

"You are pregnant," Madam Mgboji pronounced. She sat opposite them in the room where she had examined her and asked her more questions. "Though one cannot be sure because a proper test has not been done, but even from the way you look and how you tell me you feel, I know you are

pregnant. Your breasts feel heavy, you said, and your nipples
are tender and you feel as if you are going to vomit. Did you
say that saliva comes readily to your mouth?"

Ginika nodded.

"These are signs that follow pregnancy," she intoned.
"Take care of yourself; you don't look well at all. You can
come and register in the maternity when you are ready, but as
soon as possible. As this is your first pregnancy, you need to be
properly looked after."

"Thank you." Her aunt got up and beckoned to her.

"Thank you, ma," Ginika looked at the midwife.

"It will be all right," Madam Mgboji consoled her. "It is a
good thing to get pregnant; it's only that the hardship brought
by war makes women afraid to get pregnant. But you are
young and should have no problem."

Ginika staggered out of the room behind her aunt.

When they got outside, her aunt asked, "What do we do
now?"

"Auntie, I want to ask you a favour, please."

"Go ahead, ask."

"I want to go to Etiti to look for Eloka. I can't bear the
thought of this pregnancy let alone carry it through the nine
months it will grow inside me. I will die if things remain as
they are now. I want to find Eloka and tell him what happened
and beg for his forgiveness. I want you to go with me to find
him."

For a long time her aunt said nothing. They walked side
by side in silence. Then she said gently, "All right, I will go
with you."

Ginika smiled. It was a very sad smile. They parted after
agreeing to set out for Etiti the very next day: there was no
time to waste. Ginika felt better after visiting her aunt.

Later that evening, while they ate dinner, she told her father-in-law she would go to her aunt's house to help her look after her children because two of them were sick. She lied deliberately, but she saw no other option left to her. She couldn't tell them what had happened or where she was going and why. It was best to keep her problem secret. Only her aunt knew – even Janet did not know.

She was grateful they did not try to stop her and knew she would have gone anyway with or without their consent. She put a few clothes in a bag and left for her aunt's house, as darkness was falling.

THEY SET out early, before dawn. They stood at the old Orie market, waiting for a lift or a commercial vehicle they would pay to get seats. Two hours later they were still waiting – no vehicles passed. A car came soon after and they ran forward. An army officer was sitting in the back.

"Yes, come in, pretty lady," he said to Ginika.

"Sir, we're two." Ginika pointed to her aunt. "Please, help us. We have been standing here for a long time."

"Driver, move," the officer said, looking away.

Ginika shook her head. "He thought I was alone."

Her aunt laughed. "He was already thinking of a pretty girl he would ravish. Idiot, let him go. That's how they spoil our girls."

Ginika winced. She knew what her aunt meant, for she had been a victim. She had even forgotten the name of the officer that got her pregnant. Tears stung her eyes and she rubbed at them.

"Ginika, don't start crying again or I'll leave you here and go home."

Two more cars stopped but when the occupants learned that Ginika was travelling with her aunt, they started their cars and sped away.

Another hour passed before they saw a lorry jolting down the road. Ginika waved frantically and the driver stopped. The roofless vehicle was stacked with bundles of straw mats and grass mattresses and Ginika knew the driver was going to a refugee camp. Similar mattresses and mats were occasionally supplied to the camp where she worked.

"Yes, *ebee*, where to?" the driver yelled.

"Etiti."

"How many of you?"

"Two. We are two, sir."

"Jump in and find space for yourselves on the mattresses."

"Driver, how do you expect me to jump into this huge monster you call a vehicle?" her aunt cried.

The driver got off and assisted her and Ginika. When they had settled down well enough, he said, "You will pay me. And I will stop you at Dikenafai, and from there you look for another vehicle, as I am going in the opposite direction."

"How much," Ginika asked.

When he told her, she paid him without argument. She had the money Eloka had given her which she had hardly touched. Each time the vehicle jolted or turned a sharp corner, they clung to the body of the lorry so as not to fall forward or sideways. At Dikenafai, they climbed down from their high patch and thanked the driver. Ginika watched the lorry rattle down the road.

"We have made some progress," her aunt said.

"Yes, and we may be lucky to find another vehicle soon." She stood by the roadside, ready to flag down any vehicle that passed.

One woman who passed by saw them and said, "Move a little to that side, that is where the vehicles pass. You will wait here until you are tired and still will not find a vehicle to board."

"Thank you, my sister." Her aunt beckoned her over with a wave, and they moved forward to the far side of another road. "If only we can get to the small town where they have a branch of the Research and Production Unit, not far from Anara," her aunt said. "Ray's friend works there. I'm sure he will help us get to Etiti."

Soon another car appeared. "Stay here, Auntie," Ginika whispered. "Let me go forward to meet the car."

She ran towards the car and waved frantically. The car stopped just in front of her. She bent towards the officer sitting at the back. Their eyes met and the man smiled.

"You're going towards Anara?" he asked. "Well, come in and I'll drop you. It's on my way."

Ginika opened the door and put in one leg and then beckoned to her aunt. "I hope you don't mind, sir. We are two – my aunt is travelling with me. Thanks so much, sir."

The officer frowned, but it was too late to zoom off, especially as one of Ginika's legs was inside the car and the other outside and her aunt was already opening the door of the passenger seat to sit with the driver.

When he dropped them in front of the Research and Production Unit thirty minutes later, and they watched him drive off after thanking him, they burst into spontaneous laughter. Even Ginika had forgotten temporarily her depression.

"He will not stop to pick up any girl again until he has made sure she is alone," her aunt said, still laughing.

They were shown where to find Mr Ukandu, Ray's classmate and friend. He was tall and skinny and bald. As her aunt had said, he gave them a vehicle and driver to take them to Etiti with the instruction that the driver should return immediately he had dropped them.

"Thank you," her aunt said. "You have solved our problem. We do not know how to thank you."

"The pleasure is all mine." Mr Ukandu smiled. "How are Ray and the children?"

"The children are well. We have not seen Ray for some time. He's with Military Intelligence."

Ginika saw her aunt's eyes cloud over. Weighed down by her own problem, she had completely forgotten her aunt's problem. How kind of her to come readily on this journey, leaving the children with Nne and pushing to the background her own worries.

Soon they were on their way. They got to Etiti before six o'clock and a soldier directed them to the commanding officer's house. When he saw the logo of the Research and Production Unit, the sentry opened the gate and the car drove in. A man in uniform ushered them into the lounge while he went for the CO. A few minutes later, the CO came and they told him they were looking for Lieutenant Odunze.

"Give me a few minutes, I'll be back."

"The driver has to return immediately," her aunt explained.

"Let him go. You will be taken care of." The short and stocky commanding officer was gone before they could say more.

"Well, we are here already. I'm sure we'll see your husband soon. Let me tell the driver to go." She got up and went out.

Ginika looked up when her aunt returned. "The CO has not yet returned," she told her.

"Do not worry. We have reached our destination. When the man comes, he'll direct us to Eloka's house."

Ginika nodded. She felt nervous now she was so close to seeing Eloka. How would he take her story? Would he be empathetic or reject her? She squirmed in misery.

"Listen, Ginika, I've been thinking." Her aunt looked at her and hesitated.

"Yes, Auntie?"

"That husband of yours does not strike me as someone who would forgive what happened that easily. You acted unwisely and wrongly, no doubt, but some husbands would forgive you and put the ugly experience behind them. Do you think Eloka is one of such men?"

Ginika stared at her aunt, frightened. "I don't know. I can't say what he would do if he found out."

"That is it – if he found out." Her aunt's eyes locked with hers. "Listen, when you see him tonight, don't tell him yet what happened. Just enjoy the night with him. Don't tell him at all. He will think the baby his when it is born."

"Auntie, I'll do as you advise." Ginika's voice sounded anxious – it had a catch to it.

She was composed when the CO returned. "Yes, what can we do for you?" he asked, beaming.

"We came to see Lieutenant Eloka Odunze," her aunt replied. "Please, can you help us by sending one of your soldiers to take us to his house?"

"Oh, Odunze. He's a captain now. He is not here any

more and unfortunately I can't tell you where you can find him. The truth is that I don't know. Officers and men move locations frequently."

Ginika's courage failed her and tears flooded her eyes. To get this far and not find Eloka – it was too much for her to bear.

Her aunt frowned deeply. "Why did you not tell us . . ." she began, but realising she was talking to a very senior army officer, she stopped and then continued, "Well, we have a problem, sir. The driver from the Research and Production that brought us has gone and we are stranded."

"Not to worry. You can stay the night and tomorrow we'll drop you at the Research and Production Unit."

The CO was friendly all through and invited them to have dinner with him. After the meal, he took them to show them where they would pass the night. "Madam, this is your room." He opened a room and they saw a narrow bed in the middle of the room. Her aunt went in to inspect the room. He took Ginika to another room nearby. "And you, young lady, can sleep in this one," he stated, as he opened the door to a similar room with another single bed. He wished her good night and went away.

Her aunt hurried to the room where Ginika was as soon as the CO had left. "We are not going to sleep in separate rooms, do you hear me?"

Ginika nodded.

"Let's move this mattress to the other room. Let's do it quickly. Tonight, I know I will sleep with one eye open, as Ama-Oyi people say. The door does not have a lock, so we cannot lock it."

They decided to sleep immediately so as to wake up early

the next day. Ginika lay on the mattress on the floor while her aunt took the bed. For a long time Ginika tossed in bed, unable to sleep. But she eventually slept fitfully.

In the morning, her aunt told her that in the middle of the night, someone she strongly suspected to be the CO had opened the door, stood at the door for a while and then left.

"I don't know who it was, but I was ready to scream the house down if the person had attempted to enter the room."

The CO kept his word and gave them a vehicle to take them to the Research and Production Unit. But they never saw him again, as he had sent his orderly and a driver with the necessary instructions.

GINIKA WAS almost five months pregnant before she decided to tell Eloka's parents about her experience and her condition. She and her aunt agreed it would be worse if she delayed too long and they found out by themselves. She could win their empathy if she explained to them how it had happened.

Ozioma had returned home but Ginika had not confided in her. Janet knew now, but there was nothing she could do to help. Ginika knew she was alone except for the support of her aunt and her grandmother who also knew.

Ginika told her mother-in-law, in the morning, after they had had breakfast. Rain fell in torrents, like a water-fall pouring down the side of a mountain. It drummed so hard on the roof and caused such a racket that Ginika had to repeat herself several times before her mother-in-law could hear all she said. In fact, she had begun to regret breaking such bad news on a day like this, but eventually her mother-in-law appeared to have all the facts.

Though Ginika had expected she would be shocked and disappointed, she had not expected her to react the way she did.

"*Hei! Hei! Hei!*" she yelled three times. "What are you saying? Ginika, what did you just say? You are pregnant? For whom?" She ran out of her room, screaming to her husband – from whom she had been estranged for many months – to come and listen to *his* daughter-in-law. "Onwaora, Onwaora, where are you? Where are you? Come and listen to your daughter-in-law. Abomination! My ears have gone deaf after listening to an abomination."

Ginika heard every word in spite of the rain. Her mother-in-law's voice reverberated throughout the whole house. With her head bent, tears dropped on her hands which lay folded on her thigh. She thought that if she had the power to undo what had happened, she would do so with her whole heart even if it meant losing an eye or a hand in the war. But she knew that there was nothing she or anyone could do to reverse what had happened.

Ozioma was the first to run into the room. "Ginika, is what Mama is saying true? Are you pregnant for another man that is not my brother?"

Ginika stared at her but did not see her, did not hear or understand her question.

"Where is she?" she heard her father-in-law bellow. He came into the room which she was sure he had not entered since Nwoyibo left Ama-Oyi. He pushed aside Ozioma who was standing at the door, and stood before her. "Ginika, what is this I heard? You are pregnant? For whom? *I mee aru*, you have committed an abomination! I want you out of this house today. I don't want to see you when I return in the evening.

And from today, don't report for duty at the refugee camp. If I see you there again, I will have you arrested. Mr Asiobi will be informed that you have ceased to work there." He stormed out.

He didn't even ask me what happened or how it happened, Ginika thought. She was very sad that she could not work any longer – it was a way of keeping busy and, more importantly, the relief materials she got from the refugee camp were useful to her aunt and to Udo's mother. She watched Ozioma walk out of the room silently; her face was screwed up, as if she was about to burst into tears.

Her mother-in-law returned and glared at her. "You are still here? What are you still doing in my room? Get out and don't enter this room again. You stink. You heard what Onwaora said? Pack your things and return to your father's house." She hissed.

Ginika spoke only once after they had all denounced her. "Can't I stay until Eloka returns? He might come again soon?"

"Are you mad? So you think my son will stay married to you after what you did. If you don't know it, this is a decent family. Now get out of my room, you win-the-war wife."

Ginika burst into tears. She got up and left the room, stumbling as she stepped on the doormat.

FOUR MONTHS had passed. Ginika thought they were the most difficult months in her life. Things had gone from bad to worse for her. Rejected by Eloka's family, abandoned by her angry father and unsympathetic stepmother, she had clung to the only two people who gave her unflinching support – her aunt and her grandmother – with whom she had lived since her father-in-law threw her out with the connivance of her mother-in-law. Janet had kept away at first because Ginika had not wanted to see her after what happened, but later she had come and brought her things. What happened in Nkwerre had cast a shadow over their friendship. The past months had been traumatic for her and for everyone. She wished she had made things easier for her aunt who cared for her in spite of her own troubles. Food was scarce and she did not have enough to feed her children, herself and Nne. And she had joined them to share what little food there was. "Ginika, eat, try and eat," her aunt would chide. "Remember you are pregnant and need to eat well. Not that we eat well here but, at least, eat what is available." But she didn't have any appetite. Sometimes for a week, she would eat nothing. She wanted to die, but death refused to come. Being cowardly, she couldn't take her own life. This would have ended her misery and perhaps made most people happy – if she ceased to exist, to be an embarrassment to a family with a good name, as her mother-in-law had said.

She sat on the veranda, watching the children shelling melon seeds. She wanted to join them but wasn't feeling well enough. Her body felt strange. Whether she sat on a chair or lay in bed, a feeling of discomfort assailed her.

"That baby is ready to come any time now," her grandmother teased her. "Are you ready to be a mother?"

"Nne, you think the baby will come soon?" she asked, frightened. Would she be able to cope? How would they take care of a baby in this house where food was not available most of the time? Would her breasts produce milk for the baby? Was she ready to nurse a baby fathered by a man she hardly knew and whom she spent the greater part of the day cursing? If curses could kill, the man would surely be dead now.

"Bring the plate here, let me help with the shelling," Ginika said to Obika who sat astride a bowl containing unshelled melon seeds.

He got up from the floor and passed the bowl to her. But the next moment it had fallen from her hand and spilled its content on the floor because Ginika was screaming in pain. She held her waist, panting and groaning at the same time.

"Ah, the baby is on the way," her grandmother cried, rising to her feet with difficulty. "Obika, call your mother. Where is she? She must take Ginika to the maternity home."

Obika jumped out in search of his mother who had gone to the back of the compound to fetch the vegetables they would use to prepare the evening meal – a few cups of rice a friend had given her the previous day.

Ginika knew that she was in labour even before her grandmother announced it. She knew because she had just experienced two of the three signs the midwife had explained indicate that labour had started. The first was the sudden sharp pain which almost unhinged her mind, as it hit her lower back, and this was followed by a gush of water between her legs. She was surprised the two signs came so close together. She tried to get up, but fell back in her chair.

"Wait for her to come to help you, my child," her grandmother coaxed. "She will soon be here."

"Nne, is she going to have the baby now?" Ona asked, wide-eyed, staring at Ginika.

"Yes, my little one, the baby is coming," Ginika heard her grandmother say.

She held her breath, anticipating the next bout of pain. She saw her aunt run into the compound, followed by Obika. "Obika, hurry to my room and bring the bag I left on the cupboard." Turning to Ginika, she said gently, "Now, I'm going to help you to your feet, okay. Don't be afraid, my hands will support you." Presently Ginika was on her feet, groaning. "Good. Now, shall we walk very slowly to the gate? But first be careful as you climb down the steps in front of the veranda. Good, good, one step at a time."

At the gate, another contraction came and stabbed her so violently that she cried out. The pain was so fierce that she almost fell to the ground, but her aunt's hands held her up. "Obika, run ahead and tell Madam Mgboji we are coming. Take the bag with you." As Obika ran off, her aunt said, "We'll have to go to her house. We can't make it to the maternity home. I'm sure she will be able to deliver the baby in her house."

Madam Mgboji was waiting for them. She had prepared for the birth in a small room she used as labour room when women who could not get to the maternity home came to her house instead. She immediately took over from Ginika's aunt and led the young woman into the room.

"You should not have any problem because your body is well developed" the midwife said, looking at her. She helped her to undress and then examined her. "The baby is coming soon," she announced to them. "You are fully dilated," she told Ginika.

In a short time, the baby's head showed and once that came out, the rest of the body came sliding into the midwife's welcoming hands. As she took it away, Ginika and her aunt heard a feeble cry. Ginika sighed. It was not as difficult as she had feared. Her aunt held her hand.

Madam Mgboji stood at the door and Ginika looked at her quickly, thinking she was bringing the baby to show them.

But it was her aunt the midwife had come for. "Come with me," she said.

When they entered again, it was to tidy her up and leave her to sleep for a while.

"Where is the baby? Is it a boy or girl? Can't I see it now?"

"You had a male baby and he is premature," the midwife said. "You cannot see him now. I'm taking care of him at the moment. But try and sleep. When you wake up, I'll take you to see him."

Ginika nodded. She was so tired she soon fell asleep. They allowed her to sleep for about an hour. When she woke up, she asked to be taken to see her baby. She told them she wanted to see the little thing that had grown inside her for nine months.

Then they told her. "The baby died," the midwife said in a gentle voice. "It is better that way because he would not have survived for long. He was not well-formed."

Ginika gave a loud cry and began to weep.

"Ginika, don't cry," her aunt consoled. "It is best he should go. I saw him: he was too tiny and was malformed. Each of his hands had two fingers missing. His breathing was laboured and I watched him breathe his last."

Her aunt's words distressed rather than comforted her. "Oh, I killed the baby, didn't I? I starved him to death while he was inside me. I neglected him and didn't give him a chance." She was hysterical, as she thrashed about on the bed on which she had rested.

The midwife gave her an injection. In a little while, she fell asleep again.

31

The attack came exactly at dawn. *Gbim! Gbim! Kagbim! Kagbim! Kakadudu! Kadum! Kadum! Kakakakakaka! Dum! Dum! Kakagbimgbim! Kagbim! Kakaka!*

Eloka jumped out of bed and ran out of the room to wake Udo, Uzo and Adim, but saw they were already up, packing things and throwing them into the estate car.

"Just get a few essentials and let's get going," he shouted, as he rushed back to his room to gather a few things. He picked up his Madison and pistol and threw some clothes in a bag. He put on his uniform and dashed out carrying the things he had collected. The front had been so quiet yesterday. Before he and the other officers returned to their quarters yesterday evening, they had left the boys in the trenches playing games – ludo, cards, snakes and ladders, draughts and *nchorokoto*. Who would have thought the vandals would be on the offensive this morning. That was war for you, he mused. He was sure the recapture of Owerri by Biafran forces recently had annoyed the vandals so much that they decided to step up operations in other sectors to make up for the embarrassment of losing Owerri which they had captured and held for some months.

"Are you ready? Get into the car!" he yelled at Uzo, Udo and Adim.

As the bombardment continued and shells fell on the outskirts of the village of Umuoku, Eloka directed Adim the way to go. The car jolted along the road which was already flooded by fleeing villagers who dropped objects they found cumbersome on the road.

"My God, where will these people go? Biafra is shrinking fast and soon there will be no place to run to or hide in." Sadly he watched them from where he sat in the car – women carrying loads and dragging their children along; children trotting beside their mothers and older siblings, some crying. It was a distressing sight. The village had not yet been hit but the sound of shells was driving the villagers away. Eloka knew the vandals were still far away and it would take a while before they entered the village. He had to make it, though, to the war front, to the trenches to give the order for retreat.

"The vandals must be really boiling, fuming to go on like this," he mused aloud. "They are putting in everything they have into this offensive." As he listened, he could hear the sound of heavy artillery. The sound of shells exploding was nerve-wracking and he could appreciate the villagers' panic. He saw a woman carrying a mattress and dragging two little children with her and wondered why she could not drop the mattress and carry the smaller child so that they could move faster.

"Head for the location where the soldiers are," he instructed Adim. "And watch out for the villagers. Some of them run as if they are drunk, swaying this way and that way."

"Yes, sir," Adim replied. He sat hunched up, his hands clamped on the steering wheel as he strove to keep the vehicle on the road without crushing the fleeing villagers. By the time he got to the war front, the officers and men were waiting for him to give them a command.

"Retreat!" he ordered. "Let it be orderly." He watched, as the soldiers jumped out of the trenches and began an orderly retreat. He looked up for signs of an air raid – there was none – but he knew it would not be long before the enemy increased the attack. He needed to get his soldiers holed up in new trenches some kilometres away before this happened. From there they could launch a counter-attack. He knew their present location would be overrun before the end of the day as the enemy advanced.

It took a while before the troops concluded their retreat. They began immediately to dig trenches and by late afternoon they were done. They holed in, waiting for further instructions.

Eloka had stayed till the retreat was completed and then took the road leading to Ngbo, the village that would be his new location. By this time, shells had started falling inside the village of Umuoku. The stragglers among the fleeing villagers – those unable to move fast either because of sickness or old age – waddled along the road like ducks. Eloka knew some of the aged would prefer to remain in the village, hoping the vandals would pass through without harming them. Some, who feared the uncertainty of the future if they left the village where they had lived all their lives, would prefer to die in Umuoku rather than take the risk of becoming refugees in strange towns and villages.

Eloka was sure the vandals had advanced significantly, for shells were exploding in Umuoku. He could feel the vibration as it shook the car. *Gbim! Gbim!* He could distinguish the sounds of the different weapons they were using: Bren gun, light machine-gun, heavy machine-gun and armoured car. It was a major offensive, he thought, wondering if it was happening on other war fronts or just this one.

"*Oga*, I can hear the sound of a plane in the air," Eloka heard Udo say.

He heard it too. "Quick, Adim, turn to the right and drive into that grove." There was a crunching and a rustling noise as Adim steered the car swiftly in between rows of trees. Before he stopped completely, Eloka shouted, "Now get out of the car all of you and take cover!" He yanked open the door and jumped out just as the others spilled out of the vehicle. He ran a short distance and threw himself on the ground. He tilted his head back a little, as he heard the plane, streaking past. *Warawarawara! Fiiiii! Fiiiii! Gbim…Gbim!* Eloka shuddered when he heard the sound of bombs exploding, as the plane strafed the road. He hugged the ground which was littered with dry and decaying leaves. When it was over, he stood up and picked out pieces of dead leaves from his uniform.

"Are you all right?" he asked Udo who was still trembling. He smiled when he saw how shaken Adim and Uzo were. These ones had not tasted battle, he thought. "Back to the car and let's get cracking," he said briskly.

Adim started the car and steered it back to the road. Eloka shook his head when he saw the havoc caused by the plane – dead bodies lying by the roadside, craters defacing the road and the roadside here and there. Fortunately the road was still motorable and Adim managed to manoeuvre the car along the now deserted road. But soon Eloka saw people emerge from the bushes where they had taken cover and continue on the road.

The shells continued to fall behind them, but he was sure the vandals were advancing faster. He had to get to location as fast as he could: there was no time to waste. He noticed also that the fleeing villagers were moving faster, and he was sure they had realised the enemy was not far behind. He knew they would not stop to rest until they could no longer hear the sound of shells.

"Stop!" he ordered the driver. By the side of the road lay an elderly woman who seemed dead or almost dead and a very light-skinned young woman bent over her, weeping uncontrollably. People passed by them without stopping or talking to the girl. "Uzo, go and bring the girl. That woman is probably her mother and is dead."

Uzo jumped out of the car and went to the girl. "*Oga* is calling you," he said loudly, pointing to the car.

The girl lifted her head and looked at the car without interest. She bent over the woman and continued weeping.

"Are you deaf?" shouted Uzo. "I say *oga* says you should come."

The girl shook her head.

Uzo walked back and reported that the girl refused to come, but Eloka and Adim and Udo knew because they had watched and heard.

"She's going to kill herself," Eloka said sadly. "The plane could come back and get her if a shell doesn't do this first. Let's go." But the car had hardly moved when Eloka asked Adim to stop again. He got out of the car and went to the girl.

Eloka bent over the woman and saw that she was bleeding profusely from a deep wound around her neck. He thought she must have been hit by shrapnel from the air raid. "Come with us," he said to the girl. "There's nothing you can do for her from the look of this wound, but you can at least save yourself. The plane could come back and there are the shells too."

"No, I can't leave my mother here," she wailed. "I must stay with her."

"That's not a wise decision." As he was about to straighten up, Eloka heard the woman mumble, with a weak voice, "Go with them, my child, go. I'm almost dead."

"No, Mama, I can't leave you here." The girl began to weep again.

As Eloka and the girl watched, the woman's body jerked twice and lay still. The girl shrieked and fell on her mother's body. Eloka lifted his hand and closed the woman's staring eyes.

"Let's go. We can take you to the next village."

The girl got up, picked up a bag that lay beside the dead woman and followed him to the car. She got into the car and sat beside Eloka.

"What's your name?" he asked the girl who was still snivelling. He wanted to help her get her mind off her dead mother.

"Queen." She dabbed her eyes with a brown handkerchief she took from her bag.

"Queen? Your name is Queen? Who gave you such a name?" He smiled at her, looking at her properly for the first time. She was a beautiful woman, he thought.

"My mother gave me the name."

"Is there no other name one can call you? Don't you have a second name as most of us do?" He wasn't going to call her 'Queen'. Only one woman deserved to be called queen by him – and that woman was his Mermaid.

For the first time the girl smiled. Her teeth were perfectly white and well-formed and her face looked even more beautiful when she smiled. "My other name is Boma. My grandmother gave me the name."

"Well, Boma sounds good to me. I'll call you Boma."

She nodded.

"What about your surname? Don't you have one?"

Boma smiled again. "Talib. My father was a Lebanese."

"I can now understand where you got your very light skin."

She looked at him shyly and nodded.

ELOKA KNEW the counter-attack was partially successful. They were not only able to halt the vandals but also push then back. Ironically, they now occupied Eloka's former location in Umuoku while Eloka and his men settled in Ngbo. He knew his men enjoyed the quiet that had reigned on the war front for some time. He heard that the soldiers socialised with the vandals. Both sides visited each other surreptitiously and exchanged mementoes. The vandals gave the soldiers cigarettes, tinned food and drinks. He wondered what they gave the vandals in return. To the enemy Biafrans were 'rebels'; to Biafrans, the enemy were 'vandals'. Rebels and vandals consorting, he smiled at the expression. He didn't think this kind of relationship should be encouraged, but was it possible to stop it? The soldiers had their way of getting round orders at times.

Eloka worried about many things. One of them was the fear that they were not combat-ready in case the vandals decided to attack again. Their arms and ammunition were seriously depleted – in fact they had nothing at the moment – while the enemy had all the sophisticated weapons imaginable. They had everything – small arms, large guns, heavy artillery, armoured vehicles and tanks. They had jet fighters and bombers; they had food and drinks galore for the fighting men; they had uniform, boots and helmets for the soldiers. On the contrary, Biafran forces lacked all these. Eloka wondered how he would cope in the face of imminent attack. He was also worried about the quality of soldiers being sent to the war fronts now – they were poorly trained. He wondered how these ill-trained conscripts could storm the vandals' trench and dislodge them from their location.

"Straight to headquarters, Adim," Eloka instructed, as he left the war front. He hated administration, but as officer commanding – OC – he had to do some administration. He saw himself more as a technical, practical person and felt more at home with fighting than being cooped up with administrative duties – writing reports, arranging for the feeding of troops and chasing contractors who did all they could to maximise profit to the detriment of the army, of the country. He called them Shylocks – they were greedy and selfish. Eloka was so busy with his thoughts he did not know when they reached headquarters.

"*Oga*, sir, we are there," Adim told him.

Uzo leapt out of the car and pulling the door open, saluted.

Eloka nodded and hopped out of the car.

As soon as he sat down in his office – a modestly furnished room in an old bungalow with wooden shutters on the window – he sent for the contractor whom he understood had been waiting for him. He looked round the room. A table behind which he sat on a wooden chair, a small chest of drawers for the files and documents and a dictionary were all he had in the room. Oh, there were, of course, two chairs for visitors.

Eloka passed his index finger over his moustache and thought he should trim it as soon as he could. It felt bushy to the touch. He looked down at his camouflage uniform and noted how rough the shirt was. Udo had not ironed it properly. Yes, now that his mind was on the boy, he remembered that Udo seemed to have behaved badly in the past month. He was not as cheerful as he used to be. Was Udo trying to avoid him? What was on the chap's mind? he wondered. Only last week, he had caught him with an angry look written all over his face, but when their eyes met, he looked away swiftly. What was eating him up? He hoped to find out. He hoped he would remember, as there were so many things to think about.

Eloka wondered why the contractor had not come in. "Cyprian!" he called. "Where is Cyprian?"

Cyprian, his office assistant, rushed in. "Sir, I went out to look for the contractor. He went to urinate. He will be here soon."

"Good afternoon, Captain Odunze," the contractor greeted. He was fat and short, with a scar on his forehead.

"Good day, Chief Ogamba, please sit down." Eloka's face was bereft of a smile, as he continued. "Chief, we are not happy with you. My people complain about the food you supply to us. The beans are full of weevils in spite of the exorbitant price you charge; the palm oil is not fresh: the cooks call it *eketeke*. It is complaints all the time about your supplies. You have to do better than this if you want us to renew your contract. We would be happy to keep you as our contractor because you are from Ngbo and know how to get supplies quickly, but we won't if your services don't improve. In that case, I'll have no option but to look for someone else. In fact, I may even decide to buy from the locals direct and not go through middlemen or contractors. I hope you understand me, Chief."

"I have heard you, Captain, and will try to do better. I didn't know people were complaining about my supply – no one told me."

Eloka smiled but there was no mirth in it. He knew the chief was lying, as he had been notified before of his failing. Anyway, he would let that go, but he was determined to terminate his contract if his services did not improve.

"All right, Chief, thank you." Eloka shook hands with him and he waddled out of the office.

He stared at the roof for a while, thinking that he might have to try buying straight from the locals. He would be able to save money for the battalion as well as buy food that was in excellent condition.

Eloka settled down to write reports – the aspect of his administrative duties he detested most.

LATER, WHEN his work was done, Eloka came out of the office and told Cyprian to ask Adim to bring the vehicle. He had instructed Adim to park the car in a hidden place, near the bushes, in case the vandals decided to bomb their location. At home he had built a temporary shelter with palm fronds and the car was parked there in the evenings and at night.

On his way home, he stopped and bought some bananas for Boma and the rest of the people staying with him. He was still not sure what to do with the girl he had rescued from the jaws of death during the evacuation of Umuoku. He had taken her to the refugee camp, but as soon as he saw the state of the camp, he knew he would feel guilty leaving her as she was, in a terrible place like that. The smell, the exposure and the lack of privacy he saw there were dehumanising, to say the least. He had brought her back to his house. Three months later, she was still with him.

"Adim, stop and let's buy some maize," he said, pointing to a woman who carried on her head a basin full of fresh maize. "Uzo, go and buy some." He gave him some money. He liked roasted fresh maize and would have it tonight.

His thoughts returned to Boma. Yes, she had been with him for three months. He had wanted to take her to Owerri to see if he could help her find work in the recaptured city; he knew some people there who could help. But the discovery he made last month had made him change his mind, at least for now. He had found her vomiting in the bathroom and she confessed she was four months pregnant. She had fooled him, living in his house without letting him know of her condition. He was displeased with her and had asked, "Why didn't you tell me you were pregnant? You knew, didn't you? You've been here for two months which means you were two months pregnant when we saw you." She had told him a soldier had got her pregnant, and she said she didn't tell him because she was afraid he would throw her out if he knew. He had not touched her anyway, so she couldn't have pinned it on him. Now that he knew her condition, how could he just send her away? Where would she go? She had no one who could help her, and her mother, the only person she had, was dead. He found himself in a big dilemma – what to do with Boma.

When he arrived home, Boma and Udo came out to welcome him.

"Good evening, sir," Udo greeted. His eyes were averted.

"Udo, how are you?"

"I'm fine, sir,"

Eloka watched him collect the corn and hurry into the house. In the past he would not only greet him, but also linger to say one thing or the other in his cheerful way.

"Can you roast the maize, Udo? I want to eat it tonight."

"Yes, sir."

"Welcome home," Boma greeted, taking his folder from him. "Did you have a good day?" She smiled and her teeth shone like silver.

"Thanks, Boma. How are you?" He noticed she wore a close-fitting dress and glanced at her belly. Her pregnancy was beginning to show, he thought. How sad for her to be pregnant at this time. This was why he and Mermaid decided not to have a baby in this war period. Where would Boma have the baby? He hadn't even thought of it? He would ask her to go into the town and see if there was a hospital or some other place she could register and be attended to. He would be willing to give her money to do so. But he had to come to a decision fast about Boma. What a complex situation he had got himself into!

ELOKA DECIDED to retire early to bed and left Boma in the sitting room reading a paperback she told him she had borrowed from a girlfriend of one of the officers.

"It looks like a thunderstorm is brewing. Don't stay up too late," he advised, as he passed where she sat. "You're five months gone now and need to rest, don't you?"

She laughed. "How do you know, Captain? Are you talking from experience or what?"

He smiled. "No, my wife is not pregnant yet, so I'm

hopelessly inexperienced, but I have heard people say women in this condition need a lot of rest." It was a good thing there was a spare room in the house which she now occupied, he thought.

THE RAIN storm began at midnight. It came with violent wind and flashes of lightning which lit up everywhere, including his room. The rumble and clapping of thunder shook him awake and he got out of bed to make sure his windows were securely locked. He went back to bed, but could not return to sleep. The drumming of rain on the corrugated iron roof and the weird map the lightning was drawing in the sky kept him awake.

He got up to adjust the flimsy curtains that covered the windows, but this did not shield his eyes from the flashes of light. He decided to just lie prone in bed, hoping that eventually sleep would steal him away. His mind turned to the past and the image of his wife glided to his memory. What was she doing now? Probably she was having her beauty sleep. Was rain also drumming hard and lightning flashing with venom in Ama-Oyi? He missed her so much – so much that sometimes his body ached for her. When would he see her again?

He turned his head towards the door; he thought he heard something that sounded like a knock though he couldn't be sure. It could have been vibrations from the thunder that rattled the door. But the knock came again and louder this time.

"Who is it?" he called. "Come in."

The door opened and he was surprised to see Boma standing there in her night clothes. He frowned and asked, rather coldly, "Yes, Boma, what do you want?" He rolled over and lay on his back. He only wore a singlet and shorts. He watched her draw nearer and at that moment the lightning flashed again and lit up her face. He was shocked by the terror in her eyes and the tears streaming down her face. He was sure something was seriously wrong with her and that it had to do with the baby in her womb. He hoped she was not bleeding, for he feared he wouldn't know what to do.

He jumped out of bed and dashed forward. "Boma, what is it? Are you ill?"

She clung to him weeping. He could feel her body trembling and as he folded her in his arms to comfort her, she pressed her face to his body.

"Now, if you don't tell me what the matter is, how can I help you?" he asked. "Come and sit down." He led her to the bed and made her sit down. He sat next to her. "Tell me what's wrong."

"I had a nightmare," she babbled. "I was frightened and had to come to you."

Eloka felt himself relax and almost laughed. He was relieved there was nothing seriously wrong with her. A nightmare and she was so distressed, he thought. "Tell me about it. What was the nightmare about?"

"I saw my mother and she was calling me to help her. But I couldn't help her. Something held my hands and legs. As I watched, she was snatched away and I saw her being killed though I didn't know what was killing her."

"Stop crying. It was only a dream – a bad dream. But you're all right now. Come, I'll take you back to your room. I'm sure you'll fall asleep in no time."

She refused to get up. "Eloka, please, let me sleep with

you. I can't go back to that room this night. I'm frightened. Please, let me stay here."

He was so taken aback that she called him by his name – she had always called him Captain and he hadn't minded. It maintained a distance between them which he studiously cultivated. He would be lying to himself if he said he didn't find her attractive, but he was determined there would be no intimacy between them. He enjoyed chatting with her when he was in the house, for she was a lively person, but he would not go beyond that in his relations with her. She reminded him of his wife probably because they were about the same age.

"Listen to yourself, Boma: a big girl like you afraid of thunderstorm, like a little girl of five," he joked. "Come, be a good girl and allow me to take you to your room." He held her hands and attempted to pull her up, but she resisted him.

Nothing he said or did would make her budge. She clung to him and he was painfully aware of her soft and splendid body pressing his eagerly. Her night-dress was transparent and her peaked breasts seared his almost bare chest, igniting a fire of desire around his groin. "All right, you can stay here till morning. Lie down."

She withdrew her hands from around him, and lay on his bed. She had stopped crying now and stared at him with lustrous eyes whose appeal was heightened by the flashes of light that penetrated the room.

"Just a moment," he said, and went out. He returned with some cushions he had taken from the sitting room. He arranged them on the floor and lowered his body. "Boma, go back to sleep," he said, before he turned and lay on his right side, facing the door, so that he would not see the lightning that still flashed and lit up the sky outside as well as the room.

32

Udo sat on the steps in front of the house, looking at women going in and out of the officers' quarters. He frowned, wondering why girls flocked to officers instead of busying themselves with serving the nation or getting married, as Sister Ginika did, and living a respectable life. As he watched, two girls came out of the house next to theirs and burst out laughing. What was making them laugh? he wondered. They looked happy and carefree in spite of the war. Above all, they looked fresh and well-fed like Boma who had occupied their house and his *oga* allowed her. Udo hissed.

He watched the girls walk away down the road that led into town. They wore sandals made from disused vehicle tyres. Biafran shoes, he murmured, remembering that Sister Ginika had worn similar shoes. Oh, Sister Ginika, he thought sadly, a strange woman has taken over your husband. What could he do to drive away this girl, Boma, from the house? He had to find a way to save his *oga* from this Jezebel, this Delilah, who had hypnotized and bewitched him.

He saw Boma come out of the house and stand beside him. He flinched, as if she had struck him. He didn't want her near him and turned his eyes in the opposite direction.

"Udo, what are you doing here?" Boma asked. "Don't forget to wash Captain's uniform and iron the spare one." She flashed him her bewitching smile with which, he knew, she held his *oga* captive, but which would not work on him.

"You don't have to remind me," he replied tersely. "I know my work and will do it without your reminding me."

"Well, I thought you had forgotten." Her voice was gentle. "I just thought you should do it in time before the sun goes down. Captain will not be happy if the uniform does not dry today…"

He interrupted her. "Please, don't tell me what my *oga* likes or does not like." His eyes flashed. "What do you know about it anyway?"

"What is eating you today?" Boma asked, surprised. "What have I said or done to deserve this attack? You don't like me, do you?"

Udo sensed the hurt in her voice but he was neither remorseful nor apologetic. "It's you something is eating, not me. Just leave me alone, okay?"

Boma hissed loudly and went into the house.

Udo blinked maliciously and muttered, "Foolish girl." He went to the back of the house to wash the uniform which he had already soaked in a bucket of water.

Later his *oga* came back with Adim and Uzo, looking tired. Did he go to the war front? Udo wondered. He hoped things were not bad in the war front and that the vandals had not advanced again.

"Welcome, sir," he greeted.

His *oga* grunted and went into the house. A few minutes later, he called Udo. "Can you peel the pineapple I brought back? Do it now."

"Yes, sir."

He brought it back in a flat plate nicely diced and put it on a small stool close to where his *oga* sat in the sitting room.

"Quick job, Udo. It looks good too. I hope you left some for yourself and the others? "Yes, sir. This is yours."

"What of Boma? Is her share here or there?

"Her own is in the kitchen, sir."

"Go and bring it here."

For a fraction of a second, he hesitated and then walked out, annoyed. Was he expected to serve this girl too? He hoped his *oga* knew what he was doing. This was too much – asking him to serve this…this husband-snatcher.

"Here it is, sir." He had the plate in his hand and in it was a small piece of pineapple.

"Give it to her," his *oga* instructed. "Oh, that looks quite small – I hope you have some left for you, Adim and Uzo. I think you gave me too much; bring the plate and let me give Boma some more."

Udo felt like throwing the plate on the ground, but he did not. He presented the plate to his *oga* who put a generous portion of his share in it. He went to where Boma sat and gave it to her.

"Thank you, Udo." She took the plate from him.

He did not say anything, as he turned and left the room. Back in the kitchen, he shared the remaining pineapple into three plates. As he cut his into pieces, he could hear his *oga* and Boma chatting and laughing. He boiled with anger and cut his finger with the knife which Uzo had sharpened the previous day against a stone at the back of the house.

UDO LAY on a mattress on the floor of the room he shared with Uzo. He had used the spare room until Boma came and his *oga* asked him to move in with Uzo, so that Boma could have the spare room. As they did after supper, before retiring for the night, the three of them – Adim, Uzo and himself – were in the room chatting. Though Adim was much older than Uzo and himself, Udo knew he was happy to chat with them. He knew he had learned a lot from Adim about the army and about life generally more than he had from the more reticent Uzo.

Adim sat on the only chair in the room while Uzo sat on the bed in which he slept. The walls were stained and Udo had often wondered what the stain was. Was it blood or human excreta? It looked dirty brown. He wondered who had occupied the room before Uzo. Who had lived in the house before his *oga*? Who was the owner and where was he now since the army had commandeered the house?

"The war front is still quiet," he heard Uzo say. "The boys were chatting and playing ludo and draughts before we left for home."

"I wish I had gone out with you," he said. "I was alone with that witch and she insulted me today." Udo hissed, shaking his legs, as he lay on his back, knees bent and feet planted on the mattress.

"Be careful with that girl, Udo," Uzo warned. "She's *oga*'s girl and he will be angry if you quarrel with her." He laughed. "It seems to me she is even pregnant for *oga*. Sometimes I think her belly is protruding more than when she came here. But I'm not sure."

Udo jumped to his feet, almost falling, as his feet got entangled with the sheet on the mattress which was not properly tucked in below it, so as to prevent it from being dirtied by the dusty floor. "What did you say – that she is pregnant for *oga*?" His mouth was open, his eyes glazed and his face dejected. "But she has been here only two months." He stood there moping, unable to bring his mind to think of Sister Ginika.

Uzo laughed derisively. "You talk like the small boy you are. How long does it take for a woman to get pregnant? It takes eternity, eh?"

"Uzo, you yourself know little," Adim mocked. "So you are just noticing the girl is pregnant. The first day I saw her, I knew she was pregnant. I pitied *oga,* but who am I to talk. I kept quiet. Maybe she has even told *oga* that he impregnated her. *Chei*, women – they are more cunning than tortoise!"

Uzo laughed. "But how did you know she was pregnant the first day you saw her?"

Adim sneered and tilted his head back. "You want me to give you a lesson? Wait until you get your own woman then you will know. I have a wife and children, so I know when a woman is pregnant. That girl was in early pregnancy when we picked her up on the road."

Udo sat down on the mattress, worried. "But what will happen now? *Oga* is already married. What will happen to his wife who is my sister? And you say, I should not quarrel with this girl. I feel like beating the pregnancy out of her and I will do it."

"You want *oga* to court-martial you? Okay, try it and see what he will do to you." Uzo grinned, exposing a row of crowded teeth. "Who will blame *oga*? Boma is too beautiful. She fine too much. See her skin . . ."

Udo interrupted. He did not want to listen to him talk

about the girl's beauty. He couldn't even bring himself to call her name. He latched on to the first point Uzo raised. "*Oga* cannot court-martial me unless I commit an offence against military law. They taught us this in the camp. Anything I do to that girl cannot be against military law." Udo looked at Uzo and Adim with a superior mien and a triumphant smile, as if he wanted them to realize that he was a properly trained soldier which they were not. But his pleasure only lasted a moment, for the pain he had experienced when he learned that Boma was pregnant for his *oga* returned to torment him.

Adim and Uzo discussed many things after this, but he did not join them. He wanted Adim to go to his room so that he could reflect on what he heard and wallow in his misery, without any disturbance. He was determined to find a way to rescue his *oga* from this temptress.

Adim left for his room at eleven o'clock. Uzo lay down on his bed and soon after, Udo heard him snoring. He lay in the darkness, resenting Uzo's snores which grated on his nerves. He was angry with the girl who had taken his room and forced him to share Uzo's room and he hated her for stealing Sister Ginika's husband. If only he knew what to do to destroy the baby inside the girl – like something he could put in her food when she was not looking or in her drinking water. Would he have the courage to tell his *oga* that he was not the one who got her pregnant, as Adim said? The main problem was that his *oga* was a man who did not care what people thought or said about him. He believed he was always right, but he wasn't. He tried to do the right thing but what he thought to be right might not always be right. For instance, why should he keep that girl here instead of putting her in a refugee camp where displaced people like her were sent? It was right to help her that day, but it was not right to bring her to live here.

He felt his head swell and threaten to explode. Frightened, he shook it vigorously and turned to lie on his side. His frenetic mind invoked Sister Ginika's image on the day she saved him from being conscripted into the army by the officer from 11 Div. He remembered all she did to persuade the officer to release him. And she had arranged for him to be where he was now.

Tears stung his eyes and flowed horizontally until they dropped on the old mattress. He did not try to wipe them away. He could hear an owl hooting in the tree at the back of the house and crickets chirruping away without a care in the world. It was hours later before he fell asleep.

ON MONDAY morning, Udo dressed in his uniform ready to go out with his *oga*, Uzo and Adim, as was the routine most days, except when his *oga* went to the front and took only Adim and Uzo. He was about to get into the car when his *oga* spoke.

"Udo, don't get into the car. You stay in the house."

"Yes, sir," he said, saluting. He glanced at his face and saw that his *oga* was frowning. Did something upset him? Why was he looking despondent? It could only mean things were not going well on the war front. Could it be something else? His uniform looked as if he had slept in it – it was rumpled and didn't look fresh. He knew because he had washed and ironed it the other day. There were bags under his eyes, as if he had not slept at all. He wore his beret at a different angle – not completely different, but different all the same.

Udo watched him get into the car. "How's the car behaving?" he asked Adim.

"The car is all right, sir." Adim scratched his head dotted with grey hair.

"Let's get going then."

Udo looked round and was surprised the girl was not present – she usually walked his *oga* to the door any time he went out. Had they quarrelled? His heart jerked excitedly. He wished his *oga* would throw her out. Let her go to where refugees like her were. Why shouldn't she live in the refugee camp in Ngbo?

After the car drove off, Udo went into the house. As he walked past Boma's room, he heard her humming a song. He hissed and went to his *oga*'s room to tidy it up and see if he left some clothes for him to wash. When he finished sweeping and dusting the room, he went to the front of the house and sat down on the steps, looking forward and observing the few people that walked past. He noticed how cool the morning was; even the sun was slow in rising and coming alive. He liked the cool fresh air wafting to him from the mango tree in front of the house. His eyes scaled the tree in search of an off-season fruit, but there was none. When he looked down, he saw two soldiers in uniform running towards their house.

Udo jumped to his feet, watching them warily. Their movement made him suspicious and before he decided what to do next, he saw the batman of the officer who lived down the road being dragged away by a hefty man in uniform. He did not wait to find out what was happening and ran into the house, locking the door. He ran into his *oga*'s room and hid under the bed. From where he hid, he heard someone banging on the door persistently. He lay under the bed, trembling and sweating though the day was cool.

He heard Boma shuffle to the front door. Angry voices floated to him and his body shook.

"Where is the soldier that ran into this house just now?" he heard a voice demand.

"No soldier ran into the house," he heard her say. "This is Captain Odunze's house. He's not at home. I think he has gone to the front."

Udo heard a different voice shout, "Madam, don't obstruct us. We saw a man in uniform outside but before we got here, he ran into this house."

He heard nothing more, but he was sure they had not gone because Boma had not returned and he had not heard the door shut.

"Now go and tell that soldier to come out or we will enter and search the house. And if we catch him, it will be worse for him and you." The voice spoke so forcefully that he heard every word, as if the speaker was in the room where he was.

He was wondering what to do when he heard her speak again, "There is no one else in this house except Captain Odunze's relation who is a very young boy. Could it be he was the person you saw?"

"We don't care, just tell the person that ran into the house to come out and meet us."

Udo crawled out and beat the dust out of his clothes. He came out and saw her coming to call him.

"I'm sorry, but there are two soldiers outside and they want to see you."

Udo said nothing to her and continued to walk steadily towards the door which was open. Instinctively, he knew they were going to take him away. They would drag him away as he saw that hefty soldier do to their neighbour's batman. He felt sad. If he had gone out with his *oga* this morning, they would not have caught him. And if he had stayed inside the house, they couldn't have seen him. He shrugged his shoulders.

As soon as he stepped out, they grabbed him.

"You are going to the front right now," said one of the soldiers – the taller one. "You stay in the rear idling away your time while boys are suffering in the trenches. You are going to smell battle today. Come on, move. Idle!" He prodded Udo and pushed him along.

"But you can't take me away. I am Captain Odunze's batman. He is an officer in Tiger Battalion." He looked from one to the other and his heart failed him when he saw them sneering. They were not impressed and continued to pull him along. "He takes me to the front," he lied. "It's just that I was not feeling well today and he left me behind."

Frantically he looked round, but help came from nowhere. He saw Boma standing at the window, watching. Her eyes were full of fear. He almost cried from the irony of the whole situation – he was being taken away but the person who should leave the house was standing at the window, wide-eyed, staring at him, as if she thought this was the last time she would see him and so must look at him thoroughly to be able to remember what he looked like.

When he saw they were not prepared to let him go, he stopped struggling. They in turn stopped pushing and cursing him. When they got to the main road, he saw a lorry which looked like it would go to pieces any moment and knew it was to take him and other captives away. And when he looked at the other side of the road, he saw a group of young men like him, who had been similarly captured, waiting. He felt like bolting way, but he knew they would shoot him if he tried to run – some of the soldiers carried guns. He counted thirty captives, some in uniform like him. He saw their neighbour's batman and moved near him – he was the only face he could recognise.

"Jump into the vehicle, all of you," commanded a corporal with a wide mouth and a flat nose.

Udo thought he looked like a gorilla. He obeyed and found himself sitting close to his new friend. He had forgotten the man's name though he had met and spoken with him once or twice. To save himself the embarrassment of asking for his name, he said, "I'm Udo. Remind me of your name."

"I'm Ubochi."

"No nonsense from any of you," the corporal bleated, as he took the front seat next to the driver, after his men had settled down with the captives in the back. "If you try any tricks, we shoot you. We don't want to do this because our bullets are for vandals and not our people. But if you try to run away, we see you as an enemy and shoot you dead. We don't shoot to wound or maim; we shoot to kill. So, be warned."

Udo watched as the lorry jolted away down the road, taking him further and further away from where he called home in the last few months. The lorry smelt badly, as if it was used to transport pigs or decaying vegetables. Even the air that rushed into it as it rattled along did not suppress the fouled odour. At first he held his breath, but when he thought his lungs would burst, he took a breath and then covered his nose with the back of his hand in such a way that their captors would not think he was covering it.

There was silence, the type found only in a graveyard. Udo wondered if he was dreaming. Or was he dead and in another world marked by solitude and penance? He worried about the front. Was he in the right frame of mind to fight? He had never fought before, but there was always a first time. However, he knew he was not prepared for battle. Would he survive it? Worst, his *oga* would not know where he was taken to, so he could not look for him. Was this how he would end his life? He thought about his mother. She lost her husband – his father – in Jos and now she would lose her only son. She would lose the two men in her life and not know where their bones lay. He felt tears gather in his eyes and bent his head to hide his weakness.

The smell nearly choked him. He pressed his face to a crack on the side of the lorry where he sat and tried to draw fresh air into his lungs from this source. His effort was hardly rewarded, for the odour persisted, making his stomach churn. He felt vomit rising to his throat and choked it back. They were sitting so close together that if he threw up, the vomit would spray at least four people.

He thought this would have been an occasion to sing the war songs taught during training, but no one seemed to remember the songs or perhaps they were not in the mood to sing.

The lorry passed a few villages and he noticed how some women who walked along the road stopped and stared at the lorry as it passed them. He understood they knew the lorry was heading for the war front.

NO ONE told Udo that they were close to the war front. They had been driving for about an hour, it could be longer – he did not have a watch to check time. But he noticed the lorry was moving slowly and without light. There was darkness everywhere. Udo felt something like smouldering fire ravish his stomach and he pressed his belly with both hands. Then involuntarily, he stretched one hand and felt about until he found Ubochi's hand and held it. Ubochi also responded by pressing Udo's hand. They sat motionless until they were asked to get off. Communication was now in whispers. The corporal's garrulous voice had turned into a whisper.

When eventually they had been deployed to their positions and told what to do, Udo clutched the gun he was given and lay on the clammy soil of a shallow trench, alongside three other soldiers. Was it a Mark IV or a Madison they gave him? He was not sure. He did not know how long he lay there – whether a day or two days. The sound of small arms and shells which had been muffled before now became more distinct, louder. As each shell landed and exploded, Udo shut his eyes and prayed, remembering he had not prayed regularly since the war started. "God, I didn't forget you, please don't forget me," he prayed. "Save me." He tried to prevent his mind from focusing on the present terror by thinking of his mother, his sisters and Sister Ginika. Would he see them again?

Then bedlam erupted, as shells began to rain down into the trenches, as if the machines and guns were guided by an unseen power. Each shell that exploded took lives with it. Cries of men rose and commingled with the sound of explosion. As Udo lay trembling and calling on his mother, a solid but wet object fell on his back and rolled down beside him. With the gentlest of movements, he stretched his hand and touched it. He gave a stifled cry – it was a human head severed at the neck which still nestled in the steel helmet that it had worn when it belonged to a body that was intact. His hand and body were covered with blood. Udo discovered himself shivering and no matter how he tried, he could not stop his body from shivering. Then he lost consciousness.

He came round at dawn, opened his eyes and heard

nothing. Everywhere was quiet. Where were the men in the trench with him? They had abandoned him when they retreated, thinking he was dead. He lay still for a while, afraid to get up in case there were vandals lurking in the surrounding bushes. Cautiously, he raised his head and saw the mess around him – the head in the steel helmet, pieces of human flesh and shrapnel littering the trench and the surrounding. He felt his body and saw that though he was covered in blood, he was not hurt. He picked up his gun and was sure it was a Madison. Gradually, he sat up, came out of the trench and looked around. It was a terrible sight to see dead bodies lying about and holes dug by exploding shells, but there was no movement anywhere. Gingerly he stepped forward and began to walk away, cautiously, at first and then swiftly. He didn't know where he was going, but he kept moving in the forest, keeping away from roads and hugging the anonymity and the eternal silence of the jungle. Even animals seemed to have fled, for he saw none in his way, except a few bush rats and squirrels.

He was lost in the forest for three days, walking and sleeping, stumbling and falling, picking himself up and continuing to walk. At a point, he sat down and removed his shoes to allow his oppressed feet and toes to breathe. It was a miracle he was wearing his boot the time the soldiers caught him. How could he have entered this thick forest without such good shoes? He did not remember he had not eaten in days.

Udo crossed a stream and later passed a narrow foot bridge. His uniform was wet but he was able to remove some of the dirt that had stuck to it. He heard movements and voices from afar and became cautious again – he felt sure he had reached a place where people lived. He found himself in a clearing and ahead of him was a hut in front of which a woman and her three young children sat, talking. When they saw him, they ran into the hut and shut the door.

"Mother, please, don't be afraid," he called out. "I'm a Biafran soldier and have lost my way. Please help me." He stood in front of the house where the woman could see him clearly if she looked.

She peeped at him through a tiny window, saw the emblem of the rising sun on his shoulder and opened the door. She stared at him. "*Ndewo*, we thought you were one of them: enemy soldiers." She smiled. Her children came out and looked at him curiously.

"I lost my way after a battle," he told her. "Can you tell me where I am and how I can get to Ama-Oyi?" He slung his gun behind him and smiled at the children."

She shook her head: she did not know where Ama-Oyi was but said he could follow the main road which led to Umuahia if he turned left and to Okigwe if he turned right. He thanked her and walked away – he had an idea where he was. Mbano lay between the two towns – Umuahia and Okigwe. She called him back.

"We have no food in the house, but you can have some *utu* we gathered yesterday from the forest."

Touched by her kindness, he smiled and took the fruits from her outstretched hands. There were five of them and they were ripe and fresh. "Thank you," he said.

On the way, he ate the *utu* and they tasted better than any he had eaten before, probably because he was quite hungry. He had only just realised how hungry he was when he saw the succulent *utu*. He followed the main road, anxious about meeting soldiers especially military police looking for soldiers who were *away without official leave* – AWOL, as it was referred to in the camp, during their training. He saw a checkpoint ahead and stilled himself to play the part he had rehearsed while wandering in the jungle – a shell-shocked soldier.

Before he reached them, he began to march, as if he were on parade. Two women and a soldier manned the checkpoint. "Ha, ha, work dey go fine!" he cried. "I dey front dey fire artillery gun dey finish vandal." He did a little dance and threw his head backwards, laughing. Then he pulled at his gun and, clutching it, aimed at the sky. "Die, vandals! Die, now!"

The two young women at the checkpoint ran into the bush. One of them cried, "He's shellshocked. He is *arti-ngbo*! He is *arti-ngbo*!"

Udo continued his funny dance until he came face to face with the soldier. "Old boy, how *kwanu*? How you dey? You get smoke for this artillery boy? Find me Mars!" He stared at the soldier with wild eyes.

"Sorry, old boy, I don't have cigarette," the soldier apologised. "Where can you see cigarette in Biafra except with people coming in from overseas? I don't have Mars to give you, sorry."

Udo nodded and swayed to the left and to the right, singing a war song, and shouting on top of his voice.

Biafra, win the war

Armoured car, shelling machine

Heavy artillery, *Kamdum*

They can never defeat Biafra

"Old boy, help me find lift to Ama-Oyi or Dikenafai or Ekwulobia," he drawled, fixing his gaze at the soldier. "Anywhere at all."

"I will try," replied the soldier.

The two girls returned to their duty post, eyeing Udo with dread. He ignored them and they relaxed and started to chat as they did before he arrived.

Soon a military vehicle trundled to a halt. It carried a few soldiers and some supplies. The soldier at the checkpoint explained to the second lieutenant sitting beside the driver. "Let him jump in," the officer said. "But tell him we don't want any trouble from him. We are going to Nnewi and can drop him at Ama-Oyi which is on our way."

Udo jubilated in his heart. He couldn't believe his luck. He would get to Ama-Oyi before long. He walked round to the front and saluted the officer, "Officer, I salute you, sir. My name is Artillery Joe – *na* de name given me in de front, as I kill vandals like chicken." He saw pity in the eyes of the officer.

"Get into the vehicle. We will drop you in Ama-Oyi," the man said.

As he moved to the back, he heard the officer say to the driver, "The boy is not up to sixteen years and he is a soldier. This war is evil; it has turned children into adults overnight. He is luckier than many others suffering from shellshock – at least he has a home to return to and perhaps a mother to care for him."

Udo jumped into the vehicle and sat in the innermost corner, fearing he might be recognised in one of the places the vehicle might stop. He saw bags of rice and beans and sat on one of them. The three soldiers in the truck left him alone and he ignored them. He was pleased to be left alone and sang a song to himself from time to time, to keep up the act. When they reached Ama-Oyi, the officer came out and asked him to get off. The truck had stopped at the old Orie market.

"This is Ama-Oyi," the officer said. "Can you find your way?"

"My fatherland, I come home with heavy artillery," Udo said in a singsong. "Artillery Joe don come home to Ama-Oyi!"

He stamped his right foot hard on the ground and saluted the officer and then adjusted his Madison ready to take off.

"Artillery Joe, I have to take this gun from you," the officer said gently. "You will not need it in Ama-Oyi. Let me take it with me and give it to a soldier who will kill the remaining vandals you did not kill." He stretched his hand to receive the gun.

Udo hesitated, displeased that he was being asked to part with his gun, but he knew the officer would take it from him with force if he refused to give it up willingly. Trouble was the last thing he wanted, so he gave it to him and said, "My gun go kill plenty vandals. Give am to another artillery boy to finish de vandals."

"Thank you, Artillery Joe." The officer returned to his seat and the vehicle jolted down the road to Nnewi.

Udo looked round to see if he was being observed. The market was deserted and he knew it was the fear of air raid that drove people away from there. He looked up. The sky was so clear and cloudless – a good day for air raids, he thought and hurried away. He walked swiftly and whenever he saw someone approaching he put up his little show. He would snigger as he watched the passerby pause, shake his head in pity before walking away. "Poor child," the passerby would murmur.

Udo knew his ploy was working. He was deeply satisfied.

He had decided even before he reached Ama-Oyi that he would go straight to see Sister Ginika. He was heading for the place he knew as her home when he sighted her coming towards him. He wanted to run forward and hug her but that would be foolish, he thought. She carried an empty bag and he wondered where she was going because she was not walking in the direction of her home – rather she was walking away from it. She passed him without looking at him, but he had taken a good look at her. He was shocked to see that she was thinner and her skin did not glow as before. He continued down the road a while and then turned round and retraced his steps, keeping her in his view. She turned round once and seeing him coming towards her, she quickened her steps.

He realised she was going to her aunt's place and followed her at a good distance. The way she walked told him she knew he was following her. Before she reached her aunt's house, she broke into a run and when she got to the gate, she began to bang on it frantically.

"Obika, where are you? Please, open the gate!" She turned and saw him coming nearer towards her and became almost hysterical, "Auntie, Auntie, please open the door quickly," she screamed. She continued to bang on the gate.

Udo was shocked by her reaction. What was happening, he wondered? Something was wrong with her. He remembered his *oga* and that girl and anger overwhelmed him. His *oga* harboured another woman in his house while his wife was pining away in Ama-Oyi. Did it make sense? He regretted he had not spoken his mind to him before he was bundled to the war front. His mind jolted back to the present when he heard her yell, "What do you want? Why are you following me?"

He saw her aunt and Obika standing at the open gate behind her and staring at him with animosity.

"Sister Ginika, it's me, Udo," he said, walking swiftly

towards them. "Have I changed so much that you cannot recognise me?" He laughed.

"Udo? Did you say you're Udo?" she asked, peering at him, as if she were short-sighted.

"Yes, I'm Udo," he said, watching her closely, wondering why it took her long to recognise him. Was it because he was wearing a military uniform and she had not seen him in uniform before? What if she had seen him when he played a shell-shocked soldier, she would have been completely fooled, he thought?

Laughing, she dropped the bag on the ground and simply walked into the arms he had thrown wide open to receive her.

33

"You said Eloka is well?" Ginika asked for the tenth time or more. It was the morning after Udo's return. She had hardly asked him any questions, sensing he needed to rest. This morning he looked quite refreshed and she knew he was already feeling much better. They were behind her aunt's house, in the space between the back wall of the house and the wall that fenced the compound. Udo sat on a chair while she stood near a big fire, with a stout stick in her right hand. She turned away and began to stir with the stick the content of a large iron pot that was bubbling over the fire.

"Yes, he was quite well when I saw him last," Udo replied. "Did I tell you he is a captain now?"

"You didn't, but I know . . ." She stopped remembering she had decided not to tell him what had happened to her while he was away. She didn't want him to know she had gone to Etiti with her aunt to look for Eloka.

Udo quickly looked at her. "You know? Who told you?"

She smiled. "*Nnunu mgba-ama*, the little bird that tells me things whispered it into my ears."

Udo laughed. "Did the little bird tell you other things?"

"You'd be surprised what it told me about you in the

army!" She could see the look of surprise die in his eyes only to be replaced by a mischievous glint which gladdened her heart, reminding her of old times.

"How long are you going to boil my uniform in that steaming pot?" Udo asked, coming over to join her. He stared at his uniform and under garment which were completely submerged in the boiling water.

Ginika stirred the clothes and turned them round and round. "Until all the *kwarikwata*, the body lice are killed. They don't die easily, you know. Janet told me so and she said they are found in both Biafran and Nigerian trenches. That's how I got to know about them, so when you complained about your body itching all over, I knew you got them when you were lying in the trench."

"I would never have known," he admitted, shuddering. "They look so flat and ugly. I almost hated my body when we discovered the *kwarikwata* yesterday. Thank you, Sister Ginika."

"Don't mention it," she said in the characteristic voice she used to tease him with and they laughed again. "They are probably all dead now, but I will allow the pot to boil a little longer just to be sure."

"Shall we go to the WCC camp after this?" he asked in a solemn voice. "I'll pretend I'm shell-shocked and I'm sure we can get some food from the people there. I didn't know the situation is so bad."

The smile on her face slipped away. "Yes, it is very bad and has been for some time. We hardly have anything to eat these days. I went to the WCC centre a number of times but stopped when I couldn't get anything. The man in charge wanted to have sex with me before giving me anything and I refused." Her eyes clouded over. She sighed deeply.

"So this is what they do?"

"Yes, that is the way it is now – you get what you want with what you have. I heard that even some Roman Catholic priests slept with girls before they gave them relief materials. I don't know if this is true, but I don't want to find out."

"I'm sorry about Nonso, your aunt's youngest child who has developed signs of kwashiorkor. It's shocking."

She stirred the pot and sighed. "My grandmother also has the signs, did you notice? This terrible disease afflicts mostly young children and old people. I've never seen anything so terrible." She shuddered. "Nne has not eaten for one week because she wants her food to be given to the children, but the problem is there is no food in the house. My aunt is out of her mind with worry. I have gone to relief centres but there is no hope. Many of the centres have nothing to give anyway, not even to refugees to whom they usually give priority. So I am planning to go to *ahia attack – attack* market – next week."

He stared at her. "No, you can't go, please. It's too dangerous."

"What can I do – watch my aunt's children and my grandmother die? Udo, I have to go. Perhaps I'll be able to bring food back. The situation is desperate as you can see."

"Yes, but what about your life? Do you want to throw it away? You could be killed. You could be caught in crossfire?"

"I know. I have been told of the dangers, but I still want to go because there is no other option." She stirred the pot slowly.

"Let's try the WCC centre today. Remember, I'm shell-shocked."

They laughed. She recalled the story he told her earlier about his escape from the front and how he pretended to be shell-shocked on his way home. She didn't know he was such a good actor though she knew the will to survive would make people do things they never dreamed they could ever do. "Okay, but be careful. There are military police everywhere looking for deserters. This is why I am reluctant to allow you to go out. Stay with us here though we don't have much food in the house."

"Did you see my mother recently?" he asked anxiously.

She avoided his eyes. "Yes, I saw her last week. It's hard for everyone, so she too is suffering. But she is managing – I think she gets a little help from her brother." She saw his eyes dim and was sorry to cause him pain but she had to tell him the truth.

"I will go and see her this evening."

"I suggest you restrict your movements. I will find a way to tell her to come here and see you. I don't want the military police to come here looking for you."

"Will they take me away if they see I'm shell-shocked?"

"You cannot predict what they can do at any time," she breathed. "I heard that once the war front is not going well, they come looking for deserters and anyone they see – even shell-shocked soldiers – they grab and take them to the front. Since Umuahia fell, I was told, we have been losing grounds steadily and the morale of soldiers is very low. I pick up these rumours and gossips as I pass people talking in groups or from the market when my aunt sends me there. They say Biafra is in a bad way. We have no battery to operate the radio, so we are cut off from news."

GINIKA DECIDED to go with Udo to the WCC centre. She told him that if there was any sign of trouble, he should leave immediately. She followed him at a considerable distance until they got there. From afar, they heard the buzzing sound made by the throng that besieged the centre. Ginika shuddered when she saw the attendants flogging the desperate neatly-dressed as well as the shabbily-clad *beggars* who jostled one another on the winding queue. She was sure there were more than two hundred people there. Udo had arrived long before her and she heard his voice abusing and threatening people before he began to sing in a croaky voice.

"Hippy Yaa-yaa, hippy hippy yaa-yaa, I remember when I was a soldier…" he sang loudly, marching up and down in front of the centre. He was dressed in his uniform which looked rumpled after it was dried in the sun. He had deliberately buttoned the shirt badly and rolled up the sleeves and the trouser legs. Suddenly he stopped singing and yelled, "WCC, Artillery Joe is here. Please, give him some food. He will kill all vandals with heavy artillery!" When the workers paid him no attention, he began to wave the club he had in his hand – the stick Ginika had used to stir his uniform in the boiling pot – swearing at them and cursing them. "I am going to fire all of you with my gun." He swung the club and then aimed it like he would a gun.

The people fighting in the queue paused and watched him. They burst into laughter. A woman said pityingly, "See how young the boy is and they sent him to fight in the war front. Now he is mad. He is only a child. Oh, mothers, we have seen something in this war. He is mad at his tender age." She sighed.

Another cried, "WCC, please, give him something and let him go."

One of the workers gave him two tins of corned beef, some dry milk and a small packet of rice. He was fat and had a round face. His white overall was stained yellow by corn flour. Ginika who stood at the side recognised him as the worker who had asked for sex before giving her relief materials. "Now go away from here," he said harshly. "Don't come back again." He waved Udo away.

After collecting the things, Udo shouted, "Is this all you can give Artillery Joe? Give me stockfish and some beans." He waved the stick before the worker.

Angry, the man cried, "If you don't go away now, I will call the two military police in my boss's office. They will carry you to the war front today. *Arti-mgbo!*" He glared at Udo.

Laughing raucously, Udo turned away from the man and began to sing and dance, "Military police, come and take Artillery Joe to the front to kill all the vandals." Walking backwards, he withdrew from the centre. Not long after he returned to the house, Ginika arrived. When they saw each other, they burst into laughter.

"You are an accomplished actor," she cried.

He gave her the relief materials and said, "It's not much but at least we came away with something. The children can eat well today."

Her aunt heard them laughing and came out from her room. Ginika gave her the things. "Look what Udo got from WCC centre and they are for the family." She was pleased to see the light that flooded her aunt's face.

"Ha, my children will eat today," she rejoiced. "But, won't you give some to your mother?"

Udo shrugged. "It is not much. Take them."

"No, take something for her," she insisted.

Ginika saw her aunt looking at her and said, "Let me have one tin of corned beef. I'll give it to Udo's mother when I go this evening to tell her he's here."

"That's a good idea," her aunt replied, giving her a tin of corned beef.

❧❀❧

A FEW days later, Ginika met a group of men and women at an appointed venue – the old Orie market. Among the twenty people assembled under the *ugiri* tree, she knew only two people – Eunice and Nkeonyelu, the refugee woman in the camp where she used to work. Janet had told her Nkeonyelu traded behind enemy lines and she had gone to her to find out more about the business. She had mentioned it to Eunice and she decided to take part.

Here she was on her first mission – an adventure she knew was fraught with danger, but was determined to get involved in if her aunt's children and her grandmother were to survive, to escape from the clutches of kwashiorkor. She could no longer bear to see the despair in her aunt's eyes. For too long she had lived with the agony of seeing the children cry for food, her grandmother lie in the sitting room, gazing helplessly and hopelessly at the wall and her aunt weep silently in her room at night. Her grandmother would sigh and groan when she thought no one was observing her. In the morning her aunt's eyes would be swollen and red.

Ginika had not told her grandmother she was embarking on the dangerous adventure. If she knew, she would not allow her to go. Her aunt and Udo had watched her leave with fear in their eyes. "Take care of yourself," her aunt had whispered, pressing her to her bosom. Udo had simply embraced her and squeezed her hand. She had smiled and warned Udo not to step out of the house until she came back. She hoped he would take her advice seriously.

Ginika saw there were only five men – the rest were women. She was not surprised, for most men were either in the army or the essential services, and a few hid in their homes to avoid conscription. She studied the group. The men were young probably in their twenties. One behaved so confidently that she was sure he was the leader of the group. He heard him addressed as Achara and wondered if this was his real name or a nickname. Some of the women were middle-aged; a few could be in their mid-twenties, while she and Eunice were the youngest.

"Now that we are all here, we can begin our journey," Achara said, putting on a black cap. He was athletic and lively and moved effortlessly like a cat.

This one was a survivor, Ginika thought. She was sure he was not the reckless type and was pleased Achara was the leader of the group. "I like our leader," she whispered to Eunice. "He appears confident and sure of what he's doing."

"Yes, I agree with you," Eunice said quietly, looking at Achara.

"Let us now go to where our lorry is parked." He led the way.

They walked behind him. Ginika made sure she was close to Eunice and Nkonyelu. She carried a large brown bag she had borrowed from her aunt. It had been filled with her children's toys and school books and her aunt had had to put the things in a carton. She saw that everyone had similar bags in anticipation of the things they would buy from traders on the other side. Each of them had as many coins as they could find or purchase. Only Nigerian coins were legal tender on the other side and she had had to buy them from people who still owned them. Her aunt had helped her to make contacts with such people. The money Eloka gave her was useful – though she had spent a substantial part of it, she still had enough to buy the coins she needed for the trip. She also took some of her most beautiful dresses which she would sell to realise more money to buy things when she got to the other side. Yes, she came prepared, as she was sure each of them was. Eunice had told her the effort she and her mother made to find the coins she had with her.

They followed a narrow path until they came to a clearing where she saw the lorry standing under an iroko tree. It looked rundown and she hoped it would make the journey both ways.

"Here we are," Achara said with a smile. "I do not need to tell you that this journey is a dangerous one. We will be together as much as possible and when necessary, but remember that you are responsible for your own safety. You are to look out for yourself, but this should not stop you giving a helping hand to another person when you are in a position to do so."

Listening to Achara, Ginika felt her heart skip and lurch about in her breast. He was warning them of the dangers they would face. Was she getting into something that would swallow her? Was it wise and reasonable to undertake this journey? Was she unwittingly swimming into the jaws of the shark of death?

"If you follow instructions closely and use your senses, you should be all right," she heard him add. "One more thing before we enter the vehicle. How many are going for the first time?"

Ginika, Eunice, two other women and two men raised their hands. Achara looked round and noted each of them. "All right, six of you are new in the trade. It is to you I speak particularly. Be careful and act wisely both on the way and when you get to the market. For your information, the towns that *attack* traders visit include Mbiama, Ahoada, Nkwere-Inyi, Ugwuoba, Oji River and Otu Ocha. Is there any of you who does not know that we are going to Oji River?" He waited and then nodded with satisfaction. "Good, we are all sure of our movement. It is important to know where you are going. I will say no more until we get nearer to our destination." He asked them to pay their fare and went round immediately collecting it from everyone. He beamed at them. "Thank you very much. You can enter the vehicle."

Ginika clambered into the lorry which smelt of rotting vegetables and fermented cassava. She was sure the lorry was used to carry these goods before the organisers of the trip hired it. She sat between Eunice and Nkeonyelu. She was grateful to have them in the group – she needed the comfort of known faces in this adventure into the unknown.

By the time they set out, darkness had descended and enveloped everywhere. The driver was careful and used only dim light. Ginika could hear the lorry squeaking and groaning. She knew when they got to hilly ground, for the lorry would slow down to a snail's pace, groan and shudder. When it descended a hill, it would rattle and jolt down at a more aggressive speed. Ginika soon felt Nkeonyelu's head lolling forward and knew she had fallen asleep. Before long, she felt the pressure of Eunice's body against her left shoulder and knew she too had slept off. She couldn't sleep no matter how much she willed to embrace sleep and be lulled into its oblivion. She knew her mind and body were too tense to relax – so many things troubled her mind. First, Udo and her fear that the military police might arrest him for desertion and second, her intuitive feeling that gave her the impression that Udo was hiding something from her about Eloka. What was it she saw in his eyes when she had asked him about Eloka and if women were after him as she saw them go after army and air force officers in Ekwulobia, Etiti and Nkwerre? She was told stories of how women pursued officers to the trenches. She shuddered and prayed God to protect her Eloka. But, would he still be hers if he found out what had happened to her? Would he forgive her and would his parents allow him to if he wanted? His mother had called her a win-the-war wife and told her she would make sure Eloka married a virtuous woman when the war ended.

She had many worries – too many. She was worried about her brother, Nwakire, who hadn't visited again. Was he alive or dead? She was worried about her father who denounced her when she told him and her stepmother about the pregnancy and how she came about it. He had shouted at her and said he didn't want to see her and asked her not to return to the house. When her stepmother rebuked her for getting pregnant, her father had shouted her down and spat, "If you had been a mother to her as you should have been, she would not have turned out the way she did." She had stumbled out of the house and left them to their recrimination. Yes, her worries were many, she thought. She was anxious about Uncle Ray – what would happen to her aunt and the children if he didn't ever come back? Finally, she was worried about herself and what her fate would be if the war ended and Eloka rejected her and there was no one to send her back to school. As for the war, she wanted it to end and didn't care anymore who won or lost. She had gone through so much that she no longer cared either way. What she wanted most was for the war to end.

She noticed that the vehicle stopped a number of times and heard voices. She knew the stops were made at checkpoints where Achara was asked questions by soldiers or militiamen on guard duty. Wide-eyed, she sat in the lorry, swaying this way and that way, depending on which side the vehicle inclined. Her buttocks were numb from the pressure of the hard wooden bench on which she sat. She thought about what she would buy. She had discussed this with her aunt. Someone told them that the popular commodities were salt, rice, beans, sugar, tea and tinned tomatoes and fish. She had agreed with her aunt that she should buy salt, beans, rice and tinned fish. Salt fetched lots and lots of money in Biafra and they planned to sell some of the salt she would bring back.

"We have arrived at the spot where we will have to leave the lorry and walk," Achara shouted from the front of the vehicle where he sat with the driver.

Ginika shifted and felt pain in her buttocks. She put her hand under and rubbed vigorously to allow blood flow freely. She clutched her bag, as the lorry jolted to a stop. She adjusted and pulled down her dress. She wore a cat-suit – she had received it from Mr Asiobi when it came in a bale of clothing sent to the refugee camp – and on top of it wore a gown with long sleeves. She had rolled up the cat-suit from her legs to her knees so that no one would notice she wore a one-piece trouser-suit. She did this to protect herself from being violated. She also had a penknife with which she would cut off any dangling *thing* that came at her. She was determined to defend herself from any such attack during the journey. Ginika jumped down from the lorry and stayed close to Nkeonyelu and Eunice.

Achara was waiting for them. "We have reached the end of the safe zone and are about to enter the area controlled by the vandals. Remember what I told you. The driver will take the lorry and wait for us in this village. We will return here in three days, and then return to Ama-Oyi. One day to trek to the market; the second day to buy and assemble the things we buy and then the third to return here to meet the driver. We shall be guided by the natives of this place. They know where the vandals are and will guide us through a safe route. Is it clear?" He spoke in a low tone.

Ginika saw that they had been joined by two men whom Achara introduced as natives of Ugwuoba who would act as guides. She took in a deep breath and exhaled air with some force. Her heart pounded like a drum and she pressed her bag against her chest, as if this had the power to stop the pounding.

They walked in darkness inside a thick forest. They were following a path and Ginika was aware of the silhouette of trees by her left and right. She tried to estimate the distance covered as they moved. She could not identify anyone anymore, not even her friend, Eunice. They walked in silence until after about an hour, they halted.

Achara asked them to touch and feel a big tree that had fallen in the forest. "This is a silk cotton tree," he stated. "Touch it and feel how big it is. This is a signpost for all of us in case anything happens to cause a separation. Make sure you get to this fallen tree and wait for the others. We will make sure no one is lost."

Ginika felt a prolonged tug at her stomach, as if a hand gripped her insides. She shuddered.

THEY REASSEMBLED at an agreed location in the market. Ginika placed her bag on the ground in front of her and stood close to Eunice and Nkeonyelu. She was pleased with all she had bought – salt, rice, beans and tinned fish. She had even bought a packet of sugar and tea which she was sure her aunt's children would love. They would drink tea with the dry milk Janet had given her the previous week. It was the evening of the second day and they were ready to set out for the return journey.

"Carry your loads," Achara instructed.

Ginika tried to lift her bag but it was so heavy she needed help. One of the guides came to her rescue. Soon everyone carried his or her load. By the time they entered the forest, darkness had descended. They walked in a single file in total silence. Ginika felt the weight of her bag, as it pressed down on her, but she didn't mind. She trotted behind the person in front of her in absolute concentration, as she didn't want to stumble and fall.

They had walked for about an hour when shooting erupted from the right. *Kakakakaka! Kakakakaka!* Ginika was too shocked to think and stood trembling, not sure of what to do.

"It is an ambush," she heard someone cry, but was not sure whether it was Achara or one of the two guides. "Run for your life."

"Let us meet where the fallen tree is." She recognised Achara's voice and it seemed to yank her out of her confusion and inertia.

There was a stampede followed by cries of pain. Ginika

knew some of the traders had been hit by bullets. She started running to the left, following the sound of feet making rustling noises as they crushed the dry leaves littering the forest. The bag was impeding her movement and she threw it down and belted away like a comet. She stretched her hands in front of her, so that she would touch any obstacle in her way before she crashed into it. Steadily she followed the sound of pounding feet. She fell when her feet touched very soft ground and suspected she was in a marshy area. She got up immediately and pursued the fleeing feet. She heard the sound turning right and swerved to the right. After an hour or more – she was not sure – the feet stopped abruptly. Ginika stopped, trembling.

"Who is following me?" she heard a strange voice ask.

With her body shaking like a leaf, she whimpered, "It's me, one of the *attack* traders."

"Come, don't be afraid," the male voice intoned. "I am one of your guides. We have reached the fallen tree."

Ginika breathed in and out, until her body relaxed. She came near and vaguely saw the man's shape.

"Sit on the tree while we wait for the others," he said gently.

Ginika relaxed further and sat on the huge trunk of the tree. She was sad she lost her load but pleased she was not killed in the ambush. They waited for an hour and were joined by Achara and three people. Ginika was optimistic that Eunice and Nkeonyelu would appear any moment. Nkeonyelu and another woman came and sat on the tree trunk, breathing hard. The second guide appeared and joined them on the trunk.

"It will be daybreak soon," Achara said. "We cannot wait

here anymore, but must return to the village. We'll come back in the night to see if some of them arrived."

As they trekked back to the village where the lorry was, the traders wore miserable faces. Only Achara and one other man had their loads. They spent the day lolling about in the lorry. Only the thought that they were alive kept them from being despondent. Ginika worried about Eunice, but comforted herself with the thought that she would be found later.

In the night, Achara and the two guides set out for the place of the fallen tree as they now called the rendezvous. There were eight of them in the lorry and before long they all fell asleep except Ginika. If she closed her eyes, she saw Eunice standing before her. Night insects and birds kept chirruping all night, worsening her insomnia until she gave up the thought of ever falling asleep that night. She could hear Nkeonyelu snoring beside her.

At the crack of dawn, Achara and the guides returned with another trader, a man. Ginika saw that only eight of them made it apart from the two guides. Twelve of them were missing – one man and eleven women.

"We have to go back to Ama-Oyi," Achara said with a sad voice. "We waited for long and even walked about in case any of them was hiding in the forest but we saw no one." He shook his head, "We found him waiting by the side of the tree," he pointed to the man who had come with them.

Ginika couldn't believe her eyes and her ears. What did it mean – that Eunice and the others were shot in the ambush and were lying dead in the forest? As the lorry jolted out of the village, she wept beside Nkeonyelu who was too depressed to say a word to her. She wept for Eunice – another flower has withered in the land, another promising shoot, like Njide.

Part Four

THE END

34

Ginika and her aunt went to see her grandmother where she lay with her face turned to the wall. She had a bowl of watery *akamu* in her hand. She sighed, as she looked at the feeble body lying on a mat in the room. The legs were glossy, as if lubricated with palm oil and her feet were slightly swollen. Her headdress had fallen to the floor leaving her thinning white hair exposed. Battling to keep her voice steady, Ginika said, "Nne, here is *akamu* for you. Get up and drink it."

The old woman stirred but did not turn round. Ginika noticed she faced the wall all the time now. She drew her knees up and coughed.

"I will not drink it," she said between bouts of coughing. "Give it to the children. They need it more than I do. I have told you not to worry about me. *Onye ara na uche ya so*, a mad person has more sense than is attributed to him. I know what I'm doing. Leave me and let me die in peace." She coughed weakly.

Ginika understood that talking weakened her more than anything. "Nne, do not talk; just sit up and eat something. I will not leave this room unless you take the *akamu*. So if you want me to leave you alone, you will have to drink it." She spoke strongly, hoping this would make her grandmother do as she was told.

"Ah, my child, you will stand there until your feet become sore, for I will not take that thing you brought."

Her aunt pushed forward. "Nne, why do you make us unhappy like this? What do you want me to do? To watch you die? Do I not have enough troubles already? If you die, what will I do? You know my husband is not here and may be dead and you say you want to die. All right, I too will die and we will know who will bury the other."

"*Ewo*, my daughter, you will not die." She sat up with difficulty. You are my only child since I lost my first daughter. Do you think I am happy to see you suffer as you have been doing for a long time? I would rather die than give you trouble. It is this disease they call *kwashiriokpa* that I am afraid of. It has attacked my legs. I want to die before it ravishes my body."

Ginika looked at her aunt and would have laughed if the situation was not so painful. "Nne, it is kwashiorkor and not *kwashiriokpa*."

Her aunt persisted. "Nne, the only way you can give me trouble is to refuse to eat what we give you. So if you want me to be happy, drink the *akamu*."

"Give it to me." She stretched her claw-like hands and as she took the bowl, they shook.

"Can I feed you, Nne?" Ginika asked.

"Am I a baby to be fed by you? Give me the spoon; I can feed myself."

They stood over her until she had taken all the *akamu*.

Ginika took the bowl from her. "Thank you, Nne," she cooed. "Well done, you took all of it."

"What could I do?" she asked with a sour voice. "You forced me to finish it."

They laughed and left her to sleep.

They went into the children's room where Nonso, the youngest lay in his bed. The others were playing outside. Her aunt bent down and lifted the child and carried him to the sitting room. Ginika followed her. Her aunt settled in a settee and she sat next to her.

"Ginika, see my child? See his colour? See his skin and his feet. What will I do? Shall I lose this child?" Her aunt burst into tears.

Ginika put her arm round her aunt and pressed her body to her. She couldn't find the right word to comfort her, so she too burst into tears. Their tears dropped on the child who slept fitfully.

"Ah, Nonso, my son, what will I do if I lose you? I don't know where to turn to for help. I'm lost. Ray, where are you? Your baby is dying."

"Please, Auntie, don't say these things. Nonso will not die."

"What are you saying? Can't you see his eyes and his legs? Look at him properly!" she yelled. "I say, look at him."

Ginika was frightened. Her aunt was suffering and she was not able to help her. She thought about the attack market and wondered if she should try again. But, where would she find money to buy the coins she would need? She had sold all her good clothes to buy food and her aunt has sold every valuable thing she had – her jewellery, her *abada* and all *Intorica wrappa*. They had nothing left to sell.

She took Nonso in her arms and cradled him. "You will not die. I will do anything to save your life." She heard the gate squeak and looked through the window to see who was coming in. Janet rushed into the compound and ran up the steps, past the veranda and into the sitting room. She was breathing hard. In her hand was a small package.

"Janet, what happened?" Ginika exclaimed. "Why are you so excited?"

Janet began to dance round the room, colliding with chairs and stools. They watched her.

"You haven't heard then? The war has ended." She laughed and shouted. "I came to find out if you heard."

Ginika gave a shout and the children ran into the house to find out what was wrong. Udo who was in the room where he stayed all day since he returned ran out to see why there was so much noise. She saw her grandmother staggering towards her, fear written all over her eyes.

"The war has ended," she yelled. "Janet came to tell us." Her eyes glowed.

"There was an announcement by one of the army chiefs. One of the women in the camp – an *attack* trader who has battery to power her radio – told us. When she heard it in the news, she ran out shouting the news for all to hear. She ran round the camp like a mad woman, proclaiming that the war was over. I followed her to her room and listened to the broadcast. The man who spoke said His Excellency and a few others had left Biafra to look for peace or something like that. I didn't understand what he meant. He told everyone to go about peacefully."

"I'm shocked. What a disaster!" Udo said, shaking his head. "So, this is the way the war ended? Just like that? After so many people suffered and died."

"Janet, it is the truth you are telling us?" Ginika heard her aunt ask. "This is not April fool, is it?"

"No. How can I joke with such a matter? It's the truth.

I'm going back to the camp to get my things ready. I'll leave as soon as I can." She was about to leave when she remembered the package she had brought. "Oh, this contains beans. I brought it for you." She gave it to Ginika.

"Janet, thank you. As if you knew we needed it so much."

"You're welcome."

"Thank you, Janet," her aunt greeted.

Her grandmother who sat near the door looked up and touched Janet as she passed her. "My child, thank you for the beans and for the news you brought us. Maybe I will not die after all."

Everyone began to laugh.

Ginika and her aunt went into the kitchen and cooked all the beans. When they finished, they carried the pot into the house and put it on the dining table. They shared it carefully in different plates. It was enough for everyone. Her grandmother ate hers with relish.

Later in the day, word reached Ginika that some people in Ama-Oyi had broken into the Caritas store and were carting away the relief materials stacked there.

"Udo, go quickly and see if it is true," she urged. "Bring anything you find. It's probably finished by now, but just go and check."

Before long, Udo ran into the house carrying half a bag of beans. He threw it down and ran out again for more. Ginika and her aunt started dancing in the sitting room.

"So my children will not starve to death?" her aunt cried. "God, I thank you. The war may have ended, but who knows when there will be food? Who has the money to buy it even if there is food?"

Udo returned after being away for a longer period than

the first time. "Everything has been taken," he said. "If you see the store, it looks like a place where mad people fought – broken glass, torn paper and empty cartons everywhere. I didn't know so many men are in Ama-Oyi until today and most of them are young men. They were there at the store fighting over everything and grabbing whatever was within their reach. Women were there too and more people were rushing there to get their share only to discover everything was gone. One woman broke down and wept. I saw refugees carrying loads on their heads – they were going back to their villages and towns. This is the only thing I could find." He showed them a tin of corned beef.

"How did you find it if everything was taken?" Ginika asked.

"A boy of ten had six tins and I asked him for one. When he refused, I told him I'm *arti-ngbo* and my name is Artillery Joe. I said if he did not give me one, I would beat him up and take all six from him. He gave me one and ran away."

Ginika began to laugh and her aunt joined her. "Well, you will not be able to play a shell-shocked soldier after today – not even to fool a child. The war is over but, it still seems like a dream to me."

"It is the same with me," agreed her aunt. "I feel as if I'm dreaming and will wake up to find that the war is still on and that all we have heard exists in our imagination."

"Well, it certainly isn't a dream judging from the half bag of beans Udo brought and the men he saw who moved about without fear of conscription. They were in hiding before and now feel liberated."

"You're right." Her aunt stared in front of her.

Ginika said, "Auntie, what do you think? I suggest Udo should take some of the beans to his mother."

"Of course, he should do that."

"When you get home," Ginika turned to Udo, "stay there and let me know as soon as Nwakire returns." Her heart beat rapidly as she thought of Nwakire and Eloka who should be back soon if they were still alive.

Udo nodded. "I will let you know the moment Brother Nwakire returns. I will also tell you when your husband comes home. I will check the house regularly to know when he returns."

She emptied some of the beans in a bag for Udo to take away while he went to collect his uniform.

"Good bye, ma," Udo said to Auntie Chito. "Thank you for allowing me to stay here and taking care of me. Don't worry about your husband. I feel strongly he'll return home. I'll come to see Sister Ginika and all of you regularly."

Ginika watched her aunt hug Udo. "Thank you, Udo," her aunt said. "You're a good boy. I wish you well and I'm glad you survived the war. Many soldiers perished."

As Ginika was seeing Udo off, she saw Janet coming towards her, carrying two bags. She waved to Udo and watched him walk away down the road. When Janet got to where she stood, Ginika asked, "You're returning to your home? Is it not too soon? Wait for a day or two longer." She thought it might not be safe to travel at this time and there was no transport. So how would Janet get to her town?

"No, I'm not returning home. Let's go into the house and I'll tell you all about it."

They sat on the chairs in the verandah and she looked enquiringly at Janet.

"I came to ask you to come with me to Uga Airport. You remember my boyfriend in the air force? He told me there are two planes there that will fly out tonight. I want to try my luck and see if I can leave the country. I was told some people left last night and more would leave tonight. Are you interested?"

Ginika stared at Janet, horrified. "You want to fly out of the country? Where will you go after that? You want to endanger your life after the war ended? Janet, I don't think you should go? Assuming it is safe to fly out, do you expect me to abandon Eloka, my husband, and leave the country?" She remembered how she had followed Janet to the phantom dance in Nkwerre which landed her into trouble and messed up her life. She wouldn't dream of entrusting her life in Janet's hands again. She shook her head vigorously.

"You're not coming?" Janet asked. When she shook her head again, Janet requested, "Can I leave one of these bags with you? I don't need to go with it but if I fail in the attempt, I'll come for it."

"That's all right. You can leave the bag with me."

"Thanks, I've got to go. I'll keep in touch anywhere I am. I have your aunt's address in Enugu which you gave me and I know the school in which she and her husband used to teach. I'll surely reach you through one of them. Goodbye."

"Take care," Ginika said, as they hugged. She knew she would miss Janet.

GINIKA HEARD that a detachment of soldiers had occupied Ama-Oyi Primary School compound which the refugees had deserted as soon as they heard the war had ended. She heard that the teachers' quarters were occupied by officers – the commanding officer lived in the headmaster's house – while all the classrooms and the hall were converted to quarters for the other ranks. She also heard that some of the soldiers came with women and that many Hausa and Yoruba traders followed them to Ama-Oyi and sold all kinds of goods in Orie market.

"I've been thinking," she said, turning to her aunt who sat next to her in the verandah. They did this every day, for she waited for news of Eloka and Nwakire and her aunt for news of her husband. "I believe I should fry *akara* while we still have some of the beans Udo brought and sell to the soldiers and their wives. With the money I realise, we can buy more beans and other things we need. If we do nothing, the beans we have will finish soon and there'll be nothing to eat." She hoped her aunt would agree with her plan. The children and her grandmother looked healthy again because they were eating nourishing food. But what would happen if they ate up the beans? They had no money to buy more.

"I have been thinking too about what to do." Her aunt frowned. "You are right. The beans will finish soon and we'll have nothing to fall back on, but I'm afraid to allow you to go to the soldiers. I have heard stories of how they seduce women and make them live with them in that place, not bothered whether they were married or single. Did you not hear of Ukandu's wife who now lives with one of them? Will you be safe? This is my worry."

"I can take care of myself, I assure you," she said firmly. "I won't fall into the same trap two times. We need money – Nigerian money. Biafran money has ceased to be legal tender, not that we have it anyway."

GINIKA WOKE up early the next morning, cleaned and ground some of the beans together with pepper. She added salt to taste and fried the mixture. She fried the *akara* in sets. She would scoop up some of the mixture with a big spoon and drop it in the hot oil and allow it to turn golden brown before bringing it out. She continued in this way till she fried all of it.

"The aroma of this *akara* woke me up," her aunt said, yawning. "I smelt it right in my room. Tell me, where did you learn to fry akara like this? I probably have asked you this question before."

Ginika laughed, wiping sweat from her brow with the tail of her wrappa. "People have asked me this question more times than I can remember – even my stepmother who hardly compliments anybody has praised my skill. I always answer that it is a gift. I didn't go out of my way to learn to do it."

"It is a wonderful gift," her aunt said, admiringly.

"I want to leave immediately while the *akara* is still hot. Hopefully the soldiers and their wives will buy. I'm leaving some for the house." She went into the house and changed into clean clothes. She was ready to set out.

"Go well and good luck to you and to us." Her aunt took the *akara* she had put in a bowl into the house.

She nodded, laughing as she headed for the gate.

When she reached the primary school compound, it was about seven. She hesitated at the gate.

"What do you want?" the soldier on sentry asked. He stared at her and she cringed when she saw the lustful look in his eyes. He was tall, very dark-skinned and skinny.

"I'm from this town. I have some *akara* I want to sell to soldiers and their wives."

"Go inside." He told her which way to go.

She thanked him and hurried inside. She saw soldiers

going about in uniform. In the distance, some were on parade, and this reminded her of her days as a special constable in Mbano. She walked to the side where she saw some women.

"I have *akara* to sell," she said to the first woman she met.

"Let me see," the woman said. She showed her and the woman said, "Follow me."

Ginika smiled. She knew from the look in the woman's face that she liked the smell of the *akara*. Inside, she saw how the hall had been partitioned with cardboard to give privacy to each soldier and his woman. The woman bought some and called the other women. Before long, Ginika had sold all the *akara* she brought.

The only man who bought her *akara* was a sergeant with a pleasant face whom she heard the women call Sule. He told her to keep the change. Ginika was astonished because the change was much. She wondered why he was not in the field with the other soldiers.

"Thank you, sir," she murmured. Before she left, the women told her to bring more the next day because they were sure people in the other blocks would want to buy. She observed that the women were not all Hausa and Yoruba – some were Igbo, Ibibio, Efik and Ijaw. She knew the soldiers had befriended them in the places they invaded in the course of the war. She shuddered. She wouldn't want to be like these women.

"Your *akara* is very good," the woman she had met outside said.

When she left the compound, she counted her money and was amazed at how much she had realised. She went straight to Orie market and bought more beans, onions, tomatoes and two tins of milk. She still had some money left, thanks to the sergeant.

35

Ginika fried *akara* regularly and sold to the soldiers and their wives. More people bought from her. She noticed that Sule was there each morning to buy *akara*. Once he asked her name and she told him. "You have a beautiful name," he remarked and she smiled. She avoided his eyes which stubbornly sought hers.

After selling all the *akara* she brought, she would go to Orie market and buy more things for the house. When she came home one day, carrying all she had bought in the market, her aunt met her at the door. Ginika saw fear and anxiety in her eyes and trembled.

"Auntie, what's the matter?"

"Come and see," was all her aunt said.

She followed her to the sitting room and then cried out as she gulped air into her lungs. "My God, where did all this come from? Is Uncle Ray back?" She stared at her aunt.

"So you know nothing about it?" her aunt asked, her face marked by disbelief.

"Of course, I don't. If I knew about this, would I go to the market to buy these things I'm carrying?" She looked down at the bag in her hand and laughed because each of the things she bought was duplicated a hundredfold and more items added on top. Her eyes widened as she took in the foodstuffs occupying the sitting room floor – a bag of rice, half a bag of beans, a carton of Peak evaporated milk, two packets of sugar, two large pieces of stockfish, a dozen tins of tomatoes, a small basket filled with melon seed, a small basket of onions and two packets of tea.

"They were brought a few minutes ago by two soldiers who came in a Land Rover." Her aunt stopped and stared at her, as if she wanted to see how she took her words. Ginika stared back blankly.

"When I asked where these foodstuffs came from, they told me Sergeant Sule Ibrahim asked them to deliver the things in Ginika's house. So I concluded you knew about it." Her aunt's eyes were frightened.

Ginika sat down, dazed. "Auntie, this sergeant has never spoken to me except to buy *akara* from me each morning. The first day he asked me to keep the change. We have never had any conversation inside or outside the army quarters." She looked at the foodstuffs again and then at her aunt. "What do we do? We can't keep this. What does he want?"

"I agree with you – we can't keep these things." Her aunt stared again at the foodstuffs. "When a man behaves like this towards a woman who is nothing to him, there can be only one interpretation. This man wants you."

Ginika shivered. Her mind turned to the smiling soldier who greeted her cheerfully and had a kind word for her each morning. She did notice a look in his eyes that told her he liked her, but she usually received such looks from men, so she didn't think much of it. She had not encouraged him in anyway. Besides, they had not interacted in any special way different from her interaction with the women and few soldiers who also bought *akara* from her.

"You will not go to that place again to sell *akara*," her aunt intoned. "By the way, how did he find out where you live?"

"I don't know. Perhaps he sent someone to follow me. I will not go there again. I hope he comes to take these things away."

The next two days she did not go to the army quarters, but the soldiers did not return so that she could ask them to take the foodstuffs back. However, Sule Ibrahim came alone the following day. He had a gun slung over his shoulder. Her aunt had gone out, so she received him alone. They sat in the sitting room where they had left the foodstuffs. She saw the surprise in his eyes when he saw his gifts untouched and left where they were dropped on delivery.

"Please, sir, my aunt and I want you to take these things away. We cannot take them." She eyed his gun which he placed by his side.

He laughed. "Why can you not take them? You think I will poison you?"

"No, it's not that. We don't see the reason why you should give us these things." She wanted to be plain, but at the same time she didn't want to annoy him. After all, they did what they liked since the war ended. There were stories of how they seized women and took them away while their husbands watched, helplessly.

"The things are for you. I want you to be my woman," he said gently. "I love you very much. Since the first day I saw you, I cannot sleep or concentrate on anything. Ginika, please, say yes. I want to marry you."

"I'm very sorry, but I can't marry you because I'm already married."

He laughed. "You are married? That is what you all say. Where is your husband?"

She hesitated. Should she say he was in the Biafran Army and had not yet returned from where he was before the war ended? Was she sure Eloka was alive? He had not yet returned, but she knew that all the soldiers could not return at the same time. Every day they heard about those that returned, so she was optimistic Eloka and Nwakire too would return.

"I know you are not married. You said that to send me away, but I will not go away. I must marry you. I like you too much."

Ginika trembled and wished her aunt were in the house. How would she be able to convince the sergeant that she could not be his wife? In desperation, she blurted it out, "I'm telling you the truth; I'm married. My husband was in the army but has not yet returned, but I know he will return. I'm waiting for him." She stared at him, hoping what she told him would not anger him and make him shoot her or Eloka when he returned.

"Are you sure he did not die in the war? Why is he not back? Even if he returns, I will take you away from him. What can he give you that I cannot? Eh, Ginika? I will make you love me more than you ever loved him. You will see." He laughed again.

What could she say to put him off, to discourage him? What reason could she give him to make him understand how impossible it was for her to marry him or be his woman? An idea occurred to her and she voiced it immediately. "Are you circumcised? I'm sure you are not. I can never marry a man who is not circumcised. It's the tradition in our family and if I do, I will die." She looked at him steadily, without blinking, hoping he would believe her.

For some time he said nothing and then he asked, "So any man who wanted to marry you must be circumcised?"

"Yes, he must," she replied, eagerly. "I swear; it's the truth."

When he got up to leave, she asked him when he would come to take away the foodstuffs.

"I said they are for you. What do you take me for – to give you something and then take it back? I will never take them back even if you continue to refuse me." He picked up his gun and left.

Ginika stood at the window watching him. At the gate, he came face to face with Obika who was returning from an errand. Ginika saw the terrified Obika press his body hard against the gatepost until Sergeant Sule Ibrahim had passed. Then he ran into the house.

A few days later, when there was no food left in the house, Ginika and her aunt began to cook the foodstuffs from Sule Ibrahim.

Ten days after the war ended, Ginika and her aunt were sitting in the verandah after breakfast when someone knocked at the gate which they had begun to lock to protect themselves from unwanted visitors.

"Obika, go and see who is at the gate," her aunt called.

As soon as Obika opened the gate, he shouted loudly. "It is Papa. He has come back!"

Her aunt ran out shouting and she followed her. Uncle Ray stood at the open gate, smiling broadly. Her aunt fell into his arms and he held her close. To everyone's surprise, her aunt burst into tears.

"What is this, my darling?" Uncle Ray said. "I'm home and instead of rejoicing and thanking God, you are weeping.

Stop now unless you want me to go back to where I came from."

Her aunt lifted her face and laughed, though her eyes were still full of tears. "I'm happy," she said. "Welcome Ray. Where are the children? Obika go and tell them your father is back. And tell Nne too."

Ginika laughed, as Uncle Ray turned and stretched his hands. They hugged. "How are you, *nwayi oma*? Is your brother back?"

"No, he's not back yet."

"Don't worry, he'll return home. People will keep returning for a long time to come. At Orie market, when I alighted from the vehicle I travelled with, I saw other people who had just arrived – many of them were ex-Biafran soldiers." He turned her round and took a good look at her. "Still as beautiful as ever," he teased. The children came running to him and diverted his attention from Ginika and her aunt.

IT WAS indeed a period of homecoming for many people especially those who had been in the Biafran army and displaced persons who had been refugees. So when Nwakire visited Ginika in her aunt's house the very day Uncle Ray returned home, she found herself dancing around the compound, jubilating.

"Welcome, Kire," she greeted him, clinging to him, as if she would not let go. "I was afraid something bad had happened to you. We never saw or heard from you after your training."

Nwakire gazed at her for a long time, pleased to see she

looked well. She knew from his eyes that he had been told about her pregnancy and her disgrace. "How are you?" he asked. "Your husband is not back yet?"

"No, I haven't seen him, but I believe he will return. I'm waiting for him." Her upper lip quivered. She looked away, as she didn't want him to notice the anxiety, the fear in her eyes whenever she thought of Eloka. Would he forgive her? Would things be normal again between them?

"Let's sit down," Nwakire suggested.

She led him to the sitting room which was free. She knew Uncle Ray and her aunt had been in their room since he arrived, catching up on lost time, no doubt.

"We can chat for a while before I go," he continued. "I arrived not long ago and was told what happened to you. I'm very angry, but I'll wait and see how things go when your husband returns. Do you know I told Papa I was coming to bring you to the house and he said he didn't want you there? He said you should go to your husband's house or to the man who got you pregnant if your husband and his family didn't want you."

Ginika saw his eyes flash and said quickly. "I know, don't worry about it. Papa told me as much when I went to see him after what happened, after my father-in-law threw me out. My own father told me he didn't want to see me. Yes, he did!"

Nwakire shook his head. They sat in silence for a while.

"How did you come home? You hitched a ride?"

"I walked along bush paths to avoid the soldiers who blocked the roads and stopped people to ask them foolish questions. I didn't want them to search me either. Someone I met gave me an old shirt and trousers and I discarded my uniform. We were in the war front when we learned the war had ended, so I lost everything I had."

"Thank God you didn't lose your life," she commiserated. How was life in the army after you left us? Were you promoted again?"

"Well, I fought at different places. It was hard, but that's a soldier's life in wartime, especially non-professional soldiers like me. I did my best, though. I was a captain when it all ended. I hate the way it ended, as if we had wasted our time and lives in vain – so many perished. At first I didn't want to come back. I wanted to end it all, but I kept seeing your face. It was you more than anything else that made me want to continue living." He smiled sadly. "I'm glad to see you're well in spite of your experience."

"Who told you?" she asked.

"Udo told me and then Papa."

"Udo? I didn't tell him. I was even hiding it from him. I wonder how he found out. No wonder he never asked me why I was living with Auntie Chito and I dreaded his asking the question."

"He said his mother told him. Why didn't you tell him?"

"I don't know. Perhaps shame, perhaps I felt he was too young to be told such things."

He laughed. "Too young? A young man who was in the army and saw so much evil? I don't think he is too young to be told."

"Perhaps you're right," she remarked and then changed the subject. "Kire, I have wanted to ask you, but is there no girl you care about? You haven't met any girl you like?" She had wanted to ask him this question but didn't know how. She knew this was a good opportunity to ask because they were being frank with each other after the experiences they had had while the war lasted.

He shrugged. "Not really, I never met a girl I could respect. Most of the ones that came my way slept around with officers and I despised them. Perhaps I was too idealistic and expected too much from them. Some of the other officers thought war has a way of compromising morals and so they didn't think the girls were doing something outrageous or immoral. They argued that the fear of death, the ever present threat to life in a war situation makes people reckless and increases their sex drive. They argued too that people in wartime are more likely to fall in and out of love easily and would have sex with any available partner. Well, they may have a point there, but I think differently. I don't believe in having sex with just any available partner, and so kept away from the girls."

She gazed at him with shining eyes because her beliefs were identical with his. "Kire, do you know that I agree with you completely?" She thought Eloka held the same belief.

Nwakire smiled. "Let's not talk about me. I want to listen to you. Can you tell me what happened? I want to hear it from you."

She told him everything, from the beginning to the end.

36

When Eloka arrived in Ama-Oyi two weeks after the war ended, it was already dark. He was grateful for the darkness which seemed to envelope everything in sight. With the very pregnant Boma waddling by his side, he didn't want to be stared at or hailed by anyone he passed on the way. They had hitched rides on the way until they reached Ekwulobia. They stood near the main road for about thirty minutes before a military truck appeared and picked them up – he couldn't believe that those he was fighting barely two weeks before offered him a ride, especially when he recalled what some of the victorious soldiers did in some towns and villages, seizing and raping women and confiscating people's property with impunity. He supposed Boma's condition helped to win sympathy from a few people who had vehicles and were willing to give them a ride.

What a tragedy the war was! What an anti-climax to him and those who fought with commitment for a cause they believed in and died for! Left to him, he would have preferred to die in the battlefield than to face defeat in this way. But he had mustered enough courage to embark on the journey home – he had a wife to love and care for, and he had to see

Boma through and later help her to return to Port Harcourt where she said her seventy-year-old grandmother lived. He hoped the old woman survived the bombardment of Port Harcourt before it fell.

Here they were at last in Ama-Oyi, close to home and to the people he loved. He was not sure he did the right thing to bring Boma home, but she had cried and begged him not to abandon her when they learned, like everyone else, that it was over, that Biafra had surrendered. Whether right or wrong, they were in Ama-Oyi and there was no going back.

"Boma, this is my hometown, Ama-Oyi," he said. "It's dark, so you won't be able to see a thing. How do you feel?"

"I'm fine, Captain." She leaned on his arm. "Just a little tired, that's all. But I'm glad we have arrived. The baby is kicking furiously and making me uncomfortable."

"Let her not come yet. We still have at least a kilometre to walk."

She giggled. "Won't it be terrible if I went into labour now? What would you do?"

"I'll abandon you and her and run away."

"How do you know it is female – you keep referring to it as 'she' or 'her'? I want a boy."

"That's your business," he said, laughing. "When my wife and I have our first baby, I'll want it to be a girl as pretty as her mother." But would his wife want a baby girl first? He recalled he had debated the issue with her when he was courting her and she had disagreed with him, saying she would like their first baby to be a boy. He wondered why women always wanted a boy as first child. He knew his sisters, Adaeze and Ijeamasi, had expressed this wish openly a number of times even before they got married. What about Ozioma? He never heard her comment on the subject. He supposed it was because she was young and such things had not started to bother her. His heart gave a jerk and he smiled; he would soon see them – Mermaid, Ozioma, his parents and the rest of the family.

He noticed that Boma was unusually quiet – she was talkative. He asked, "Have you decided the name to give the baby when it is born?"

"I'll wait until it's born, Captain." She replied curtly.

He wondered why she seemed to be upset. They continued in silence until they reached their destination.

When Eloka knocked on the gate, Osondu opened it and took the two bags he was carrying from him.

"Welcome, Brother Eloka," he said with a broad smile.

"How are you, Osondu?" Eloka smiled back, remembering how Ozioma had welcomed him the last time around. He knew that if she were the one that opened the gate, the whole house would hear her explosive shout.

Osondu stood aside for them to enter first and, shutting the gate, followed them into the house.

As soon as he stepped into the veranda, he heard footsteps stumping down the stairs. A lantern was placed on a stand and he could see the lengthy passageway clearly. He moved forward and stood at the door leading to the sitting room and waited. He knew it was his mother, for she had a way of stamping on the stairs, as if to protect herself from falling. His head tilted backwards as he waited. Boma stood behind him. His mother's eyes were focused on the stairs as she descended until she reached the ground floor.

"Mama, I'm home," he said, stepping aside, so that Osondu who was carrying his and Boma's bags could pass. "Put the bags in the sitting room," he told Osondu.

His mother turned sideways and, when she saw him, she gave a thunderous cry. "It is Eloka! Ozioma, where are you? Your brother has returned home." Her face lit up, as she beamed with joy. "*Nna*, welcome!"

Eloka moved towards her and they hugged. She looked at him closely and burst out laughing. She began to thank God. Eloka saw Ozioma belting down the stairs and said, "Ozioma, take it easy. Don't push us down," and then he hugged her too. When he turned to his mother, he saw her gazing at Boma, as if she was a messenger from the gods who had brought her a gift.

"And who is this beautiful woman you brought home?" Her eyes were focused on Boma's protruding belly and Eloka saw clearly the look of astonishment mixed with pleasure in his mother's eyes. He knew what she was thinking and shook his head with disgust.

He ignored his mother's question and asked instead, "Where is my wife? Has she gone to bed?" He saw his mother and Ozioma look at each other and remain silent. "Ozioma, didn't you hear me? Where is Ginika?"

"She went to her place," Ozioma answered.

He remembered his father and asked, "What about Papa?"

"He came back from a council meeting late and went to bed after dinner. Do you want me to wake him up and tell him you're back?"

"No, let him sleep. I'll see him in the morning."

"Why are we standing in the passage? *Nna*, come into the sitting room first," his mother coaxed. "And you too, my dear." She smiled at Boma. "You must be very tired after your journey. Come in and sit down. We will find you something to eat."

Eloka began to speak but changed his mind. He beckoned to Boma and they followed his mother into the sitting room. "Sit down," he said to Boma, but remained standing himself. "Ozioma, get me another lantern. I want to get to my room first and change these clothes I have worn for two days. What about the guest room? Can you get it ready for Boma?" He looked at his mother and saw her watching him.

"Mama, what do you have in the house? We are very hungry." He smiled and continued. "Food first and then we'll talk. I know you are dying to ask me questions but you will have to wait."

His mother laughed. "So you read my mind, my son? We can talk whenever you want – seeing you alive is enough for me. I have dreamed and waited for this day. God, I thank you for bringing my son home to me."

Ozioma returned with two lanterns. She gave Eloka one and then said to Boma, "Come and I'll show you the room you will sleep in."

"Boma, follow her," Eloka said. "Will you like to have a bath first?"

Boma, who had practically not said a word, nodded. "Yes, I'll like to have a bath."

"Ozioma, show her the bathroom," his mother said. "And warm the jollof rice in the pot for Eloka and Boma."

After Ozioma and Boma left, Eloka turned to head for his room only to see his father shuffling towards it and rubbing his eyes. "Eloka, this is you, eh? Welcome back." His father hugged him before sitting down.

Papa, I didn't want to disturb your sleep." Eloka saw how tired he looked and wished he had not woken up. "I thought I would see you in the morning and had told Ozioma not to wake you."

"Ozioma did not wake me," he said. "I heard when your mother shouted and would have come down immediately, but I just couldn't find my slippers." He laughed. "I searched and searched until I looked under the bed."

AFTER THEY had eaten, Boma retired. Eloka had seen how tired she was and had urged her to go to bed. Eloka had felt better after taking a bath, but he felt even much better after the meal. However, he didn't quite feel so himself and he knew why. He was sure he would not be able to sleep without finding out why Mermaid had gone to her family instead of remaining in his home – which was her home too – as they had agreed before he enlisted in the army. Why did she leave the house? He hoped his father was not too tired to talk, but he was determined, this night, to find out what happened. He looked up and was pleased that neither his father nor his mother had left the room. He sensed that they too wanted to stay and talk – this suited him very well. And they were waiting for him to open the discussion. His father sat in his favourite chair and rested his feet on a low stool. His mother sat on a settee, opposite the door.

He said to his father, "When I asked about my wife, I was told she was with her family. I want to know what happened. I left her here before I joined the army and expected to find her here."

His father stared at the ceiling for a while before looking at him. "Eloka, I sent your wife away because of what she did. I don't have the mouth to talk about what happened, but I suppose I have to say it. Our people say that an adult should not stay in the house and allow a goat in tether to give birth. Your wife committed an abomination…"

Eloka was irritated and wished his father would go straight to the point. He was not happy with the way he spoke about Mermaid. "Papa, go to the point. I'm listening."

"You have come again with your impatience; you will not allow me to talk," his father chided. He hissed and looked away.

"Papa, I'm sorry, but you can understand my anxiety. Please, go on." He vowed not to interrupt no matter how he dallied in his narration. He heard his mother sigh and then hiss.

"Eloka, your wife was pregnant and refused to say who got her pregnant. She said she didn't know who he was. She told us a story that even a child would not believe. I told her I would not allow her to live here carrying someone else's baby."

Eloka was dazed by what he had just heard, as if an unseen assailant dealt him a stunning blow. He felt his stomach flutter, as if something was running around there. When he found his voice, he cried, "My wife was pregnant! How did she get pregnant? Are you sure? When was this? Has she had the baby?" He was babbling, asking so many questions without waiting for answers.

"Yes, she was pregnant and we didn't know until she was almost five months gone," his mother said angrily. "Imagine! She was here carrying someone else's baby and I was feeding her and sheltering her. God forbid! I heard the baby died after she gave birth to it."

He listened to his mother narrate the rest of the sordid story; the more he listened, the more distressed and appalled he became. Eloka groaned and, bending his head, covered his face with his hands.

"*Nna*, do not think of her anymore," his mother advised. "She does not deserve such attention. Now that the war has ended, you can look for a proper wife and forget her. She is a win-the-war wife – a harlot. Imagine . . ."

Eloka's head shot up and he glared at his mother. "Don't say that. Don't call her a harlot again." His eyes were full of grief.

He got up to leave, but his mother said, "*Nna*, you cannot leave without telling us about the girl who came home with you. She is so beautiful. Who is she? Is she carrying your baby? " The light in her eyes irritated him and he frowned.

Eloka felt his father's eyes on him. He knew both of them would willingly accept Boma if the baby she carried were his – so desperate were they to have grandchildren who would perpetuate the family name and inherit their property. Well, he would let them know that Boma was not carrying his child. The woman he had hoped would carry his baby had disappointed him. But, shouldn't he hear from her? Should he condemn her based on what his parents said?

He looked up and saw them waiting eagerly for him to confirm their thoughts and tell them what they longed to hear. With a steady voice, he declared, "I'm not the father – I'm not responsible for Boma's pregnancy." He saw the look of surprise and disappointment in their eyes. He also saw the questions their eyes asked which their mouths couldn't utter: why then did you bring her to the house, who was the father and what has it got to do with you? He continued, "I saw her by the roadside where she was in danger of being killed and decided to help her. I brought her with me, hoping that after her baby was born, she could return to Port Harcourt to look for her grandmother."

His father and mother stared at him, as if they thought he was out of his mind and he noticed that his mother's mouth was agape. He got up and left the sitting room and went to his room.

Back in his room, he sat on the bed and groaned again and again. He knew he would not be able to sleep that night. He knew he would have no peace until he had heard from her. His world was crumbling around him and he had lost everything – first was the loss of the war and now the loss of his Mermaid. His shoulders shook as he broke down and sobbed.

THE MORNING was bright and the air fresh but Eloka did not notice, for only one thought dominated his mind – to see her and hear her version of the horrifying story his parents told him last night. He would send Osondu to her house immediately and hoped she would come as soon as possible. He couldn't bear his present state anymore – knowing and not knowing, tension and anxiety.

As these thoughts churned inside him, Ozioma came into his room to say that Ginika was outside. He was surprised, for he did not expect that she would come this morning, for it was not possible that she knew he was back. How could she have found out? He was sure she came because she heard he had returned and he was pleased that she came without waiting for him to send for her. But how did she find out, he wondered? Perhaps what he had heard was false and, when he talked with her, she would clear the air and reassure him it was all a lie.

"Thank you, Ozioma, tell her to come." He sat down on

one of the chairs and waited. He remembered that both of them had sat on the two chairs in the room the night before he returned to his battalion, facing each other and talking happily. He heard the knock – it was so faint – and waited for the door to open, but when the door remained shut, he said, "Come in."

She came in and stood at the door. She was as lovely as ever, but looked subdued, he thought. Her eyes were focused on his face and, as she hesitated, her hands were slightly lifted. He knew she wanted to hug him, but something held him prisoner and he could not get up from where he sat. The story his parents told him which Ozioma confirmed earlier in the morning was like a concrete barrier separating them. He couldn't bear to touch her or take her in his arms until he knew what happened.

"Welcome," she said, smiling. "When did you come back?"

"Please, sit down." He indicated the chair on the other side of the table. "I returned last night. How are you?"

She sighed. "I'm okay. I have been waiting for this day and I'm so glad you're all right." She looked down at her hands which lay folded on her thighs.

He gazed at the curve of her lips, the swell of her bosom and admired her rich glossy hair which she held back with a ribbon. He looked at her blue dress – he had bought it for her after they got married – and thought blue was so good for her and accentuated her beautiful complexion. He knew she wore the dress now to please him.

"How did you know I was back?" he asked curiously.

She looked at him. "Udo told me."

"Udo! How is he? We lost him, but I'm glad he returned safely."

"He's all right."

They were silent for a while. The air around them was heavy with unspoken emotion and he thought he should broach the subject at this point. He could see how uncomfortable she was, as he saw her lift her hands and put them down again. He could not believe that he was with the woman he longed for so much while he was away, yet now he was with her, he could not even stretch his hand to shake hers.

"I didn't find you here when I came home last night and when I asked they told me you got pregnant. Is this true?"

"Yes, I was pregnant and the baby died the day it was born."

He felt as if a knife was thrust deep into his heart. He sensed something die inside him, and groaned. When she looked up at him, he saw that her eyes were full of tears.

"What happened?" he asked hoarsely.

As he listened, he thought it was exactly as his parents and Ozioma presented the story, though she had added more details which their account lacked. He found it difficult to believe her as hard as he tried. How could a man have sex with her without her realising it, without her crying out and calling for help in a house where her friend and her boyfriend were? In other words, she claimed the officer had raped her and she had not resisted him. He shuddered. The thought of it almost unhinged his mind.

"I don't believe you." He spat the words in her face. "You have behaved badly. I'm totally disappointed in you."

She burst into tears. She tried to explain further but he was no longer willing to listen. "Please, go. I can't bear to see you. Go." He turned away from her.

"Why do you find it difficult to believe me? It's the truth and you have to believe me."

"I don't. Your story doesn't make sense to me – it looks like something you made up. Fabrication! Can you leave now?"

She stood up, shaking. "What about you? You not only lived with a woman in your house but got her pregnant. And you even brought her home, not caring what your wife would think. Suppose I had been here, how do you think I would have taken it? I have not judged you, have I? But you judge me. And you judge me wrongly."

"For your information, I'm not responsible for her pregnancy." He gave her a scornful look. "So you're trying to justify what you did? Is that it?"

She shook her head. "No, don't get me wrong. I'm only asking you to try to understand."

His voice was raised when he said, "I said you should leave." He glared at her and saw her flinch. Her eyes were full of despair but he was too angry with her to care. He was sure Udo told her about Boma but whatever he told her was false. He thought that what she did was deceitful and irresponsible and he could not bring himself to overlook it. It was all about trust – and not about forgiveness or about trying to understand.

"All right, I'll go, but I will not come back." She walked out of his room.

He stared at nothing in particular and was not aware that she left the door wide open when she walked out. As a thought occurred to him, he started to his feet, but changed his mind, shut the door and flopped on the chair. He heard the door open and lifted his head, wondering if she had come back. What would he say to her? But it was his mother that walked in.

"What did that wayward girl come here to do?" she

536

demanded. "She had the courage to enter this house after what she did? *Nna*, I hope you are not thinking of taking her back?"

"Mama, *pua ebea*! Get out!" He glared at her and she shuffled out of the room, downcast.

He groaned again. What was he going to do? Forgive her and take her back or part with her? He reflected over the war that had just ended – it ended badly for the side he fought on – and over his experience in the army. He had tried to be decent in his conduct throughout his days as an officer, he thought. But he knew most officers acted differently. Many behaved terribly and did things that damaged the cause they fought for. He knew there were devils as well as saints among the officers – few saints perhaps. He argued with many about their attitude to women. He remembered Captain Akudo who was addicted to sex with teenagers. To him women were beautiful objects to be ravished and thrown away. "They taste differently when they are quite young," he had said, with a careless laugh. He had been disgusted and kept away from Captain Akudo and his debauchery. And there was also Lieutenant Nandu who saw sex as delectable food which he must eat at least once a day to remain alive and sane. Many others had equally indulged excessively in the act without talking about it like these two. He knew also that women flocked to military camps and made themselves available to officers, so it was not always the officers who seduced them. Where did his wife belong in all this? Was she drugged and sexually abused, as she claimed? But, why had she gone to the military camp in the first place?

Eloka got up and walked out of the compound. He headed for his rose garden which had turned into a wilderness. He stared at the tangle of weeds, thorns and roses. Eloka sighed. He had lost everything that made life worth living, he thought.

37

Ginika locked herself in her room and refused to open the door when her aunt and later Uncle Ray came, pleading with her to open it and eat something. She lay on her back, staring at the ceiling. She wanted to die and end her suffering. Why should she suffer as she had done since she could remember? First she lost her mother as a child and grew up in a virtually loveless home. She escaped by marrying a man she thought loved her as deeply as she loved him. She made a mistake by going to a dance that never took place in Nkwerre and had paid dearly for it. But, her misfortune didn't end there. Now she had lost everything. Eloka had rejected her. How could she go on after this? They had planned together how their lives would go after the war and she had had hopes, but all had come to naught. She realised bitterly that it was not the dreams one dreamed that ruled one's life but the choices one made that determined the course of one's life. She had made wrong choices – perhaps it was better to say that circumstances conspired to propel her to make wrong choices. In each case, it was not possible for her to predict the outcome of her action.

"Sister Ginika, open the door," she heard Udo's voice. "I beg you, open the door." She sighed but lay where she was.

An hour later, she was still lying in the same position when she heard raised voices. She listened, curious.

"If you no bring her out, I go shoot you," she heard a voice spat in a mixture of pidgin and English. "And I go kill all of you here. Bloody rebels!"

"Why do you want to take her away?" she heard Uncle Ray ask. "What did she do?"

"Please, Sergeant, we don't want trouble," her aunt pleaded. "Please, leave us alone. No one here has committed any crime."

"Shut up, woman," she heard the loud voice again. "Who allow you to talk? If you talk again, *walahi*, I shoot you now. Where the girl dey?"

"Sergeant, you have not answered my question?" she heard Uncle Ray's persistent voice. "You must tell me what my niece did before you take her away."

Her heart jumped to her mouth, as she realised they were talking about her. She was terrified and knew whoever it was would shoot Uncle Ray.

"*Ajikwu* rebel, you wan die?" the voice came again, aggressive.

"If you want to shoot me, go ahead, but I cannot release her to you until you tell me why you want her."

There was a grunt and she heard the sound of a scuffle. She understood that Uncle Ray had been struck by the person her aunt had addressed as sergeant. She shuddered. Could it be Sergeant Sule Ibrahim? But he didn't seem a violent man. What was she to do now? When the sound of violence continued unabated, she dressed hurriedly and, opening the door, went out.

As soon as they saw her, the tumult ceased. Uncle Ray lay

on the ground where she had seen one of the men in uniform kick him. "Why are you beating him?" she asked the soldier. There were three of them and she looked from one to the other. She was frightened because they were armed.

"This *na* the girl, sir," one of the soldiers identified her. "She is Sergeant Ibrahim woman, *na* him."

"Arrest the *ashawo* rebel!" the sergeant barked to the two soldiers. She looked at him and cringed at the vicious look in his eyes. He was of average height and wore a cloth cap made from khaki.

They grabbed her. Horrified, she asked, "Why are you arresting me? What did I do?"

"Stupid woman! *Barawo*! You don kill Sergeant Sule. You go see pepper today. Nobody fit save you; you go pay for your crime."

"What crime?" Uncle Ray's voice shook, as he sat up with difficulty. Udo went close and assisted him. He was badly bruised and Ginika began to cry.

"You think say crying go save you? You go see. *Na* you tell Sule make him go circumcise himself before you allow him to touch you. No be so, *ashawo*? The wound get infection. You don kill better man, you bastard rebel! We dey look for the rebel nurse – abi *na* chemist – wey circumcise Sergeant Sule. De man don run for him house. But we go catcham. No rebel fit mess soldier up and go free. As for you, you go see." He moved threateningly towards her and she cowered before him.

"No, no!" she yelled. "I did no such thing! My God, he got himself circumcised?"

Uncle Ray, her aunt and Udo were appalled. She saw their eyes and knew their fear reflected her own terror. As the two soldiers dragged her away, the sergeant cocked his gun and dared Uncle Ray to make any move.

"If you move, I blow you to pieces, *Ajikwu* rebel!" Walking backwards, he followed his men, his gun at the ready to shoot at the least provocation.

Ginika gave one more backward glance before she was prodded out of the compound.

HER TERROR increased when they entered the army camp. They took her past the hall where she had rehearsed *Mammy Wota* with Eloka and the other actors. The sergeant opened a door with a key and they pushed her in. She found herself in a room with a dusty floor and a window which was permanently shut because a block of wood had been nailed across it. There was no furniture in the room. She shook from fright, wondering why they had brought her there.

"You go dey for guard room till you tire for here or you can die if you like," he spat. "If you make noise, I shoot."

"Sergeant, sir, I beg you, release me," she pleaded, her face flooded with tears. "Believe me, I never asked Sergeant Sule to get himself circumcised. Why should I do that? I have my own husband." Her voice tripped over the word 'husband'. Could she really say she had a husband now?

"You be bloody liar, rebel woman," he snarled.

"I'm not lying," she protested, one of her hands pressing the floor on which she sat. "Sergeant Sule and I were not even friends…"

"Shut your dirty mouth," he bellowed. Turning to the two soldiers, he said, "Wait outside."

She saw his face break into an unpleasant smile, as he approached her. His eyes were cloudy with lust. Her eyes widened with horror and she was about to scream when he said, "If you cry out, I go kick you to death."

"Don't touch me," she said, "or I will report you to the commander of this camp."

He laughed derisively. He lunged forward to grab her but she shrank away towards the wall. The room was not bright but there was enough light for her to see every move he made. He began to unbutton his trousers as he inched forward steadily. Horrified, she shrank away further to another part of the room. He followed her like an animal preparing to pounce on its prey. What would she do? No one would help her. No one knew where she was. The sergeant could easily overpower her and have his way, but she intended to put up a fight this time.

When he was ready, he leaped forward, grabbed her around the waist and pressed her body hard against his. She was repelled by his dark ashen skin and his thick wet lips. Remembering the self-defence tactics Captain Ofodile had taught her and other special constables, she kicked the sergeant's groin and heard him cry out. He abandoned her and staggered backwards. His eyes were full of hate. He turned to the door but it opened before he reached it and the two soldiers came in, their eyes questioning.

"Hold the witch," he barked. And as they pounced on her, and held her hands, he picked up his gun, which rested against a wall, and aimed it at her head. "I go kill you now," he roared. She cried out in terror. He changed his mind, swung it before her and then hit her ankle with the butt. The pain caused her to cry out again. After he had returned the gun to its former position, he reached for her body and tore off her blouse, exposing her breasts. Her skirt suffered a similar fate and soon lay at her feet.

She struggled to free herself but they held her and pushed her to the ground. She screamed and one of them clamped a rough hand on her mouth. Divesting himself of his clothes, the sergeant grabbed her legs and prised them open. He entered her with force and as her naked body heaved under his, he stretched his hands and squeezed her breasts until they were sore. As he strove to reach his climax, his thrusts became frenzied and he taunted her. "I go fuck you, *ashawo*. You kill Sule. He be better man pass all your rebel brothers. Dat thing you no give Sule, I go take am today. *Ashawo!*"

She whimpered and groaned, unable to cry out because of the strong hand covering her mouth. Her eyes popped out like those of a rat gripped by a cat. At last, she felt his body shudder and then he rolled off her. She felt bruised all over from the pressure of his lean hardy body. Her body sweated profusely.

He glared at her and grinned cruelly. "Make you do your own," he said, pointing to one of the soldiers. Ginika sobbed, as she watched helplessly. It was the soldier who had not said a word since the cruel drama began.

The man shook his head and said, "No, sir." He turned his face away.

"If you no do, I go deal with you." The sergeant's nostrils flared in anger. "I go come back to you." He turned to the other soldier – the one that had identified her in her aunt's house. "Make you do your own."

The soldier leered at her and, as he pulled at the button on his trousers, Ginika gave a throaty cry and lost consciousness.

38

Udo followed Uncle Ray to the military camp to lodge a complaint against the three soldiers who abducted Ginika.

"What do you want?" barked the man on sentry duty at the entrance.

"I want to see the commander," Uncle Ray said. Udo stood behind him.

"Why do you want to see him?" The man who had two rows of tribal marks on either cheek stared at them disdainfully. "Go back, Commander no dey for camp. I don go Enugu."

"It is very urgent," Uncle Ray pleaded. "Please, let me see the second-in-command if the commander is not around."

Udo was sure the man was lying. He could see it from his eyes. When the soldier's eyes turned to him, he looked away and drew closer to Uncle Ray.

"Now go away. We no allow bloody *Ajikwu* soldier into the camp." He waved them away. "If you no go now, I kick you out."

Uncle Ray touched Udo's hand. "Let's go. We'll try later when this one goes off duty. His replacement may be a kinder person." They walked away with a feeling that he was watching them.

They were back three hours later and approached the gate with caution.

Uncle Ray, you are right," Udo said, "Another man has taken over."

"Let's see if he can help us." Uncle Ray walked up to the man. "Good afternoon, brother," he greeted. "We want to see the commander. It is urgent; please allow us to see him."

"Why do you want to see the commander?" the soldier asked, staring at them suspiciously. Udo observed that his English was good unlike that of the other soldier who spoke pidgin. "I asked why you want to see the commander and you stand there looking at me, as if I had water in my mouth."

Udo felt anger rise inside him but he suppressed it. He knew they had to be patient. Sister Ginika's life was in danger. Nobody knew where the soldiers had taken her. Had they killed her? His heart gave a thud, as the thought crossed his mind. He looked at the soldier again and saw that his face appeared more pleasant than the other one.

"We want to make a report about a missing person."

"Missing person? Why should you make such a report to the commander of this camp?" He looked at Uncle Ray with amusement.

"Uncle Ray sighed and replied. "I thought the commander might like to help find the person since he is in charge of security in this town."

"You think we came here to do police work?" the soldier asked. "We are here to make sure Ajikwu soldiers do not cause trouble. So go away and don't disturb the commander." He returned to his post.

"Uncle Ray, why not tell him the missing person wanted to make trouble in the town and you want to let the commander know about it?" Udo suggested.

"You are right, Udo. Thank you." He moved near the soldier again and said, "I didn't want to say this before, but the man I am talking about wants to make trouble in the town. He was a soldier in the Biafran Army and I heard him say he would kill Nigerian soldiers if he found them outside their camp. That is what I want to discuss with the commander so that the man can be arrested. He has gone into hiding."

"Why did you not say so before? Okay, follow that road and you will reach the commander's office. Ask anyone you see on the way."

"Udo, that was a clever one, eh? Thanks for your suggestion."

The commander received them in his tastefully furnished office – former refugee office and former headmaster's office. Udo was surprised that a temporary office could be so comfortable and beautiful. These officers took care of themselves and their men.

"What can I do for you?" asked the commanding officer – a lieutenant – after Uncle Ray had introduced himself and Udo. He looked pleasant and likeable. He was short and cut his hair very short. Udo saw how smooth and neat his uniform was and how shiny his boots were.

Uncle Ray explained what happened in his house in the morning and how three soldiers had abducted his niece and taken her away to an unknown place.

"Are you sure of your facts?" asked the commanding officer.

"Yes, sir. I was there when they came. In fact, they beat me up because I refused to allow them to take her."

"Wait here and let me ask if any woman was arrested and brought to the camp."

Udo's eyes were fixed on the officer, as he re-entered his office. "No woman was brought into the camp. I asked the sergeant in charge of the guard room and he assured me no woman is there. You see, if anyone is arrested, the person will be taken to the guard room."

"Sir, perhaps they took her to another place," Uncle Ray said, extremely disturbed. "I'm worried about my niece; please, help us to find her. One of the men who took her is a sergeant."

The commander hesitated and frowned. "What is his name, this sergeant?"

"I have no idea. I know he is a sergeant because he wore his rank - three bars – on his uniform and I also heard the other two call him by that rank."

"Well, if you don't know his name, I'm afraid I cannot help you. We have more than one sergeant here." He stood up.

Udo and Uncle Ray still sat down. "Sir, I can describe him to you. Perhaps this might help to identify him."

The commanding officer had lost interest. "Mr Man, you have to go now. I have some work to do."

Uncle Ray and Udo got up reluctantly and walked out of the office.

UDO DID not sleep throughout the night. He had passed the night in Uncle Ray's house, hoping Sister Ginika would come home any moment. He was sure that if the soldiers released her, she would come to her aunt's house, for this was the only home she had now. Udo wept for her all night, remembering how good she had been to him. He wept because he was powerless to help her.

As soon as dawn arrived, he dressed and rushed out. He meant to tell Brother Nwakire what had happened. He didn't think he could do anything better than Uncle Ray had done, but he thought it was necessary for him to know. When he got to the house, the first person he saw was Auntie Lizzy. She was preparing breakfast in the kitchen.

"Good morning, ma," he greeted.

She turned and stared at him, grimacing. "Udo, where have you been? No one sees you these days. You don't even care to come and help us, as you used to do."

"I'm around, ma, only that I have been busy."

"Busy doing what? Has the war not ended? Are you still hiding from conscription?" She laughed.

He waited for her to stop laughing and then said. "I came to see Brother Nwakire."

She sneered. "That one, he is always in his room, brooding. I don't know what I did to deserve two stepchildren like those two – Ginika and Nwakire. I suppose they are my own cross which I have to carry till the end of my life, or till they leave home and start living on their own." She turned over the plantain she was frying. "See how Ginika disgraced herself and her father-in-law had to drive her away..." She stopped, for Udo had slipped out of the kitchen but was hovering outside the door. He smiled when he heard her hiss loudly.

He muttered an abuse under his breath and walked away, wondering why Auntie Lizzy disliked Sister Ginika and Brother Nwakire. But, did she really like anyone?

He knocked gently on Nwakire's door and waited.

"Yes, come in," said a sleepy voice.

Udo went in and sat down. Nwakire looked at his face and sat up immediately, for Udo was weeping.

"What's the matter?"

"It's Sister Ginika. She was arrested yesterday by three soldiers and taken away. Uncle Ray and I spent the whole of yesterday looking for her. She has not returned till this morning and I came to tell you."

Nwakire sat on his bed, submerged in thought. Udo saw mixed emotion dancing on his face, but what showed clearly was anxiety.

"Why did they arrest her?" he asked in a voice that was far from steady.

Udo hesitated. And when he stared at him without blinking, he blurted, "They said a soldier had died after being circumcised and that he had done it to be able to marry Sister Ginika. So they accused her of killing him."

"The soldier got circumcised and died?" Nwakire asked, appalled. "You know, she told me about the sergeant who wanted her badly and from whom she was hiding. She also told me she had lied to him about a family tradition that wouldn't permit her to marry an uncircumcised man. Actually, we had laughed over it. You mean the stupid man took it seriously and got himself circumcised at his age? My God, how reckless and foolish can people be?"

Udo wiped his eyes with the end of his shirt. Nwakire began to put on his clothes and Udo was worried about the glint in Nwakire's eyes, as his face had become quite grim.

"Wait outside," Nwakire said.

Udo got up and waited outside the door. When he came out, Nwakire wore a black shirt and jeans. One of his trouser pockets had a bulge and Udo wondered what he had there. Udo followed him out of the compound and when Nwakire saw him walking behind him, he barked. "Go home."

Udo was frightened. "Where are you going, Brother Nwakire?" He hoped he was not going to the military camp to make trouble. He knew the soldiers would either arrest him or even shoot him. Udo remembered that Uncle Ray had told the soldier on sentry that an ex-Biafran soldier had sworn to kill any soldier he saw in Ama-Oyi. If Brother Nwakire went there, they might think he was the man Uncle Ray talked about.

Nwakire turned and saw Udo still following him. "Are you deaf? I said you should go home. I have unfinished business to see to."

"All right, I'll go home, but won't you tell me where you're going?" The anger in his face was so pronounced that Udo felt the soldier on sentry would shoot him at sight.

"It's none of your bloody business. Now run along." He stood and waited until Udo had disappeared on the path leading to his home.

But as soon as Nwakire continued on his way, Udo turned back and followed at a distance. He thought that if Nwakire looked back, he would dart into the bush, but he didn't look back, not even once. He walked swiftly, not to the military camp – to Udo's relief – but towards Eloka's house.

Udo watched him enter the compound through the open gate. He stood in front of the gate wondering whether to go in or wait for Brother Nwakire outside. Since Eloka – his former *oga* – took Boma into his house and lived with her and since he had sent away Sister Ginika, Udo hated him – "disliked him strongly", might be a better way to express his feelings. He vowed never to visit him or talk to him again until he had sent Boma away and taken back his wife, Sister Ginika.

So, he waited outside. But after some time, he became worried. What was Brother Nwakire still doing in the house?

Did he go to tell Eloka that Sister Ginika had been arrested by soldiers? What good would that do except make him dislike her the more? Udo's worry increased when a thought perched on his mind and grew in strength as time passed and Nwakire did not come out. Suppose what he had in his pocket was a pistol? Did he go there to shoot Eloka? He had said he had an unfinished business to do.

Udo walked into the compound – a house he had visited frequently when Sister Ginika lived there. He saw Eloka's mother and that girl, Boma, sitting in the veranda. Her belly was big and her face looked puffy. "Good morning, ma," he greeted Eloka's mother and completely ignored Boma. "Is Brother Nwakire here?"

Eloka's mother blinked and hissed loudly. "Can't you hear his voice? He has been arguing with Eloka. I have gone in there and asked why they were quarreling but they ignored me. I do not know why people will not stay in their own house, but want to make trouble for others in their own home. Have we not had enough nonsense from that family and their wayward daughter?" She hissed again.

Udo was too shocked at her cruel words to say anything. He stood there, wondering whether to go into the room and ask Brother Nwakire to come away. Suddenly there was a loud explosion. Udo knew it was the sound of a gunshot.

"What was that sound?" cried Eloka's mother.

The sound came a second time and before Udo could move, he saw Brother Nwakire striding towards him. His face was ghastly. He passed without looking at any of the people on the veranda. Udo was sure he did not even see him. Eloka's mother rushed to her son's room, followed closely by Boma. Udo walked behind them. When they got into the room, he saw Eloka lying in a pool of blood. Brother Nwakire had shot him twice at close range and he was hit in the neck and chest. His mother fell beside him, shouting and weeping. Udo's and Boma's eyes met and he pushed past her and left the room and the compound.

Outside, Udo looked frantically for Brother Nwakire. His body shook and he couldn't think straight. At last he decided to head for the house – Nwakire might have gone home. He walked and ran and then walked again. He knew people he passed stared at him. When he got to the house, he met a frightened Auntie Lizzy descending the stairs.

"Udo, I heard a sound like gunfire," she said in a shaky voice. "Did you hear it?"

"No, I've just arrived," Udo said, breathing hard. "Let's check Brother Nwakire's room. He may have shot himself."

"What do you mean? Why would he shoot himself?"

Udo ran past her and took the stairs two at once. He rushed to Brother Nwakire's room and tried the door but found it locked. He pounded against the door with both fists. "Brother Nwakire, open the door. Please, open the door."

Auntie Lizzy stood beside him. "Are you sure he is in there?"

Udo nodded, as tears flowed down his face. "He's there. I think he has killed himself. I'm going to break the door. Where is Uncle?"

"He went to Enugu to find out if the government will give him back his job."

Udo did not wait for her to finish. He was already running down the stairs. He knew where a hammer was kept and he ran to fetch it. It took him a while to break the door. He found Brother Nwakire lying on his bed like someone asleep. Udo bent down and saw that he had shot himself in the head. There was blood everywhere.

39

Ginika lay on the dusty floor, groaning. Her right ankle was badly swollen and the skin around the wound had turned purple. Since she regained consciousness, she had not stopped weeping and marvelled that her eyes could produce such a copious amount of tears. The tears would not stop, no matter how hard she tried to suppress them. She knew the tears would keep flowing until she stopped wallowing in self-pity. She wished it were possible for her to die, so that her star-crossed life would come to an end. What did the sergeant want to do with her? Leave her to die here and bury her secretly? He had not offered her any food, but she had not expected him to. After all, he wanted to punish her for Sule Ibrahim's death. Why had no one come to look for her? She looked down her bruised body. She had covered it with her torn blouse and soiled skirt. She heard a sound as if a key was being inserted in the lock to open it. She cringed, pressing her back hard against the wall.

The door opened and the sergeant came in and she glanced at him in terror. His face was grim. He had a paper bag in his hand and he threw it to her.

"*Ashawo*, wear de dress inside dat bag quick quick," he ordered.

As she hesitated, he shouted, "You deaf? Make you no waste my time."

She was afraid he wanted to take her out to shoot her in a secret place. She had been afraid throughout the night, thinking he would come and take her out in the cover of darkness and execute her. But he had not come during the night. What did he plan to do this morning – or was it afternoon? She was not sure what time of day it was.

"If I say it again, I go kick you." He stood over her.

"Where are you taking me? Whose dress is this and why do you want me to wear it?"

He lunged forward and hit her. "Wear de dress before I kill you. I tell you, you no fit put me for *wahala*, rebel woman."

She tilted her head and the blow landed on her left shoulder. She removed her torn blouse and put on the dress. It was her size and fitted her.

"Stand up!" he commanded.

She tried to stand up but collapsed on the floor. "My leg is broken," she wailed. "I cannot stand on my own."

She looked at him and saw fear in his eyes. She understood that someone had at last come to look for her and he had been asked to produce her. In spite of her broken body, she felt joy surge in her heart. Perhaps her aunt and Uncle Ray or her brother, Nwakire, had reported to the authority and found where she was. She watched him, her eyes full of scorn, and she felt a burning desire for vengeance well up inside her.

He turned towards the door and she wondered what he was up to. Should she shout that she was in the guard room? Would help come faster if she did this? But before he got to the door, a short man clad in army uniform walked in and the sergeant stepped backwards. From the stranger's demeanour she knew he was an officer – probably the commanding officer of the military base. As she watched, more people entered the room – Uncle Ray, her aunt and another soldier. Then lastly came the person she never knew she would see again – Miss Miriam Taylor, her teacher and friend.

She read the horror in Uncle Ray's eyes though he tried to hide it. She saw her aunt's face crumple like a dry leaf squeezed by a fist, as her eyes brimmed over with tears. She knew she was a dreadful sight.

She tried to get up, but failed. She flopped on the dusty floor and looked from one person to the other until her eyes had perched on everyone including her captor, the sergeant. Then she broke down completely and wept, but she knew it was not grief alone that called for these tears but relief as well.

"I'm very sorry about this," the commanding officer said, shaking his head. "I didn't believe such a thing could happen in my command. It's unpardonable." He turned to the sergeant and said, "Sergeant Bala, you will be court-martialled for this. I'll see to it."

Miss Taylor and her aunt bent over her. "You're safe now, dear," Miss Taylor said. "No one can harm you now. We'll take you straight to hospital to have your leg attended to and to have you medically examined." She smiled at her.

She nodded and smiled through her tears. "Thank you, Miss Taylor." Uncle Ray and her aunt helped her to get to the vehicle that had brought Miss Taylor to Ama-Oyi and then they drove out of the military base.

Part Five

AFTER THE END

40

Ginika sat at the departure wing of the local airport in Lagos. She was glad that she was returning home after being away for nearly six months. She was her old self again, she thought, except that she was wiser and more mature. She had been a school girl when the war began, but three years after she was a woman with enough experience to last her a lifetime. She had experienced grief and she had known loss, but she would not allow these to harden her or make her forget the joys of life. She was saved by love and friendship though, ironically, she had been hurt by love. The naïve girl of nineteen had turned into a patient and confident woman of twenty-two. It was after she had been discharged from hospital that Miss Taylor told her about Nwakire and Eloka. She still didn't know how she managed to survive the shock and the depression that followed. Without Miss Taylor and her missionary colleagues and friends who had counselled her, she could not have survived. Miss Taylor told her that when the war started, she had first gone to Asaba before moving to Lagos to teach in another mission school.

She picked up the magazine – *Spear* – Miss Taylor had given her to read while waiting for the flight to take off. She smiled. What a privilege to fly in a plane! She recalled the horrible air raid she had survived in Orie market in Ama-Oyi during the war. Now she was going to fly in a plane for a second time – the first time had been when Miss Taylor took her from Ama-Oyi with a broken ankle and drove her to Enugu in the official car she had brought from Lagos and both of them had flown to Lagos. The hospital in Enugu where Miss Taylor first took her could not handle her case and referred her to the National Orthopaedic Hospital in Igbobi. Miss Taylor had spoken to some people who spoke to others and soon after she had been flown to Lagos in an air force plane, accompanied by her friend. And now she was returning to Enugu by air, and she knew Miss Taylor had contacted her aunt and Uncle Ray, who would meet her at the airport.

"Please, can I look at your magazine?" asked a fat woman who sat in a chair opposite her. Beside her sat a stout army officer who looked younger than the woman, though Ginika suspected they were husband and wife.

She nodded and gave the magazine to her.

"Thank you." The woman said and began to leaf through the pages.

Ginika watched a major in full uniform, whose rank was clearly displayed on his shoulder, lift a child of about two and kiss her on the cheek. The child giggled happily and then impulsively kissed the man on his lips. A pretty and fair-skinned woman sat near the major and Ginika took her to be his wife and the child's mother. She smiled sadly, remembering that she too had had a child, though under extremely painful circumstances, but who would have been about this child's age if he had lived.

She looked round the lounge where she and other

passengers waited for the arrival of the plane that would fly them to Enugu. There were more men than women and most of them were military personnel and a few civil servants and business people. She saw the soldiers and gazed at their faces – lucky ones who had survived the war and who had fought on the winning side. The officers who fought on the losing side had been demobilised, as they were not recognised; they were labelled rebels. Those who had joined the army during the war simply returned to their former life and tried to pick up the pieces and continue living – as traders, students, farmers, artisans and teachers. To this category belonged her loved ones who had survived and were alive today: Udo, Leonard, Bartie, Ezeonu, Belu and Monday, the houseboy-turned-carpenter. If Nwakire and Eloka had survived, they would have returned to the university to complete their undergraduate studies as many had done. Nsukka University had reopened and other universities had also taken back their former students who fled to the East during the massacres.

"Madam, is this seat taken?" a man in suit asked.

"No, sir, the seat is free."

"May I sit near you then?" he smiled, displaying pink gums and white teeth.

"Please, do. The seat is free." She watched him sit down before she relapsed into thought.

Ah, Nwakire and Eloka – both gone for ever. She wept for Nwakire and for Eloka, two wonderful young men who were destroyed by the war and the evil it spawned. She had been shocked that her gentle, loving brother could kill anyone, but then he had killed at the war front. The war had taught him to shoot to kill. She shuddered. She knew she would mourn Nwakire and Eloka for a long time. Life was a mystery, she thought. How could she lose the two people she loved most in life the same day and almost the same hour? One shot the other and then shot himself. Double tragedy which almost destroyed her too, but for the care and encouragement she had received from Miss Miriam Taylor. She owed her life to her. She had taken her to hospital promptly and saved her leg. The doctor had said she was lucky gangrene had not set in or the leg would have had to be amputated. She was in hospital for three months and now could walk as well as she did in the past. She had survived the war – many had not. Eunice and Njide had died needlessly – flowers that withered too soon.

Ginika heard the cultured voice of an announcer inviting passengers to board the plane. She got up and, picking up her hand luggage, joined the queue that formed outside the lounge. A big coach stopped in front and passengers began to enter it. When it was her turn, she got in.

IT WAS a short flight, less than an hour, but in her excitement, Ginika was impatient for it to end sooner than it did. She looked out of the window and saw the sprawling city down below and thought the houses looked like match boxes. Enugu was her favourite city in the whole of eastern Nigeria and she would like to settle there when she finished her education and started working. She was fascinated by the landscape and gazed at what she thought were Iva Valley and 9th Mile Corner. She saw cars moving slowly on the roads but they were very few. Most people had lost their cars during the war, she thought. Now the plane was descending and she shut her eyes because she felt as if she was falling into a deep hole.

Her heart fluttered and jumped up, as if it would fly out of her body. She had felt exactly the same way during the other flight, six months ago. Was this the way it was with everyone? She hated the take off and the landing, but felt better afterwards.

Ginika lifted her hand luggage and joined the other passengers as they descended the gangway. In the distance, behind a fence made from barbed wires, she saw people who had come to meet their friends and relatives and knew she too would be met by people who loved her – her aunt and her husband. Her eyes searched the crowd, as she looked for the familiar figures she would recognise anywhere. Then she saw her aunt waving frantically and Uncle Ray with that radiant smile that never left his face. Since she had not checked in any luggage, she bypassed the passengers waiting for their luggage and trotted off to meet them.

"Ginika, welcome back!" cried her aunt, as she opened wide her arms. Ginika dropped her hand luggage and walked straight into those arms which had always acted as a protective umbrella to shield her from the rain of adversity.

"How wonderful to see you again, Auntie!" She pressed her cheek against her aunt's and shut her eyes. After what seemed an eternity, she heard Uncle Ray say, "Aren't you going to greet us? Is she the only one that came to receive you?"

She laughed and drew away from her aunt to hug Uncle Ray and then saw that there were indeed more people than she had expected. Her eyes widened when she saw Udo, looking taller and more handsome than ever, and – what a miracle! – Amaka Ndefo, her friend, who had flown to America with her family in a relief plane as the war raged. She hugged them one after the other.

"Amaka, when did you return?" Her face glowed with smiles. "I thought you were at school in America?"

"Yes, we're on vacation and I came to see my dad. I'm returning next week."

"How are your mother and brothers?" she asked. She thought Amaka had added some weight and her skin looked lighter. "Are they as healthy as you are?"

Amaka nodded. "This is for you." She gave Ginika a bunch of red roses which she had wrapped with a colourful sheet of paper. "I know you love red roses and I cut these from the garden in front of our house. This is a special welcome for a special girl!"

"Oh, Amaka, how thoughtful of you!" she exclaimed, as her eyes became misty. She buried her face in the blood red roses and inhaled deeply. And for a moment, she remembered the red rose Eloka had given her the day he proposed to her. "Thank you, Amaka. You cannot imagine what this means to me."

"You're welcome." Amaka smiled.

She turned to Udo. "Haven't you gone back to school? I thought school has reopened."

"Yes, it has." His eyes shone, as he continued, "Sister Ginika, I want you to thank Uncle Ray and Auntie Chito. They put me in their school, St Augustine's College, and are taking care of me."

Ginika turned to her aunt and uncle. "This is great news. Thank you so much." She knew Udo could not have gone back to Jos – just as she couldn't have gone back to Port Harcourt with the atmosphere of hostility bristling there – and his mother could not have sent him back to school.

"Udo is a good boy and we are happy to do what we can to help him," her aunt said and then added, "Do you know the government has taken over all mission schools and renamed them? Ours is now called Hilltop Boys' High School."

"Taken over all mission schools!" Ginika's voice echoed her aunt's. She was shocked. "Why?"

Her aunt shrugged. "They said schools belong to the community and not to the churches – whatever that means. Are the churches not part of the community?"

"Will the government be able to maintain the high standards set by the missions before the war?" Ginika wondered if her former school in Port Harcourt had also been taken over by the government there.

They reached the park and got into the car which looked refurbished and she thought Uncle Ray must have spent a lot of money to put it back on the road. Her aunt sat beside Uncle Ray while she, Amaka and Udo sat in the back. Uncle Ray started the car and drove slowly out of the airport.

"Someone who returned from overseas brought this letter for you last month," her aunt said, as she handed her a blue envelope. "Ray and I were not at home but Obika received it."

She was curious to know who wrote her from overseas and tore the envelope. As she read the letter, her eyes widened and she kept saying "Ha, ha, ha," until she came to the end of it. Amaka turned and looked at her and she knew she and the other listeners were eager to know who wrote it, and why she was so excited.

"The letter is from Janet," she announced, folding the sheet. "She is in America where she ended up after escaping in the last relief plane that flew out of Biafra at the end of the war. She met a young Igbo man there and married him. He brought the letter when he visited home briefly."

"*Hmm*, that Janet is fast," her aunt sniped. "She is an opportunist and knows how to make a way for herself in every situation."

"She is, indeed." Ginika stared out of the window.

Uncle Ray negotiated a sharp bend and then said, "We have arranged for you to finish Higher School at Queen's School, here in Enugu. We know you cannot go back to your former school in Port Harcourt. Teaching started four months ago but I'm sure you can catch up."

"Oh, did you?" Ginika smiled. "But that isn't necessary, for I've been offered admission to two universities – to study journalism in Nsukka University and education in a new university that opens this September in Benin City. The two universities admit students with O/Level subjects, so I took the qualifying examinations after I was discharged from hospital. I passed the two examinations, but I prefer journalism to education, so I'm going to Nsukka University in September – less than two months from now. Miss Taylor arranged everything and she also helped me to win a scholarship."

"This is great news." Her aunt's eyes glowed. "That teacher of yours is wonderful. She saved your life by coming to Ama-Oyi to look for you when she did. Her supervening presence compelled that Commanding Officer to investigate your abduction by that horrible sergeant. And she saved your leg too – I was afraid it would be amputated. We learned the sergeant was dismissed from the army."

Ginika shuddered, as she remembered her ordeal. "The man is evil," she whispered.

"People like him give the army a bad name," Uncle Ray said.

As the car meandered along damaged roads, she looked out of the window and saw houses with bullet marks and cracked walls and wondered why they were still in this appalling condition six months after the war ended. Perhaps the owners did not have the money to repair the houses. The war had impoverished most people in the East. The wreckage of war still defaced the city, she thought, sadly. Lagos was the opposite. There was no sign at all in the city that a gruesome war had been fought in the country for almost three years . . .

Amaka, who sat between Ginika and Udo at the back, said, "Do you know my mom said I should ask you if you would like to come to America to study, but it seems you've been taken care of here?"

"What, study in America!" she exclaimed. "Well, that's very kind of her, but I'll settle for Nsukka University for my first degree; later I'll go to America for a Master's degree."

ACKNOWLEDGEMENTS

I gratefully acknowledge the support of Royal Holloway, University of London, Egham, United Kingdom, that granted me a one-year Fellowship as a Visiting Research Fellow in 2006/2007 and thus empowered me to complete the first draft of A Million Bullets and Roses.

I am greatly indebted to my late editor and friend, Dr T.C. Nwosu, who expertly edited the first draft of the novel. How sad that he did not live to see the birth of the book which he commended so highly. May his kind and gentle soul rest in perfect peace.

I express my thanks to Jalaa Writers Collective for publishing the first edition of the novel.

I thank Odili Ujubuonu and Jude Dibia for reading the manuscript and making useful comments and suggestions. I benefited immensely from the critical perceptions of Drs James Tsaaior, Patrick Oloko, Udu Yakubu, and Mrs Hannah Okeke, my doctoral student – who passed away before the publication of the book – and members of my family especially, Chris, my husband, friend and companion of many years, and my daughters, Nwanneka and Chidinma, who read the manuscript and made suggestions.

I am grateful for the kind support of my cousin, Barrister Harriet Nkechi Gore, when I was writing the novel in the UK in 2006 and 2007. Emma Dim and Chris, who were both officers in the defunct Biafran Army, provided valuable information about military terms and formations.

I thank Onyeka Nwelue and the editors at Abibiman Publishing UK, for finding my work worthy.

Finally, I thank the following friends for their support and encouragement in the course of writing this book – Pat Bryden, Stephanie Newell, Robert Hampson, Joy Odewumi and Uche Odili.